LEGACY

BOOK ONE OF THE DEAD GOD SERIES

C.J. PYRAH

To my endlessly patient wife.

ACKNOWLEDGMENTS

Thanks are due to many people, but above all Rebecca Frew, Emma Sanford and Hannah McGregor-Viney for their patience and kindness in reading those first, hastily-formed words on a page, and to all at Next Chapter.

PROLOGUE

The crash of hobnailed boots filled the hallway as a tight-knit group of guards stormed through the palace. Their shields where up, ready, swords drawn and spears levelled. The early morning sun glinted off their polished armour, the growing heat of the day embracing the soldiers as they ran, coaxing beads of sweat to drip from under their helmets and down their faces. The guards, however, had no intentions of stopping.

From the neighbouring corridors and palace rooms, they could hear the sounds of battle raging. Screams of pain, bloodthirsty war cries and the pillagers' whoops of adulation let loose within the halls. The men and women revelling in their bloodlust and newfound riches had once been loyal, and the guardsmen knew it. All of them knew the punishment for desertion, especially when faced with the enemy.

The formation followed the winding corridor until it opened out into a huge feasting hall. The walls were covered in monumental mosaics showing the glories of the Kingdom of Dazscor. Now the chiselled faces of the kings and queens of old stared proudly down on a scene of chaos. The feasting tables had been overturned, the ornaments scattered and broken on the floor.

The looters, picking through the debris and stripping the corpses of the courtiers they had found there, eyed the guards hungrily as the formation skidded to a halt in front of them. One of the looters, a tall bald man with a blood-splattered face began to walk slowly towards the bristling knot of spears that had emerged from the corridor. As he approached, other looters began to draw in behind, hands creeping towards sword hilts. Stopping a few metres from the guards, he spread his arms wide and grinned broadly.

'Brothers, sisters, welcome to our court! You have nothing to fear from us, we are comrades, all of us. We have all loyally done our duty for king and country and now some other fat-arse wants to take his crown. Why should we stand in the way? Come lay down your arms and join us, let us take our share of the spoils before the new order takes it for themselves. The royals are all dead—we have nothing to fear from them now!'

'I would disagree with you on that!'

The guard's front ranks parted to let a smaller figure wearing much more elaborate armour than the others and sporting a green cloak emblazoned with a red rose, pass through. She possessed long auburn curls and an upright, regal demeanour. She stood, feet set defiantly apart.

'Oh, Princess, had I known it was you, I'd never have dreamed of saying such things in the presence of your divine majesty …'

The looter's voice oozed sarcasm as he fell into a grossly over-exaggerated bow, the men behind him howling with laughter as he did so.

The princess continued to stare at the man, the icy ferocity of her glare stifling the laughter of the mutineers before her. 'I don't care what you think of me, or my father. I'm not here to defend him. All I need to know is if you're going to let me and my troops go on our way, or whether you and your filthy accomplices wish to die?'

The looter captain's wide smirk remained as he drew his

2

sword and started to pace back and forth. 'So, the little precious princess wants to play soldiers, does she? You certainly came dressed for the occasion. How much do you reckon that pretty, shiny armour would sell for, boys? I'll enjoy taking it from you, from your dead body if I have to, though I'd rather you were alive for the experience.'

He lunged forward, his sword point aimed at the princess' throat. Around him, his men surged forward, leaping at the guards, trying to tear their shields away. The formation, however, held firm.

The guards took one step back as the tide of looters hit, then shrugged them off, spears snaking out from in-between the shields, ripping open throats and lodging in bellies.

The looter captain's eyes were filled with hunger as his sword flew through the air, his gaze fixed on his target … but then the princess was gone. Nimbly, she sidestepped the clumsy blow, hand slipping to her shoulder where the hilt of the sabre was barely visible through the thick, cascading curls. The sabre whistled through the air, gouging a deep red gash in the looter's back. He screamed and fell to his knees, silenced as the sabre took his head.

Wordlessly, the guards re-formed around their princess and continued across the hall; the remaining looters scattered into nearby corridors. She approached a mosaic behind the raised royal table: a queen with arms outstretched in welcome. Carefully, she pressed a jewel set in the centre of the queen's mosaic belt, which sunk into the stone behind. There was a dull scraping as the mosaic split to reveal a hidden staircase plunging into darkness.

The vault was filled with an eerie green-blue light that flickered on the walls and gave a sense of drowning. The sea of treasure that filled the space and disappeared into the recesses of the vault glimmered in the strange light, but was barely recognizable. Gold, silver and jewels made up the hoard. Imperial guards were rushing around, bringing more boxes of precious stuffs to add to the treasure trove from a side passage, their contents spilling out as they desperately tried to finish their task.

They skirted around the edge of the vault's antechamber, avoiding a large marble altar where a pale figure and his hooded assistant were chanting strange words and drawing odd symbols in the air ... the place where the mysterious light emanated from.

There was a clatter as the princess and her guards entered the vault from the central passageway, to be met by a fraught-looking bureaucrat trying desperately to organise the madness.

'Your Highness, what are you doing here? It's not safe, you should be making your way to the harbour!'

'Where's my father? I thought that he would be down here?'

'No, he's already left for the ship. Please, you must go; the spell they are casting is far too unpredictable for you to be here.'

'What is going on here, Lord Chamberlain? Why are these men not defending the people of this city?'

'The king gave orders for his treasure hoard to be moved here and protected by enchantment. The Aramorians are already assaulting the walls and half of our men at least have turned against us. The city is lost and we must safeguard Dazscor's legacy for the future!'

There was a deep, reverberating hum from the altar as the light swelled, causing all of the people in the vault to shield their faces. As the light died back down to its unsettling glow, the princess blinked and rubbed her eyes.

The figure of the sorcerer was still standing at the altar, arms desperately circling as he continued to trace symbols in the air, shouting words of power at the top of his voice. His assistant dashed from the altar to the Lord Chamberlain, clutching a large round object in her hand. 'Here, someone must take this to the king. Hurry, we can't control the spell for much longer!'

'One of my guards will take it, Ebor!' The princess beckoned one of the guardsmen, who stepped forward. 'Take this object to the king as fast as you can. He'll be making his way to the Royal Barge, so you'll have no trouble finding him.'

'But, Your Highness, my place is by your side …'

'I gave you an order Ebor, now go! I shall not be far behind you, and I'll have your comrades to protect me. Go!'

Ebor dropped his spear and shield, took the object, and sprinted down the side passage.

'Now, Your Majesty must go too …'

The Lord Chamberlain's words were cut short as another surge of power rippled from the altar. This time, a large crack appeared in the ceiling of the antechamber. The princess' guards barely managed to drag her out of the way as a huge chunk of the ceiling collapsed, crushing the Lord Chamberlain beneath it.

The guards tried to drag the princess behind the altar, towards the side passage, their feet slipping on coins and jewels as they moved.

The sorcerer's voice was drowned out by the rumbling and crackling of the spell he was trying to contain. His assistant, tugging at the hem of her cloak, tried to free herself from the rubble.

Another swell of light and the spell exploded, knocking everyone in the vault and antechamber off their feet.

The princess was thrown further into the vault and she struck her head on a treasure chest. She blinked, her vision swimming before her. She could barely see the guards scattered about her, trying to rise to their feet, the body of the sorcerer lying crumpled nearby. Then … darkness.

1

There's a particular freshness to the air at that time of year when Winter starts to give way to Spring. This effect is particularly noticeable in the early hours of the day, when the sunlight is new and clean. When the world is still trying to rouse itself from a night of slumber. Breathing in this air focuses the mind, quells those annoying erratic thoughts that float unbidden through conscious thought. This natural changing of the seasons is the perfect time to dwell on changes that we might make to our own lives.

This, at least, was what Torben thought as he walked across the field that morning. He'd always seen himself as a pseudo-philosopher, and he often felt that he was closest to answering life's deepest questions when carrying out mundane tasks, particularly early in the morning.

As he walked across the field, dipping a hand into the sack around his neck, pulling forth a handful of seeds and scattering them across the field, he could feel himself lost in the monotony of the task. Dip and scatter, dip and scatter, dip and scatter.

The only thing that could distract him from his thoughts were the distant sounds of Master Amos further up the field as he guided the plough through the earthen sea. He steered the oxen skillfully, a little left, then a little right, picking the best course, leaving the straightest, truest furrows in the wake of the plough. You could tell that Master Amos had been living and breathing farming since he'd been born.

Torben's mind continued to wander. By the end of the working day, he'd have done enough thinking to solve all the world's problems, at least thrice over. That is, if he actually came to any concrete conclusions. As with all of his musing, Torben always seemed to be on the precipice of a breakthrough, only to be distracted by the next question that swam into his consciousness.

By the time he reached the end of the field, the thread of philosophy had turned from the elemental nature of seasonal change to the still unanswered question of where exactly he'd left his dominos. He reached into the sack and scattered the seeds amongst freshly turned sod.

'All out, Master.'

Master Amos raised a hand in acknowledgement from the upper end of the field as he brought the oxen round and started to drive them back towards the gate. Torben strolled forward and sat with his back against one of the many trees that lined the limits of Master Amos' field, and, with a sigh of relief, removed the sack from around his neck and laid it on the ground.

He didn't have to look to know that his neck and left shoulder had been rubbed raw by the thick hemp sack. He rubbed both meditatively, mulling over the prospect of what the rest of the day would bring. More walking up and down the fields behind the plough, dip and scatter, dip and scatter. It was enough to make a man go crazy.

'Give us a hand with this lot, lad.' Master Amos had drawn the plough and its pair of oxen level with Torben and the tree that he was leaning against.

As Torben stood, his shadow enveloped the much smaller figure of Master Amos, who must have been at least a foot shorter than him. Torben lifted the haft of the plough and Master Amos unhitched the oxen, then led them to a nearby post. As he tethered them, Torben could hear him whispering softly, keeping them calm.

He was a kindly, ageing man. To be honest, Torben had no idea how old Master Amos actually was. For as long as he'd known him, Amos had existed in a perpetual state of elderliness. His weather-beaten face had barely registered change but, of late, Torben had noticed that he walked with more difficulty, and that his back seemed more bent with fatigue.

'Good lad,' Master Amos said as Torben brought over an armful of fodder to lay down before the oxen. 'I reckon we'll get this next field and the one up top done by the end of the day, if we're lucky. It's meant to rain tomorrow, that'd be bad news for ploughing.'

Like all farmers, Master Amos seemed to have a sixth sense when it came to predicting the weather. Torben liked to think that it was all blind guesswork, but he'd lost count of the amount of times that Master Amos had predicted the weather and been right.

As Torben straightened, Master Amos lowered himself gingerly onto the ground next to the tree. He began unwrapping a cloth bundle and proffered a chunk of bread to Torben when he sat down next to him. Torben drew a small knife from a sheath attached to his belt and handed it to the older man, who'd taken a wedge of hard cheese from the bundle. Wordlessly, he took the blade and divided the cheese in two, handing Torben half, as well as the knife.

Master Amos was a man of few words. There'd been many days when Amos hadn't spoken a word, neither to Torben nor to his long-suffering wife. It wasn't that he was unfriendly, far from it; he was one of the kindest people Torben had ever come across. Amos, it seemed, didn't feel that small-talk was a necessary part of existence.

Torben picked up a water skin that he'd dropped at their feet and took a large mouthful. He wiped water droplets from his mouth and passed the skin to Amos. 'Are you going to bring in any more labour for the rest of the season?'

Amos looked at him, weariness heavily lining his face. He sighed deeply and ran his hands through a greasy tangle of silver hair. Torben new exactly what the answer would be.

'Don't think I'll be able to scrape together the brass to do that this year. I know that last year I said that I'd get some hired labour, but ...'

'I know, it was a tough winter again,' Torben replied dejectedly.

Master Amos looked away, the weary, worried expression still lining his face. It *had* been a tough winter, and he was starting to wonder how many he had left. 'Look, Torben, I know that you must find life here with us a little suffocating, but until I can pull things back from the brink, there's nothing that I can do.'

Torben didn't answer, but stared despondently into the distance. The field laid along the side of a hill and offered an excellent view across the surrounding countryside. From this vantage point, he could see the small collection of buildings that made up Master Amos' farmstead. Beyond the farm were the rooftops of Bywater Village and beyond those the sprawling valley that made up Burndale. Barely perceptible tendrils of smoke curled up from village chimneys, the only sign of life in the landscape.

The fact that Master Amos couldn't again afford to bring in temporary labour to help out on the farm meant that Torben was, for all intents and purposes, tied to the farm. He'd been telling himself for the last two years that once he got the money together for hired help, he'd go off and explore, stretch his legs and let the road whisk him away, far from Bywater and the depressing little valley. He'd never set foot further than seven miles from Bywater and had never been to the borders of Burndale.

But three harsh winters in a row meant that Master Amos

was closer than ever to toppling over the brink, into destitution. If Torben left, it would be a death sentence for the old man, and he couldn't do that to him, not after all of the kindness he and his wife had shown him.

'Right lad, let's get on; the fields won't sow themselves thou knows.' Amos looked at the forlorn youth next to him. Torben's blue eyes stared emptily across the valley as wind tugged at the heap of messy brown curls on his head. He could tell that Torben was lost deep in thought, and he didn't need to guess what he was brooding about.

He'd been ruminating on how to best show his gratitude to Torben for days now, but the shortage of money meant he could do little for the young man. 'And think about it,' Amos continued, 'if we get this all done today, you can take tomorrow off. I need to take the plough to the blacksmiths to get straightened anyway, so they'll not be much for you to do.'

This was a lie. There was always plenty of work that needed to be done on the farm, but it was the only thing Amos could think of that he could afford to give. In any case, the statement jolted Torben back to reality and for a second he looked genuinely taken aback. He couldn't remember the last time that Master Amos had freely given him a day off. 'But what about the repairs that need to be made to the cow shed?'

'That can wait," he replied, trying to sound as carefree as his gruff nature would allow. 'It's going to rain tomorrow. I don't want you scrambling all over the cowshed roof; like as not, you'd do yourself a mischief.' Amos stood, using the tree at his back and the staff he used to steer and goad the oxen, to help pull himself up.

As he did so, Torben continued to sit on the ground, stunned by the gift that had been handed him. A whole day off! He could go to the tavern in Bywater—he hadn't managed to get there in over two months—and he could, well … Torben couldn't think clearly about what he'd be able to do. It had been so long since he'd been allowed free time.

'Come on now, don't just sit there gawping at nothing,' Amos exclaimed. 'We still have work to finish today!'

'Right you are, Master!' Torben sprang to his feet, grabbed the sack from the ground, and rushed towards the gate further down the field to replenish the supply of seed grain.

Amos watched him go. The newfound energy Torben was exhibiting made the old man smile; it had been a long time since he'd seen the lad get excited about anything. Farming life was hard and it took a certain sort of person to do it, and Torben was *not* one of those. Sure, he could carry out the labour as good as anyone. Sure, the lad's body had become conditioned after weeks on end of back-breaking labour. But Amos knew that he lacked the resilience to last as a farmer. He had too much wanderlust in his soul, itching to be let loose. It was only a matter of time before Torben would leave Bywater.

Amos made his way to the oxen and untethered them from the post. Torben had sprinted back up the hill and was already lifting the plough into position. It only took a couple of minutes to get the two beasts ready and, with a click of his tongue, they once again lumbered across the field, dragging the plough behind.

Torben fell into line and began scattering seeds into the fresh furrows. Every now and then, when the wind dropped, Amos heard the jaunty tune that Torben was humming as he worked.

The enthusiasm of the promised day off had decidedly waned by the time both fields were sown. The sun had sunk low on the horizon and the surrounding features in the landscape had become fuzzy silhouettes. The forest to the east of Bywater was a single indistinct menacing mass of trees, whilst the village itself was defined by flickering lights in house windows.

By the time Torben had cast the last handful of the seed for the day, Master Amos was already unhitching the oxen and getting ready to lead them down to the farmstead. Wordlessly, Torben followed the old man down the hill towards the edge of the field. When he reached the bottom, Master Amos was trying to chivvy the oxen through the gate and onto the road.

'Bring the last of the seed grain down with you,' he called over his shoulder as they lumbered towards the farm.

Torben hefted the last two unopened seed-grain sacks onto his broad shoulders and climbed the stile out of the field and onto the road. Master Amos and the oxen, though not far away, had already become indistinct in the fading evening light. Torben set off for the farmhouse. He could feel the fatigue of the day gnawing at his muscles, especially in his shoulders, which were straining under the weight of the sacks. Nevertheless, the further that he went down the road, the easier the last part of the day seemed to become. With each passing step, he realised that the sooner he reached the farmstead, the sooner he was free … for a day, at least.

He began to pick up his pace and was soon jogging down the road, the weight on his shoulders completely forgotten. He quickly caught up with Master Amos and the oxen, and sped past them, his feet thudding loudly on the dirt track, his mind focused on his temporary freedom.

Master Amos watched him whizz past and disappear round a bend in the road. The old man sighed heavily, hoping that Torben wouldn't do anything too stupid that evening. The last time he'd gone to the Rusty Sickle, the tavern in Bywater Village, he'd spent nearly three months wages in one sitting. There was nothing to be done, though. Torben would make his mistakes and he'd have to figure a way to rectify whatever resulted.

As the oxen shuffled into the farmyard, Amos watched Torben open the byre doors, ready to receive the two hulking beasts. With a couple of carefully aimed prods from the staff and encouraging clicks of the tongue, Amos guided the oxen into their stalls. Torben had already laid out their evening fodder and was hovering outside the byre, watching Amos intently out of the corner of his eye. He was clearly waiting to be dismissed. Taking no heed of the restless youth, Amos went into both stalls and carefully fussed over each ox. They were the key to his livelihood; without them he wouldn't be able to run the farm … without them, he'd be finished.

A pointed cough from the byre threshold indicated that Torben's impatience was reaching a breaking point. Amos didn't turn around, but raised one hand in the air as he continued to intently inspect a hoof. That was all the permission Torben needed. When Amos straightened and turned, he caught a glimpse of Torben disappearing into the farmhouse. 'Gods watch over you, boy,' Amos whispered under his breath. 'I pray you don't need their help tonight'.

Mrs Amos didn't need to be told where Torben was going when he entered the kitchen. His beaming smile said it all. The young man nodded a greeting and closed the door behind him. He turned to climb the stairs.

'So, Amos decided to let you have a little time to yourself then?'

'Aye, he did' Torben said, regarding Mrs Amos patiently. He'd been hoping he'd be able to slip in and out of the farmhouse without being accosted, but clearly that wasn't to be. He could already see the makings of a temperance lecture in Mrs Amos' beady eyes.

Despite her obvious age, the woman was still sharp as a pin and her eyes, which flashed with keen intelligence, peered down the length of her long, hooked nose. Even though his size and bulk made him seem overly large, Mrs Amos had a knack for making him seem small. She knew exactly what Torben's plans were for that night, and she didn't approve.

Torben could feel her steely gaze pierce him, probing for a sign of potential mischief. Subconsciously, he shuffled nervously and, in a matter of seconds, she'd managed to reduce the tall robust man into a tiny guilty child, and he hadn't even done anything … not yet, anyway.

'And what are you going to do with yourself tonight, young

man?' Mrs Amos' voice held an icy tone. 'Will you be going into the village?'

'Aye, I reckon I might. Just to stretch my legs, change of scenery, and all that, Mrs Amos.'

'I hope that you'll carry yourself with more dignity than the last time you went down to that … *tavern.*' The word seemed to physically pain her to utter, and it was quite plain that she didn't approve of such places.

Torben didn't reply and averted his gaze. He knew that there was nothing he could say that would placate her, and he'd learned from experience that the best thing to do in such a situation was to play mute.

Mrs Amos turned, picked up a poker from beside the fireplace, and set to work tending the blaze. 'If it had been up to me, I certainly wouldn't give you time off. We've barely got enough time as it is to do everything that needs doing, without you gallivanting off to drink yourself senseless.'

Slowly, Torben began to edge towards the stairs; he daren't turn his back on Mrs Amos, lest the sudden movement prompted more scolding.

'You were an absolute disgrace the last time you went to that godforsaken cesspit.' There was no disguising the malice in her voice. 'I thought I'd never get over the shame of seeing you being carried back, slung over the back of an ox! Couldn't even walk! How you managed to get yourself into such a state is beyond me.' She shook her head. 'None of that would have happened had Amos not left you to your own devices. He's much too soft on you, but then I always knew he was a cretinous pushover. Thank the Gods that he has enough brain cells to work the farm; otherwise, we'd have been out on our ears long ago thanks to his idiocy …'

Mrs Amos continued to mutter bitterly under her breadth, lamenting the state of the farm, her husband, and anyone unfortunate enough to be younger than herself. As soon as Torben felt his boot touch the bottom step, he wheeled and took the first steps two at a time to be out of sight as quickly as possible.

Unlike her husband, whose gruff exterior belied a genuinely kindly and forgiving soul, Mrs Amos didn't appear to have a decent bone in her body. Ever since Master and Mrs Amos had taken Torben in as a child, Mrs Amos had treated him with contempt. She'd made it plain on many occasions that her husband should have left Torben in the cold, and not taken on the burden of looking after him. Torben had no idea how Master Amos had been able to put up with his wife's verbal abuse for so many years, though the lines on his face and his noticeable depressive nature were signs that the old man was close to breaking point. Had Torben been in Master Amos' shoes, he'd have left the haughty witch a long time ago, but Master Amos would never be able to bring himself to do anything like that. It wasn't in his character.

When he reached the top of the stairs, the spring had crept back into his step. He strode to the end of the corridor, lifted the door latch, and stepped inside. His room was small and sparsely furnished. Then again, there wasn't much space for anything more than a bed and small table, which acted as a stand for a washing bowl and a large wooden box. He pressed himself against the rough stone of the whitewashed wall to allow enough space to close the door, and sat down heavily on the end of the bed. It sagged visibly under his weight, and creaked as he started to pull off his boots.

Torben had been sleeping in the same bed since he'd been taken in by the couple, and it was now a good foot too short, barely wide enough to take the breadth of his shoulders. Mrs Amos would never conceive of spending any money on getting the bed replaced.

He pulled his tunic over his head, moved over to the washing bowl, and began to remove the day's grime from his hands and face. In all honesty, he had no idea how Master Amos had been able to get away with giving Torben the day off. Mrs Amos had made it quite clear that she didn't approve of the idea, and if she didn't approve, it usually meant that the idea was immediately scuppered. Of course, there was a strong possibility that the old woman simply wanted Torben out of her sight. Yet one of her favourite pastimes was to scold him for anything and everything, which made it odd that she wasn't being too obstructive.

When Torben had finished washing, he took a small towel from a hook on the wall, dried his hands and face, and moved to the wooden box. Lifting the lid, he surveyed the contents. Everything that he owned was in the box. He shifted through the few items of clothing at one end, trying to find a tunic that wasn't too shabby, not that he had a great deal of choice. Apart from the clothes, the box contained a few odds and ends: a couple of well-thumbed books, a money pouch, a small square of mirrored glass, and half a bone comb that was missing most of its teeth.

Torben found the most presentable of the tunics and removed it. Bundled up, it was a bit creased, but that didn't matter. No one at the Rusty Sickle would care how he looked. He unravelled the thick woollen tunic and gave it a shake, hoping the creases would fall out. As he did, an object fell from the folds and landed with a thud on the floor.

He dropped the tunic and snatched up the item, turning it over several times to ensure that no harm had come to it—the item in question was a silver arm ring which, though dulled with age, glinted faintly in the evening light struggling through the small window. The surface was etched with intricate flowing patterns that swam across the metal and terminated in two knots at the end of each arm. Torben could clearly make out the shapes of human figures and a writhing Wyrm that snaked across the face of the arm ring.

Torben's father had often told him the story of the Triskedale Wyrm when he was a child. He must have heard the tale a thousand times, but each telling was as fresh and captivating as the last. Every time he recounted the story, he'd lift up the sleeve of his tunic and show Torben the arm ring. On cold winter nights, the flickering light from the fire made it seem like the etched warrior figures sprang to life, whilst the Wyrm writhed and thrashed around them.

Torben picked up the tunic and polished the surface of the metal. When he was satisfied that the arm ring hadn't sustained any damage, he grabbed a scrap of cloth from the chest and wrapped it around. As he placed the bundle back into the chest, he paused, and slipped the arm ring on his upper arm. It had been made for his father and Torben sensed a definite connection to him as the arm ring sat snuggly on his arm, as it would have on his.

He put on the clean tunic and fastened a belt over the top, then pulled on his boots, still spattered with muck from the day's work, and made sure the bottom of his trousers were tucked inside to preserve them from the elements. Standing, he grabbed his long, rough leather overcoat from the hook on the back of the door and picked the money pouch from the box.

Opening the door to his room carefully, he listened for signs of life. He could hear Mrs Amos delivering her usual evening lecture down in the kitchen. He'd have to move fast to avoid being caught up in the tirade that she was no doubt delivering to her husband.

He walked quickly and quietly across the landing and down the stairs, without passing through the kitchen, and stepped out into the night. He could hear Mrs Amos calling after him as he strode purposefully across the farmyard, but he kept his head down, and focused on getting away as quickly as possible. He vaulted over the farmyard gate and started down the track towards Bywater Village. The lengthy, winding path was illuminated by the light of the rising moon. He sighed with relief and a smile crept across his face. He was free!

2

T he track that led between Master Amos' farmstead and
Bywater followed the line of the hillside for a mile before
veering off at a right angle and leading towards the village.
Indeed, the track took the walker very much out of their way
and there didn't seem to be any reason why the makers of the
track hadn't created a more direct line between Amos' farm and
Bywater.

The farmstead had been on the hill overlooking the village
for almost as long as Bywater had been in existence. Amos
always used to boast that one of his very distant relatives was on
the first village council, close to three hundred years ago. It was
unlikely, therefore, that the field system lying between Bywater
and Torben had been long established when the Master Amos of
yesteryear had chosen to homestead on the hillside.

If it had been daytime, Torben would have cut across the
fields and taken a more direct route but, in the dim moonlight,
he knew it was safer to stick to the track, even though it led him
almost a mile out of his way. The fields that lay between Bywater
and Amos' farm were ill maintained and boggy, and Torben had
no desire to get muddy or to break an ankle in a rabbit hole. In
fact, no one in the village could actually remember a time when

any crop had been cultivated, or any animals grazed on the fields; they were of the general opinion that the fields were the subject of a long-forgotten land dispute that no one wished to breathe life into again.

Not that any dispute in Bywater would have been particularly ferocious. The most exciting thing that had happened in living memory was when the village cooper had gotten into a fistfight with a travelling salesman outside the tavern who, he claimed, had cheated him on the price of a shipment of barrels. The story was still told by the old folks that propped up the bar in the Rusty Sickle, even though the event had taken place over thirty years ago and the fist-fighting cooper was long dead.

The dirt crunched softly under Torben's boots as he made his way. The sound of his footsteps seemed intrusive in the still night air. There wasn't much life in this part of Burndale. Behind Amos' farm, the land sloped up to the Burn Downs, a desolate and infertile area of rolling chalk hills that almost completely surrounded Burndale, and where only gorse, heather, and the occasional pine tree could scrape a living. No one in the valley knew what lay beyond the Downs, nor indeed how large the Downs even were. A consensus had been collectively reached that they weren't worth thinking about and, as a result, no one strayed far to the north, east or west of Bywater. Having said that, even if one *had* wanted to explore the Downs, the lack of paths or tracks, the treacherous carpet of bracken and heather, and the rolling mass of ditches and hillsides made it nigh impossible to make much progress. Occasionally, some of the village's young men attempted to cross the Downs, but they inevitably returned a few hours after they'd set off, muddy and dejected.

Beyond the fields that stretched in a rough circle around Bywater was a sprawling mass of woodlands that made up the majority of Burndale. The woods were cut only by the course of the river and the road that hugged its banks, which meandered to the end of the valley and into the rest of the Kingdom of Dazscor and Aramore, to which Burndale belonged. The path that Torben was travelling took him to the very borders of the woodland before veering back towards Bywater, which stood as the only beacon of civilisation in Burndale.

As he approached the bend in the road and the edge of the woodland, darkness loomed oppressively and trees began to block out moonlight. Subconsciously, he held his breath and slowed, trying to minimise the noise made by his footsteps. There was no particular reason for him to be worried and he knew it, but there was something about being in, or near, woods at night that filled him with a strange sense of unease. You never knew who, or what, might be lurking in the darkness, peering from behind trees and waiting for an unsuspecting passerby.

The woods remained still and empty of robbers or cutthroats as Torben skirted the edge and turned down a bend in the road towards the village. He was almost disappointed; an attempted robbery would certainly have livened up his night and, in a heartbeat, would probably have made him the most interesting figure in the dale. However, it was not to be, which was probably for the best.

Now that Torben was nearing the village, more signs of life emerged from the gloom. He passed the fields and farmhouse that belonged to the Ketch family, a surly farmer with two bullish sons and a downtrodden daughter. Everyone in Bywater avoided the Ketch family; indeed, the only people to venture close to their land were Torben, Master and Mrs Amos, and the few folks who made the journey to Amos' farm on business. The Ketches had long been marked as 'outsiders'. Even though the family had been resident in Burndale for over four generations, people still viewed them with suspicion. It was probably this collective suspicion that made Mr Ketch so irritable, but there was nothing to be done about it. The Ketch family card was marked and 'once marked, never erased', or so ran the saying in Bywater Village.

There was no sign of life as he strolled past the Ketch farm. All the windows were dark and the majority of shutters were closed. There was one window, he noticed, whose shutters were still open, and he suspected that this was the room that Mr Ketch's sons shared. The two of them were notorious for sneaking out to the tavern in the dead of night, and they were often seen drinking themselves into a stupor in a corner of the Rusty Sickle. No doubt his sons' constant disobedience was another reason Mr Ketch was so crotchety. That being said, he was a saint compared to Mrs Amos.

In the distance, Torben saw village lights winking and flickering in the night, and soon sounds of habitation were heard. It was as if he could hear the collective breathing of the community drifting through the night. The village was home to less than two-hundred people, but as the track started to wind between outlying houses, it felt as if he were walking into a metropolis. After all, he'd never been to a place larger than Bywater, and the majority of his time was spent either in the fields or amongst the three buildings that made up Amos' farm.

Most of the village structures were clustered along the road that ran through the community. The road widened at the northern end to form a rough square, before continuing further up the valley and petering out three miles from Bywater, where it met woods. The village square marked the northern extremity of the settlement, where the majority of life was focused. Gathered around the edges, was a tavern, the blacksmith's and cooper's workshops and the single odds and ends shop that provided the scarcity of luxuries that made their way from larger towns to the south. The only focal point in the square was a well that had long ceased to function; the village folk had to draw all their water from the river.

Torben emerged from the track onto the main road and headed towards the epicentre of the village. There were a surprising number of people out and about, which made him suspect that there'd been a meeting of some kind in the tavern or out in the square. Not that he was particularly concerned with village politics. When Torben had turned sixteen, and been eligible to attend council meetings, he'd trekked to the village every week so that he could be present. He soon learned, however, that nothing was ever done at these meetings … but, then again, nothing needed doing in Bywater. The council meetings were merely a sounding board for the old men to complain about poor harvests, lack of rain, or a fall in the number of livestock—nothing that they could do anything about.

As Torben stepped into the village square, the tavern stood out clearly against the other buildings. Light spilled out of un-shuttered windows, and muttering and laughter flowed from within. Swinging gently in the breeze above the door was an old sickle, once lime-washed white, but now with orange rust clearly visible on the blade. The malty tang of ale wafted through the door as Torben stooped to enter.

The interior of The Rusty Sickle was dimly lit and vaguely obscured by the fog of wood smoke that drifted from a blazing fire and congregated in the beams of the low ceiling. The makeshift bar rested to one side, consisting of a large wooden table with stools in front of it; behind were stacked ale barrels on their sides, taps driven through their lids. There was a dirty sheet of an undetermined hue draped over the bar, covered in a multitude of stains. Above the beer barrels ran a wide shelf covered in wooden tankards, horn mugs, and occasional dusty glassware. The middle of the room was dominated by a fire pit, sunk slightly below the flagstone floor. It held a roaring blaze, which provided most of the light. Gathered around the fire and the walls were a motley collection of chairs and tables, a surprising number of which were occupied. Torben had expected the tavern to be fairly empty—not that he minded it being full of patrons, because the buzz of so many people was enlivening.

As he negotiated his way towards the bar, he saw Johnny, the proprietor, a youngish man with a wispy, scruffy beard that barely clung onto his chin, tending to the punters. Johnny was almost as tall as Torben, which meant that he was stuck in a stooping posture, thanks to the low ceiling. Indeed, Johnny walked with a permanent hunch when not in the Rusty Sickle but, inside the establishment, it was barely noticeable, given that the majority of patrons were too tall to stand up straight in the low room anyway.

Johnny raised a hand in greeting as he caught sight of Torben. 'Long time since I've seen you in here. Let you out again, did they?' He didn't need to ask whether Torben wanted a drink and half turned to fill a tankard from one of the barrels.

'Aye, the old man finally relented, and I got away before that wife of his could stop me,' Torben replied with a wry smile.

'I don't see why you stick around up there. There's nowt there for you but misery and hardship. You're giving that man the best years of your life—for what, eh? One night off every three months? That's no way to live if you ask me.'

'Well what else have I to do? Anyway, I couldn't leave Amos up there alone with only his godawful wife for company. She'd probably kill him and, if not, then they'd starve to death. He can't run the farm by himself.'

'Aye, aye, you've said so before.' Johnny placed the tankard on the bar. 'Are you eating tonight and all?' He gestured to a cauldron suspended from a tripod over one end of the fire pit. 'The stew's good tonight. I'll vouch for it myself.'

'That'd be grand,' Torben replied.

'No bother lad. That'll be three fishes.'

Reaching a hand into a trouser pocket, Torben produced his money pouch and pulled out three copper coins, so dull with age that the mark on one side was obliterated, whilst the leaping fish on the other could barely be detected.

Johnny took the money and turned around, rooting under the bar to look for a dish and spoon to serve Torben's meal. As he did, Torben raised the tankard to his lips and took a long quaff of the amber ale. He sighed audibly and wiped droplets from his mouth.

'Good?' Johnny had completed the exploration beneath the bar, and was surveying Torben with a thin smile.

'Like drinking liquid gold, Johnny!'

'Hah, that's what I like to hear!' The barkeep proffered a wooden bowl and poorly carved wooden spoon. 'Help yourself to stew. There should be bread there too but, if not, the missus will be bringing some fresh out shortly.'

With a nod of thanks, Torben took the bowl and moved to an unoccupied table near the fire. He placed his tankard on the table to mark his spot and made his way to the cauldron. Lifting the heavy lid, he surveyed the dark brown liquid that bubbled beneath. He couldn't discern many of the substances in the murky depths, but it smelt good so he ladled several large spoonfuls into the bowl. He picked up a chunk of crusty bread from a small crooked table beside the fire pit before taking his seat and digging into the simple but hearty meal.

As he ate, he surveyed the patrons. There were a lot of familiar faces, but Torben couldn't conjure up many names. He noticed one table where the patrons were clearly having a similar dilemma trying to work out who Torben was. Faintly, he heard the whispered conversation wafting through the general hubbub.

'Isn't it one of them Ketch lads?' asked one thin sallow man who Torben believed was a labourer on one of the farms east of Bywater.

'Don't be silly. The Ketches look shady as anything, and have been beaten once or twice by the ugly stick! Look, they're over there in *that* corner!'

The incredibly large, muscular man, who took up one side of the table and was speaking, was the village blacksmith. Torben couldn't quite remember what name he went by, but the enormous jet-black beard and thick eyebrows were distinctive enough in their own right … not to mention that the blacksmith was still wearing his heavy work apron, pockmarked with singes and burns, which testified further to the man's trade.

As he spoke, he pointed a beefy finger to the darkest corner of the tavern where, sure enough, the massive bulk of the Ketch boys could be seen slumped against the wall. The table in front of them had already gathered an impressive collection of horn cups and they were busy ploughing their way through another set.

The debate finally ended when one of them asked Johnny as he gathered tankards from recently vacated tables. Torben didn't hear Johnny's response, but the answer didn't seem to help them connect the dots.

'I don't recall an Amos ever having lived in the village,' the sallow man uttered.

'Aye, he works that piss-poor farm beyond the Ketch place, and beyond the abandoned fields,' declared the blacksmith.

'I didn't realise that they had a son,' piped up another man, who Torben couldn't see because he was almost entirely obscured by the blacksmith's shadow.

'No, he's not their son,' an older man stated, and held up a bony finger to add further weight to his years and authoritarian manner of address. 'The boy was taken in after his parents died of the sickness, the last time it came to Burndale. They were tenants on Amos' land and he felt duty-bound to take in the bairn.'

'I thought they only took him in because the parents owed Amos' wife money and they wanted to work it out of the lad,' added the sallow man.

Torben let the conversation fade into the background noise. He didn't want to hear the debate as to his origins, nor did he wish to hear people slander Master Amos. Regardless of why he'd taken him in, he'd always been kind to Torben, even if he'd made him work hard. Torben concentrated on his stew, hoping that the act of eating would take his mind off the conversation he'd overheard.

With a soft sigh, he made his way back to the cauldron and helped himself to another bowlful. As he was about to make his way back to the table, his eye caught a peculiar individual entering the tavern. Indeed, the attention of most of the other patrons was drawn to the figure that ambled to the bar where Johnny stood, warily eying the new customer.

Before him stood the stocky figure of a male dwarf, standing no more than four feet in stature. He looked up at Johnny and politely requested a drink, clearly trying his best not to let on that he sensed everyone's eyes inspecting him intently. It wasn't that the people of Bywater had never heard of dwarves before, but it had been many years since one had last been in the village. Indeed, there were few people alive in Bywater who could claim to have seen a dwarf in the flesh.

As the dwarf took a tankard of ale from Johnny and turned to survey the rest the room, the noise level immediately increased; everyone began talking to mask the fact they'd all been watching the newcomer—all except Torben. Having no one to strike up a random conversation with, he remained staring at the dwarf, who stared back. After a few seconds, the dwarf raised his tankard, took a swift drink, and made his way around the fire pit with the clear intention of sitting at Torben's table.

'Good evening,' said the dwarf amiably as he drew level with the table. 'Mind if I join you?'

'Go ahead stranger, you're welcome,' Torben responded with a quick nod. He'd always enjoyed meeting new people, and the chance to converse with such an exotic character as this dwarf was one that, in his eyes, was *not* to be missed. A meeting such as this was likely to be the most exciting thing to happen to him all year, if not all decade.

He surveyed the dwarf as he placed his tankard on the table and pulled out the other stool. He looked young, or so Torben guessed. There were no flecks of grey in the full head of thick long black hair, roughly pulled from his forehead and held in a short ponytail, nor in the neatly trimmed beard that ran the full length of the oval face and jutted from the square chin. The dwarf had twisted the end of his beard into two braids, held together with etched silver beard rings, and he'd done the same to the ends of the moustache that dangled down to his chin.

Although the dwarf's thickset brow and large squashed nose gave him a slightly dim-witted appearance, the vibrant bright green of his deep-set eyes made it clear that he was as sharp as a pin. He was dressed in a wool jacket trimmed with sheepskin, a faded blue tunic and thick wool trousers, all which looked dishevelled, and a pair of very road-weary boots. It was clear that he'd been on the road for quite some time. Removing a large rucksack from his back, he sat opposite Torben with a heavy sigh.

'The name's Gwilym.' He extended a meaty looking hand across the across the table, several silver rings on his thick fingers glinting in the firelight.

'Torben.'

The two shook hands and Torben was surprised by the strength of Gwilym's grip. The dwarf surveyed the tavern, turned back and leaned in, confidentially, across the table. 'No offence, but this place seems a little rustic.'

'Aye, you're not wrong there,' said Torben with a quick smile. 'Not many people round here have ever seen a dwarf.'

'Why? When was the last time a dwarf passed through these parts?'

'The Gods only know. Possibly whenever the last trading caravan ventured to these parts, but that would have been … over six months ago. In fact, so few of your folk are seen in these parts, most people here probably think that dwarves are creatures taken from stories.'

'Creatures taken from stories.' Gwilym bristled. 'You folks want to get out a bit more and see the world! Though by the looks of it, the sight of the wider world might kill off a few of the people in here.'

'You're not wrong there!'

'Outside this valley, people are a lot more open-minded, you know,' Gwilym stated. 'Used to dwarves, men, and all manner of folks wandering around at will.'

'And where outside Burndale might you be from then?' Torben stared intently, his eyes wide with curiosity.

'Me? Well, where should I begin?' Gwilym tugged his beard thoughtfully. 'I wouldn't exactly say that I come from anywhere. I wouldn't want to restrict myself to one particular geography. Things get awfully complicated when you say that you come from this area or that country. Nothing gets people to make a snap decision about you as quick as knowing where you're from!'

Torben looked confused. 'But how can you *not* be from *anywhere*?'

'No, lad, you've missed the point. I'm from nowhere and everywhere. I go where I please, I do what I please. I don't worry about being tied to a piece of earth; you get plenty attached to the earth when you're dead and buried in it.'

'So you're a wanderer then?'

'Aye, that'd be one way to put it.'

Torben sat back and sighed deeply. 'That sounds like a wonderful way to live, not having to call anyone Master, being able to get up and go where you please.'

'There's no feeling like it,' acknowledged Gwilym. 'As long as you're savvy enough to earn enough coppers to buy a decent meal now and then along the way, you needn't give a toss about the cares of normal life. It seems to me like you and I are kindred spirits.' He nodded sagely.

'I can think of nothing better than taking to the open road, leaving this godawful village, and never thinking of it again!'

'*But?*' The dwarf's eyebrows arched. He knew what Torben was about to say.

'It's complicated. I can't just up and leave. It wouldn't be fair.'

'What's fair got to do with it?' Gwilym wagged a sturdy

finger. 'You ought to look out for number one! Think of all the exciting places you're missing out on, because you're trying to be fair to someone else, and not to yourself!'

'What brings you to this remote part of the world then?'

'Pardon?' Gwilym was taken back by the abrupt question.

'How come you're here? You said it yourself. I could be experiencing all of the exciting, exotic places of the world and yet here *you* are, in this forgotten corner of boredom.'

Gwilym drank at length before replying. 'I was stretching my legs, broadening my horizons, and all that.' He ran a hand through his beard several times. 'I heard that the country round these parts was well worth taking in … the area was recommended to me by a friend.'

'Who on earth recommended that you come *here*?' Torben was visibly shocked. 'Whoever told you that this was an interesting part of the world is no friend at all! Forget broadening your horizons; if you're not careful, this place will make you forget what a horizon is.'

'I don't know about that,' he said, surveying the patrons again. 'This lot here don't seem to be worried by that. They seem quite happy in their ignorance.'

'Aye … most people are.'

The two sat silently for a moment as Torben stared dejectedly into the bottom of his tankard. 'What's stopping you from getting out then?' Gwilym fixed Torben with an intense stare.

Torben, lost deep in thought, took a few seconds to comprehend what Gwilym had said.

'How come you're still here, then? You still haven't given me a good reason why a man of wanderlust like yourself is still here. Or are you like most people?' Gwilym gestured the tavern with the sweeping wave of an arm.

'To be honest I couldn't tell you why I'm still here … truly.'

'I reckon you're afraid,' Gwilym smirked. 'You're afraid of what might happen if you leave the safety of the dully familiar!

I've seen it many times. It's often the case that people are afflicted by a fear of the unknown.'

'I'm not afraid,' Torben snapped. 'I just don't want to let people down is all. Not all of us can drop our responsibilities and go gallivanting off into the wilderness!'

'Prove it then.'

'What?'

'Prove it. Come with me tomorrow. Travel up the road with me for half a day, and if you get scared or tired, you'll still have plenty of time to scurry back home.'

Gwilym's abrupt demand left Torben taken aback. He was staring across the table, the amber light from the fire dancing and flickering in his eyes; it gave the dwarf a wicked, impish edge.

'What's the use?' asked Torben. 'Getting out of here for half a day isn't going to prove anything.'

'How do you know unless you try? In any case, it's like I said: what's half a day in a lifetime? You've got nothing to lose and you can be safely tucked in bed come the night if you want to be.'

Torben had never thought of himself as being a particularly proud man, but the dwarf's words, even though delivered in a jovial tone, held a sharp edge. Like Gwilym said, what was the harm in going on a walk? He hadn't planned on doing anything else with his day off. Going on a jaunt with Gwilym would probably be more diverting and stimulating than anything else Bywater had to offer.

'What's in it for me? If I go off with you for a day, I'll lose out on a day's wages. To a man of small means like myself, a day's coin is the difference between life and death.' The lie came more easily to Torben than he'd expected—but truly, he was only aware of what he was saying when it leapt from his tongue. Why shouldn't he earn a bit of coin though, especially if all he had to do was go for a jaunt with this strange dwarf? And depending on how foolish this dwarf was, his coin could put him a long way towards being able to leave Burndale.

Gwilym surveyed Torben intently … so intently he began to squirm self-consciously. He was certain that Gwilym would dismiss the proposed bet without a second thought.

'Hmm-mm,' the noise rumbled deep from within Gwilym. He was silent for a moment and then a grin spread across his face. 'It seems that you and I are cut from the same type of cloth, Torben. If you go out with me for a whole day, and prove to me that you aren't afraid to leave your precious village, then I'll give you this.' He reached into the folds of his jacket and pulled out a plump purse that he tossed onto the table.

The purse clinked pleasingly as it hit the wooden surface, clearly full of coin. Through a small gap at the neck of the purse, Torben swore that he could see the glint of gold reflected in the firelight. His eyes lit up and he instinctively reached a hand across the table.

'But!' Gwilym's hand swept across the table and scooped the purse back into the safety of his cloak. 'If you don't hold true to your word and leave my company before dusk, I'll demand that as payment.' He pointed to Torben's arm, where the arm ring peeked from the short sleeves of his tunic and gleamed in the firelight.

Torben leaned back, his hand covering the arm ring from Gwilym's beady gaze. He couldn't risk losing the one connection to his family, his father, could he? But then, why should he lose it? How could he? There was no way that he would lose the bet. Gwilym was a fool and would soon be a much poorer fool.

Torben leaned forward again and placed his elbows on the tabletop. He smiled and felt a new air of confidence. 'Alright, I'll head out with you.'

'That's the spirit!' Gwilym grinned. 'Could do with a bit more conversation on my travels. It's been mighty lonely recently.' Holding up a hand, and placing the other upon his chest, he adopted a serious tone. 'Now, as a sign of good faith that I shall not lead you too far astray from this boring shadow of civilisation, let me buy you a drink!'

Gwilym sprang to his feet and made his way to the bar with surprising speed. Torben watched, curious. What was the harm in it? It would do him good to get out of Bywater, stretch his legs, and spend time with someone whose family history he didn't know inside-out. There was nothing of note, or excitement, to the north of Bywater, save the sprawling mass of the Downs. Like as not, Gwilym would give up hope of finding diversions and head back to the village with Torben by midday.

Gwilym startled Torben by appearing alongside him, as if from thin air, holding two overflowing tankards. He plonked one down in front of Torben and raised his in the air. 'To the morrow!'

'To the morrow!' Torben grabbed his tankard and joined the dwarf in toast.

3

Torben awoke as dawn crept its way through Burndale and bathed everything with a soft yellow light. The air was thick with the musty smell of the rain, which had fallen during the night. The moisture in the air and the raindrops that clung to the buildings and trees surrounding Bywater added a sharp edge to the morning light, and painted a glossy sheen across the village.

Sharp fingers of reflected light forced their way under Torben's eyelids; they brought him groggily back into consciousness. He was lying on a pile of dank straw in the small stable block that abutted the Rusty Sickle. The straw was intended for the bedding down of animals, but no one in Bywater had the capital to afford a horse. The nearest one came to a horse in Burndale was the odd mule or donkey that brought some of the wealthier farmers' produce to market, and those beasts were far too precious to be left outside the tavern.

The stable was in poor repair, as evidenced by the shafts of light that poured through the holes in the ceiling and the puddles that had accumulated on the floor beneath. For the most part, however, the stable provided comfortable enough lodging for an inebriated patron and was deemed, by Johnny, to be a suitable resting place for customers who had taken enough drink that they couldn't face the journey home, but not enough so that they'd become troublemakers.

With a groan, Torben sat up and held his head in his hands. If he started moving, he knew that he'd feel better. He grasped a stall partition and used it as a crutch to haul himself up. As he rose to his feet, the room swam and he resisted the urge to fall back to the floor. He stood still a moment, hanging onto the beam as he fought the sick feeling that sat like a lead weight in his stomach.

After a few fraught moments, Torben felt human enough to take stock of the surroundings. As far as he could tell, the other stalls in the stable were unoccupied. The door to the stable was ajar and next to it was a bucket of water and a small loaf of bread. This was typical of the hospitality that Johnny offered his regular patrons.

He staggered to the bucket and splashed water on his face. It was shockingly cold and it made him gasp and splutter. Torben slumped down on the floor and leaned against the door lintel. Pulling off a chunk of bread, he began to chew meditatively. The bread, however, was incredibly stale and the first mouthful stuck fast in his throat. The coughing fit that followed left him doubled over on the floor as he coughed up the sawdust-dry bread.

When the coughing subsided, Torben could hear rustling sounds from one of the nearby stalls. He tried to see the source of the noise, but his eyes watered heavily, and everything in the stable was a blur. From the stall in front, Torben could make out a shape in the hay as it moved slowly towards him and grunted softly.

Suddenly the figure erupted from the straw and filled the room. Torben leapt back towards the door of the stable, desperately trying to rub the moisture from his eyes so he could see the creature clearly.

'What in the world has gotten into you?'

The voice was familiar and as he wiped the last of the tears from his eyes, he saw the diminished figure of Gwilym standing knee-deep in the straw.

'Oh, it's you!' He slumped against the wall and waited for the pounding of his heart to slow.

'Did I scare you?' the dwarf asked, an odd smile of satisfaction pulling at his lips.

'I thought you'd left.' Torben tried to make himself seem calm and composed, but he was keenly aware of the fact that he was still breathing heavily and that his face felt flushed.

'Now why would I leave? We have a deal, remember? You were going to prove to me that you were brave enough to leave and experience a little bit of the world ... unless, of course, you've changed your mind?' His eyes scanned Torben's forearm, searching for the glint of silver—and, undoubtedly, looking forward to collecting his spoils from the wager.

'No, of course I haven't changed my mind. I was just taken aback is all.'

'Ha, and here's me thinking that I was going to win our little wager so easily. Glad to hear you're still in the game.' Gwilym strode to the bucket of water, splashed some on his face, and filled a water skin that he'd removed from his pack, buried deep within the straw.

Torben attempted to eat more of the stale bread, but did so cautiously. He watched Gwilym rescue his pack from the straw and take down his belt from the nail where it hung. It was only then that he noticed the short sword attached to the back of the dwarf's belt; it had remained almost completely hidden from view when he was wearing the woollen jacket.

Nervously, Torben fingered his knife that he likewise carried on his belt. It seemed very small compared to the weapon that Gwilym carried, no more than a child's toy.

Gwilym saw Torben inspecting his blade as he adjusted the belt around his waist. 'It always pays to be prepared lad. You'd struggle to find a dwarf that doesn't travel with a trusty seax to keep themselves safe.' He reached behind him and drew the seax from its sheath, and gazed at his reflection. Gwilym held the weapon nonchalantly, but it still gave off a menacing air. 'This blade has seem me through many scrapes on the road, all part and parcel of the travelling life, I'm afraid.' He slotted the seax back into its sheath and looked directly at Torben. 'But I'm sure you'll discover that for yourself soon enough.'

Torben didn't answer, but tried to look relaxed.

Gwilym pulled his arms through the sleeves of his jacket, hoisted the pack onto his shoulders, and peered past the stable door, inspecting the tavern yard. He sniffed the morning air, then breathed deeply. 'Right lad, we'd best be off! Can't be wasting good daylight now, can we?' He stepped across the threshold, leaving Torben alone in the stable.

He dithered for a second, he no longer possessed the confidence that he'd found last night. It seemed that the brash, carefree attitude had come from the bottom of a tankard. On the other hand, if the dwarf had wanted to kill him and take what little wealth he'd had on him, he could have easily done so during the night. It would have been a lot easier than luring Torben into the wilds; no one in Bywater would have intervened or stopped Gwilym had his crime been discovered. The villagers would have been far too concerned about preserving their own hides than avenging one who they barely knew, or cared about.

Torben could hear Gwilym whistling outside and this goaded him into action. He grabbed the rest of the stale bread, scooped his overcoat from the floor, and half strode, half jogged out of the stable. The lure of coin was too much for him and this seemed too good an opportunity to be missed.

Most of the people who'd frequented the Rusty Sickle the night before had been marked as drunkards when they'd returned to their homes with talk of dwarven travellers abroad in Burndale. There'd been much clucking of tongues and wagging of fingers as wives and parents warned against the tricks that strong drink could play on the mind.

It wasn't surprising, therefore, that Torben and Gwilym

attracted many stares as they walked through the centre of Bywater, following the road to the east, towards the woodland. Considering it was only an hour after dawn, the village was bustling with people going to and fro—gangs of labourers heading to the fields, women and children carrying vessels to the river to collect water, the blacksmith hammering diligently in his workshop.

Many passersby stopped dead in their tracks and stared at Gwilym as he trudged by, and many viewed Torben with suspicion. Barely concealed mutterings drifted through the village.

'Isn't right for that lad to be gallivanting off with strangers.'

A group of villagers began to follow Torben and Gwilym through the village. They kept their distance, but it was clear that they didn't like the intrusion by an outsider, nor the obvious collusion of one of their own with the stranger.

'Well,' Gwilym said sotto voce, 'it seems the folk round here are even friendlier in the day time.'

'Just keep walking and don't look them in the eyes. You don't want to frighten them, or they might get rowdy.'

To Torben, the walk through the village was a bit of a joke. He enjoyed being the centre of attention; it made a change from people ignoring him. And what did he care if the villagers whispered about him behind his back? As they passed people, Torben nodded acknowledgements, waved a hand, and occasionally hailed someone he recognised with a greeting.

As they reached the eastern outskirts of the village, the disgruntled gaggle of villagers began to peal off, satisfied that the dwarf wouldn't cause mischief. The murmurings of conversation continued though as the villagers dispersed, wondering what could have lead Torben to take up with such a strange outlander. Almost every conversation ended with the same conclusion: Torben had always been a bit of an odd one. Being trapped up in that tiny farm with Amos and his fiend of a wife, with no real parental figures, must have addled the poor lad's mind. Had Torben heard any of these conclusions, he'd certainly have had a few strong words to throw back in retaliation, but he and Gwilym simply continued to stride from the village.

As they left the last house behind, the road cut a straight line through rows of fields north of Bywater. Most of the fields on this side of the village were divided into small plots, and as the soil was very poor, cultivation barely extended more than a mile-and-a-half beyond the village boundaries. Hardly anyone tended this land; the majority of labour focused on more prosperous plots to the south and west, where most of the village's food was grown.

The few people that Gwilym and Torben came across as they followed the road were the older men too sore and world-weary to be of much use in the big work gangs and tended the scrappy vegetable and fodder patches in this part of Burndale. As a rule, they weren't very talkative and those that did acknowledge Torben and Gwilym, only did so through a curt nod or hollow grunt.

As they passed through the fields, the road became noticeably more rugged and unkempt, and as the two figures came closer to the eastern woods, trees began to encroach the road.

'So what exactly are you looking for out here?' Torben broke the silence that had settled over the two of them since they'd left the village.

'Huh?' Gwilym had seemingly been dwelling on the xenophobic attitude of the villagers and didn't register Torben's question. 'What do you mean, what am I looking for?'

'You must have had some reason for coming out this way. There's nothing that I know of this side of Bywater, and the road only carries on for another couple of miles.'

'How do you know that there isn't anything on this side of the dale? Have you ever even been to the end of the track?'

'Well, no.' Torben paused and scanned the area. 'But

everyone in Bywater knows that there's nothing to the north. If there was, they'd have continued building the road.'

'No wonder you've never made it out of your village, if that's how you've been brought up to think.' Gwilym regarded the young man walking next to him. 'People aren't logical, and most things in life aren't clear-cut. There could be any number of reasons why they didn't continue to build the road, but then think laterally: why did they bother to extend the road beyond the confines of the village in the first place, if they knew there was nothing to the north?'

'Errm.'

'See!' Gwilym jumped in before Torben could gather his thoughts. 'No logic behind it, is there? Which makes me think that there's something of interest and potential profit for anyone savvy enough to go and sniff around.'

Torben thought hard, trying to come up with a response, but he couldn't deny the logic of the dwarf. He took in the scenery they were passing through. By now, the two of them were deep into the woods and the path was becoming rougher and more unkempt by the foot.

The bright summer's day felt murky as a thick cover of foliage reduced light to a more gloomy, emerald hue. The only noises that cut through the dense silence were the sounds of Gwilym and Torben's boots crunching along the dirt path, the occasional caws and trills of birds flitting between trees, and the rustling of four-legged creatures in the brush.

Torben didn't like woods. Having spent the majority of his life in open fields, so being deep in woodland was intensely claustrophobic. As he walked along, Torben's eyes constantly darted left and right, scanning the undergrowth. Gwilym, on the other hand, didn't seem phased by the change in scenery. He was whistling under his breadth and there was a definite spring to his step. Being back in the wilds had obviously improved his mood.

'Is there anything, dangerous, in these woods, do you think?'

Torben was trying to make his voice sound calm, but there was a distinctive quaver in his tone.

'There are a lot of things in the wilder places of the world that could harm you … wolves, bears … hell, I've had wild boars come at me in the past … especially if you get in-between them and their bairns.' He smiled dryly. 'Though you never know when locals might band together and jump a passing traveller for the sake of a few coins. One time I passed through a village that had never heard of my folk, let alone seen a dwarf—aye, even more backward than your lot. I arrived in the evening, after everyone in the local tavern had had several ales, so they welcomed me graciously. I had as much food as I could eat and as much drink as I could sup. Never had to spend a single penny. I woke up the next morning, expecting the situation to be the same, and was ready for a spot of breakfast. To my surprise, I was met by an angry mob who tied me up and threw me in the Well.'

He chuckled to himself. 'I found out later the people in that village—Hamden, Horden, Harden?—had a folktale about a *little man* that lived in the Well, and the tale ran that if he emerged and walked around the village at night, he should be showered with gifts, well fed, and treated like a king. However, if the little man appeared during the daytime, he needed to be thrown back into the Well, or else the village would be struck with bad luck for the rest of the year. I've no idea how the tale came to life or if they had ever seen a dwarf before, but that damn fairy story nearly cost me my life. Two days I was stuck down that wellspring before I was able to climb up and escape! The bloody villagers placed a guard up top to make sure I wouldn't get out and eat their children, or whatever it was that the *little man* was supposed to do.'

He shook his head and shrugged. 'At one point, I thought the situation was going to turn south when we were leaving your homestead but, thankfully, they weren't quite as backwards as these other folk. Not that that's saying very much … but, then again, the villagers you come across are normally the least of your worries. There are a number of other creatures and folks that can spell trouble. A lot of cruel, heartless folk lurk by the roadside and roam the wilds. Sadly, there are decidedly more of them wandering about than there used to be.' Gwilym looked at Torben, who'd turned decidedly pale. 'I'm sure there's nothing like that in these woods though. It seems very quiet, in a good way that is, peaceful and tranquil—aye that's the word, *tranquil!*'

Although Gwilym had brought Torben out of his comfort zone purposefully, with the aim of trying to win himself another trinket, the young man was starting to grow on him and, despite the fact that he was still very wet behind the ears, he couldn't help but respect him for following through with the wager. Most of the time when he challenged small-minded country-folk to brave the wilds, they didn't turn up the next morning, or surrendered their money to the dwarf without a fight when he came to collect payment. They were more concerned with getting rid of the stranger than questioning the validity of the wager. If they did meet with the dwarf, they rarely lasted more than an hour before becoming overly nervous and scurrying home—with a little encouragement from Gwilym himself.

Torben looked uneasy, but Gwilym didn't think that he would bolt anytime soon; the lad was made of sterner stuff than the majority of village-folk he'd met. If nothing else, the lad would make this a slightly more challenging fleece than he'd previously tried to pull.

Silence fell again upon the pair as they continued up the path. By now, the sun was well on its way towards its midday zenith, and the temperature had started to rise under the smothering canopy of leaves. The path had begun to climb steeply up the valley and the laboured breathing of the travellers grew louder.

The path continued its ascent for another forty minutes, until the sharp pitch of the incline suddenly relaxed, allowing Gwilym and Torben respite. The two stopped and leaned heavily against a tree that had rooted itself across the path, and caught their breaths.

'We must be reaching the top of the dale. Look, the path up ahead is levelling out.' Torben peered through the gloom, trying to glean more to report about the way forwards. 'It's running out by the looks of it.'

The woods were impinging more and more onto the path, and looked completely overgrown in places. The track, for the most part, was now just a bald strip of dirt.

'Keep your eyes peeled, Torben. If there's going to be anything of interest around, it'll be up here.' Gwilym set off again and Torben followed directly behind.

It was hard work determining where the path was leading; in some places, the track disappeared altogether, and they had to rely on the spotting of bald patches of dirt further up the hillside. When the path finally did level out, it brought them to a circular clearing in the woods. Around the edges of the clearing, a couple of tall and sturdy oak trees had taken up residence, their long gnarled branches invading the clearing, almost as if they were straining to keep the light from the ground. All the trees looked very old and it seemed to Torben that they were probably the oldest things that he'd ever set eyes on. He could easily imagine them glowering down from the hillside on the first settlers as they arrived in Burndale all those years ago.

'Here we are, end of the line. You know, after what you said last night, I was hoping that there'd be a pot of gold here, or a feast laid out and waiting for a curious traveler.' Torben was feeling very smug. He'd told the dwarf that it wasn't worth following the track and now he was a sack of gold richer for Gwilym's naive optimism.

To Torben's disappointment, however, Gwilym wasn't listening, but had instead set off across the clearing and was poking around the far bushes.

'What you doing? I said there's nothing up here. You might as well pay up now and be done with this little adventure.

There's nothing but trees here, common garden trees, no treasure, no riches, no gold, just boring trees!' Torben waited for a second, hoping that the dwarf would respond, but he continued investigating the bushes.

Torben was becoming exasperated; he'd enjoyed a nice stroll with Gwilym, but now victory had presented itself and he wanted to be off backdown the hill with his coin. He wanted to enjoy a good hearty meal before he was obliged to traipse back to Amos' farm and work. He was about to launch into another observation of the tree-dominated hillside when Gwilym let out a small cheer and dived into the brush.

Torben ran across the clearing, fearing that the dwarf was giving him the slip, and abandoning him without paying him his due. When he reached the point where Gwilym had disappeared, the dwarf emerged from the undergrowth, grinning from ear to ear.

'Nothing up here, he says. How wrong you were, my lad!' Gwilym beckoned Torben to follow and left the clearing again.

To Torben's surprise, the track continued on the other side of the clearing and led into the woods, where it stopped at the base of a dilapidated stone tower that rose towards the canopy of the trees. The tower was covered in thick moss and spiralling ivy, effectively allowing it to blend in with the surrounding growth, and it looked as if it had abandoned for quite some time. At the base of the tower was a large wooden door with a simple latch. Gwilym was tugging at it.

'Well, I'll be damned,' Torben exclaimed, staring at the tower, his mouth hanging open.

'Now do you appreciate what I was talking about? Consider this as an education in the wonders of the world, Torben! I like to think that today I have opened your eyes.' Gwilym grunted as he pulled the door latch. 'Bloody thing is rusted shut. Give me a hand with this, will you?'

Torben, now as enthusiastic to explore as Gwilym, helped him with the door. Gwilym's efforts had only opened the door a couple of inches, but with Torben pushing as well, they managed to make a gap wide enough to enter.

The door hinges squealed as it opened and flecks of rust flew off, testament to the amount of time that they'd been unused. Gwilym squeezed through the gap first and Torben followed, barely managing to fit his broad frame through the threshold.

The interior of the tower was dim. The walls were studded with small windows along its whole length, so it was just about light enough to see without the aid of a torch. The only thing immediately visible to Gwilym and Torben was a spiral staircase. They looked at one another and then began to climb.

'I don't suppose you know of any reason why someone would have built a watchtower up here?' The dwarf's voice bounced and echoed in the small interior.

'No idea. No one in the village knows that it's here. Or at least no one in living memory knew of it.'

'Hmm, interesting. Do you have any folktales about invaders or wars in your village?'

Torben thought for a moment 'No, none. Why?'

'Often military fortifications, or watchtowers, can be absorbed into folk memories and tales of battles and conflict, and these tales can often outlast knowledge, or existence of the structures themselves. I was thinking that if you had a tale in Bywater about two barons fighting over land, or beasts or brigands coming down from the surrounding hills, or whatever, it may explain why this tower is here.'

'As far as I know, there were no battles or anything like that around here. Nothing exciting at all happened in Burndale. Perhaps people built this tower because they were bored.' Torben could barely conceal the bitterness as he said this.

'Ha,' Gwilym snorted. 'I could certainly believe that!'

As they ascended, Gwilym used his seax and Torben his knife to clear vegetation that had grown across the windows so there'd be more light. Beyond the windows, there were no other observable features and the interior of the tower was consumed by the curve of the spiral staircase. They climbed for what seemed like an age before they popped out onto an interior platform where the spiral staircase abruptly stopped.

The platform extended across the tower, except for the side where the spiral staircase emerged. There were windows with two-foot spaces between them, running all the way around the walls. The platform was bare, save for the remains of a very old fireplace, in which hung a rusted cooking pot suspended from a chain. On the wall furthest away from staircase was a thick wooden ladder that ascended to a trapdoor in the ceiling.

Gwilym scratched amongst the dry leaves that had collected in the tower, looking for anything that might be of interest, whilst Torben inspected the trapdoor. He tested the strength of the ladder by placing a foot on the bottom rung. It held his weight well enough, even though the wood groaned ominously as he began to climb.

Gwilym came and stood next to the ladder, looking dejected. 'Well, there's nothing that we can take home with us, save that useless looking pot.' Gwilym scanned the trapdoor. 'We should be able to get a nice view from up there.'

Torben stood to one side and let Gwilym ascend the ladder. The dwarf grunted as he fiddled with the trapdoor fastening, and then recoiled and covered his eyes with one hand as he flung open the trapdoor. Light burst into the chamber below. He climbed the remaining rungs and vanished onto the watch platform.

Torben stood for a moment, letting his eyes adjust to the light, and then ascended the ladder himself. A breeze tousled his curly hair as he emerged into open air. He hauled himself onto the watch platform and stood next to Gwilym, who was surveying the view. Before them stretched the whole of Burndale, as far as the eye could see. The builders of the watchtower had chosen the perfect spot, taking advantage of the natural slope of the dale to allow for a full, unobstructed view of the valley, whilst allowing the tower to be virtually impossible to spot amongst the trees to anyone who was looking towards the eastern end of Burndale.

'You know this place doesn't look half bad from up here. I almost feel bad for what I said about it last night.' Gwilym stared across the dale, his hands on his hips, the disappointment of not having found anything valuable temporarily gone.

The line of the river was clearly visible to the west, cutting through the western woods. A small lake that bowed next to Bywater Village glistened in the midday sun. Bywater itself squatted as a rather more ungainly sight in the landscape; the dull-roofed and dark-walled houses looked out of place in the landscape compared to the deep lush green of the surrounding woodlands, the gentle gold of the wheat fields to the north and west, and the shimmering azure of the water.

'You know, this reminds me of the time that I travelled to the city of Makesh a couple of years back. The approach to the city from the north, where I was coming from, was through the mountains, and once you crested them you spent the rest of the journey looking down on the city until you reached the desert floor. I spent hours admiring the towers and minarets from the mountain paths. The whole place seemed so much more peaceful and beautiful when you were looking down. Having said that, this isn't at all like being in the desert ... a terrible place to travel ...'

Torben let Gwilym's voice wash over him as he launched into the full flow of his story. The dwarf was right though, Burndale, and even Bywater, looked a lot more picturesque from a distance. Perhaps being distanced from the place was allowing Torben to truly appreciate its beauty. The drudgery and exasperation of life in Burndale seemed very remote from the watchtower.

Torben's philosophical train of thought was interrupted by a dark smudge encroaching the corner of his vision. He turned his head and focused his gaze on the western part of Bywater. At that end of the village, thick black smoke rose from the houses—

it was far too thick, however, to be smoke from household fires and hearths. It was slowly spreading from house to house and creeping through the village.

By now Gwilym had spotted the smoke too and stopped his story. Like Torben, he turned to better view the scene.

'What's going on?' Worry was clearly audible in Torben's voice.

Fire had started to spring up across the rest of the village, no longer in a consistent swath as in the west of the village, but in isolated spots unconnected to the houses ablaze in the west.

'There isn't enough wind for the thatch to be blowing around and setting light to the other houses. Someone must be setting the fires in other parts of the village. Why would they do that?'

Gwilym was oddly quiet and Torben spun, hoping it would prompt Gwilym into answering his question.

The dwarf's brow was heavily knitted and his expression dour. 'I think it's best if we stay up here for the time being. It's not safe to go back down there. I've seen this happen before. Believe me, there's nothing but trouble down there.'

'What do you mean? Is someone attacking the village?' Torben could barely keep still; he was growing increasingly agitated.

'Aye, like as not. I'm sorry lad, but there's nothing we can do. Best stay out of trouble for the time being and—Torben, no!'

Torben was climbing back down the ladder. He skipped the last few rungs and sprinted down the stairs. He needed to know what was going on; he needed to help! Bywater was all he knew and he wasn't about to let it be burned down in front of his eyes.

Gwilym stood on the watch platform. He was torn as to what he should do. On the one hand, following Torben and going back to Bywater village went against every feeling of self-preservation he had. He was certain that the village was being laid to waste, and he didn't want to get caught up in that. On the other hand, he didn't want to see Torben charge back into the village and get killed. He dithered, shuffling his feet unconsciously.

'Bugger it all!' With that, Gwilym climbed down the ladder. As he set his feet down on the platform, he could hear the squealing hinges as Torben tore open the tower entrance. The lad was quick; he didn't have a moment to lose. He sprinted down the stairs, calling Torben's name. As he careened down the spiral staircase, he couldn't help but think that he was making a big mistake.

4

Torben didn't think, he just ran. Within seconds of leaving the top of the watch platform, he'd forced open the tower door and had smashed his way through the undergrowth that covered the path. He crossed the clearing in the blink of an eye and began to thunder down the hillside, back towards Bywater.

Had he taken a few moments to consider what he was doing, it might have occurred to him that blindly charging into the village, unarmed and unprepared for a fight, was not the brightest of ideas. Indeed, he might even have stopped to consider his reasons for wanting to protect the village in the first place. As he'd often said, all he could dream of was escaping that backward, introverted community and never returning. What had the villagers ever done for him that warranted him to risk his life for them?

As he ran, however, the only thought that went round his head was that, in reality, Bywater and Master Amos' farm was all he knew, and that without them, he'd have nothing.

Torben's brain only fully kicked into gear when he reached the bottom of the dale. He was back on the main path that ran out of Bywater, and the houses of the village were clearly visible where they lay just over a mile from the edge of the woods. Scrubby vegetable plots were all that lay between Torben and the village, and they offered a scant amount of cover; instinctively, he knew that he had to tread more carefully from now on.

He was also exhausted and now that he had stopped running, that exhaustion hit him like a lead weight. Torben had no idea how long he'd been running. The journey, which had taken them the whole morning, had passed in a blur, and Torben's sense of time had completely abandoned him. His breath became more and more strained as the adrenaline in his body dissipated.

It was clear that the fire in the village wasn't the product of some horrific accident. From the border of the woods, he heard screams echoing across the fields, and now and again he also heard piercing, guttural howls. He'd never heard anything like it before, and it chilled him to the bone.

The wind had also changed direction and the thick smoke was blowing towards Torben, across the fields from the village. Heavy ash and soot, carried by the wind, made him cough as he struggled to breathe evenly after the descent from the dale, and his eyes began to water in reaction to the pungent smoke.

Now that he was back in the valley, no longer running blindly, Torben didn't know what to do. His small hunting knife was almost certainly no match for whoever, or whatever, was running rampant through the village. Then again, did he even want, or need, to go to the village? He'd easily be able to skirt the houses, flit across the fields and return to Amos' farm without setting foot in the village. If he did that, he'd be able to return with minimal risk. It would be slower, but much safer.

Still, he needed a plan … he needed—his train of thought was broken as Gwilym burst from out of the undergrowth, not expecting Torben to be standing stationary, and ran straight into him. Before Torben knew what was happening, he was pinned to the ground. He tried to speak, but Gwilym's head had made perfect contact with the small of Torben's back and had knocked the wind out of him. There was a moment of silence as he tried to recover, broken only by Gwilym's ragged post-run breathing and Torben's wheezing.

'You … stupid … pillock,' Gwilym managed to say. 'You could have been killed, running off like that without a second thought as to what might be down here. You seem to forget that you're a farm-boy, not some lance-waving knight charging off to battle!' He rolled off Torben's prone form and managed to stagger to his feet doubled over by the young man.

With the weight of the dwarf lifted, Torben gasped for air and sat up.

Unlike Torben, Gwilym was less used to prolonged bouts of physical activity, and his face was bright red and his dark hair slick, dripping with sweat. It trickled from his hairline to the tip of the squat nose in an unbroken stream. 'What the hell were you going do once you got to the village, eh? Challenge whoever's there to a fist fight?'

'I don't know. I hadn't thought that far ahead. I was trying to work out a plan when you barged into me!'

Gwilym opened his mouth to retort, but a shrill scream pierced the air. Torben and Gwilym's heads snapped round, trying to pinpoint the location of the woman who'd screamed and, more pressingly, her assailant.

The field in front remained empty, and there was no sign of anyone advancing. Nevertheless, the two crouched down, painfully aware of how exposed they were on the road.

'We need to get to cover.'

'What are you planning to do?' Gwilym was still scanning the field, intently inspecting each clump of sad-looking vegetables, as if expecting to see an aggressor lurking within.

'I need to get back to the farm.' Torben was likewise surveying the field, trying to work out the best way to stay concealed. 'We might be able to get there before anything happens.'

'Are you sure that it's worth ...' Gwilym stopped mid-sentence. 'Are you sure that's what you want to do?'

'Aye, positive.'

'In that case, lead on.'

Torben looked at Gwilym. The dwarf was tightening straps on his pack and making sure that it wouldn't unexpectedly throw him off balance. His face was set in a grim expression, his brows so deeply furrowed that the bushy eyebrows almost connected with his beard.

'You don't have to come with me if you don't want to.' Torben's eyes met the dwarf's. 'I won't hold anything against you if you want to turn around and head back up the dale. These aren't your people, and you don't owe them or me anything.'

'I know that, but I'm not someone to abandon a man in his hour of need. It's best to stick together in a situation like this. Besides, you know the lay of the land here better than I do. We stand a much better chance of getting through this as a pair rather than as two lone desperadoes.' Gwilym pulled tightly on the straps one last time and crept level with Torben. He nodded at the young man and surveyed the field once again.

Although Torben didn't know Gwilym in the slightest—they'd only been aware of one another's existence a matter of hours—he was very glad to have the dwarf by his side, and that he wasn't alone. 'Right, follow me then.'

Torben, still crouched low to the ground, dashed from the cover of the trees with Gwilym close behind, rushing toward a large tree in the middle of a nearby field. As they entered the open land, Torben half expected to be struck down, but no surprise blow came. He thought that the sound of his heavy breathing, let alone the noise of his and Gwilym's feet crunching gravelly soil would alert attackers. This field and the surrounding ones, however, were empty; there was no one to be seen.

As they neared the tree in the centre of the field, Torben became more nervous about what their next move would be.

Nothing stood between the tree and the abandoned fields to the east of the village other than scrappy patches of carrots and cabbages, which would provide no cover whatsoever.

On reaching the tree, Torben pressed himself flat against the trunk, trying to maximise the amount of cover it afforded. Gwilym, instead, lay flat on the ground behind a small amount of scrub that had grown around the tree's base, and used this as a watch point to survey the village. The tree itself lay at the top of a small hill, which afforded the duo an unobstructed view of Bywater below, but this also meant that the tree was the most obvious focal point in the landscape for anyone looking out from the village.

'What can you see?' Torben hadn't dared survey the village thoroughly. He was worried about what he might observe. 'Can you see any of the bandits still in the village?'

'Yes, but they're not bandits … they're Lupines.'

'They're what?' Torben stuck his head from behind the tree as far as he dared to glimpse what was happening. It was hard to distinguish much. The black smoke pouring out of building windows and doors obscured much of the action. Clearly visible, however, at the edge of the village were two tall lean figures that were humanoid in form, but definitely *not* human.

They resembled large gangly wolves, standing on two legs with front limbs serving as arms; long-fingered hands replaced forelegs or paws. They were completely unconcerned by the roaring blazes before them and stood leaning on spears, talking amongst themselves. Not far behind them lay the body of a woman. It was hard to be exact with details from their observation point, but the large pool of blood that surrounded her plainly showed that she was dead.

'Lupines,' Gwilym repeated quietly. 'They're not truly man or beast, but something a lot more dangerous. I've seen their handiwork before and it's not pretty. It's typical of their raiding tactics for part of a pack to set fire to a settlement and drive the inhabitants into the arms of their colleagues waiting at the other end. After that, they push their victims into a place they can't escape from and … well … these two look like they've been left on sentry in case anyone slips the net and tries to escape. There'll probably be sentries posted on each side of the village. We need to get a move on. If we linger here, they'll spot us soon for sure, or pick up our scent when the wind changes direction.'

Torben shuffled back around the tree and looked in the direction that they needed to go. From where they were hiding, they needed to cross a quarter of a mile of open fields, until the vegetable patches met the densely hedged boundary of the abandoned fields that lay between Bywater and Master Amos' farmstead. Once they reached the abandoned fields, the hedge would easily shield them from the village; the long grass, thick brush, and scattered trees would provide ample cover for them to reach the farm.

'Which way are we going?' Gwilym had joined Torben on his side of the tree and was looking up expectantly.

'We need to get there.' He pointed down the hill towards the hedge-line.

'There? We'll never make it there with all that open ground. They'll spot us for sure, and believe you me, you do *not* want to start a footrace with Lupines!'

Torben squinted at the sky. 'How long do you reckon it is until nightfall?'

'That won't be for hours yet. We can't stay here that long. Like as not, they'll sweep the surrounding countryside soon, looking for anything or anyone that they've missed.'

'Alright, alright. Just let me think.' Head in hands, Torben squatted on the ground. At this point, the only way forward was to retreat back up the dale and to the tower to wait for nightfall. If they did that, then Amos and his wife would almost certainly be dead by the time they got to the farm.

A shrill howl from the village made Torben bolt upright, his hands scrabbling at his belt for his knife. He wheeled round, ready to strike, but there was no attacker bearing down. Gwilym, once more lying on the ground and peering through the brush, kicked Torben sharply and shushed him.

'Have they found us … have they picked up our scent?' He pressed against the tree again.

'No, it's not us they're after … yet. This might be our chance though. Look!'

With great care, Torben eased his head from behind the tree and gazed at the village. With spears ready, the two Lupines on sentry were starting to encircle a man running at full speed from the village, obviously hoping that his exit was clear. Echoing howls from inside Bywater made it clear that the man was being pursued..

The man himself was huge and well-built, with a distinctive bushy beard. It didn't take Torben long to recognise him as the village blacksmith he'd sat near in the Rusty Sickle the night before. He was still wearing the heavy work apron, which must have protected him from the flames as he made his escape through the village. In his meaty hands, he carried a scythe.

As he spotted the two sentries approaching, the blacksmith skidded to a halt, quickly checked behind him, and then charged towards the sentries.

'Quick, this is our chance!' Gwilym sprang to his feet and sprinted across the field.

For an instant, Torben was transfixed by the sight of the blacksmith, bloodied and singed, hurling himself at the sentries in a desperate bid for freedom. The blacksmith swung the scythe in a huge arch, trying to catch one of the Lupines with the curve of the blade. The sentries leapt out of the way, one of them losing its footing and crashing to the ground, its spear flying from its grasp.

It looked as if the blacksmith might have gained the upper hand as he deftly avoided the other sentry's thrust and sent them reeling back with a blow to the face from the scythe haft.

More Lupines, however, swarmed down the main street towards the blacksmith. He mustn't help him; he *couldn't* help him. But what if he could buy the blacksmith time? Provide a distraction so he could escape? It was best to stick together in situations like this. Torben stood a moment longer. He took several deep breaths to calm his nerves and sprinted across the field after Gwilym.

Behind him, Torben could hear the clash of metal on metal, the howling of the Lupines, and the guttural bellowing of the blacksmith as he fought for his life. Torben daren't look back; if he did, he'd lose the precious seconds that the blacksmith's life had bought him and that would be that.

Ahead, Gwilym had almost finished hacking a hole in the base of the hedge with his seax. He quickly looked up to make sure Torben was drawing near and threw himself through the hedge. As Torben broke stride to dive through the hedge, he heard the harsh, bitter scream of the blacksmith as he succumbed … and triumphant howling of the Lupines.

As he leapt through the hedge, broken woody stems and thorny prickly leaves scratched his face and arms. He thudded onto the other side and lay in the brush, dazed by the force of the impact, before Gwilym's burly hands picked him up and set him on his feet.

'Let's keep moving. I don't think our friend back there is going to buy us anymore time.'

Torben nodded and the two of them hastened across the field. The thick hedge-line around the abandoned field system shielded them from the road. Anyone who wanted to survey the landscape would have had to enter the fields themselves to see what was going on inside the hedge-line. Even then, it would have been hard to spot someone amongst the grass, even a person as tall as Torben, who stood well over six foot. Nevertheless, the two kept low as they moved through the fields, Torben leading and Gwilym following not far behind.

The going was tough because the long grass twisted itself

around their boots, as if trying to trip them, and the field held countless invisible rabbit holes and plough furrows that lay beneath the sea of green. They lost count of the number of times that they pitched forward upon losing footing in unseen depressions, but Torben and Gwilym pushed on as fast as they dared. As they ascended the hill towards Amos' farm, the village grew more and more distant. As they periodically looked back to make sure that they weren't being followed, they could see that the smoke in Bywater was dissipating. All that was left of the houses were blackened skeletal support timbers and a few stone chimneystacks from the more prosperous dwellings.

After thirty minutes, they reached the hedge-line at the other end of the field system. Gwilym drew his seax, ready to cut an exit through dense undergrowth, but Torben held up a hand to stop him and beckoned Gwilym to follow.

Torben had gotten his bearings and tracked along the side of the hedge-line until he came to an opening he'd previously created to pass to and from the abandoned fields as he wished. He brushed aside loose branches that he'd concealed the entrance with and tentatively poked his head through the hedge.

'The coast's clear,' he said as he retreated into the field. 'The farmstead is just around the bend, and it'll be far easier to follow the road than cut through the hedge to get to the fields on the other side.'

'Fine, lead on.'

Torben edged his way into the hole in the hedge, surveyed the length of the road once more, and stepped though. Because of his size, Gwilym passed through the gap more smoothly and, when he emerged, he followed his companion up the road towards the farmstead.

Approaching the turning, they pressed against the hedge and edged their cautious way around the corner. Torben, in the lead, stopped and peered into the farmyard. 'Bollocks!' Quickly, he slipped back into the hedge again.

'What? Are there Lupines in the farm?' Gwilym's voice was so quiet that it was barely audible over the breeze.

'Not that I can see, but they've definitely been here already.'

Gwilym started to speak, but Torben had already edged his way into the gateway and entered the farmyard.

As Torben crept forward, he became increasingly certain that the Lupines had moved on. Debris from the house lay strewn across the yard—clothes, furniture, and anything that hadn't been valuable or portable enough to be worth taking. The doors to the barn had likewise been flung open and the remaining sacks of seed grain had been torn open and cast into the yard; presumably, the raiders had been looking for loot.

Torben unconsciously straightened as he surveyed the carnage and walked across the farmyard. It was then that he saw Master Amos, or rather his body, lying spread-eagled on the ground before the barn. The old man's hand still gripped the haft of a pitchfork, but the improvised weapon had clearly done no good. A deep cut ran the length of Amos' back and his face and neck was gashed with deep claw marks.

There was no sign of Mrs Amos, but Torben didn't care. She'd been much lighter on her feet than her husband, but there was no way that she'd have been able to flee the farm. Doubtless, she was still inside the house.

Crossing the yard, Torben knelt and closed the old man's eyes. There had been many times when Torben had resented him, even hated him, but now he felt as if the only family he had left in the world lay before him … bloodied and motionless … gone forever.

Gwilym, who'd followed Torben into the farmyard and had been standing at a distance with his head bowed, looked up suddenly, his gaze fixed on the house. 'We're not alone,' he whispered. 'We need to get out of sight, *now*!'

'Quick, into the barn,' Torben ordered.

The two of them darted into the interior of the barn. Torben crouched in one of the ox stalls. The floor was sticky and the compartment reeked of blood. He picked his way around the dead ox so that he could look into the yard through a crack in the wall.

Three figures had emerged from the house and were bickering over a sack of goods looted from within. The Lupines were tall and lanky, easily standing over six foot, covered from head to toe in greyish fur like that of a wolf. They were humanoid in form, except that they bore the long distinctive muzzle and ears of their wolf cousins. Their yellow eyes were clear, bright, and displayed a sense of keen intelligence. They were clearly more than primal savages.

They spoke and Torben could make out rows of sharp pointed teeth lining their mouths. As the Lupines gesticulated and tugged at the sack with long dexterous fingers, their claws flashed under the dazzling sun.

Their only clothing: crude leather shorts down to their knees. No shoes or boots. The talons on their feet were clearly visible, even though they stood twenty from the barn. They had an array of weapons strapped to their bodies, though the blood that matted the maw of the one closest the barn was proof enough that they weren't averse to using the natural weapons they'd been born with.

The Lupines made their slow way across the farmyard, talking as they did so. Torben could only hear the odd word; the guttural tone of their accents, coupled with the odd growl or bark, meant their speech was hard to make head or tail of when at a distance.

As they made their way back to the road, Torben had to shuffle along the barn wall to keep the Lupines within the sightline provided by the crack he was peering through. He was concentrating so hard on watching the Lupines, he didn't notice the bucket at the back of the ox stall.

A thud resounded as his foot connected with the bucket and shoved it a foot and half across the stall. In any other situation, the noise would have been barely audible, but it seemed to boom around the otherwise silent barn. Gwilym, with his back to Torben, watching the barn door, flinched when he heard the noise—and he wasn't the only one that noticed. The ears of the Lupines pricked as they registered the sound; they turned, their eyes fixed on the barn.

Torben hadn't dared move from his position against the wall for fear of making more noise. He could still see what the Lupines were doing. Indeed, as the three stared at the barn, it felt to Torben as if they were staring through the wooden wall, straight at him.

One of the Lupines moved a couple of steps forward, head cocked and raised to the sky. He sniffed. After a couple of seconds, the Lupine turned back to his cohort, muttered something, and they strode onto the road and out of sight.

'Phew!' Torben sank to the floor and released a long sigh of relief. 'They're gone. I thought they'd come and investigate the barn for sure.'

Gwilym made his way to the wall, looking for himself to ensure the coast was clear. 'Had they not killed these oxen, they'd have picked up our scent for sure. Thankfully, the stench of this place kept us covered.'

During the stress and excitement of watching the Lupines, Torben had stopped noticing the smell of the blood that filled the barn, but now that he was fully aware of it again, it began to make him feel sick. 'What now?' he whispered anxiously. 'Is it safe to move on, do you think?' He was very wary of making too much noise, and even his soft whisper reverberated around his head like a bellow.

Gwilym ceased staring at the farmyard and withdrew from the crack in the wall, straightened up, and curtly nodded. 'I reckon they're long gone now. There was nothing keeping them here, and I imagine the rest of them are camped down in the village. I don't think we should stick around for too long though, just in case they decide to come back, but we've probably enough time to sweep the house for provisions first.'

'Where are we going to go?' Torben's voice sounded forlorn. It had occurred to him that he didn't know where else to go. The only geographical knowledge that he had to draw on were the names of a couple of villages in the next dale, and he wasn't even sure of what the next dale was called. He had no idea of how to get to these places, either. All the directions from Bywater that he'd heard people give, had been to follow the single road until it left Burndale where, the locals assumed, everything would be signposted. At present, however, travelling by the road wasn't an option.

Beyond his scanty knowledge of the next dale, the only other place Torben knew about was Triskedale … from the stories that his father had told him. But Triskedale might not even be a real place, just a made-up setting for a fanciful tale a man had told his little boy on long lonely winter nights by the fire.

'I think it's best if we make for Gallenford. It's well protected there. They'd just finished repairing the palisade when I last left, so I doubt the Lupines will have bothered them. They'll have sought out softer targets elsewhere, I imagine. I have a good friend that lives there who will put us up and, like as not, help you get back on your feet. It'll be a long trip, but it'll be worth it, and who knows how many undefended villages these Lupines have targeted, or have their eyes on between here and there. Best not to take the chance, but to get somewhere we'll definitely be safe.'

The confidence in Gwilym's voice comforted Torben a great deal. He'd heard of Gallenford before, albeit only once. He seemed to recollect that a merchant caravan had taken the wrong road several summers past and had accidentally ended up in Bywater after having set out from there. They'd tried to sell wares to the sceptical villagers with little success before packing up and trying to find their way back to profitable civilisation. Not that this meant that he had any idea of where Gallenford was. The place could have been ten or ten-thousand miles away for all he knew.

'How long will it take us to get there?'

'That doesn't matter now. Let's get out of immediate danger before we start plotting our route. Come on, let's go.' Gwilym made his way towards the barn door and beckoned Torben to follow.

They stood by the door as Gwilym peered out, double-checking to see if the coast was indeed clear. Satisfied that it was, he darted into the farmyard and strolled toward the house, Torben close behind. The first they knew of the trap that had been set for them was when an arrow whizzed past Torben's face and thudded into the barn door.

From the road, the three Lupines reappeared from where they'd been lying in wait. Two sprinted across the farmyard towards Torben and Gwilym, whilst the third stood in the gateway knocking another arrow to his bowstring.

'Follow me!' Torben bellowed.

There was little point in seeking shelter in the house. They'd only be cornered and, even if they were able to barricade themselves in an upper room, the Lupines would only summon more of their fellows to help, or would simply set fire to the house.

In the split second that Torben had to think, it was clear that the best chance for survival was to head for the western woods. If they were lucky, they might be able to lose the Lupines in the trees. Night was fast descending on Burndale and, if they drew out the chase for long enough, Torben thought that the Lupines might give up and return to the village rather than tracking them down in the dark.

Torben dashed behind the farmhouse and through the open gate of the field that lay to the back of the dwelling. It had been one of the largest fields that Amos had owned and it stretched from the farmhouse to the borders of the woodlands.

Now their survival came down to a footrace across the field. Torben glanced quickly over his shoulder as he ran. Gwilym was hot on his heels and the two Lupines weren't much further behind. The third Lupine was rounding the corner of the house, bow half-drawn, ready to let fly.

Another arrow tore through the air over Torben's head and he crashed through the undergrowth at the edge of the field and into the woods. He didn't make it far, however; a thick, serpentine briar hooked itself around his boot and he crashed to the ground.

5

For a few seconds, Torben lay dazed in a bed of nettles, unable to bring himself to move. He'd managed to save himself from the worst of the fall, but the momentum had sent his head smacking into the ground. His vision swam as his brain tried to make sense of what had happened. Behind him he could hear branches snapping underfoot and what must have been Gwilym's voice shouting at him, but it sounded as if he were miles away.

Then, the adrenaline kicked in again. Torben rolled onto his back just as the Lupine lunged at him with its spear. The heavy iron point buried itself deep into the ground, inches from his face. The Lupine didn't bother trying to prize the spear out of the ground and strike again, but threw himself onto Torben, jaw gaping, going for the throat.

Torben managed to raise his arms up in time as the Lupine crashed into him. The weight and speed of the creature's descent nearly brought its jaws within striking distance of Torben's neck, but instead the two became locked in a bitter struggle for survival. He could feel the Lupine's hot breath on his face, and smell the horrible stench of blood as it leered down at him.

Torben could clearly see the Lupine's yellowed blood-stained fangs, and the wild look in the dark glaring eyes.

Claws slashed at Torben's eyes, attempting to blind him, but somehow he managed to beat back the angry blows. He brought up his knee and connected with his enemy's rib cage. The beast flinched from the force of the blow and this bought Torben enough time to fasten a hand around his neck and squeeze.

The Lupine grabbed Torben's wrist with both hands and claws dug deeply into his arm as it tried to prize away his hand. Torben could see blood trickling down his arm and knew that he couldn't keep up the momentum much longer.

Luckily, Torben had managed to buy enough time to scrabble at his belt and locate the knife. He drew the blade; it was barely longer than three inches, but it was enough to save his life. Determinedly, he jabbed the knife deep into chest of his attacker and he felt the horrible, grating sensation of the blade punching past the Lupine's ribcage.

The Lupine let out a bloodcurdling howl and released Torben's arm, scrabbling at its side, desperately trying to retract the knife. Torben was able to heave the weakened form off him, and slammed the Lupine into the ground. He withdrew the knife and thrust it into its neck. The beast fumbled with the knife and Torben's hand, which doggedly held the weapon, but then its limbs went limp as life drained from its body.

Torben let out a huge sigh of relief when he saw the Lupine's yellow eyes grow dim and as he crouched over the corpse, breathing heavily and recovering his strength, determined to keep moving. The third Lupine on the hill must still be pursuing him. He had no idea where Gwilym had gotten to, but he certainly hadn't come to help. Presumably, the dwarf had been chased and had kept on running into the woods.

A strange cold sensation crept across Torben's upper body, followed by the barbed prod of a blade being pressed, gently but firmly, into the base of his neck.

'Stand, whelp!'

Another Lupine's voice startled him—it was gravelly with a savage edge to it—and it pressed the blade a little harder into Torben's neck, just enough so that it punctured skin. Torben rose slowly and turned to regard the Lupine, who tracked the blade upwards with Torben's cautious movements, and then held it against his throat.

This one stood slightly taller than Torben and the deep-set, dark yellow eyes glowered over the long muzzle. The blade was a battered, rusty scimitar that had likely been a fine weapon once upon a time, but now only hinted at its former glory.

'What are you going to do with me?' Torben's voice was oddly calm now that he was staring death directly in the face.

'What do you think?' The beast nodded to his fallen comrade on the ground and smirked, revealing razor-sharp fangs. 'That one was just a pup you killed, hot-headed and young, but I'll still see that he's avenged.' He raised the scimitar, forcing Torben to raise his chin skyward, restricting his field of vision and making him strain his neck. With a snarl, he whipped back the blade, away from Torben's throat.

Torben closed his eyes, not wanting to see the blow. However, instead of the triumphant howl that he'd expected, he heard a whimper. He opened his eyes and caught sight of a blade protruding from the Lupine's navel. The creature groaned, spluttered, and collapsed to the ground. The scimitar clattered to the ground. Gwilym stood behind.

'You took your bloody time!'

'In order to surprise him, I had to lose him first, didn't I?' Gwilym had a cheeky little grin, apparently quite pleased with his handiwork. He wiped the blade of his seax against a trouser leg before slotting it back in its sheath with a firm click. As he opened his mouth, a Lupine's piercing cry reverberated around the dale from behind.

The two whipped around and saw the third Lupine standing on the crest of the hill, head thrown back and howling. For some reason, the creature had chosen to stay on the hillside and watch the mêlée unfold rather than help its now dead comrades.

'What's it doing? Coward should come down and have a go at us, rather than stand up there crying!' Torben's blood was up and now that he'd come out on top in the scuffle, he was spoiling for a fight.

Gwilym, on the other hand, had lost the smarmy smile that he'd previously worn. What little of his face wasn't covered by the beard, had grown ashen, and he looked decidedly nervous. 'Come on, let's go, there's no time to waste!'

'Why? We can take on that furry bugger, no problem! He deserves no less than his friends here for what they did!'

There was an air of excitement in Torben's voice that Gwilym didn't like. The young man stepped forward and would have made his way back out into the field had he not grabbed him by the arm and restrained him.

'What are you doing? He might get away if we just sit on our arses here,' Torben snapped.

'If we go back out into those fields, we're dead for sure,' Gwilym retorted. 'Do you know what that creature's doing? He's calling for help, not because he's afraid of us, but because he thinks we'll be exciting to hunt. If we don't move, all the Lupines in the dale will be on us before we know it and tear us to shreds.'

Grabbing his arm, Gwilym pulled Torben further into the woods. At first Torben resisted—he wanted revenge for Amos, and the smouldering remains of what had been his life, his world. After a few·steps, however, he relented and the two of them began to run through the woods.

The dwarf had been right so far and now didn't seem like the best time to test his knowledge. After all, what was the point in killing one Lupine in the name of revenge if it led to his own death?

As the two fled through the woods, the Lupine's mournful howling rang out from the hill ... and down in the village answering calls drifted across on the breeze.

Gwilym and Torben didn't stop running until night had completely fallen over Burndale and, even then, they only stopped because to continue in the pitch-black woods was nigh impossible. For fear of being spotted, they dared not light a fire or use torches to guide the way. Though they hadn't heard the Lupines for some time, that didn't mean that they weren't still being tracked.

While there had still been light, to put the Lupines off their scent, Gwilym had made sure to lead Torben through as many streams and pools of water as they could find; occasionally, the dwarf had changed direction to make their tracks as confusing as possible. Torben had been surprised at how much knowledge the dwarf had of attempting to lose pursuers, but he didn't question Gwilym's tactics. At least one of them seemed to know what he was doing.

When they finally stopped, the pair had been blundering around in the dark for over an hour. Their limbs were tired and heavy, and their clothes, saturated with brackish water from streams and pools in the woods, weighed heavily. In the blackness, they made out the profile of a huge oak tree and they slumped to the ground with their backs against it.

'This seems as good a place as any to stop,' Gwilym exhaled noisily.

'I guess so. I lost track of which direction we were going in three hours ago. For all I know, we might be back in the woods near that godforsaken tower.'

'For both our sakes, let's hope that isn't the case—'

A howl resounded through the night air. Both sat in silence, desperately listening for more noises or clues that they'd been discovered, but they heard nothing else.

'Must have come from the village,' whispered Gwilym.

'You sure about that?'

'No … but I don't think I could take another step if my life depended on it. Hopefully, by now, they've given up and gone back to their camp.'

Silence descended again. Their ears strained to hear unwelcome sounds, but the woods remained quiet, save for the hooting of an owl from a nearby branch.

Although Torben's body was exhausted, his brain was wide awake and now that they'd stopped for the night, question after question raced through his mind. 'So, what are those things, the Lupines?' Torben wasn't sure he really wanted to think about them after the day they'd been through, but he couldn't help asking.

Gwilym shifted and pondered. 'To be honest, I don't really know." He spoke slowly as he considered the answer. 'I'm sure there's someone in the world who knows what they are, but all I've heard is rumour and speculation. A man I met out west told me that they were once a group of men tortured beyond recognition and became savages who'd lost all reason. I don't buy that myself. They've never struck me as being particularly human, there's too much beast in them, and they're far too intelligent to have been tortured into insanity. You only have to look into their eyes and you can see the vicious cunning and scheming there.

'I came across another traveller who'd heard that they're descended from a group of werewolves that tried to cure themselves. She said that they made a pact with a witch, who promised to permanently fix them in human form … mind you, for a huge sum of money. The werewolves tried to fleece the old crone out of some payment and, enraged, she fixed them in their wolf forms instead of their human ones. Not sure how much of that I believe, either. Never been a big believer in magic, me.' He smiled wryly. 'All I've seen are parlour tricks to entertain children. If there were witches and other magic folk in the world, they're all long gone now, and I warrant that they'd all have been smart enough to not make bargains with a group of desperate werewolves. Having said that, I haven't seen any proof for the existence of werewolves either. Just stories to keep people in their beds at night instead of in the taverns.'

'So what do *you* think they are?' Torben sat forward, making sure that he caught every one of Gwilym's words.

They continued to speak very softly, not wanting their conversation to draw the attention of anyone lurking nearby.

'Personally, I reckon they were born and bred the way they are. Same as I'm a dwarf, you're a human, and other people are other things. Lupines have existed as long as anyone can remember, and their tribes have been roaming around the land killing, looting and pillaging as long as anyone can remember. What does it matter where they come from? No one's origins make them culpable for their actions. I thank my lucky stars every time I come across a Lupine and manage to escape to tell the tale, and that's a lot more than most people today can say.'

Torben slumped against the tree. Gwilym's words brought home the facts of what had taken place in Bywater. Like as not, no one would come back and settle in the village. The only people outside of Burndale who'd been vaguely aware of the place would know that the village was a dead-end and not bother to repopulate the area.

Gwilym must have noticed Torben's mood sink back into melancholic brooding, and that what he'd said would not have helped. He fidgeted awkwardly before deciding that he should at least attempt to console Torben. 'I'm sorry, by the way, for your loss.' He struggled to find the right words, but carried on regardless. 'It must be hard to lose your parents like that.'

'They weren't my parents,' Torben replied quietly. 'I lost them a long time ago.'

There was a somewhat expectant silence that followed this statement. Gwilym clearly wanted to know more, but didn't know how to prompt Torben to tell the tale.

Torben, not wanting the awkward silence to continue, spoke again. 'My mother and father weren't from Burndale. To be honest, I can't remember where they were from. For one reason or another though, they turned up in Bywater and, unsurprisingly, no one would take them in. You saw yourself how they reacted to strangers, and they were even less disposed to taking in an unknown man and his heavily pregnant wife.

'Luckily for them, Master Amos happened to be in town that day, took pity on them, and brought them to lodge with him and his wife on their farm. He took my father on as a full-time field labourer, and my mother helped out wherever Mrs Amos wanted. Two weeks later I was born.' He closed his eyes as he recalled the past. 'The three of us lived in one small room in the farmhouse, though we took our meals with Master and Mrs Amos, and that was the arrangement for six years.

Then, one day, people got sick. A group of traders had come to the village and brought a disease with them, and it ran through Bywater like wildfire. Amos and my father were struck down, both of them bedridden for weeks. My mother used to go down to the village and tend to people. She had a marvellous knowledge of herbs and medicines, and she was able to bring many village folk back from the brink.'

He drew a long, desolate breath. 'It was the children that got hit hardest; every family lost at least one child, apart from us. For one reason or another, I escaped. Talk began to go round the village that my mother was a witch who saved her own son from the plague, but didn't care for the children of others … indeed, she propagated the disease in other children. Seems a ridiculous way to think, given that she saved so many lives, but people become incredibly narrow-minded in situations like that.'

Gwilym murmured agreement.

'In any case, her work caught up with her. Despite all her medicines and poultices, she couldn't save herself. The sickness took her, and without her help and wisdom, my father succumbed as well. That didn't satisfy the villagers though. They were baying for my blood as well, thinking that my parents had gotten what they deserved for cursing the village, and that my death would be the last piece of justice they needed. Thankfully, Amos managed to dissuade them from their course.

'Given that my mother had saved his life, he claimed

responsibility for me, and began to treat me as a son … but his wife hated every fibre of my being. She lost her whole family to the sickness and she blamed me for it, and constantly berated the old man for taking me in … and near broke both our spirits. As for the rest of the villagers, they treated me with suspicion ever since. I was allowed to take part in village life, attend council meetings when I turned sixteen and the like, but I was never truly one of them, and they made sure I knew it.'

Torben spat into the darkness, trying to dispel the bile and anger that telling the story had created. 'But I guess we shouldn't speak ill of the dead now, should we?' He bowed his head. 'And now, I never have to go back.'

'If it's any conciliation, I found leaving home one of the most thrilling and liberating experiences I ever had, ever will have,' Gwilym affirmed. 'Once you leave, that weight of having to fall in line with the status quo, live up to peoples' expectations, all falls away. You can carve your own life rather than fit into a niche that someone, or some community, has made for you.'

'So what made you leave and set off on your *liberating* new life?' Torben's tone displayed bitterness.

'Ah, no particular reason, I guess. Just got tired of the boring farming life—like you. I decided that if I had to plant another row of wheat, I'd probably go insane. So I picked up my pack, strode down the road, and haven't looked back for, hell, nearly twenty years.'

Torben was disappointed by Gwilym's response. He'd morbidly hoped that they'd both been forced into a wandering life. It would have given Torben a small crumb of comfort to know that Gwilym knew what he was going through. Instead, it appeared that Gwilym existed in a charmed universe, where he could do whatever he wanted, without consequences.

'We should think about getting rest; it'll be another long day tomorrow.' As he spoke, Gwilym settled himself into a more comfortable position at the base of the oak.

'How far are we from Gallenford?' Torben still wasn't ready to sleep yet, his head filled with many rogue thoughts.

'No idea. It'll take us a good few hours to get our bearings while we travel, and only then will we be able to tell. We could have been running in completely the wrong direction for all we know.'

Gwilym rolled away from Torben, the implication being that he wanted to sleep, not answer questions.

Torben tried to settle into the thick grass, which made a reasonably comfortable sleeping mat, but thoughts, questions and doubts continued to dance around his head.

He inclined his head towards Gwilym, about to ask another question when he heard a snore from the sleeping figure. He turned and peered upwards, trying to spot stars through the thick covering of the foliage.

Gwilym's snoring continued, growing in strength with every breath, and Torben was alone with his thoughts.

***

When he awoke the next morning, Torben lay still, his eyes shut, listening to sounds. He could hear the wind caressing leaves above his head and chirps and tweets from birds. Everything *seemed* safe.

Opening his eyes, he sat up. The surrounding area was densely forested, except for the twenty-plus feet around them. The massive size of the tree they'd slept under only allowed for bushes and small plants to grow beneath its boughs.

It took him a few moments to process the fact that Gwilym wasn't there and when he realised it, he stood and searched for signs as to where the dwarf may have gone. Gwilym's pack and jacket lay near the depression that his body had made in the long grass, so he couldn't have gone far. Like as not, he'd gone in search of water or perhaps a more secluded place to relieve himself.

Torben sat back down, his back against the tree, and fished around his coat pockets, taking stock of what his worldly possessions had boiled down to. Apart from the knife that hung from his belt, the clothes on his back, and the arm ring he still wore, all he could find in the pockets was twine, the odd grain seed, and the chunk of bread he'd taken from the tavern the morning before. He sighed loudly. People surely must have started out with less?

At the sight of the bread, his stomach churned and complained. Given he'd not eaten since the previous morning, he was starving. The bread had grown harder with age, but he didn't care; he just wanted to eat. After a few small cautious mouthfuls, he felt better, though a little unsatisfied with his lot. He'd just about finished eating the sad little meal when he heard Gwilym's voice coming from nearby woods.

'Now look, there's no need to do anything too hasty!'

Torben peered around, but couldn't see the dwarf. Then another voice replied, much quieter than Gwilym's, so quiet in fact that he couldn't make out any words.

'I don't know what you think I've done, but why don't we sit down and discuss this in a sensible, rational manner?' Gwilym was speaking in a much more nervous tone than Torben had heard before. And the volume was very loud, which wasn't wise, considering that Lupines might still be roving around the forest looking for them. The only explanation: Gwilym was in trouble and hoped that Torben would hear and help.

Trying to make as little noise as possible, Torben hopped upright and crept in the direction of Gwilym's voice. The thick undergrowth made it hard to be completely silent but, after a few feet, the brush began to thin out and a small clearing came into view.

As he started to see more clearly, Torben tracked around the edge of the clearing. He saw Gwilym through the tall grass, though he still couldn't clearly see the person that he was talking to. A hooded and cloaked figure was slightly visible, but he didn't dare poke his head too far past the cover to get a good look until he knew that he'd not be in their line of sight. He could, however, hear more clearly what the figure was saying, and he listened intently as he moved around the clearing.

'There's no use trying to make a run for it—that is, unless you want a bolt in your back.'

'I'm sure we both know that would get us nowhere.' Gwilym was still speaking very loudly, and his voice echoed. 'Having said that, with all the Lupines around here, perhaps it would be best if we continued this conversation at a later date.'

'Don't worry,' the hooded figure declared, 'you'll be *much* safer with me. The boss made it clear to get you alive and I'll do everything to make sure that happens.'

'I don't know how much your boss is paying you, but let me assure you that if we can come to a reasonable agreement, I could—'

'Shut it, dwarf! You can't pay me off and you can't trick me into letting you go, either. You might as well stop the plotting and the scheming. The game's up!'

By now Torben had made his way around the clearing and was directly behind where he thought the voice of the hooded stranger was coming from. He darted behind a tree and peeked out, assessing the situation. From his perspective, Gwilym stood at the far end of the small clearing and the figure was only feet from where Torben was watching. It was tall and wore a long green cloak that almost touched the ground; a large voluminous hood covered the head and masked the face. The figure held a crossbow in slender brown-skinned hands; it was aimed directly at Gwilym, who had his hands raised above his head.

Gwilym's eyes flashed for a moment in Torben's direction when he saw the man's face poking out from behind the tree, and then quickly made eye contact with the figure again. The dwarf shuffled and edged, almost imperceptibly, away from Torben, and the figure adjusted slightly, tracking Gwilym's movements with the crossbow, and in the process, turning away from Torben.

He readied himself and burst from his hiding place, leaping onto the hooded figure. There was a sharp snap and a high-pitched whistle as the figure pulled the crossbow trigger; they fell under Torben's weight and the bolt flew into the trees above Gwilym's head.

In an attempt to subdue the stranger, Torben repeatedly aimed several punches down into the swirling mass of cloak but, every time he brought his fist down, the figure seemed to slide out of the way and avoid the blows. A heavy boot emerged from the folds of the cloak and struck Torben squarely in the face. He reeled back, clutching his jaw. He could taste blood in his mouth and a tooth felt decidedly loose. The force of the blow completely unbalanced him and he threw out his free hand to break the fall.

Now the figure seemed to be everywhere at once and lashed out again at Torben's face, striking him in the nose and forcing his head back. Before he had time to recover, the figure had grabbed his hair and, standing behind him, held a long curved dagger to Torben's throat. 'Drop the weapon, dwarf!'

In the short time that Torben and the hooded figure had been tussling, Gwilym had made it halfway across the clearing. He had his seax drawn and ready, but he stopped dead in his tracks when he realized the gravity of the situation.

'Drop the weapon *now*! Or your friend here won't thank you for what'll happen to him.'

'Oh, bollocks!' Gwilym threw the seax onto the ground and stepped back for good measure.

'Now on your knees, and if I see any movement from you, this one dies!' To emphasize the point, the figure yanked Torben's hair, making him inhale sharply. Deftly, the figure pulled Torben's hands behind his back and tied them with rope produced from the folds of the cloak. The attacker then kicked Torben face-first into the ground and bound his feet.

Torben heard footsteps as the figure strode past, the knee-high boots nearly hitting his face. As he looked up, he could see Gwilym being bound in similar fashion.

'Where's your pack?' The figure stared down from within the folds of their cloak as they spoke. 'I was told to bring all your possessions as well as you, dwarf. We can do this the easy way or the hard way,' came the chilling threat as the figure lifted Gwilym's chin with the back of the dagger.

Gwilym didn't say anything, but thrust his head in the direction of the oak tree and his pack. The cloak gathered snugly around them as the figure disappeared into the woods, blending in with the surrounding trees.

'Bugger it all,' Gwilym exclaimed.

'What the hell is going on?' Torben tried, unsuccessfully, to worm his way across the ground towards his colleague.

'It looks like we're being arrested. An old acquaintance of mine seems to have got it into his head that I wronged him and has sent a lackey to bring me to him.'

'Wronged him? Are you wanted for something?'

Gwilym searched for the right words. 'It all depends on your definition of *wronged*, doesn't it? I mean, in some senses, maybe I did wrong him, yes.'

'Great. Just bloody great! I escape certain death only to be trussed up like a hog, and probably killed for no reason, just because you *may* have wronged someone!' He rolled onto his front, fighting with the bonds on his wrists, trying to find a weakness in the rope, but with no luck. The cord might as well have been woven from iron.

'Stop struggling or I'll give you something to squirm about!' The figure had returned, holding Gwilym's pack and woollen jacket. 'Is this everything you had with you?'

'Aye, that's all of it. Hardly worth robbing us, really.'

The figure threw the pack at Gwilym's feet and swept back the hood to reveal the face of a young and slim, athletic-looking woman, the brown skin on her forehead glistening from the tussle with Torben. She was obviously no stranger to the wilds or a dangerous lifestyle, as exemplified by a discernible scar that ran across her right eye onto her cheek and the hardy nature of the leather jerkin beneath the cloak. Her black hair was arranged into a single plait that curled around her slender neck and dangled over a shoulder; her ears terminated in blunt points rather than being curved like those of Torben or Gwilym.

She sheathed the dagger and retrieved the crossbow from where it had been knocked out of her hands. Turning, she surveyed her two captives, amber-coloured eyes darting across the bonds binding their hands and feet. 'This is how it's going to be; the two of you are going to get up and walk until I tell you to stop, and if you don't do exactly what I say, people are going to get hurt. Understand?'

Torben and Gwilym muttered acceptance and didn't make eye contact with their new captor. The woman took a bolt from a pouch by her side, threaded a foot though the stirrup of the crossbow and drew back the string with one swift movement. As she straightened, she slotted the bolt into place, her cloak billowing around her as she did so. As the folds of the fabric settled back into place, Torben caught a glimpse of a longsword, as well as a curved dagger hanging from her belt. Whoever this woman was, she meant business. 'On your feet, let's go!'

The two struggled to their feet and shuffled in the direction that the young woman steered them. She had linked their feet together in a way that allowed them to move, but with no way of escaping without cutting the rope.

'This is a fine mess you've gotten us into,' Torben hissed as they waddled through the woods.

'Aye … well, if nothing else, I feel a lot safer with her at my back than the Lupines.'

'Shut up, both of you, and keep walking!'

6

As Gwilym and Torben made their slow way through the woods, the woman walked on one side, watching them intently and keeping her crossbow trained on one or the other of them at all times. The trio travelled in silence, except for the odd occasion when Gwilym or Torben, restricted by the binding ropes around their feet, fell and grunted or groaned when they hit the ground.

Torben had no idea where they were going. The thick canopy of leaves above heavily restricted a view of the sky, which meant there was no sun by which he could tell where they were heading. He guessed that they were going south, but that was because the only way out of Burndale lay that way.

After a few hours of walking, they heard running water grow louder and louder. This could only mean that the woman was leading them to the river, known to the residents of Bywater simply as 'the Burn'.

It wasn't known whether the dale had been named after the river, or the river after the dale, but no one really cared. The people of Bywater had taken very little heed of the river, save as a place to draw water from after the well dried up. A few older folks used to fish along the Burn, or from the lakeside but, generally, people largely ignored the water.

Given that the road ran alongside the river, Torben assumed the woman meant to continue leading them wherever the eventual destination was. The thought of taking the road and being in open view of any Lupines that might still be lurking about made Torben nervous. It was surely only a matter of time before the Lupines extracted all the loot they could carry and looked to leave the dale —of which the fastest and most direct route was the road.

As they walked, Torben wondered whether he should say something to her. Surely though, she'd have taken all variables into account? Was she taking a calculated risk that the Lupines had already left Burndale ... or weren't going to leave for some time?

Every time Torben mustered enough courage to say something, he'd somehow make eye contact with her. Her severe scowl made him think twice about speaking and he quickly faced forwards again, continuing to struggle along.

By what must have been midday, they came upon the river and the road. As the undergrowth cover became sparser the closer that they got to the road, the three of them instinctively reduced sounds of their movements, and stuck to the thickest areas of cover.

'Stop!' The woman spoke briskly and quietly. 'The two of you are going to wait here. If either of you try to escape, you'll have me to answer to.' With that, she crept closer to the road, with the obvious intention of seeing whether the coast was clear.

Torben and Gwilym sat down without speaking and watched her go; they couldn't have escaped if they'd wanted to. They were exhausted from the strain and exertion of walking with bound feet through thick undergrowth and over uneven ground, and constantly scrambling to their feet without the use of arms, which were still tied behind their backs. Despite this, Torben scanned their surroundings, determining the best line of escape.

There must be a way that they could slip into the trees, lie low until nightfall, and then make good their escape. If only they could get far enough away from their captor …

'It's no use,' Gwilym muttered, cutting through Torben's train of thought. 'We can't escape. She's good, this one. I've come across her before and I know what she's capable of.'

'Who is she?'

'Her name's Eleusia, blade for hire. Her services are always in high demand.'

'But surely we can do *something*?' Torben's whisper was thick with exasperation. 'There's two of us and only one of her; if we jump her together, we might be able to subdue her long enough to get away.'

'That'll never work, lad. I've seen her fend off an entire battalion of Imperial Guards with a broken arm. She came out of that no worse for wear than when she'd gone in, and she took out a couple of dozen of the Emperor's finest in the process. She could deal with the two of us in her sleep!'

'How do you know all of this?'

Gwilym offered a limp shrug. 'Let's just say the two of us used to be colleagues once upon a time.' He didn't seem disposed to offer more information at that moment.

Torben started to ask another question, but Eleusia re-emerged from the undergrowth and beckoned them to get on their feet and follow. Wearily, the two men picked themselves up and shuffled after their captor.

Despite what he'd said before, in reality, all of the fight had left Torben's body. His mind might still have been seeking every possible avenue of escape, but his body had decided to lie down and be carried along by the currents of fate.

At the edge of the tree line, the three stopped and checked the road up and down several times. Even though Eleusia had already reconnoitred the way ahead, she didn't leave anything to chance, especially when it came to her own safety. Satisfied that the coast was clear, she prodded Torben and Gwilym into the road with the end of her crossbow, and led them quickly across the road and into a bowl in the riverbank.

Lying hidden in the depression was a small boat that looked as if it would struggle to hold the three of them at the same time.

'Get in, and be sharp about it!'

Torben approached the water's edge and managed to tip himself into the boat. He landed with a painful thud and wormed his way to the bow and away from Gwilym as he began to negotiate his way into the boat.

Unfortunately for Gwilym, who was much shorter than Torben, gaining entry to the boat was a lot more difficult. He almost made it over the side of the boat, but with his arms tied behind his back, he wasn't able to gain a grip on the inside. He slipped back over the edge and toppled into the water.

Eleusia cursed as she waded into the river and picked up the struggling dwarf by the scruff of his neck and heaved him into the boat, before leaping in herself and pushing the craft into the main stream. Once in the boat, she swiftly raised the small sail and the craft began to zip along. She seated herself in the stern and took the rudder. Torben noticed that she kept her crossbow on her lap, loaded, just in case he or Gwilym caused trouble.

Torben leaned against the side of the boat and watched the countryside roll past. He had no idea how far they were from Bywater, but he knew that the village was getting further away with every second. Despite this and despite the rather awkward situation he and Gwilym found themselves in, Torben couldn't help but feel excited at the prospect of being taken somewhere new.

Gwilym, on the other hand, sat stony-faced and very damp next to Torben in the bow. To him, the situation was hopeless. There was no foreseeable way that the two of them would be able to overpower Eleusia, and if they escaped by tipping themselves over the side of the boat, they'd be as good as dead. The current of the river had become increasingly stronger with every passing minute, and with their bound hands and feet, they'd quickly sink to the bottom and never be seen again.

'How long will it take us to get to Gallenford?' Torben asked.

Eleusia turned her gaze from the river to look at him. 'I'm not taking you to Gallenford. What makes you think I'd take you there? I've had enough of little tin-pot settlements for the time being. Besides, you can't get to Gallenford by river, and it would take us *weeks* to get there.'

Torben appeared disappointed. 'When we were escaping the village, Gwilym thought Gallenford would be the easiest and the safest place to get to.'

'I'd hardly call it easy to get to from here, let alone safe.' Eleusia returned her gaze onto the river, reading the currents and looking for rocks or obstructions. 'I passed through Gallenford nearly three weeks gone, and it looked about as safe as your village does now.'

'Lupines?' Gwilym asked. The conversation had drawn him out of his melancholy and he sat forward, staring intently at her.

'Sadly for Gallenford, yes.' Eleusia's voice was steady and unemotional. 'They passed through there a day before I did, burnt it to the ground, poisoned the well, killed the livestock and any of the inhabitants not clever enough to escape whilst they still could.'

'What about the palisade?'

Torben had never actually seen a palisade before, but his father's stories had often included descriptions of bygone towns protected by palisades, and his impression of them had been that they were practically unassailable.

'What, that sad little row of sticks?' Eleusia scoffed. 'Nothing will keep a pack of hungry Lupines away except cold hard rock … and colder steel.'

Although Gallenford was merely a name to Torben, the news of its destruction chilled him to the core. The fact that he'd never been there made it worse. The place had come into existence and been destroyed before he'd had a chance to see it.

Torben scanned the road to the east and the undergrowth covering the western bank, half expecting to see hundreds of piercing Lupine eyes staring at them, waiting for a chance to strike.

'So where are we going?' Torben asked.

'Karpella,' Gwilym replied. 'That'd be my guess; am I right, Eleusia?'

'You always were a sharp one, Gwilym. It's a shame that it's inflated your head a bit too much.'

'How do you know where we're going?' Torben, confused, turned to Gwilym, who was staring sullenly at the bottom of the boat again.

Eleusia reached out her foot and nudged Gwilym's leg. 'Well, aren't you going to tell him?'

He shuffled awkwardly for a few seconds. Torben could practically hear the dwarf's mind ticking furiously as he fished for an answer. 'Let's just say that Eleusia's employer and I may have had a slight disagreement over something I did for him recently.' Gwilym collected his thoughts. 'And, it would seem that our current situation means that he still feels *very* strongly about it, and wants me to return to Karpella … to discuss the situation.'

'I'm not sure that there'll be a huge amount of discussion on the topic.' Eleusia's face was grim.

'Wait, so what exactly did you do, Gwilym?' Torben was beginning to worry that Gwilym may have mixed him up in something quite serious.

'Nothing. It's just a misunderstanding!'

'I doubt Björn will see eye to eye with you on that,' Eleusia butted in. 'He seems very certain about what happened, and all he wants is for you to agree with him.'

'Look, I told Björn everything I had to say the last time we met, and my story hasn't changed since then!'

'Who's Björn?' Torben interjected into the conversation.

Eleusia ignored him and continued to address Gwilym sternly. 'You're a thief, dwarf! Admit it and Björn may be a little more lenient towards you. You know what he's capable of.'

'Thief?' Torben muttered under his breath. He wasn't so much full of disbelief at the accusation, but rather of sad acceptance at what he'd become involved in. With the credibility of his only companion rapidly falling into disrepute, he felt more lost than ever.

Gwilym could tell that the situation was making Torben nervous, so he addressed him directly. 'Believe me, this is a big mistake. Believe me, I'm no thief! I've certainly engaged in some activities that were decidedly shifty in past, but never thievery. Björn and I just need to talk things out and, doubtless, we'll come to an amicable agreement.'

'I wouldn't count on that.' Eleusia's dark, neatly shaped eyebrows arched in surprise and then her face settled back into its typically stern expression. 'Björn is going to make sure that he gets only honest answers from you. We *all* know how good you are at worming your way out of trouble with that silver tongue of yours ... how good you are at convincing others to go along with you. Is that how you ended up with your manservant here?' She inclined her head, indicating Torben, who straightened and bristled visibly in reaction to the question. 'What did you do?' she continued. 'Offer to give him all his heart has ever desired if he followed you? Or ... what was that fence you used to run? That's it! Did you offer him gold from that trick bag of—'

'No,' Gwilym snapped.

'Ah, so you *do* still use that one,' Eleusia crooned. 'I reckoned you might. Very useful little bit of trickery that.'

'What bag? Gwilym, what's she talking about?' Torben's head flicked from one to the other as he tried to understand what they were talking about.

He was about to speak in his own defence when there was a

heavy chink as the purse in question was thrown before Torben. It was the same purse that Gwilym had shown him, albeit briefly, in the Rusty Sickle the night they first met. Eleusia had fished it out of Gwilym's pack, which lay at her feet in the bottom of the boat.

Torben leaned forward, trying to see what the fuss was about, but his bonds stopped him from picking up the purse and investigating. Instead, he peered at it, as if expecting its secret to be written on the front of the leather. The purse was nothing particularly special to look at. It was made of strips of deep brown leather, an inch in width, sewn together, with the stitching standing out prominently on the exterior. Its neck was secured by a small length of red rope and there was a small brass loop near the neck so the purse could be secured to a belt if need be. All in all, the article seemed fairly ordinary.

Gwilym began to speak loudly again, attempting to regain Torben's attention. 'Look, there's really no need for this. I tell you, Torben, that everything will be much better if you let me explain what the situation is. I—'

'Be quiet!' Eleusia ordered. She secured the rudder of the boat so that it kept the intended course without her having to physically guide it and squatted in front of the purse, facing Torben. She picked it up, untied the rope, and held it towards him so he could see inside.

From the depths of the purse, Torben saw the gleam of large lustrous gold coins that threw a warm golden light from the interior.

'What do you see?' Her voice was hushed.

'Gold coins. What do you expect me to see?' The golden light reflected in his blue eyes as he stared into the purse, completely bewitched. He couldn't take his eyes away from it, completely transfixed by the huge amount of money that she held in her hand.

Gwilym had stopped trying to interject, but was looking dejectedly at the wooden deck of the boat, his head bowed, refusing to look at the other two. He knew what Eleusia was about to do.

Turning her head to watch Gwilym's reaction, she slowly inverted the purse. As she did, the coins clinked against one another when they slipped through the purse's neck and thudded onto the wooden decking. When the purse was completely empty, she tossed the leather pouch next to the pile of coins and settled back in the stern, one hand on the rudder.

Torben couldn't see any discernible difference between the gold when it had been in the purse and when it lay in a pile on the deck. He looked at Eleusia, expecting her to give further instructions as to what he was supposed to do. Was he supposed to test the quality of the coins? He had no idea what made a good or a bad coin, and he'd only seen gold a handful of times—never held it—so the idea that he'd test the quality of the gold was laughable.

Sensing Torben's stare, Eleusia inclined her head toward the gold, indicating that he should watch it, and then turned to survey the course of the river.

At first, he only saw the heap of gold pieces, glinting pleasingly in the sun but, as he watched, the gold began to lose its lustre. Slowly, the coins grew dimmer and dimmer, and the colour too began to change—from the pleasing deep yellow of gold to a speckled grey. After a minute, all that lay on the floor was a collection of pebbles and a single, particularly worn gold coin, which peeked from beneath a stone.

'Neat, isn't it?' she asked, smiling to herself.

Torben didn't reply, but sat in stunned silence, staring at the pebbles.

'Very rare thing to come across nowadays,' Eleusia continued casually. 'I don't think that there are many who could skillfully make a trick purse like that. The leather of the purse is enchanted, so whatever you place in there will take on the appearance of something else. Place a single gold coin in there with a collection of pebbles, like our friend did, and you can make yourself look like the richest man in the world. Shame that the enchantment wears off after a few seconds after the bag is emptied. We were all jealous of you, Gwilym, for possessing it, but Björn felt that it would help you the most in your work.'

He, like Torben, didn't react. He continued to sit and watch the deck of the boat rise up and down with the current.

'When I was tracking you, I heard an interesting story in every village that I passed through, about a dwarf that would appear out of the wilderness, seemingly out of nowhere.' Eleusia didn't care that neither was listening. She was enjoying her victory too much. 'This dwarf, so all of the village people said, would find a tavern, take his fill of meat and drink, and then challenge someone, usually the biggest or toughest or most generous in the tavern to a wager, to—'

'To prove to him that he was brave enough to leave the village and walk with him in the wilds.' Torben spoke softly, but there was bitterness in his voice.

'Yes, that's exactly it,' Eleusia said triumphantly. 'I guessed that he tried to pull the same trick on you. Clearly, he didn't have time to take your money before the Lupines attacked, and you both became somewhat distracted. Mark my words, Torben, if that hadn't happened, then he'd have fleeced you for everything you had. I spoke to one of his victims; they said that he took them into the middle of nowhere and then threatened him at knife point to part with his gold.'

'Don't listen to her. There's more to this than meets the eye. Just let me explain!' Gwilym couldn't sit idly by and listen to Eleusia anymore, and sat forward on his knees, trying to capture Torben's attention and implore to him directly.

Torben, however, sat staring vacantly into the distance.

'He doesn't want to know, dwarf. He's heard everything he needs to know about you.' Eleusia was stretched out in the stern, enjoying the spectacle, her hand barely touching the rudder.

'You stay out of this,' Gwilym retorted. 'It's not like you've never done wrong yourself. Even I shiver to think of some of the jobs you've pulled off, without a second thought as to what you're doing or who gets in your way.'

'I never said I was clean,' she said carelessly. 'But I'm not the one on trial now, am I?'

'Please, Torben, just hear me out and you'll understand why I did what I did, I promise you!'

'Don't!' Torben's eyes flashed dangerously as he surveyed Gwilym. 'I've heard enough. I should never have listened to you in the first place! I'm not sure what's worse; having you run me through to the top of that godforsaken tower for the sake of a few ounces of silver, or whatever the hell is going to happen to us when we're delivered to your *friend*. You've truly screwed me over and, sadly, that's the only concrete thing I have left now.'

'You know what? You're right.' Turning to Eleusia, he spoke imploringly. 'Look, I know we've had our differences, but the lad doesn't have anything to do with this. Can't you let him go? Make me answer for my mistakes, but don't make him answer for them, too!'

'I wish I could do that for you, I really do.' Eleusia looked decidedly unmoved. 'My orders were to bring you, your possessions, and anyone I found in your company to Björn, no questions asked, and that's exactly what I intend to do. I don't renege on my deals like you.'

Casting around for anything that he could say to make things better, Gwilym turned desperately to Torben once more. 'Look, you're right. I *have* buggered things up well and good for you, but you have to believe me: things aren't as black and white as they seem. You just have to let me explain things. I can fix *all* of this!'

Torben didn't reply or look at Gwilym, but continued to stare at the passing river, hoping that the water would rise up and whisk him from this mess that he'd landed in.

Gwilym sat back in his corner of the boat, knowing that there was nothing that he could say to him at that moment that would cool his anger and he couldn't come clean, either. Not with

Eleusia within earshot. In any case, there'd be no way that she would let the two of them confer in secret; she was far to watchful a guard to let that happen.

He shuffled in his space, getting as comfortable as possible, though with his hands tied behind his back, getting comfy was nigh on impossible. Once he'd reached as good a sitting position as he was going to find, he sifted through the problem facing him.

Although the situation appeared pretty bleak, he'd found himself in tricky situations before and managed to come out relatively unscathed. He knew that he'd not be able to provide an argument of any weight to Torben—to convince him to trust him again—until the two of them were alone. Before that happened, he was fairly sure that he'd have to survive the first round of grilling from Björn, and, knowing him, his words would likely not be the only way he'd try to extract an answer.

After that, he'd have to formulate a form of escape, with or without Torben. If the boy wouldn't listen to reason, then there was no point in trying to drag him along with him. Having said that, even if he did manage to escape, he'd have all sorts of problems to deal with, Eleusia more than likely being one of them.

As he thought through scenario after scenario of what might happen once they reached Karpella, Gwilym absently stared at the boat deck once more, and his bushy brows knitted and unknitted as ideas swam around his head.

Neither Torben or Eleusia noticed the dwarf sink into a trance. Eleusia's amber eyes were too busy scanning the channel ahead, keeping the boat in the deepest and fastest part of the river to make as much haste as possible.

She knew that her prisoners wouldn't trouble her. Torben was staring broodily at the passing riverbanks whilst Gwilym scarcely moved from his corner. Eleusia had no doubts, however, that Gwilym was trying to think his way out of his predicament;

she knew him too well. Still, there was little that he could do for the moment.

By this time, they'd sailed the entire length of the Burn, which ran from the lake alongside Bywater all the way down Burndale, and drained into a much larger river. It was into this river that she steered the craft and, after a bumpy transition, they picked up speed rapidly when they joined the flow of the river and were swept downstream towards their destination, Karpella.

7

'Wake up!'
     The voice swam towards Torben from what seemed miles away. It echoed in his head as he slept, intruding on his thoughtless dreaming and shattering the private world that he'd retreated to.

'Wake up,' the voice repeated.

Where was the voice even coming from? In his mind, Torben was striding across the fields back in Bywater, trying to sow seeds into plough furrows, but the land undulated constantly, throwing him off balance, making it excruciatingly hard to even walk, let alone get on with the task at hand. And then, there was that horrible piercing voice that wouldn't stop echoing around and around. It almost sounded like the tone that Mrs Amos had addressed him with every morning, rattling his door and shrieking like a harpy for him to get up and work.

'Wake up!'

This time the voice was accompanied by a kick, and this jolted Torben back into consciousness. However, he lay with his eyes still shut. He felt that opening them would be an acceptance of his fate, and that if he held on a little longer he would wake and see the bare whitewashed ceiling of his room in Amos' farmstead. Instead, he received another kick for his trouble.

'All right, all right, I'm awake.'

'We're nearly there,' Eleusia said. 'I need the two of you ready to move; there'll be no dallying once we moor the boat, understand?'

'Aye, we hear you,' Gwilym grumbled.

With a heavy sigh, Torben opened his eyes. All he could see was blue sky above and the top of the mast. In his slumber, he'd slipped down the side of the boat where he'd rested; the awkwardness of his sleeping position revealed itself through the stinging in his hands and arms, being crushed under the weight of his own body. He struggled into an upright position, trying to let the blood-flow return to normal in his limbs, and surveyed where the river had brought them.

Before he'd fallen asleep, they'd been the only boat on the river, whereas now there were boats everywhere, nipping to and fro between the shorelines, which must have been over two miles apart. The river's banks were lined with jetties and warehouses of all shapes and sizes, and everywhere could be heard the bustling of people going about the business of the river.

There were also larger ships travelling up and down the passage, much larger than their small craft. They were ocean-going vessels, Torben imagined, huge beasts with multiple masts that stood over three stories in height above the waterline. One such craft sailed right in front of them, and it towered high above. To Torben, it looked as if the entire population of Bywater could have easily been accommodated in that ship, and they still wouldn't have had the manpower to crew it.

There were scraping sounds of wood and metal as the pilot somewhere above them in the ship guided the hulking leviathan into one of the docks. As the ship turned and faced them broadside on, Torben could see that the back of the ship had been built much higher than the rest of the vessel, and looked as if it had been fortified to prevent, or discourage, attack. Occasionally, the head of a helmeted guardsman was seen peeking over the ship's crenellated of the ship's fortifications, and at several points ballistae could be seen, used to protect the ship and her cargo.

The sight of this ship alone would have been different and exciting enough for Torben. No one back in Bywater would ever have been able to imagine that such a structure could exist, let alone sail. As the ship turned from the main course of the river, Eleusia was able to guide their craft swiftly around it. Laid out in front of them was Karpella, the capital of the Kingdom of Dazscor and Aramore.

The city was situated along the southern bank of the river Arlen and across two islands that jutted from the water to the north. The entire metropolis was surrounded by a huge stone curtain wall with fortified towers along its length. The walls screened most of the city from view but, here and there, a tower was tall enough to peek over them. The northern most part of the city was dominated by a huge castle that took up the bulk of that island and guarded the passage of the rest of the river to and from the sea, which lay way off to the west.

There was only one gate on the southern landward side, but the channels in between the city's islands flowed through, joining the river at both ends. The channels were wide enough to easily accommodate smaller boats, such as barges, dinghies and small transportation craft, and were protected at both ends by portcullis that spanned their entire width.

It was towards the southern channel that Eleusia steered and the closer they got to the walls, the dimmer the light became as they travelled into the shadow of the fortification. As they passed underneath the arch, Torben looked up and could see the metal teeth of the portcullis protruding from the gap in the ceiling that it descended from. As he surveyed the portcullis' rust-orange teeth, Torben felt a lump in his throat and he winced as they passed directly below, fearing that the metal edifice would come crashing down onto their boat.

Clearing the walls, their surroundings became light again as the sun shone onto the streets of Karpella. Lining the channel were a multitude of small landing points, and buildings of all shapes and sizes crowded the waterfront. Most of them were made of wood and the upper floors stuck out over the channel, vying with one another for space.

There were people everywhere, of every race and creed that Torben could imagine, and many more beside; they unloaded ships, pedalled wares along the waterfront, and bustled about their business. Their shouts and cries reverberated along the channel and through the streets, and there was movement everywhere.

How could anyone make their way through the swarming streets here, Torben wondered. There were so many bodies passing here and there, not to mention the carts, wagons and animals that attempted to move through the streets as well.

Eleusia and Gwilym were unfazed by the surroundings. They'd both visited Karpella many times and had long ago lost the sense of wonder that Torben was feeling. Gwilym continued to lie in the boat, not bothering to take in the sights. His brow was still furrowed in thought and his face was lined with weariness, a testament to his night of restless rumination.

In front of them was one of the three bridges that spanned the channel between the mainland and the first of Karpella's islands, and as they approached Torben could easily pick out the figures of the city guard. They maintained a large presence upon the bridges. Both ends were protected by small forts through which the passage of goods and personnel could be monitored.

He wasn't the only one watching the guards on the bridge. Eleusia was also staring at them intently, studying their movements. She'd covered her crossbow with one of the folds of her cloak and for the first time Torben saw a slightly nervous expression cross her face. She was, after all, not carrying typical cargo and if any guards inspected their boat with too keen an eye, they'd have easily spotted the fact that Torben and Gwilym were bound hand and foot.

The same thought had clearly crossed Gwilym's mind for he sat bolt upright as they approached the bridge. He opened his mouth as if he were about to hail the city guard above.

Eleusia, however, was too quick for him. She kicked him hard in the small of the back, sending him flying onto the floor. 'Utter one word, Gwilym, and I swear that I'll plant my dagger in your back, guards or no guards!'

He sat up on his knees and looked back at her with pure malice. He didn't say anything, but turned and spat blood into the river. Torben could see him running his tongue across his teeth, checking that they were intact.

Eleusia didn't stop staring at the top of the bridge until they were well beneath its arch. Once under, she steered towards the southern bank of the channel. It didn't take much guessing for Torben to work out which jetty she was aiming for. At the end of one, a couple of feet away from the other side of the bridge, and shielded from view by the upper floors of a house that veered dangerously over the river, stood two large thug-like men.

Both looked as if they'd seen many a brawl, and they carried barely concealed weapons beneath ragged coats. One of them raised a hand to Eleusia as he spotted the boat, and the other one reached out and caught the rope that Eleusia tossed him, and secured the craft to the jetty.

'You took your time,' one of the thugs growled. 'The boss has been waiting for weeks for word from you. He's not happy!'

'I'm here now, aren't I?' Eleusia fixed the man with a steely stare. 'We need to get these two off the boat and into the compound as quickly as possible. Do you have the cart?'

'Aye, on't road,' the other thug replied.

'Good, gag them before we leave. This one,' Eleusia indicated Gwilym, 'is likely to try and draw attention to us.'

The two men grunted in obedience and hauled Torben and

Gwilym out of the boat, stuffing dirty rags into their mouths as they did so. Eleusia placed Gwilym's possessions into his pack and slung it onto her back before stepping from the boat and onto the jetty. Her crossbow was half concealed under her cloak, ready, just in case they should run into trouble.

'Come on, to your feet!' one of thugs snapped, cuffing Torben round the ears with a hand missing several fingers.

As soon as the two prisoners struggled to their feet, the thugs jostled them along, as fast as the foot bindings would allow, into an alleyway. The other pedestrians that passed them as they crossed the road that ran along the waterfront averted their gaze. They simply hurried past, clearly not wanting to get involved.

The alleyway was dark, dank, and full of rubbish. A small stream of muck ran through the middle and down a sewer grate at the end, where a covered cart hitched to a dishevelled looking pony waited for them.

The thugs pitched Torben and Gwilym into the back, one climbing in with them to make sure they didn't cause trouble whilst Eleusia and the second thug sat in the front. The thug in the back drew rough dirty fabric across the two men to block any view of the street, as the cart started to make its way through Karpella.

The journey in the cart could only have lasted ten minutes, but with the curtain drawn against the outside world, it was hard for Torben to tell exactly how far or where they'd gone. All he knew was that after an indeterminable amount of time, the cart drew to a halt and the thug jumped down and beckoned them to follow. 'Come on, I haven't got all day,' he said gruffly.

Gwilym eased his way out of the cart first and Torben followed, blinking and shielding his eyes as they emerged from the dingy interior into the sunshine once more. After a few seconds, Torben's eyes adjusted to the light levels and he was able to take in his surroundings.

The cart had drawn up before a large stone building, which had a sturdy wooden fence surrounding it on all sides and formed a compound. Before the heavy wooden gates were shut by two guards, Torben turned and caught a brief glance of the street they'd travelled along, which looked a lot more rough and ragged than the waterfront.

'Stop gawking and move!' The thug smacked Torben in the back of the head and pushed him forwards, driving him towards the house.

Eleusia had gone on ahead, pulling Gwilym behind her, and was passing through double doors into the interior. 'Bring him up as well,' she said over her shoulder. 'Björn will want to see both of them.'

Torben staggered up the stairs as the thug urged him on with curses and blows. He tripped on the last step and tumbled through the open doors into the building, and landed flat on his face inside.

A roar of laughter erupted and looking up, Torben saw a large room full of rough-looking folks eating and drinking around heavy oak tables. The sight of Gwilym's capture and Torben's fall through the door was highly amusing, and as the two prisoners shuffled through the room towards stairs at the back, they were pelted with insults, food, and stale beer.

'Traitor!'

'String 'em up!'

'Thieving piece of filth!'

Torben and Gwilym were glad to make the safety of the stairs and, to avoid the hail of missiles that had greeted their arrival, they scrambled up as fast as the bonds would allow. At the top was a long corridor with rooms branching from it at regular intervals. The sound of Eleusia's steady, confident footsteps resonated through the stone corridor as they were led towards a particular door at the end.

The door itself was nothing special, but clearly the room was of importance because a monster of a man stood before it, his meaty arms folded, guarding the entrance. At least Torben thought that it was a man. As he drew closer, he realised that the guard who towered over them and made Torben seem diminutive, had a large single yellow eye in the centre of his forehead that glowered as they approached. Before the creature was an immense wicked-looking axe, whose head was on the wooden floor with the cyclops' hands resting on the haft, ready to swing into action.

They stopped before him and he spoke with a deep and powerful voice. 'The boss gave orders that you were to be admitted as soon as you arrive, Eleusia.' With that, he pushed open the door.

Eleusia entered, Gwilym and Torben nervously following. The cyclops dismissed the two thugs with a wave of a massive hand and entered behind the trio, though he had to duck under the door lintel to do so. He pulled the door shut behind and took up position in front of it, arms folded once more.

The room they stood in was sizeable, with a large curved ceiling that gave Torben the impression he was standing in an upturned stone boat. There were no windows and the only light was provided by a huge fireplace set into a wall and several candle brackets; the room was not only dimly lit, but very warm. The walls were bare save for a large bookcase at the end, and in the centre of the room was a large low-set desk covered in papers, scrolls, and thick account books. Bent over the desk was the bald head of a dwarf, busy writing with a quill on a piece of parchment.

Eleusia led her prisoners up to the desk and then stood in silence, and waited for the dwarf to finish writing. No one spoke. All that could be heard was the scratching of the quill as it raced across the page and the occasional plop as the writer replenished it with ink. The silence made Torben feel very nervous and the intense heat in the room made him realise how long it had been since he'd had a drink of water. Suddenly, he became intensely aware how dry and scratchy his throat felt and, before long, he experienced a coughing fit.

The sound shattered the dwarf's concentration and he looked

up and surveyed Torben over the rims of small round spectacles that clung to his face. He stared, saying nothing, and as the coughing subsided, returned to his writing.

The dwarf was Björn, so Torben assumed, and he was much the same height as Gwilym, but stouter. At first, one could have been tricked into calling him fat, but the way his bones carried his weight indicated he was very strongly built. His head was completely bald and the slight sheen of sweat that covered it reflected the flickering amber candlelight. Despite his baldness, he sported an enormous silver beard, flecked with the original bark-brown colour, that covered most of his torso.

After a few more minutes, he set down the quill, crossed heavily scarred hands on the desk in front of him, and surveyed the two prisoners for what seemed an eternity to Torben. Then, he removed the spectacles from the bridge of his bulbous nose and turned to Eleusia. 'I wasn't expecting you until nightfall, Eleusia.' Björn's voice was husky and so soft, it was almost a whisper. 'It was careless of you to enter the city with them in daylight. I have enough problems with the city guard as it is without you adding to them.'

'I thought you'd want them in your possession as soon as possible. I felt the risk was worth it to save time.' There was a distinct quaver in Eleusia's voice. Clearly, she was afraid of Björn and avoided making eye contact, staring at the wall behind him as she stood at attention next to Gwilym.

'Well, it was still careless nonetheless. No matter though, you brought me what I wanted.' He picked up a small roll of parchment from the desk and held it out to her. 'Take that to the Paymaster and he'll see that you get what you're owed.'

Taking the scroll, Eleusia turned as if to leave, studying the parchment as she did so, but she didn't get far before she wheeled and stormed to the desk, anger written across her face. 'What the hell is this?' She waved the parchment before Björn's face.

'What you're owed, Eleusia.' The dwarf's voice remained low and level.

'We agreed thirty gold for delivering Gwilym and his belongings, plus another ten for anyone I captured with him. This says I'm only to be paid fifteen!'

'Aye, we did agree to that figure, but that was before you flouted your orders to get them to me.' Björn's voice had taken on a more dangerous edge. 'Our scouts spotted you sailing up the Arlen in broad daylight and brought the news of your return barely two hours before you arrived. Only just enough time for me to work my contacts in the castle to get the bribes to the right guards stationed in the right places. Or did you think that the Karpella city guard had become more lenient towards our activities since you've been gone?

'I had to call in several favours to get out those bribes in time —several *expensive* favours. I can't afford to pull so many strings at the last minute for the sake of you. Too much running around at the eleventh hour makes people careless, and that's when the wrong people notice things they shouldn't. You're lucky I'm paying you anything at all.'

'What about the money for him?' Eleusia gestured Torben.

'Him?' Björn snorted. 'Look at him. He barely looks as if he'd know which end of a sword to hold, let alone swing it. You get ten gold for the thief, five for the boy. Now get out of here before I change my mind. I'll send for you when I need you again.'

Björn's point was brought home by the appearance of the cyclops at Eleusia's back. He laid a huge hand on her shoulder and, without resisting, she allowed herself to be escorted from the room. As he closed the door after her, the cyclops returned to his guard, the single eye taking in every movement Gwilym and Torben made.

'Now, what should I do with you?' Björn turned back to stare Gwilym in the face. 'Are we going to have a conversation here and now, or are you going to make my life difficult?'

'Well,' Gwilym began quietly, 'you know that I would always

prefer to have a nice, civil conversation with you Björn … level with you, dwarf to dwarf. But—'

'But what?' he demanded, the menacing tone returning.

'I don't have anything to say that I haven't already told you.'

'Really? You're really going to stick to that cock-and-bull story you tried to sell the last time you stood here in front of me? And here I was, thinking you were smart. I'm going to ask you once, nicely Gwilym, and after that I'll be forced to move into other realms of persuasion. Where is the Keystone?'

'I don't know, Björn.' Desperation had crept into Gwilym's voice and he wrung his hands in front of him as he spoke. 'I've already told you everything that happened, truthfully! After we found the Keystone, we set off to bring it back to you, but then Meckel gave me the slip and tried to kill me when I pursued him. There was nothing I could do, Björn. I have no idea where he is or where the Keystone is. He's disappeared and, like as not, we'll never see him again!'

'*Nothing* you could do?' Björn hissed. 'I've seen you fell a cony from over two-hundred feet with that sling of yours, and you're telling me that you couldn't bring down something your own size? If nothing else, you could have died trying to stop him. That's the level of commitment I demand from my people!' By now Björn was standing and leaning across the desk towards Gwilym. His voice still possessed a dangerous hiss and he speckled Gwilym with spittle. 'It seems to me there are only two logical reasons behind this bollocks you're telling me; either you've been in cahoots with him this whole time and let him go, hoping I'd buy your story or you let him go because you didn't have the guts to do what needed to be done. Neither of these options I like.'

'Please, you have to believe me!'

'Shut it,' Björn bellowed. Taking several deep breaths, he resumed his seat behind the desk and ran a hand across his bald head.

Gwilym had retreated several steps and seemed to be making himself look as small as possible.

'And what about *you*?' Björn addressed Torben.

'Me, sir?'

'Aye, you!' He looked him up and down. 'If you're involved with this fool, then I expect you have some inkling as to what has actually been going on.'

'No, sir. I don't.' Torben spoke truthfully; he had no idea what the two dwarfs had been discussing. Keystones? That mysterious Meckel person? None of it made any sense to him, but it didn't seem as if Björn was in the mood to take 'no' for an answer. As he'd feared, merely being associated with Gwilym was enough to make him a suspect in all this.

'Look boy, I don't know you and for all I know, you might have a brain hidden somewhere underneath that curly mop of yours, so I'm giving you a chance to tell me what I want to hear and I'll make it worth your while.'

'I wish I could tell you something, sir.' Torben shot a dirty look in Gwilym's direction. 'But I—'

'Don't know anything,' Björn finished Torben's sentence. 'It seems that you are as stupid as I thought. What kind of idiot enters into a venture like this without establishing what it's all about?' Placing the spectacles back on his nose, he picked up a piece of parchment and dipped the quill in the ink. As he began to write, he spoke without looking up. 'The two of you have until morning to come to your senses and give me a straight answer. After that, I shall *not* hesitate to resort to all the methods at my disposal to get what I want. It won't be pretty and it won't be quick. Gord!'

The cyclops moved swiftly, his heavy footsteps reverberating through the floorboards, and stood behind the prisoners, looking at his boss over their heads.

'Put these two in the attic cells. I want two men outside the door at all times. If I catch anyone shirking their duty whilst guarding them, the consequences will be severe ... understand me?'

'Aye sir,' Gord rumbled.

'Good, take them away.'

Using the axe haft to shepherd Gwilym and Torben out of the room, Gord guided them towards the door. As they entered the corridor, they heard Björn shout after them.

'Until the morning then!'

Once in the corridor, the twosome were ushered back the way they'd come. When they reached the landing that overlooked the dining hall below, they were greeted by the sight of Eleusia, leaning against an arch. Gord looked her up and down with his single piercing eye as he passed, growled menacingly, and steered Torben and Gwilym up a flight of stairs. Eleusia clearly didn't heed the cyclops' warning for as soon as Gord turned his back to ascend the steps himself, she'd disappeared back down the corridor, her green cloak billowing around her.

The stairs they ascended became increasingly narrower the higher they climbed, until they ended on a small landing. In front was a small open door that Gord pushed them through, then pulled sharply behind them. On the other side, the two of them heard the scrape and thud of a heavy bar being dropped.

There wasn't much to see when Torben surveyed the prison cell. They were in an attic room, the only light source a tiny slit of a window high on the gable-end wall, opposite the door. There was however, a single bucket filled with dirty, brackish water—but water, nonetheless.

Torben fell to his knees before the bucket, dunked his head in and took several big gulps. At that moment, it was more refreshing than any ale he'd ever taken. Falling back against a wall, he watched Gwilym drink his fill in a similar manner. After the short-lived elation of quenching his thirst, the creeping sensations of dread and hopelessness began to edge into his heart once more.

'Ah!' Gwilym smacked his lips as he rose, water droplets cascading down his beard and hanging from his moustache. 'Well, Torben, that could have been much worse.' The timidity he'd displayed when speaking to Björn had completely disappeared and he spoke with his usual jocularity.

Torben had already decided that he'd do his best to ignore Gwilym and not communicate with him in any way. He'd determined that listening to the dwarf's idle conversation would only sink him deeper and deeper into the abysmal situation they were now in, but the dwarf's statement shocked him and he couldn't help but respond. 'What? How on earth can you say that? Here we are, trapped in a tiny room, awaiting what seems our execution, and you don't think it could get *worse*?'

'Oh, it could have been much worse,' Gwilym said nonchalantly. 'We've got our lives, and all our digits come to think of it, and that's a plus right there. I once attended a similar meeting, as a captor not a captive, where Björn got so angry that he put out a man's eyes purely because he sneezed, and that's not even the angriest I've seen him.'

'You say that, but how do you know he's not going to change his mind and send that hulking brute to finish us off?'

'Björn's not going to kill us. He can't afford to kill us until he thinks we've given him all the information he wants.'

'That's *another* thing.' Torben's voice rose as anger welled. 'You've got a damn lot of explaining to do! What the hell have you been playing at? Argh, if my hands were free right now I'd give you a damn good hiding!'

Gwilym had rather hoped he'd forgotten the revelations that Eleusia had forced on the boat, but clearly they were very much at the front of Torben's mind. Indeed, his face was already resuming the flushed, angry red hue it had turned on the boat when it appeared as if he'd have strangled Gwilym there and then … had he been able to move, of course. Gwilym took a deep breath. 'Look, Torben, perhaps I wasn't completely honest with you when we first met; I can't deny that what Eleusia told you was true, in part.

'When I met you, you looked like the sort of man that I could bait into falling for my scheme, but that changed as soon as we started walking. You had one thing that all of those other idiots didn't: you were discontented with your lot in life. The people I robbed were all happy to do the same monotonous thing over and over again, and by the time I parted with them, I felt like ending their life just to release them from the boring torment they were willing to subject themselves to—not that I *did*, mind you!

'But you, you wanted—still want I reckon—to see the world, stretch those legs on the open road and live a little … and I saw myself in you.' Gwilym smiled wryly. 'I didn't want to resort to jumping people like a common thief in the wilderness for the sake of a few copper coins, but that's what I had to resort to in order to make ends meet, and ensure I could get as far away from Björn as I could, not that it's done me much good now.

'Another thing I realised is that you've got guts, lad. You may not know much about handling yourself in a serious scrap, save what your instincts tell you, but you're a damn sight braver than nearly every other man I've met. And that got me to thinking that maybe you'd be able to help me claim one of the biggest hauls that anyone has ever seen.'

By now, Torben was leaning forwards and hanging on to Gwilym's every word. His face had returned to its normal pale hue and his previous anger was beginning to dissipate. There were, however, still a few grains of scepticism floating around his mind; he couldn't completely forget the fact that Gwilym had been only a few 'sympathetic' thoughts away from robbing him, perhaps even killing him. Nevertheless, he motioned the dwarf to continue talking.

'I take it that the Keystone that Björn mentioned meant nothing to you?' Gwilym asked.

'No, absolutely nothing.'

'Well then, let me fill you in on a little history. You may not know it, but all of the land that runs for hundreds of miles on either side of the Arlen River, from its source to the sea—including, I'll warrant, your sleepy dale—was and is ruled from the same royal seat here in Karpella.

'Before the current dynasty ascended to power, there ruled a king called Sarper the IV ... over a land that was then known as the Kingdom of Dazscor. Sarper was an entrepreneurial soul, alongside being one of the greatest misers to ever tread the world. He established Karpella as the great trading port that it now is, brought in goods and treasures of unimaginable value from a number of distant lands, and all the profits were carefully squirrelled away in the castle.

'Sarper's wealth has been lauded for generations, but is well known to his contemporaries. Other kings grew jealous of the untold riches locked up in Karpella. Eventually, one of the border kingdoms down to the south, the Duchy of Aramore, decided to try their luck and invaded.

'Unfortunately for Sarper, he'd been so bent on saving his treasure, that many other matters, including the army, had been neglected. Most of his men were fat and idle, and couldn't stand before the aggressive, highly drilled troops of Aramore. Not to mention the fact that his miserly nature meant that there were many in his kingdom that resented him and wanted their fair share of the treasure.

'Without much difficulty, the Duke of Aramore marched through Sarper's kingdom and lay siege to Karpella. It was only a matter of time before Karpella would fall, and Sarper knew it. With every passing day, his men were deserting in droves, and the mob in the city was growing restless and discontented with the apparent lack of concern that the King showed for their welfare and that of the city.

'In his retinue, Sarper had a powerful sorcerer—there were a great many magic wielders back in those days than now—and he charged him to make safe his gold from the invaders, as well as his own people. His plan was to slip out of the city, let it fall to the Aramorians, and hope that their inability to secure his gold would mean that he'd be able to easily retake control of the city by offering gold to the right parties.

'Well, the sorcerer put such a powerful enchantment on the treasure vault, deep in the bowels of the castle, that it claimed his life. Before he died, he passed onto his King the one thing that would allow access to the treasure: the Keystone. With the gold secured, Sarper and his retinue began their escape; unfortunately for them, whilst the ritual had been taking place, the Aramorians had begun their final assault and were making great headway through the city to the castle.

'Sarper was killed escaping, cut down by an arrow to the back as he fled through the docks. However, when his body was searched, there was no sign of the Keystone. He'd given it to one of his servants with strict instructions to never let it fall into the wrong hands. This servant slipped away. The Aramorian dynasty has ruled the joint Kingdom of Dazscor and Aramore for nigh on the last one hundred and eighty years, and the Keystone hasn't been seen since.'

Gwilym paused for breath and, with difficulty, took a quaff of water from the bucket.

Torben took advantage of Gwilym's temporary silence to ask, 'Why is Björn so obsessed with the Keystone if it's lost?'

'Ah, a fair comment you might think.' He settled back in his corner. 'That's exactly what I thought when I entered Björn's office, and he told me about the information he'd received as to the Keystone's whereabouts ... that the man who possessed it was willing to sell it to him. I told him there and then that he was a fool to believe such stories, that the Keystone was lost beyond all hope of finding it, if it had ever existed in the first place. And even if it were found, we'd have no way of telling whether it was the genuine article. But I bowed to his wishes, after he told me how much my share would be if he was right ... so me and my partner, Meckel, went to retrieve it.

'We had to travel to Makesh, a journey of nearly two-and-a-half months, to find the rendezvous point far to the south, near the border of the Free States and the Sultanate of Fashaddon, where we were to meet the fellow that claimed to have the Keystone. When we reached the meeting place, the man—I can't rightly recall his name now—and an old priest were there to meet us. This old man showed us what looked like a piece of stone—nicely carved, a mystic-looking rune here and there, the sort of thing I'd carve onto a rock if I wanted someone to think it was a magic stone.

'This old priest mixed up a potion in front of us, which he said was a truth potion, and that it would make any person who drank it, or any object it was poured upon, disclose a single truth when asked by a questioner. I was sceptical about all this, so the priest gave some to Meckel and asked him where he hoarded the money Björn paid him … and out Meckel comes and tells him straight off. Meckel had only told one other person where his hoard was buried and that was me, in case he died on the job; that way I could take it to his ageing mother to provide help for her.

'In any case, the priest poured the rest of this potion on the stone and asked it whether it was the Keystone of Sarper the IV, and the stone burst into flames and then returned to normal, as if nothing had happened. I still wasn't too sure about all this and was about to ask if there was another test we could do for further proof when Meckel leapt forward, dagger drawn, and killed them both on the spot. He grabbed the stone and then killed all five of the guards the man had had lying in wait, should we try to jump him.

'When I tried to stop him, he near killed *me*. He'd been driven wild by the thought of all that gold, and ran off with the stone. I would have followed, but he struck me in the temple with a sling stone and knocked me flat; had it been any harder, the shot would have killed me.

'After I regained consciousness, I hotfooted it back to Björn to tell him what happened, but he assumed that I'd thrown in my lot with Meckel, and that we were trying to cheat him out of the treasure, as you heard today. He locked me up and would have tortured an answer out of me if I hadn't escaped. I tried to get as far from Karpella as I could to save my skin, and that eventually led to our meeting in that Bywater tavern.

'That leads us to our current predicament. My original intension, before being waylaid, was to lie low for a while and then pursue the Keystone myself. Björn has made it clear that he's in no way sympathetic to me. What do I owe a man who's imprisoned me twice, tried to kill me once, and would think nothing of trying to torture an answer from me? *Nothing*, that's what!' Gwilym scowled and drew a deep breath. 'There's no way I'd be able to pull off a haul like this without help. If we can manage to get ourselves out of this situation, how would you like a share in more treasure than you or anyone in that tin-pot little village of yours would be able to imagine?'

The offer took Torben by surprise and he sat stunned for several seconds. 'But how do you know where this Meckel bloke has gone? He could be anywhere for all you know.'

'True,' he replied with a nod. 'But I know Meckel better than anyone alive. He wasn't a trusting sort, but when you work as someone's partner for so many years and go through all sorts of dangers, you get to know them almost better than you know yourself.

'As I mentioned, I'm the only one he told about the whereabouts of his hoard. By my reckoning, it can't be a large amount of money. Meckel was far too free with his coins down at the docks to have managed to scrimp much away, but he'll need money to pay people to help him with this job, so he'll almost certainly return to his hoard. We can pick up his trail from there." He grinned mischievously. 'What do you say? Can you let bygones be bygones in circumstances such as we now find ourselves in?'

'Well ... to be honest, I don't know.' Torben mulled over

everything Gwilym had told him, but there was too much information to process—not to mention the fact that his trust in the dwarf had yet to be repaired. He couldn't bank on the fact that the dwarf wouldn't turn on him when the job was done or at the next convenient moment. 'I need to think about it. Sorry, Gwilym, but I don't know what to say.'

Gwilym was very much taken aback by Torben's response and his brows and moustache bristled when he realised the young man wasn't going to provide an answer there and then. 'Well, we've got until morning, I suppose, provided Björn keeps his word,' he said curtly. 'You'd best make your mind up fast though; once things get underway, we'll need to act quickly.'

With that, he lay on the floor and began to wriggle into a position that would let him rest easy. The limited light coming through the window had almost faded to nothing, and the room was nearly pitch black.

Torben waded through the sea of thoughts, ideas and scenarios streaming through his head. As he thought, his eyelids grew heavier and heavier, and his head nodded against his chest. Before he had even begun to fully contemplate the problem at hand, sleep took him and he lay against the cell wall, snoring loudly.

8

By the time Torben awoke the following morning, the day was well and truly underway. Warm yellow daylight streamed through the tiny slit window and cast a golden beam on the floor. Gwilym was already awake and had his ear pressed to a crack in the door, apparently listening for movement on the other side.

Torben struggled into an upright position and staggered to his feet, trying his best to stretch out his muscles, even though he still couldn't move his arms properly. If nothing else, standing helped ease aches and pains that the bonds were giving him.

'Can you hear much?' He kept his voice low, barely more than a whisper.

'Only the two guards outside and they're not what we need to worry about. We can't have long. The sun's been up for a good few hours so, like as not, Björn will begin dealing with business soon.'

Leaving Gwilym at the door, Torben shuffled to the window and craned his neck, trying to see the outside world. The window was so small, it was hard to make out much of the surrounding streets, but he could clearly view the castle on the next island, its dark stones glowing over the rest of Karpella.

Between the castle and Torben's vantage point were a sea of houses. Nothing, however, was quite as tall as Björn's stronghold on that part of the island.

'Ahem.' Gwilym cleared his throat loudly to attract Torben's attention. 'Given the fact that we're rapidly running out of time, there's no point avoiding the ogre in the room. Have you made up your mind about my offer?'

He sighed deeply. He'd been hoping Gwilym would have been too preoccupied trying to predict Björn's approach to worry about what he'd decided. In reality, Torben hadn't come to any legitimate answer per se, only realised that he was well and truly cornered. 'As far as I see it, I don't really have a choice, do I? I still don't know whether I can trust your word. For all I know, you might kill me as soon as it becomes convenient. Then again, I reckon you're my best hope of escaping.

'If we escape and go our separate ways, I'll be trapped in a city as a wanted man, with nowhere to go and no idea of where to begin rebuilding what's left of my life. There's no point in going back to Burndale to squat alone in a pile of ashes, that's for sure.' He eyed Gwilym intently. 'I'll help you with this madness, but I'll tell you straight now, if I get the slightest whiff that you're thinking of double-crossing me again, I won't hesitate to beat the living daylights out of you!'

'Sounds good to me; glad you came to your senses at last.' Gwilym didn't look up or remove his ear from the door as he spoke, but continued to listen intently. A few seconds passed and Gwilym sprang back and scrambled to his feet next to Torben. 'They're on their way. You can hear that brute Gord's footsteps on those stairs from miles away.'

'Right.' He waited, expecting Gwilym to give instructions of some sort, but the dwarf remained silent and stared at the door. 'So what's the plan? You *do* have a plan, don't you?'

'Huh? A plan? Oh yes, of course I have a plan. Just follow my lead.' He didn't offer up any more than that, just continued to stare at the door.

Torben considered pressing him for more information on what he should expect from the "plan", but the sounds of Gord's footsteps thudded outside and was followed by the rumble of the cyclops' voice as he gave the order to unbar the door.

Björn had arrived.

Light streamed into the room as the door opened and the short stature of Björn crossed the threshold into the cell, with the looming torso of Gord behind. The room was almost thrown into darkness as the cyclops glowered at the prisoners from behind his master.

Slinking into the room behind them was Eleusia; she slipped past Gord's massive bulk and leaned against a wall, picking her nails carelessly. She still sported her travelling gear from the day before, though she was now wearing a scarf wound several times around her neck, which was odd, given the fact it was relatively warm in the room.

'Now then, gentlemen,' Björn spoke in business-like fashion. 'I'm hoping that the two of you have come to your senses and are going to tell me what I want.'

Gwilym and Torben stood in silence. Moving carefully, to not draw too much attention, Torben turned to Gwilym and attempted to discern from his silence what he intended to do.

Gwilym, however, didn't react, simply stared Björn straight in the eyes; clearly, he was opting for a more confrontational stance than he had the day before.

'Well?' Björn continued, looking from one to the other. 'You've tried my patience for too long already, so I suggest that you start talking now … or this *won't* end well for you.'

Again Torben turned to look at Gwilym, and this time he saw the dwarf shake his head, almost imperceptibly, but it was a clear sign to his companion to remain silent. He then faced Björn, Gord and Eleusia, and gulped nervously.

The prisoners' continued silence prompted Gord to limber up, rolling his shoulders and his neck, and then menacingly cracking his knuckles.

Björn met Gwilym's gaze and allowed the silence to continue for a few more seconds before sighing deeply and shaking his head. 'I take it that you're not going to be cooperative. In that case then, you'll have to suffer the consequences of your actions. Gord, Eleusia? I don't expect you to leave this room until you've got an answer from the two of them.' He eyed his fellow dwarf critically. 'No offence to you, Gwilym, or your crony here, but I shan't be staying to watch, as much as I want to. I have business to attend to down at the docks.'

With that Björn left the room, though his exit lacked the menace that he had intended, given he had to weave past Eleusia and squeeze past Gord to leave.

As Björn's footsteps receded, Gord brought in a canvass roll and set it on the floor in front of Torben and Gwilym. He loosened the fastenings and spread the roll on the floor. Inside were all manner of strange, vicious looking implements and tools, which the cyclops lovingly crooned over as he ran his fingers along them.

Gwilym's mind was furiously working, trying to formulate a plan to get the two of them out of a situation that was rapidly going downhill. He glanced at Torben, trying to catch his eye and reassure him that he had some sort of strategy, even if he didn't.

Torben didn't meet the dwarf's gaze, but stared in horror at Gord's toolkit. All the blood had drained from of his face and he stood as pale as a ghost as he watched Gord draw a wicked looking hook from the roll and hold it up to the light. His huge eye looked up at Torben and he smirked as he noticed the affect the hook had on his prisoner.

The smirk, however, didn't last long. A sharp crack broke the intense silence and Gord slowly but surely pitched forwards, and lay spread-eagled on the floor, all his senses, temporarily at least, knocked from his head.

Beyond Gord's prone body stood Eleusia, the wooden bar used to secure the door in her hands. One end of the bar had a significant dent; the wood had cracked under the force of the blow she'd delivered to the cyclops' head. Gwilym and Torben stood stunned, staring with open mouths at the scene before them.

Eleusia dropped the bar onto Gord's body and, stepping over it, approached the prisoners, her dagger drawn. At the sight of the unsheathed blade, Torben and Gwilym instinctively shuffled back, but their backs were already pressed against the wall and there was nowhere to retreat.

'We haven't got time for the two of you to act all stupid,' Eleusia said with annoyance. 'If I wanted you two dead, I'd have let Gord do it for me. I'm trying to help you.'

Reluctantly, Gwilym turned his back on Eleusia so she could cut the bonds around his hands and feet. 'So why exactly are you helping us now? I mean, it seems a bit strange considering all the trouble you went to bringing us here in the first place.'

'Look, we can either stand here gossiping like cretins until that oaf wakes up or we can actually get out of here.' As Eleusia spoke, she moved over to Torben and cut his restricting bonds, too. 'All you need to know for now is that I'm willing to help you until we get to a safe house, where we can discuss what my cut will be for pulling off this stunt of yours.'

'Whoa, hang on a minute. *Your* cut from the scheme?' Gwilym looked astonished. 'We've been telling the truth the whole time, and—'

'Knock it off, Gwilym,' she cut in brusquely. 'It's obvious you at least know where to start looking for Meckel and the Keystone. That must be how you got Torben back on your side so quickly. I was half expecting him to sell you straight out when Gord got his toys out. Frankly, I'd be damned surprised if you aren't mentally running that gold through your hands right now!'

As the rope yielded to Eleusia's sharp dagger, Torben let out a sigh of relief; he was finally able to move his arms and legs freely again. He began to massage his wrists, heavily abraded from all those hours the rope had constrained him.

She sheathed the dagger and walked swiftly towards the door, and turned as she crossed the threshold. She eyed Torben and Gwilym, who still stood at the back of the cell. 'We need to leave *now*! Cyclops have thick skulls you know, so Gord won't be down for much longer.'

'What are we going to do?' Torben muttered to Gwilym.

'Do what she wants, I say. This seems to be going a lot more smoothly than I imagined it would.'

'Why? What was your plan?'

'I hadn't thought of one in time. I was hoping something would come up,' Gwilym said with his usual jovial tone as he clambered over Gord's massive bulk.

Reluctantly, Torben followed the others, shaking his head in disbelief at what was happening.

'You couldn't make this up,' he thought with a sigh.

As he left the cell, Eleusia closed the door behind and barred it with another plank of wood that had been left on the landing. 'That might buy us a little more time once he wakes, but not much. Here.' She handed Gwilym his pack, belt and seax that she'd brought onto the landing, and then passed Torben his small knife. She was already wearing the sword and dagger beneath her cloak, and her crossbow was suspended from one shoulder by a leather strap.

'Let's go,' she urged. 'They've started doling out breakfast in the mess, so there should be plenty of noise and movement to cover our escape.'

With that, they descended the stairs carefully and quietly. As they approached the landing above the mess hall, they could hear the hubbub of Björn's henchmen talking and eating. When they reached the landing, they crouched low, keeping below the wooden boarding that served as a bannister of sorts. Eleusia led them through an archway that marked the beginning of the corridor to Björn's office. As she veered to the left to take the corridor, Gwilym grabbed her elbow.

'What are you doing?' he whispered sharply. 'It's a dead end down there; we'll be trapped for sure!'

'Trust me, this is the fastest way out.'

'You're mad! There's nothing but storerooms down there, well apart from Björn' office, which he may well still be in.'

'Guys?' Torben whispered.

'You may think you're clever—hell, you may even *be* clever for all I know—but there's a damn sight more about this place than you're aware of, so shut up and follow me.' Eleusia ignored Torben.

'I'm not about to follow someone who's stupidity will lead me to my death,' Gwilym responded with a snort.

'Guys, if we don't move now, we'll be dead regardless of which way you want to go,' Torben raised his voice just enough to be able to butt into their argument. As he spoke, he pointed sharply in the direction of the stairs. Visible over the top of the wooden bannister was the top of a man's head bobbing up and down as they ascended.

Grabbing Gwilym by the scruff of the neck, Eleusia yanked the reluctant dwarf into the corridor with Torben close behind. As soon as they were shielded from view, Eleusia let go and ran down the corridor towards Björn's office. Torben didn't need further encouragement, but kept close to Eleusia's heels.

Gwilym paused and cursed under his breath. Hearing boots on the landing behind, he sprinted after the others and, in the nick of time, slipped through Björn's office door. Torben shut it swiftly behind as the man turned into the corridor and entered a storeroom, oblivious of all but his work.

The interior was lit only by the fire, which flickered low in the grate. Eleusia grabbed a candle from a wall holder and lit the wick in the fire's dying embers. Gwilym slumped in the chair behind Björn's desk and watched. Holding the candle high above her head to illuminate as much of the room as possible, she stalked to the end of the office and headed for a large chest in a far corner. She knelt beside it and ran her hands around the edges of the lid.

'If it's money you're looking for to help us on our way, then you're sorely mistaken to look for it here.' Gwilym put his feet up on the desk. 'Everyone knows that Björn keeps every scrap of coin in this place under lock and key in the Paymaster's office downstairs.'

'I'm not looking for gold; this is our way out.'

'That?' Torben asked, moving away from the door and leaning onto the desk. 'What are we going to do? Hide in it and hope no one looks inside the thing?'

Gwilym snorted with laughter and Eleusia's head snapped around to throw a deadly look in Torben's direction. Without speaking, she held the flame of the candle level with the chest's keyhole.

Torben and Gwilym were perplexed, but then the candle's flame flickered, almost imperceptibly, as if being manipulated by a tiny gust of wind. Sitting forward to gaze more intently at the flame, Gwilym's eyes regained their twinkle as he saw hope in the situation. 'You're kidding me?'

'Now, why would I do that?' Eleusia smirked.

'Where does it lead?' Torben moved around to take a closer look.

'No idea,' she answered with a shrug. 'But right now, the passage has to get us out of here. Gwilym, will you do the honours?'

Springing from the chair and picking up his pack from the floor, he trotted over and removed a small canvas pouch from the pack. He unwrapped lock picks and carefully studied the lock, his head cocked, assessing the situation. Selecting the appropriate tool, he inserted the pick and began to manipulate the lock, his meaty hands moving with far more dexterity that Torben would have thought possible. There was a small click, followed by a loud clunk.

He took a step back and raised a hand to Eleusia, who threw open the lid to reveal a narrow stone staircase that descended into pitch blackness. Now that the chest was open, the breeze flowed fully into the room, making the candle flame flicker violently and awakening the embers of the fire.

No one needed to give instructions. Torben quickly grabbed two more candles from their brackets, lit them with Eleusia's flame, and followed her down the staircase. Gwilym brought up the rear and closed the lid slowly above them, trying not to make a sound. He took a candle from Torben and the trio descended the stairs.

The staircase plunged down through the building and then below ground level before running straight. Everything was covered with damp moss and mould, and water continuously dripped from roughly hewn stones on the ceiling.

'I think the tunnel should bring us out on Bookbinder's Square and from there it's only a few streets to the safe house I've organized.' Eleusia spoke normally now that they were safely in the tunnel.

'Is this safe house going to be safe for all of us, or just you?' Gwilym asked with a smirk. The dwarf still treated Eleusia's involvement in the situation with great suspicion, and he had yet to see anything that convinced him of her true complicity in the scheme. Eleusia didn't respond to Gwilym's question, but continued walking, leaving Gwilym to scowl at her back.

The tunnel carried on for several more minutes before morphing into a steeply ascending staircase. Torben, bringing up the rear, nearly tripped several times on the slimy stones as they traversed the stairs, and was dazzled by a blinding light that filled the tunnel when Eleusia flung open the trapdoor at the top and stepped out into the daylight.

They entered a dusty room full of books, which were piled all over the floor, arranged on shelves that ran all around walls, and stacked precipitously on a small desk near the door to the outside world. Behind the desk sat a diminutive figure that

Torben guessed by his stature must be a gnome. Clearly the proprietor of the bookshop, he stared openmouthed at the three strangers that had just popped out of his floor. Now that the trapdoor was shut again, it blended seamlessly into the wooden floor, and they'd be hard-pressed to find it again.

Not stopping to make excuses, the three quickly made their way to the door and exited into the street. As she passed, Eleusia laid a large gold coin before the shopkeeper. 'You didn't see anything.'

Astounded at what had just taken place, the shopkeeper continued to watch as they set off at a brisk pace through the streets of Karpella.

The party found themselves standing in a small square. The ground floors of most buildings were shops, all with hefty-looking tomes and thick rolls of parchment on display. A large wooden sign painted to resemble an open book was fixed to one building and read in large round letters: Bookbinder's Square.

There weren't many people in the area and, beckoning them on, Eleusia led Torben and Gwilym into a more bustling street beyond the square, to seek cover in the crowds rushing about their business.

As much as Torben wanted to soak in the sights, smells and sounds of the city, there wasn't much time for sightseeing as Eleusia led them at a blistering pace through the streets. He quickly lagged behind as the ebb and flow of the tide of people battered him and made it impossible to walk in a straight line for more than a few seconds. Both Eleusia and Gwilym, however, passed through the crowds with no effort, seamlessly maintaining the relentless walking pace whilst slipping in between individuals and easing past wagons and animals trundling along the route.

Torben managed to keep his eyes on Eleusia, now quite far ahead of him, catching glimpses of her jet black plaited hair here and there in the crowd. Gwilym's short stature, however, meant that it was impossible to keep track of him in the mass of people.

His concentration broke when he inadvertently barged into a burly man wearing the uniform of the City Guard. The man's chainmail clinked ominously as he recoiled from the unexpected contact.

'Watch where you're going, idiot!' The guardsman glowered at Torben from beneath the rim of his conical helmet. The nose guard of the helmet ran down the man's face, nearly to his chin, and made his face almost unrecognisable as that of man's; the effect unnerved Torben greatly.

'Sorry about that. I didn't mean no harm!'

'Aye, sure you didn't. Now, get out of my way!'

Torben sprang to the side as the guardsman muscled past, barging him with a large kite shield as he did so. Torben could hear him complaining about the patrol to one of his fellows as he disappeared into the crowd.

Turning back to continue on his way, he scanned the throng, looking for Eleusia's black hair, but she was nowhere to be seen. He hurried forward, peering into every shop and looking down every side street, trying to glimpse his companions. His panic, however, was short-lived; passing a large wooden door, he caught sight of Gwilym leaning against it, clearly waiting for him.

'Ah, there you are!' The dwarf smiled. 'I was afraid you'd run off and left me alone with her.'

'Where's Eleusia?' he asked as he stepped away from the flow of traffic and stood next to Gwilym in the doorway arch.

'She's inside, making sure everything is going to plan. She wanted to speak with her contact before we seek shelter here. I don't like it, Torben. I don't like it at all.'

The two of them stood in the double doorway of a large house, its face covered with dense ivy and climbing roses. Sticking into the street above the archway was a large fan that swayed in the breeze. Its surface was painted black with bright red ivy-like tendrils painted delicately on top.

The door behind them opened and Eleusia stuck out her head, and beckoned Gwilym and Torben to enter.

'All clear then?' Gwilym asked, sarcasm evident in his voice.

Eleusia didn't acknowledge the tone. 'Yes, I'm sure you'll be glad to hear.' She disappeared back inside, and Torben and Gwilym followed.

Quickly, Gwilym scanned the street and windows looking down from the opposite buildings, making sure that they weren't being watched. Satisfied that no one had taken any notice of them, he closed the door behind.

To Torben's surprise, the doorway arch led underneath the building and opened onto a sizeable courtyard littered with potted flowers, tables, chairs, and the occasional couch. There were several young women moving around, fetching water from a little well in the corner of the courtyard, and scrubbing flagstones.

Standing in the centre was a woman who watched the travellers enter and extended her arms wide to welcome them. 'Come in, come in,' she said with a singsong air. 'Welcome to Ivy House, gentlemen! It's always good to have guests, even those a little more … ahem … problematic, like yourselves. Would you like food and drink; you must all be hungry?'

The woman was very kindly looking, though she did emanate an air of command, even when speaking in such a well-tempered manner. Whatever this place was, this woman was clearly in charge. Her sense of presence was amplified by the elaborate dress she wore, which was covered in delicate white lace embroidery, and appeared to be suspended on her body rather than encasing it. Vivid blonde hair added to her stature; it was piled on top of her head in a nest of carefully crafted curls. Her thick lips, painted a vibrant red colour, stood out starkly against the white of her skin.

'I'm Madame Fleurese and I'm the keeper of this establishment.' She clasped Gwilym and Torben's hands as she spoke. 'I've been informed that I may be of assistance to you and that the three of you, in turn, may be of assistance to me.' She winked a dazzlingly blue eye roguishly at Torben as she released his hand, and began to walk around them, assessing the two up and down as she did so.

Gwilym glowered at Eleusia, and turned and fixed Madame Fleurese with a suspicious eye. 'I'm glad you've been so well informed *Madame*, though I hope you'll humour me and tell me exactly what my associate here has informed you of?'

'No need to worry, Gwilym,' Eleusia said breezily. 'I've given nothing away, but we should retire somewhere a bit more secluded and hammer out the details of our scheme.'

'Aye, we should … the three of us, that is,' Gwilym rumbled. 'We need to sort out the relationship of the existing parts before we can think of bringing others into this.' He looked pointedly at Madame Fleurese, who instinctively picked up on his intonation.

'Yes, I'm sure the three of you have a lot to discuss,' Madame Fleurese beamed, apparently unconcerned with the seriousness with which he spoke. 'I have a lot of business to attend to before the night's work begins, so I can join your discussion later. If you'll follow me, I shall show you to the Silent Room.' With a graceful turn, her dress and underskirts billowing, Madame Fleurese headed towards a door leading off the courtyard.

The trio followed, Eleusia leading the way and Torben and Gwilym inspecting every nook and cranny of the courtyard as they walked—Gwilym because he was suspicious that they were being watched and Torben out of bemusement as he wondered what this place was.

On entering the building, Madame Fleurese led them through a large open room with a bar at one end; it was full of low-lying tables surrounded by large brightly coloured cushions. Above, a balcony ran around the room and was accessed by an elaborate wrought-iron spiral staircase painted black and covered in vivid red, decorative iron work resembling ivy, a copy of the sign hanging in the street. There were numerous, cell-like rooms branching from the first floor balcony.

Lounging against the banister, observing them, were several young women.

Torben did a double take when he first saw them, as they were clothed only in short silk dressing gowns that barely extended halfway down their thighs. They laughed when they observed Torben staring at them, mouth open, and his face flushed bright red.

Gwilym pushed Torben onwards after Eleusia and Madame Fleurese, who'd already exited via a door behind the bar. 'Keep walking, lad,' Gwilym said, barely concealing a chuckle. 'They'd be far too expensive for you right now.'

'Bloody hell,' Torben said, looking over his shoulder as he was marched onwards. 'What *is* this place?'

'What? Have you never heard of a broth …' He paused and shrugged. 'Well, I guess you probably haven't. Never you mind about them; you'll learn all about things of that nature when you're older!'

Torben ignored Gwilym's jibe. He was too transfixed by the young women hanging over the banister. As he disappeared through the door, there was a renewed bout of giggling from above, as the ladies of Ivy House waved him off.

Torben and Gwilym ambled through a kitchen, where several large pots bubbled away and two hogs turned on spits, and a small army of cooks beavered away, well on the way to having the evening meals for patrons prepared. Madame Fleurese stood by a narrow door on the other side of the kitchen, through which Eleusia had already passed. She held a ring with two large heavy keys on it, one of which had clearly been used to unlock the door. She snapped her fingers as Torben and Gwilym walked by, and two servants appeared, holding large platters of food and clay jugs of water and wine.

On the other side of the door was a narrow corridor that led to another door, significantly stronger looking than the last. The thick oak was strengthened with thick bands of black iron, and

Madame Fleurese had to use both hands to turn the massive key in the lock.

They all stepped into the room beyond, the servants silently following behind. It was relatively bare, with a single, large wooden table surrounded by six chairs and a small bureau at the far end of the room with various writing materials stacked inside.

'Put the food down there. Then you may go,' Madame Fleurese announced, addressing the servants in a business-like manner. 'Now,' she nodded and gestured as the servants left the room, 'this is our Silent Room, where our most important clients conduct business of a more, errm, private nature. I've ensured that you have the room for the whole night, and I can assure you that you won't be disturbed.

'I shall return in a few hours when you've had time to discuss things but, if you need anything in the meantime, ring the bell and someone will attend to your needs.' She pointed at a thick gold cord that hung next to the door and laid the keys on the table.

When she turned to leave, Eleusia took the keys and followed her out, whispering to her as they walked. There was a sharp click as Eleusia locked the outer door, and then returned to the Silent Room and locked the other door.

Gwilym had shed his pack and jacket, and was piling a plate with food. Torben joined him, and for several minutes all that could be heard was Torben and Gwilym breaking their two-day prison fast. Eleusia didn't eat, but sat on a chair opposite, her feet on the table and, despite the relatively early hour of the day, she poured herself a glass of wine.

'Shall we get down to business?' Gwilym asked through a hefty belch, having cleared half his plate. 'I'm intrigued to know, Eleusia, what ransom you'll demand from us in exchange for your help.'

'I hardly think that rescuing you from Björn can be classed as me holding you to ransom,' she retorted.

'Gwilym does have a point,' Torben stated. 'You must have sussed this out as an opportunity you stand to gain from ... well enough to defy your old master. From what little I've heard and seen of Björn, you'd have to have a damn good reason to cross him.'

'Well said, Torben,' Gwilym mumbled through a mouth full of bread, spraying crumbs across the table. 'How do we know that you're not about to double-cross us once you get more information? And, for that matter, how can we trust someone who's already dragging in more people without consulting us? How do we know that Madame Fleurese isn't assembling a gang of thugs right now to drub our heads in?'

Eleusia sighed and, removing her feet from the table, leaned towards the two seated on the other side. 'If it's proof you need that I'm not going to turn you back over to Björn once you've spilled the beans regarding this scheme of yours, then here.' Setting her glass on the table with a sharp clunk, she removed the scarf around her neck to reveal an angry red mark running around her throat; it was veined with deep purple bruises that stood out starkly against the brown of her skin.

'After Gord took you up to the tower cell, I went back to convince Björn to pay me my full share for capturing you. I reckoned if we discussed it when you weren't in his sight, he'd be more reasonable.' Eleusia's voice caught as she spoke. 'I was wrong. He near choked me to death. Had Gord not come in to tell him he was needed downstairs, I'm sure he'd have killed me.

'He never used to be like that; he used to be reasonable and fair, and take into account every point, good and bad, when we reported on our missions. Now ... I don't think I know him anymore. You know what I'm talking about Gwilym? Björn would never have turned on one of his own, except when he had concrete proof that they'd wronged him. But then, he wants you tortured, dead, with nothing to go against your word but his twisted thoughts.

'Last week, the others told me he killed two of his sworn

hands because one had dirty boots and the other said something that he didn't like, not even aimed at him. There was no warning; he just cut them down where they stood. Madness Gwilym, that's what it is. He's finally lost his reason, and I need out of there. I can't continue to do his bidding when I'm looking over my shoulder all of the time, wondering when he's going to turn on me! I need to get far away from here … to escape him, same as you … and we both need the same thing to be able to do that.'

Eleusia drained the last of the wine and poured herself another with a shaky hand, droplets of crimson speckling the table.

Gwilym stared hard at Eleusia, his eyes flitting up and down, left and right, reading her face to determine whether what she was saying was true. 'Well,' he said after a long while. 'Here we are, two fugitives from a madman. and an outcast without a home. Three people I'd say are more than worthy of a hearty slice of the good life. It'll be hard work to pull off the haul, and I warrant that we'll only get one chance at the prize. Who knows what will happen once we open the vault, but to chance our arm slipping into the castle under the nose of the Imperial Guard twice in the same decade would be a fool's errand.

'I propose that once we secure the Keystone, we hit the vault hard and fast, take as much as we can carry, and split it three ways. Once we have the gold, sticking together would be foolhardy. We'll get away scot-free more likely if we part ways. If, when we're in the vault, we decide that we could make another attempt at a later date, we can reconvene at an agreed time and try again. But let's not get ahead of ourselves now. Can we agree on a fair third share each?'

'What of the Madame?' Torben asked, curious.

'What of her? Eleusia brought her into all this; therefore, I reckon that she should take a cut from Eleusia's stake.'

'Use your head, Gwilym,' Eleusia admonished in exasperation. 'You've outlined everything very neatly, but you haven't considered logistics. The three of us would probably do fine on our own securing the Keystone, provided that Meckel is still hiding alone in the wilderness, but there's no way that we could walk straight up to the castle gates, swan in, and open the vault.

'We'll need a base in the city where we can target operations from, and Ivy House is the best place for that. The City Guard, and many of the Imperials frequent this place regularly, which would keep Björn and his men away for sure, not to mention making this ripe harvesting ground for information about the castle. And then there's the fact that Madame Fleurese is renowned as being the most well connected woman in the whole of Karpella. She'll be able to source any information we need about the castle and the legend of Sarper IV's treasure vault. Without that information she can secure for us, we'd sit outside the gates for years, looking for an in.'

'What makes you so sure she can be trusted?' Torben asked, his brow furrowed. 'And what makes you think that she would even hear us out? The scheme sounds mad to me, and I'm in it!'

'It may sound mad, but she's a brothel keeper; she'd do anything for good hard cash, especially when she doesn't have to stick her own neck out to get it. And she's helped us so far. Unlike the other two people in this room, she hasn't double-crossed you, or bound and gagged you. You've got a much better reason to trust her than either of us!'

Gwilym shuffled uncomfortably as she spoke. He'd much rather that the memory of his deceit not be brought back into the forefront of Torben's mind. 'She speaks the truth, Torben, I hate to admit it, but she does. In that case I suggest that whatever prize we bring back from the vault is split four ways, one for the each of us, and one to pay Madame Fleurese for her services, hospitality … and reimburse her for any expenses incurred.'

'Agreed,' Eleusia nodded.

'Aye, agreed,' Torben said.

'The only thing that I'd add,' Gwilym said, 'is that, for

security's sake, we keep Madame Fleurese in the dark about where we're going as much as possible. All she needs to know is that we're going to get the Keystone and, once we return, we hit the vault.'

Eleusia nodded again, as did Torben though his brow furrowed again as a question came to mind. 'Where are we going then?'

Eleusia chimed in, 'Yes, you need to tell us where we're going!'

'Right you are, right you are. Meckel's hoard was buried outside the town that he grew up in, near to his family, so that it could easily be taken to them in the event of his death. We need to head to *that* town.' Gwilym picked up a goblet and took a long swallow of wine, enjoying the fact he was holding Torben and Eleusia on tenterhooks.

'So where do we need to go?' Eleusia's voice was deep and threatening. She had no patience for the dwarf's games.

'Gallenford.' He drained the goblet in a single deep draught and then began to filled another.

9

Most of that night was spent arguing over plans to escape Karpella unharmed and undetected. As soon as an idea was about to be agreed upon, either Gwilym or Eleusia would think of something that might easily go horrifically wrong. The table in the Silent Room steadily started collecting piles of parchment listing all manner of ideas and showing crude map sketches.

Madame Fleurese didn't return that night; the few times a servant was admitted into the room to bring fresh supplies of food and drink, they heard the roar of Ivy House's patrons in the bar two rooms away. Clearly, the place was doing well that night and Madame Fleurese needed to keep an eye on the proceedings and make sure her girls weathered another night of custom unharmed.

Eventually, after hours of deliberating, a plan was almost about agreed upon by the three. The decision was made as dawn was breaking across the roofs of Karpella—not that they could see this from the windowless seclusion of the Silent Room. Torben was dog-tired, but there was no time to sleep. They needed to move quickly, before the morning was fully underway, to maximise the chances of successful escape without Björn's men detecting them.

When the bell within the Silent Room finally rang to signal Madame Fleurese's return, Torben's head was slumped on the table as he caught a few precious minutes of sleep. Eleusia was carefully burning pieces of paper in a brazier, making sure not one scrap of notes escaped the flames. Gwilym leaned back in a chair against a wall, meditatively sharpening his seax with a hone stone. With each scrape of the stone, a shower of sparks illuminated his face and flashed in the emerald pools of his eyes.

Despite having been on her feet all night, Madame Fleurese seemed incredibly chipper when she was admitted to the room by Eleusia, and laid down a large tray supporting breakfast. 'Well now, it seems that you've had quite the night of deliberation.' The singsong voice was far too loud for the time of day. 'I hope you haven't sat here all night in vain?'

'No', Gwilym replied, 'I think that we've made up our minds … and we have a proposition for you.' He stood, laid the hone stone and his seax on the chair, and picked up the only remaining piece of paper that rested on the table. He walked over to Madame Fleurese, nudging Torben awake as he did so, and presented the article.

'As has been agreed by the three personages present on the night of the third day of the second month in the twenty-third year of the reign of Hastel, Emperor of the joint Kingdom of Dazscor and Aramore,' Madame Fleurese read, her voice losing its jolly tone and becoming serious. 'The three shall each receive a third portion of the treasure at the time that it has been secured by the party, providing that none have reneged on the agreement. In return for services rendered to aid the three—providing information, hospitality, and any necessary equipment for the success of the scheme—they have each agreed to pay Madame Fleurese of the reputable and notable Ivy House a third of their individual share.'

Madame Fleurese continued to read the rest of the document

under her breath, skimming thick and clumsy passages that took up the rest of the paper. Gwilym had insisted that the agreement be written in as judicial a manner as possible, otherwise, 'we might as well be writing a shopping list.'

As she read over the document a second time, making sure all details were to her liking, Torben sat at the table and rubbed his weary eyes. He then, sheepishly, used a sleeve to wipe away the small pool of drool he'd left on the table.

'Well?' Gwilym asked.

'This seems in order,' Madame Fleurese chimed, the song back in her voice. 'Pass me that quill and I shall make my mark upon this very serious and esteemed document.' She winked at Torben as she knelt over the table and signed the bottom of the paper.

Gwilym scowled at the back of her head, clearly not approving of the careless jollity with which she'd referred to the agreement he'd slaved over.

'Now, I've taken the liberty of providing you with rations for the start of your journey. I presume you've decided how best to leave the city?'

Gwilym butted in before the others could. 'Yes, but we decided to keep that between the three of us, for security.'

'Gwilym's afraid that you'll blab.' Eleusia smirked and Madame Fleurese smirked in return.

'In that case, I shall leave you to make your final preparations. Your rations have been placed in the kitchen, and I shall wait in the courtyard to bid you farewell.' With that, she rolled up the parchment, turned and left the room, closing the outer door behind.

Gwilym hastily shut and locked the inner door, and turned back to Torben and Eleusia, tucking into the breakfast tray. 'Right, we should go through the plan one last time before we leave, just so we know that everyone is on the same page.'

Torben and Eleusia groaned loudly, but Gwilym shushed them. 'First off, once we leave Ivy House, we need to take a—'

'Right, down Goldsmith's Alley and across Spicer's Square,' Eleusia declared, not looking up from the cold ham that she was quickly gobbling.

'Yes.' Gwilym bristled, not caring to be interrupted. 'Then, once we get across Spicer's Square, we need to cross the bridge to the mainland and—'

'Head straight to Medallion Square and, upon arriving there, sign up to join the next caravan leaving the city,' Torben broke in.

'Well.' Gwilym harrumphed, taking a seat at the table and pulling breakfast towards him. 'I'm glad you're both taking this seriously.'

'Calm down. We know the plan and that's all that matters,' Torben said, taking a piece of chicken.

'Aye, well, I guess so,' Gwilym muttered darkly, biting into a thick slice of bacon.

After they'd eaten, the they left the Silent Room, locking both the doors behind and entering the vast kitchen. On a large workbench, next to the first of the Silent Room's doors, were two travelling packs and a bundle of rations meant for Gwilym, who still carried his battered, heavily patched pack. Eleusia didn't stop walking as she plucked the first of the packs from the table and slung it over her shoulders, deftly moving the crossbow to a suitably accessible position. Torben, on the other hand, stood by Gwilym, who reorganised the various odds and ends he always carried to make room for the food.

Passing through the main bar of Ivy House, the room was empty of patrons and staff. All doors on the floor above were closed and the only sign of the revels that had taken place the night before was the vast collection of glasses and crockery that littered the bar room tables.

When Torben and Gwilym entered the courtyard, Eleusia was in discussion with Madame Fleurese, standing by the entrance gate. Their conversation was too quiet to be overheard, but the indistinct whispering that echoed around the courtyard implied that the conversation was fairly intense. As Torben and

Gwilym drew level with the pair, Madame Fleurese and Eleusia embraced, and the older woman kissed Eleusia on the forehead.

'Keep safe, my dear. I shall look for your return.' Turning to Torben and Gwilym, she addressed them all. 'I shall wait eagerly for you all to return from wherever it is that you're going. Safe travels and happy hunting!'

Gwilym nodded thanks curtly as he walked through the gate, held open by Eleusia, and Torben clumsily kissed the hand that Madame Fleurese proffered as he exited. There was a soft clunk as Eleusia closed the gate and the three of them were alone on the empty street. The watery dawn light cast a pinky-grey wash over buildings, and the only noise heard was a light breeze playing in the eaves of the houses.

Wordlessly, the party set off at a jog, three sets of eyes scanning the streets and building windows to check for anyone that might be tracking their movements. Rose Street, where Ivy House was situated, was almost deserted, save for the occasional drunk staggering wearily home after a night of revelling.

Likewise, Goldsmith's Alley was deathly quiet as they turned off Rose Street. The position of the alley meant that the weak morning sun had yet to cast light into it; as such, it was as dark as midnight.

The trio picked up the pace as they strolled through the darkened lane. This was the part of the plan that worried Gwilym the most; Goldsmith's Alley had no other streets turning off it, and if anyone was waiting for them to leave Ivy House, this would have been the perfect place to ambush them. The lane could easily be cut off at both ends and, given that the ground floors of the Goldsmith's shops that lined it were heavily fortified and locked against intruders, they'd have been caught like fish in a barrel.

The end came into view soon enough and they popped onto Spicer's Square without incident. Unlike the alleyway, Spicer's Square was cast in a pleasing pink light that reflected off the sandstone buildings in a myriad of rosy hues. The square was also full of activity. Spicers started buying and selling well before dawn, as they were forever worried that a caravan would arrive during the night and their competitors would secure an easy profit from it at their expense.

The buildings surrounding the square were large, open-fronted shops with huge awnings that covered a multitude of barrels and boxes that spilled from the front of each shop. The open square centre was full of people buying and selling all manner of exotic spices and aromatics. The spicers moved from seller to seller, trying to buy goods for the best price, and all were accompanied by a large retinue of servants and guards forever glowering at competing parties, hands never too far away from swords. The City Guards were present in force to stop trading from becoming too vicious; there was a contingent that patrolled outside every spicer shop to prevent raiding from taking place between rivals.

The crush of people meant that Eleusia, Torben and Gwilym were reduced to a slow walk as they pushed their way through the crowd. With so many bodies surrounding them, it would have been impossible for anyone to track them for long. They walked in single file, with Gwilym first, Eleusia second, and Torben bringing up the rear—each holding the topmost straps of the other's pack to prevent them from being separated. The three travellers didn't look like they were there to deal in spices so, for the most part, they were ignored by merchants; occasionally, though, one would shove a bag of sweet or spicy smelling powder in their direction, only to be swatted by a disgruntled hand.

As they exited the trading floor of the square, a huge gatehouse loomed before them that barred the way across a bridge leading to Karpella's mainland section. The City Guard watched everyone that crossed the bridge, both ways, looking for anyone that might cause trouble. As well as the guards stationed at the gates at both ends of the bridge and those patrolling its length, there was a strong contingent of archers posted in the gatehouses.

As they approached the first gate, Eleusia drew her cloak about her and pulled the hood over her face, not only to conceal her appearance but also her weapons. As agreed in Ivy House, the three of them would split up, crossing the bridge as individuals so as not to attract too much attention. Although in theory it wasn't illegal for the public to carry weapons through Karpella's streets, to *openly* carry weapons without *good* reason was a surefire way of attracting unwanted attention from the City Guard.

Torben felt a nervous lump in his throat as he passed through the arch of the gatehouse, but a bored looking guard merely passed a casual eye over him as he walked by. Torben had deliberately loosened the straps of his pack so that the folds of his leather overcoat would flap more freely in the breeze and show he wasn't hiding anything within. None of the guards inspected him carefully enough for this to matter and he crossed the expanse of the bridge and through the other gatehouse with ease.

He spotted Gwilym standing underneath the sign of the Rose & Crown public house, the agreed meeting point. Neither of them spoke; they were too nervous to engage in idle chitchat. The two cast around, looking for Eleusia, and saw her emerge from a large group of boisterous young men heading for the public house behind them. With the group reunited, they set off down the wide thoroughfare that led down to Medallion Square.

Unlike the districts on the middle and castle islands of Karpella, the mainland portion of the city was much younger and, as a result, the streets hadn't been largely segregated into specific trades. There were all manner of grocers, potters, haberdashers, butchers, and curiosity shops lining the street and people crisscrossed the road between their favourite stalls, which added to the confusion. Unlike the exotic heady fragrances that had filled Spicer's Square, the air in this part of Karpella was much more rancid, and Torben gagged as they passed a particularly large fishmongers, whose wares were starting to sweat and stink in the steadily strengthening morning sunlight.

The street ahead abruptly ended and opened onto a huge oval piazza surrounded by immense buildings looming over the open space and dwarfing rows of tenements behind them. On entering Medallion Square, they turned sharply and ducked into a small alley. Eleusia pulled back her hood and peered into the huge square. Over her shoulder, she said, 'If I'm not back within the hour, then get out of the city without me ... if I can, I'll find you on the road.'

'Luck go with you,' Torben said softly.

She pulled the hood back over her head and disappeared into the crowd.

The centre of Medallion Square was dominated by a huge fountain crowned with a statue of a kingly character on horseback. The head of the statue was made of bright white, clean marble, which contrasted greatly with the more weathered, greyish body and horse of the rest of the statue. The head was also ill-fitting and completely alien to the body it was attached to. It seemed slightly too large, almost resembling a pumpkin head of a scarecrow in proportions, and the bloated face was at odds with the muscular athletic body.

'They change the head every time a new Emperor is crowned.' Gwilym had guessed what Torben was looking at. 'It used to be a statue of Sarper the IV, but when the Duke of Aramore seized the throne, he replaced the head with his own. Since then, every new Emperor and Empress has replaced the head with their own. Some priorities, eh? I heard that Hastel paid 1000 gold pieces for that ugly mug—a damn sight more than he's spent on any other public service. But his royal highness has to keep up appearances now, doesn't he?'

Gwilym continued to prattle as Torben continued to stare at Medallion Square. All buildings had large swinging signs, like that of a shop sign hanging above the entrance, bearing different coats of arms. Flags bearing matching sigils hung from windows and fluttered from roofs.

'What are all of these buildings for?' Torben asked, bemused.

'Ah, those are the headquarters of the Merchant Guild Houses. Each one of those sigils represents a different Guild House and each house has a presence in all of the big settlements from here to the ends of the earth, or so they claim. Hell, I've heard stories of them being so powerful in certain cities, they've brought down governments that weren't lenient enough towards them. That clumsy git on his stone horse over there is probably the only semblance of Imperial authority over them.'

'How on earth is Eleusia going to visit each of those houses in an hour? There must be fifty, at least. By the time she's learnt which caravan is leaving next, it'll already be gone,' Torben said in disbelief.

Taking Torben's arm, Gwilym leaned the way into the street and pointed to the base of the fountain, around which were an array of brightly coloured tents, each adorned with one of the Guild Houses' sigils. 'See them? Each tent is the sole point of contact that anyone in Karpella will have with the Guild Houses. You can only gain access to one of the headquarters if you're a Guild House member, or have specific permission—countersigned at least four times—from senior Guild members. So Eleusia, thankfully, doesn't have to break into each Guild House to gain the information we need. What's more, they tend to be pretty vocal when they require extra muscle. It pays the Guild Houses to take on as much protection for their caravans as they can. Otherwise, all kinds of people might try and raid them … the other Guild Houses included.'

Indeed, as Torben watched, all manner of people were entering and exiting the tents, some clearly on official business and others, judging by more rugged and well-armed appearances, mercenaries looking for their next job.

'Let's go you two. I've found us an employer.'

The sound of Eleusia's voice behind them made both of them

jump in surprise. They whipped around to find her leaning casually against the alley wall.

'Where the hell did you come from?' Torben gasped.

'I thought it best that I wasn't seen coming and going into the same alley. I'd not be surprised if Björn has men watching this place. Come, follow me.' She turned and walked down the alley, away from Medallion Square, and took a right down another side street.

'Get used to that,' Gwilym muttered under his breath to Torben. 'She always does that. I think it's a game to her to see how many times she can creep up on whoever she's working with. Some sort of power-play mind game if you ask me.'

Following Eleusia, Torben and Gwilym were led down a succession of alleyways that snaked around the back of the Guild Houses, until they popped into Medallion Square opposite a large tent with fabric made from alternating strips of bright blue and muted yellow. Outside the tent fluttered a pair of banners sporting a golden griffin against a blue backdrop, rearing on its hind legs and clutching a pair of scales in its outstretched claw. After scanning the crowds, the three of them crossed the square and ducked under the open tent flap.

An old man looked up from a writing desk as they entered and Torben could feel the eyes of two guards, who were flanking the entrance on the inside of the tent, inspecting his back as they stood before the desk.

'Ah, so you did come back then,' the man said to Eleusia with a quick smile. 'And these must be the two companions of whom you spoke. Sign your first initial here.' He pushed forward a long, partially rolled piece of parchment.

Taking an elaborate quill Eleusia, followed by Gwilym and Torben, scrawled an illegible initial on the bottom.

'Excellent.' The man's voice was incredibly bland. 'Now, all of you show me your right forearms.'

Confused, Torben regarded Eleusia and Gwilym as they rolled up the sleeves on their right arms and presented their forearms before the man's nose for inspection. Torben followed suit, though he had no idea what was going on. The man peered briefly at each and then scribbled a note underneath their initials. 'Now, how armed are you all?'

Eleusia opened her cloak to reveal the longsword, dagger and crossbow, and the old man nodded in approval. He seemed satisfied by Gwilym's seax and the sling that he produced from his travelling cloak, but sighed deeply as he cast his eyes on Torben and saw only the small knife hanging from his belt. He rummaged for a scrap of paper, wrote a small list upon it, signed the bottom and, after rolling it up, sealed it with wax. 'Take this to the quartermaster at the muster station and he'll provide you with arms, which will be deducted from your salary, understand?' the old man asked casually, handing paper to Torben.

'Yes … *sir*.' Torben felt the old man's position necessitated some form of label.

'Good. Now step over to the brazier and, once you've been stamped, you should report to the Guard Master at the muster station immediately, and he'll give you further instructions.'

Before he knew what was going on, Torben, who stood the closest to the lit brazier in the corner, had his left arm seized by a tent guard, who then plucked a red-hot brand from the flames and pressed it against his forearm. A horrible sizzling sound and stench filled the air as the brand seared Torben's forearm; he yelped in pain.

After a few seconds of agony, the guard removed the brand, pushing Torben to one side and branding Gwilym and Eleusia in the same manner.

Once the brand was lifted from Eleusia's arm, the trio were escorted from the tent by the guards. The tent flap was drawn, shielding the Guild House's bureaucracy from the outside world.

Torben headed straight for the fountain and plunged his arm

into the cool water. 'You could have warned me that they'd do that!'

'Yes, well, we thought it might put you off,' Eleusia said nonchalantly, using a hand to cup water over her own brand.

'Aye, you know, let it be over and done with quickly, so that you didn't dwell on it before it happened,' Gwilym added with an amiable smile.

Torben grumbled to himself as they headed towards the city gates. The main gate to Karpella wasn't far from Medallion Square, and the principal road through this section of the city directly linked the two, which meant they made quick headway.

The walls cast heavy shadows over nearby buildings and the gatehouse completely overshadowed the entire square laying before it. Two huge towers protected the gate and the walkway above, and towered above as they approached. The inside arch of the gate was so dark that it was lit by torches. The City Guard seemed to be everywhere, but they were allowed to pass without issue as the guards were more concerned with watching those entering rather than leaving.

Beyond the city walls was a wide road paved with huge stone slabs; it stretched from the gate into the distance, where it vanished into a vista of plentiful fields and rolling hills. Surrounding the road for over a mile on all sides were tents of all shapes and sizes and colours, and huge makeshift corrals that housed innumerable beasts of burden. Amongst the tents, here and there, were massive banners matching those of the various Guild Houses, indicating where the muster station for each caravan was.

'That's the one we want.' Eleusia pointed into the distance. 'The golden Griffin and scales of Guild House Fisel.'

Guild House Fisel's mustering station was abuzz with movement as people bustled around, moving boxes of goods and supplies, loading wagons, and calming horses and oxen that sensed the tension of their imminent departure. High above, the Guild House's flag wafted in the breeze. A makeshift but solid fence surrounded the muster station, and Torben, Eleusia and Gwilym were stopped before entering by armed guards keeping careful watch.

'Brands,' one guard demanded brusquely.

The three drew back sleeves to reveal their brands. They were a horrible, angry red colour, and Torben's had yet to stop throbbing, but the coat of arms of Guild House Fisel was distinctly burned into his arm.

'Fresh blood,' the guard said curtly. 'You'll need to see the Guard Master over there; he'll sort you out.' Stepping to one side, he waved an arm towards a tent not too far away and let them pass.

A small line of people snaked from the Guard Master's tent, which the three of them joined while waiting for admittance. When they finally reached the Guard Master's desk, he examined their fresh brands, muttered something in approval, and they were ushered to another desk at the side where a clerk made them re-initial several pieces of paper before dismissing them.

'Well, here we are.' Gwilym breathed a sigh of relief. 'I don't think I've ever felt happier to be a corporate lackey in my life!'

'Careful what you say. We haven't left yet.' Eleusia scanned the people working around them for anything suspicious.

'True, but even Björn would think twice before infringing on the territory of one of the Guild Houses, not to mention damaging its property.' He waved his brand before her face.

'Why, exactly, were the brands necessary?' Torben winced as he dabbed his with a wetted scrap of cloth.

'To show other Guild Houses where your allegiance lies,' Gwilym responded. 'You can only serve a single Guild House in your life, in theory that is, and as you may have read in that infernal paper-pushing tent, you're authorised to kill on sight anyone bearing the brand of another Guild House if they're on Guild House Fisel property without good reason. Speaking of which, we should get you something more useful than that whittling knife of yours.'

'Looks like the Quartermaster's tent is there,' Eleusia said, shielding her eyes from the bright midday sun.

Her guess proved correct as they approached the tent and saw racks of weapons and boxes of supplies. A man annotated on a wax tablet as he inspected the stores. 'What do you three want?' the Quartermaster demanded, not looking up from his work.

Torben sheepishly stepped forward and handed over the small scroll.

He inspected the seal, demanded to see Torben's brand, and then opened the scroll to read the list inside. 'Right then.' He moved to one of the weapon racks. 'Standard-issue shield, times one, standard-issue short-sword, times one, and spear standard-issue times one.' He laid the weapons on an empty table and quickly scribbled in a large ledger. 'Sign here.'

Torben approached the ledger and clumsily signed his name where the man's finger pointed. He could hear the Quartermaster take a sharp breath as Torben's poorly executed signature strayed beyond the carefully drawn lines that separated ledger entries.

'Have you three been assigned a duty yet?'

Eleusia, Gwilym and Torben shook their heads.

'In that case, go to the mess area and you shall be assigned duties shortly.'

The curt tone indicated that they should leave and they made their way towards a fairly large open area dotted with campfires and the odd, empty table. They sat on the ground, apart from the few other people who were loitering as they too waited for orders, and Torben began to look over the new arms.

Gwilym picked up the short-sword that Torben placed on the ground as he attached the sheath to his belt, and tutted as he inspected the blade. 'What do they expect you to do with this? You'd be hard-pressed to slay a loaf of bread with it.'

Rooting around in his pack, he took out his hone stone and started to work on the blade, and soon the metal started to hum and sing in his hands as he skillfully manipulated it this way and that to create a razor-sharp edge.

Eleusia continued surveying movements around her and, after a while, pointed discretely at a man crossing the mess area. He was clearly someone of importance, as his clothes were incredibly well tailored and made of fine, shiny velvet.

'There's the man in charge of this outfit, I bet', she said under her breath, 'and I'd warrant that he's the one who keeps the maps of the caravan's routes.'

'Be careful, Eleusia.' Gwilym didn't look up from his work as he whispered. 'Everyone may look busy around here, but there's still too many eyes that could be watching … and ears no doubt listening.'

Before Eleusia could reply, the sun was blotted out as a huge, hulking shadow loomed over them. 'The Quartermaster said the three of you are to come with me on patrol.'

The shadow's voice was deep and Torben was sure that he could feel it reverberating through his body. Indeed, the sound of the voice was punctuated by a succession of snorts disrupting the flow of speech. The voice wasn't the only thing strange about the shadow.

As they climbed to their feet and stepped into the sun, they could discern its features. The creature's body was that of an incredibly tall, muscled man; he had tanned, albeit extremely hairy skin, and the head was that of a bull with two long horns protruding from the sides of the forehead and curving widely over the crown of the head. Several gold rings were pierced through its horns and a much larger one pierced its nose at the septum. The fur was a dirty ginger-blonde hue and the shaggy mane hanging from its chin was tamed into a single crude plait, which swayed beneath its chin. Numerous tattoos swirled across most of its bare arms. The fur extended down the minotaur's neck and disappeared beneath a thick chainmail shirt.

'I am Antauros,' the minotaur said, fixing each in turn with beady black eyes. 'If you don't cause trouble for me, then you'll give me no reason to trouble *you*, understand?' The beast wheeled about and trudged in the direction of the perimeter fence.

Torben slung his pack on his shoulders, picked up his spear and shield, and took a step forwards, only to be stopped by Gwilym who was staring dumbly after the minotaur.

'Are you mad?' he whispered.

'What? I'm following orders. I thought that would be a good thing to blend in round here.'

Torben's voice was full of sarcasm.

Gwilym and Eleusia remained rooted to the spot, not moving a muscle; they were regarding the minotaur with what could only be described as outright fear. True enough, Torben had been unnerved by the beast's appearance, but only because he'd never seen an individual like Antauros before. The inhabitants of Bywater had all been human, but ever since Gwilym's arrival in that sleepy village had thrust him beyond the village's borders, he'd come to realize that the world was filled with all manner of diverse dwellers and denizens.

'They must be out of their minds if they expect us to follow that brute,' Eleusia hissed.

'What's your problem?' Torben asked, not lowering his voice enough for the others, who sharply shushed him.

'Torben,' Gwilym muttered with a roll of the eyes, 'that creature there is widely renowned as one of the most ferocious folk to walk this earth. If he's the Antauros of infamy, and I reckon that there are few minotaurs that bear that name as it is, then amongst other eminent deeds, he was responsible for the massacre of hundreds in the name of duty.'

'In the last war between Aramore and Rahhail, he slaughtered an entire village—men, woman and children— single handily, with no motive other than pure malice, so the story goes,' Eleusia added grimly.

'I guess he's not someone that we should get on the wrong side of then,' Torben said quietly, nodding at Antauros, who'd turned around to see why they weren't following.

Before he could react, Gwilym, Torben and Eleusia jogged over to him. Antauros flared his wide nostrils menacingly and continued walking. 'The caravan is due to leave at sundown and, until then, the Guild House wants a keen watch put on the perimeter at all times to make sure none of the other houses infiltrates the caravan, or establishes where we're going.' Antauros spoke as one used to giving orders.

In front of the perimeter was ten feet of empty space that formed a buffer zone between the tents and fence erected against the outside world. Antauros pointed to the left, following the line of the fence with his hand. 'We need another two patrols to ensure there's no gap between watches for people to sneak into the muster station. The two of you,' Antauros said to Gwilym and Eleusia, 'head that way. I'll take the boy and go the opposite way. When we meet on the other side of the station, I'll want a report from you two.'

'Yes, sir! We'll get right to it,' Gwilym's response rang out cheerily. Clearly, he was glad that he didn't have to patrol with Antauros. 'You heard the fellow, Eleusia, so let's be off!'

He and Eleusia set off along the perimeter fence, away from Torben and Antauros, at a much quicker walking pace than needed. Torben could seem them looking back over their shoulders and regarding him with concern as they whispered.

Antauros didn't pay attention to the two of them as they left, but went over to the perimeter fence and picked up a long canvas bag, which he hung across his back by a strap, a heavy war-hammer that he slotted into a belt loop by his side, and a large round shield. He eyed Torben carefully and then grunted, and began to walk around the perimeter in the opposite direction. Torben glanced at the disappearing figures of Gwilym and Eleusia and followed the minotaur.

The two of them walked in silence as they looked around for

anything suspicious. Torben had slung his shield on his back and held his spear casually as he walked, the point bobbing in rhythm with his body's movements.

'You haven't used a spear that much before, have you?' The beady black eyes of Antauros watched Torben as he walked.

'Can't rightly say I have,' Torben responded lightly. 'More of a ploughshare rather than a sword man in terms of practical experience.'

'Humph. I thought as much. The thing doesn't even look sharp.'

'Don't blame me for that; blame the armoury of Guild House Fisel.'

Antauros laughed. 'You're right there. The Guild House governors aren't fighting men and women; they're used to hiring mercenaries to protect their goods and goad their competition … mercenaries who bring their own gear that can actually do some damage.'

'Like you?' Torben bit his lip as he spoke. He didn't know whether his question, asked in all innocence, was too blunt given Antauros' background.

'Yes,' Antauros acknowledged after a pause. 'Like me, I suppose.' The minotaur pondered before speaking again. 'I heard your friends talking about me earlier, about my eminent deeds, so I'm sure, you've already heard about the cloth that most people think I'm cut from.'

'I've heard one version of a story, and I wouldn't say that the tale was enough to condemn a man on sight. Sounded more like superstition to me, as opposed to fact. I was always told that a person's deeds take on a will of their own after they've been carried out, and can grow or contract at their whim. Doesn't matter what the one who created the deed did in the first instance; it's how others nurture or neglect them that makes them what they are.'

'That's a very diplomatic stance. You'd be hard pressed to find many who'd adopt it.'

'*Did* you do the things that people talk about?'

'Depends. People say I've done many things, most of them unspeakable and farfetched.'

'I think you know which one. You said yourself that you overheard what Gwilym was telling me earlier.'

He shrugged. 'In a manner of speaking, it's true, but then again there are many parts of how people relate that tale which *aren't* true.'

Silence again. Clearly, the minotaur didn't want to delve deeper into the accusations that Gwilym and Eleusia had levelled against him. Torben could feel the minotaur's eyes still on him, and it seemed that Antauros was puzzled by the way that he was acting in his presence.

In truth, Antauros was extremely puzzled by the young man that walked at his side. He was used to people being afraid of him, or shunning him, but Torben spoke to him as if they were sharing a meal over a tavern table. The boy seemed naive and in this world one definitely couldn't afford to be so.

'If you've never used a spear before, why sign up for something that could get you killed? In my experience, only stupid or ignorant people put themselves in harm's way without good reason.'

'Necessity, I guess.' Torben skated over all but the most basic details regarding his newfound service to Guild House Fisel.

'*Necessity*? I'm sure if you'd looked harder, you'd have found another profession that didn't lead you so far from your home.'

'I don't have a home, not anymore. It was taken from me because none of us knew how to defend ourselves.'

Antauros pondered for a moment, and then muttered an apology. 'I didn't mean to cause offence.'

'That's quite alright. You had nothing to do with it.'

'You want to keep your spear up,' Antauros said quickly, changing the subject.

'What?'

'Your spear,' Antauros repeated. 'Keep the point up at all

times, unless you're actually using it to defend yourself; otherwise, you might accidentally impale somebody.'

'Oh, right.' The apology had caught Torben by surprise. He'd not have suspected a reputedly bloodthirsty killer to be so quick to avoid offending someone.

Antauros didn't give Torben a chance to continue his questioning. He picked up his pace, leaving a small gap between himself and the young man.

Torben lifted up his spear and set it against his shoulder, the point bouncing up and down alongside his head, and decreased his pace to give Antauros the space he wanted.

The minotaur was an incredibly curious creature. On the face of it, and from Gwilym and Eleusia's brief descriptions of his character, Torben had expected to be scared out of his wits by a blood-thirsty monster; instead, the person that walked before him seemed almost bashful, prickly in his conversation, but bashful nonetheless.

The rest of the patrol passed in silence, Antauros deliberately keeping communication to a minimum, only breaking silence to issue an occasional order. Night had begun to creep into the muster station, but rather than settling down, the camp grew busier and busier as the hour of departure neared.

When the figures of Gwilym and Eleusia finally came into sight, the sun sat low on the horizon, and it was hard to see in the fading evening light.

'Anything to report?' Antauros asked as he drew level with the pair.

'That patrol was as quiet as a graveyard,' Gwilym answered.

'Good. Now follow me. It's about time that the Superintendent gave his final orders before we depart.'

Antauros tramped between tents and the three followed, picking their way through the maze of ropes and tent pegs. Deliberately lagging behind the minotaur, Gwilym and Eleusia looked Torben up and down as if they expected him to be hurt.

'Well, you managed to escape unscathed then,' Gwilym declared.

'Aye. You know, I don't think that he's the fellow you think he is.'

'You may think that now,' Eleusia muttered, 'but you wait. Once the bloodlust settles over his eyes, nothing will get in between him and the thrill of the kill.'

The centre of the muster station was full of armoured men and women, waiting for instructions from the apparently absent Superintendent. The crowd parted for Antauros, who took up position in the centre, the better to see and hear what was going on.

Before the gaudy spectacle, that was the Superintendent's tent was a small group of men talking quietly. Torben, who was craning his neck over the mass of people to see what was going on, recognised one of the figures as that of the Quartermaster. Evidently, something was wrong and the mercenaries massed before the tent sensed this.

A decision had obviously been made, for the Superintendent beckoned two bodyguards, who moved forward with him towards the crowd. From behind the protection of their shields, the Superintendent addressed the crowd, but his words were carried away by the breeze; no one beyond the first few rows heard his speech.

'What did he say?'

'Speak up!'

'Did anyone catch that?'

The Superintendent addressed them again, but many were too busy discussing what he'd said; he was completely inaudible. Realising the futility of his efforts, he retreated into his tent, the small group of confidants following.

The news drifted back slowly from the front ranks and many sullenly returned to their tents; the caravan wouldn't leave that night.

'Typical,' Antauros snorted before tramping off.

'Why is everyone so upset?' Torben asked, looking around at discontented people.

'We only get paid when we're on the move,' said Eleusia, 'so another day in camp means one more day with no coin in their pockets.'

'It also means that anyone with half a brain will be able to get into the station tonight,' Gwilym added and gestured. 'Look at them. None of them will be doing duty tonight. They barely did it when they thought they were getting paid. If Björn and his lot have managed to track us this far, he could ride in here on a bloody elephant and no one would stop him! Come on, we'd best find a place to rest for the night, out of sight.'

He led the way through the crowd, trying to find a covered spot to best shield themselves from eyes that might be seeking them.

Around them, the muster station buzzed with angry caravan guards, who grumbled and shot dirty looks towards the Superintendent's tent, wishing unspeakable horrors on the man who was delaying their journey and next pay packet.

10

The dawn sun rose sluggishly over the turrets of Karpella Castle and above the roofs and towers of the city, and crept over the sea of tents that touched city walls. Slowly but surely, the rays of morning light began to pick their way deep into the muster station of Guild House Fisel and caressed the faces of sleeping guards and merchants, bringing them groggily out of the clutches of sleep. From their resting place, hidden amongst parked wagons, Gwilym, Eleusia and Torben began to stir from their slumber.

Although there was ample space in the mess area for the three to sleep with other mercenaries around one of the multitude of campfires, Gwilym had decided that they'd be safer sleeping away from the mass of unknown and discontented people who were supposed to be guarding the caravan and its cargo.

The idea seemed a lot less appealing in hindsight as Torben sat up and tried to stretch kinks out of his neck. He'd slept with his head pressed against a wagon wheel, and he gingerly tilted his head from side to side, trying to regain full mobility.

Despite the fact that the sun had already warmed the day to a comfortable temperature, the three of them were shivering in the shade of the wagons, the early morning dew clinging to their hair and blankets, chilling them to the bone.

Gwilym was the first to show true signs of life. He sat up abruptly and let out an enormous, loud yawn. 'Ah! Nothing like the smell of fresh morning dew on the grass to get a dwarf's heart singing. Come on you two, we're wasting the best part of the day!'

The dwarf's jocularity didn't sit well with Eleusia, who glowered from folds of her cloak and lashed out with a foot as he leant over to check she was awake. Wordlessly, Eleusia stood and shook the moisture from her cloak, and then stepped from their hiding place in search of food, pulling the hood so it shielded her eyes from the intrusive sunlight.

Gwilym stretched expansively and hauled himself onto one of the wagon wheels to survey the morning's activity. Apparently satisfied with what he saw, he dropped down. 'As I thought. Not a single guard on duty the whole night. I reckon they'll struggle to get anyone on patrol for a good few hours yet. Nothing kills morale like cutting wages.'

'Aye, you'd have thought Eleusia had woken up bankrupt, the way she was stomping around,' Torben said, getting to his feet and stretching his back over a wagon.

'She's always been a moody one.'

'Do you reckon we'll move today?' Torben asked.

'We'd better hope so; from what I heard last night, this is the third day in a row that the caravan's been delayed, so no wonder there's so much discontent amongst our fellow guards. I heard some leave during the night, whispering about work going in the Kingdom of Kjörnsholm's northern outposts for anyone foolhardy enough to take it. Nothing but barren steppe for miles and miles; you couldn't get me there for all the gold in the castle vault!'

'There must be something really drastic going on if we're three days behind schedule already.'

'Not necessarily. The Guild Houses are always incredibly

jumpy when it comes to moving caravans around. After all, the goods we'll be protecting must be worth thousands of gold pieces ... tens of thousands. If they get even the slightest whiff of something not being quite right, it takes them forever to work up the courage to move out. If the Superintendent moves the caravan off at the wrong time and loses the Guild House's money and goods, he'll pay for it with his life, and he knows it. Like as not, they've probably heard tell of a rival Guild House using a similar route to us, and want to avoid running into them.'

A soft thud behind them announced the arrival of Eleusia, who'd vaulted over a wagon and crouched on the ground, trying get her breath back. Her face was bright red, and there was a noticeable absence of food about her person.

'What in the blazes is wrong with you?' Gwilym appeared stunned by her sudden appearance.

'Ssshh!' She held up a hand, emphasising the need for quiet, and listened intently. After a minute, she relaxed and released a sigh of relief.

The tense atmosphere that Eleusia's arrival had generated meant that Torben, like Eleusia, had crouched on the ground so that he was no longer visible above the wagons. Gwilym's short stature, however, meant that he could stand upright in the hiding place without risk of exposure. He looked at Eleusia over the bridge of his squat nose and drummed his fingers against his crossed arms expectantly. 'Well? What's the situation?'

'They're here. Björn's henchmen must have slipped into the camp during the night. I saw two sniffing around the mess area, asking questions.'

'Surely if we lie low, they'll continue to the next muster station?' Torben asked worriedly. 'There's so much activity from the other Guild Houses in this area that they surely can't have the manpower to thoroughly search every muster station for us?'

'You say that,' muttered Gwilym, 'but it would be easy for

Björn to learn that this caravan is due to leave the soonest, even with the delay.'

'That's right,' Eleusia chimed in. 'No other Guild House has a caravan due to leave Karpella in the next two weeks.'

'Björn's not stupid,' he stated blandly. 'He knows this is the safest, most convenient way for us to leave the city. He knows we're here.'

'Bugger,' Torben sighed. 'What are we going to do? I don't like the idea of just sitting here, waiting to be found!'

'I'd agree with that,' Gwilym nodded. 'Given that we're supposed to be moving out today, it can't be long before these wagons are moved … hide in plain sight, that's what I say. Björn's cronies wouldn't dare attack us in the open with so many guards around, and they wouldn't dare travel with the caravan. Once we leave, security will become so tight, they're bound to be discovered.'

'You say that, but think this through rationally,' Eleusia said. 'You know Björn's men just as well as I do. How many of them would you say have ever had a rational thought in their lives? Like as not, if they see us, they'll jump us, regardless of how many of the Guild House's mercenaries are nearby. I agree we can't sit here, but we need to find something to deter Björn's men from attacking us as soon as they see us.'

The three of them sat, deep in thought, until Torben suddenly snapped his fingers when realisation kicked in. 'Follow me.' He gathered his things and edged his way out from their hiding place. 'I know the deterrent we need!'

'You can't just go running off, lad!' Gwilym shouted after him.

'There's no time to waste. Come along and stop grumbling.' Torben strode across the muster station, making for the mass of mercenaries gathered at the mess.

'For crying out loud,' Gwilym said, 'that boy's becoming a liability. I hope he knows what he's doing!'

'Don't worry, he does,' Eleusia stated, shepherding Gwilym from their hiding place and hurrying after Torben.

They followed Torben into the mess, both tightening the grip on their weapons as they entered the crowded area, and the three drew close together for security. It didn't take Torben long to spot Antauros, who sat at a table on the far side, his back to the rest of the world. Pushing his way through the crowd, Torben made his way towards the minotaur, the others following. They only managed to get about halfway across the mess, however, when two men stood from their spots next to a campfire and barred the way.

'Well now, look what we've got here.'

Torben recognised the fellow who spoke. He'd been one of the men who'd helped Eleusia bring Gwilym and him to Björn's compound, and had thrown him unceremoniously through the door.

'If it isn't our old friend Gwilym … and Eleusia, so good to see you.' The man 's voice was full of feigned enthusiasm and it grated heavily. 'And look here. I barely recognised the boy with his shield and all. You're starting to look like a real man, aren't you?'

Several more of Björn's men emerged from huddles of mercenaries gathered around the campfires, and they encircled the trio, fingering the hilts of their weapons. The by-standing mercenaries watched intently, though none offered to help. To them, it didn't look like Guild House business, or theirs, so they elected to keep out of it.

'Now, Tom,' Gwilym said cautiously , 'there's no need to do anything rash. You know better than to start a fight on Guild House territory. Björn won't thank you for starting a blood feud with Guild House Fisel, will he?'

'You're underestimating Björn's influence, dwarf,' Tom snarled. 'He has eyes and ears inside all the Guild Houses, and he knows how to speak to them, face to face. I would say that

'Truly? I think I prefer your other friend. She's a lot quieter, and doesn't complain as much.'

Antauros tossed his horns in Eleusia's direction, who had abandoned the box she'd been pretending to be organising, and was crouched behind tent fabric, trying to glimpse the scroll that the Superintendent was pouring over.

'How did you end up with these two?' he asked. 'None of you seem like a natural fit together.'

'It's a long story,' Torben answered with a rueful smile. 'The long and short of it is that Gwilym saved my life, in a manner of speaking, and we've been blown along by fortune to where we are at the moment.'

'I'd work on being cryptic if I was you,' Antauros said, laughing. 'Those men who accosted you in the mess—everyone knew they'd been sent by Björn. They approached us the night before, offering more money than Guild House Fisel will pay us for this job, to rat you out to them. It may not have looked like it, but all those other mercenaries were sizing you up as soon as you entered the mess, assessing how much trouble you might cause them if they decided to turn you over to Björn's men.'

'What about you?' Torben fixed Antauros with a nervous eye. There was no doubting the fact that if the minotaur decided to turn them over to Björn, there'd be no stopping him.

'Well, I could always use the extra money. That's the problem with the mercenary life; you never know where your next pay-packet will come from. I wouldn't worry though. I'm no friend to Björn or his men and I wouldn't want to help out that despicable bastard if I had a choice.'

'That's good to hear.' Torben relaxed.

'Antauros!' A high-pitched man's voice sounded from behind, and Torben and Antauros turned to see the Superintendent at the back entrance of the tent. Eleusia, Torben noticed, had moved back to the crate she'd been sorting and was lifting it into a wagon, on the face of it completely ignoring the Superintendent.

Behind the Superintendent, the tent was now almost empty. His servants were rolling up the carpets that lined the floor in preparation for disassembling the temporary edifice.

'How long until you've finished packing away all of this stuff?' the Superintendent asked curtly.

'Not long, sir.'

'Good, I want a word. Your people can sort the rest, can't they?'

'Aye, they can handle it,' he responded, following the Superintendent, who led him through the tent and walked him to the muster station.

'*Your people*,' Gwilym said mockingly. 'I'd rather eat manure than be referred to as that beast's servant again.'

It didn't take the three too long to pack away the last of the boxes and chests into the wagons, but by the time they'd finished, the Superintendent's tent had been taken down and the servants were struggling to fold it into a manageable bundle.

The day was quickly drawing to a close, and the pink hue of evening tinted the light.

'We'll be heading out soon,' Eleusia said.

All around, the mass of tents that had filled the muster station had all but disappeared, and the packed wagons were hitched to restless draught animals.

'Come on, let's get something to eat. I'm starving,' Torben said.

'A good suggestion at last,' Gwilym agreed.

The three of them set off towards the mess, though all the wagons moving to and fro in front of them, blocked their way and slowed them down. Gwilym led them towards the perimeter fence, where there was a reasonably clear thoroughfare, and their progress picked up immensely.

'What did you discover while the rest of us were working, Eleusia?' Torben urged.

'The Superintendent seems to be quite a particular man,' she responded. 'Which makes me think that he'll insist his tent is laid out in the same manner every time they erect it … which will help us vastly when we steal the maps we'll need. He also keeps the maps locked in a desk, which shouldn't cause us much of an issue. All we'll need to do is pick a night several days into the journey when the guards are less alert, and we'll be able to break in and—'

Eleusia was cut short as she fell face first to the ground, tripped by the shaft of a spear that had been thrust between her legs from underneath a wagon.

Before any of them could react, the leering figure of Tom stood before them, his sword at Eleusia's throat as she lay on the ground. Five more of Björn's men emerged from the cover of the wagons, surrounding Torben and Gwilym, and cutting off their escape.

'I must say that I'm disappointed,' Tom grinned. 'I was always told that it would be impossible to surprise you, Eleusia, but here we are, eh? You can drop your weapons, gentlemen, if you want to see your friend live.' He regarded Gwilym and Torben with a chilling smile.

Gwilym had drawn his seax in readiness for a fight, whilst Torben had levelled his spear and was vainly trying to find the most effective way to protect himself with his shield.

'How do we know you won't just kill us?' Gwilym asked darkly.

'You don't, now do you? You've just got to hope that I'm in as good a mood as I was this morning, though I must admit that having that stupid brute interfere in our business was most annoying. Now, drop your weapons.'

'Don't listen to him,' Eleusia ordered, her voice muffled by grass.

'Shut it,' Tom snapped, kicking Eleusia in the head. 'I'm not going to ask you again, dwarf. Drop your weapon and get your whelp here to do the same. Your cow's not here to save you now.'

'I wouldn't call him that if I was you,' Torben said.

'What?'

'I wouldn't call him that,' Torben repeated flatly. 'You'll make him angry.'

'Are you stupid, boy? What are you talking about?'

Torben inclined his head behind Tom.

Tom, glancing over his shoulder, threw himself to the ground and rolled clear of Eleusia as a javelin flew through the space he'd been standing in—it sent one of his men reeling backwards as it struck him in the chest.

Antauros bellowed as he erupted from behind a wagon where he'd been lurking, and smashed into the thugs with his shield, his war-hammer arching round to strike another in the face; it connected with the man's skull with a sickening crunch.

Eleusia sprang to her feet when she felt Tom's foot leave her back and fell on the leader, her longsword flashing wickedly in the evening light as it sliced the air. Tom managed to parry the blade, but was forced back by the hail of blows that Eleusia sent in his direction.

'Keep your shield up,' Antauros roared at Torben as he caught sight of the young man squaring up a thug, desperately jabbing the air with his spear, trying to deter the man from attacking.

The thug picked the right moment, dodged past Torben's spear, and shoulder-barged him, sending him sprawling to the ground. Torben yanked the shield back over his body in time to protect his torso from the man's attack. The thug's sword ricochet ineffectively off the thick wooden shield and before he could strike again, Torben had found his spear and jabbed it straight into the man's throat.

He looked in horror as the man fell to his knees, scrabbling desperately at his throat to stem the deadly tide, but to no avail. Slowly, he keeled over as the blood streamed through his fingers … and his life with it.

Antauros stooped over Torben, offering a hairy hand. 'Keep your shield up, boy.' He hauled him to his feet. 'You need to be more controlled with your feints; otherwise, you'll look like an idiot, and will end up a *dead* idiot!'

'Bit late for the lesson, isn't it?' Torben asked wryly.

The only one of Björn's men still on his feet was Tom and he was beating a hasty retreat along the perimeter fence, Eleusia and Gwilym in hot pursuit. His right arm hung limply, the shoulder of his tunic bloodied and torn; clumsily, he tried to fend off his attackers' blows with the sword in his left hand.

Seeing an opportunity for escape, he abandoned the sword and dived headlong through a gap in the fence, and rolled down a small slope, crying out in pain as his wounded arm was battered in the fall.

Eleusia stuck her sword into the ground and removed the crossbow from her back, hoping to load it and take a shot at Tom before he ran out of range, but he'd already gone to ground in a nearby ditch and was nowhere in sight. 'Bugger!'

'Do you have a natural knack for turning up late to confrontations, or is it a coincidence?' Gwilym asked, sheathing his seax, eyeing Antauros intently.

'You're welcome,' Antauros snorted.

'What are we going to do with this lot?' Torben's voice sounded faint and distant.

'Leave the buggers,' Gwilym said. 'I don't want anything more to do with them.'

Torben regarded the man he'd killed. Taking this life had affected him more profoundly than when he'd killed the Lupine back in Bywater. The body before him wasn't that of a snarling beast, but a man, like himself, and yet the man had the same steely look of a cold-hearted murderer in his eyes as the Lupine had.

'I know what you're thinking.' Eleusia put a hand on Torben's shoulder. 'Remember that if you hadn't killed him, he'd be looking down at *your* body right now.'

'The caravan will be leaving soon, and you'll need all your energy for the first march,' Antauros advised. 'Best grab a hot meal while you can. It'll be nothing but stale rations from now until we see another city.' With that, he disappeared into the mass of wagons and vanished from sight.

Gwilym spat and surveyed the remnants of Björn's men. 'You could see the bloodlust in him during the scrap. We're lucky that it didn't take hold or we'd be dead, as well.'

'You could be a bit more grateful,' Torben snapped.

'Oh come on,' Eleusia said dryly. 'I don't want to stand here and listen to the two of you bicker. Let's get out of here. Antauros is right; we need to rest before we move out.' Taking Torben's arm, she led him away from the scene, Gwilym following.

The three of them picked their way through the wagons and made their way to the mess area of the muster station. Unlike earlier in the day when they'd passed through, almost all of the free space was filled with people squatting round campfires and tables. Most of them looked like the mercenaries that were to protect the caravan along its journey, but here and there were groups of well-dressed merchants in the Guild's employ; they were all enjoying their last carefree moments.

As they joined the back of a queue, a roar of laughter erupted from a large group of dwarves who were watching two of their fellows struggling against one another in a wrestling match. Gwilym inspected the dwarves intently, muttering to himself as he tried to work out where they were from.

The food they were served was a form of rough porridge served in crudely carved wooden bowls, but it was warm. Taking a large chunk of flat bread, Torben joined Eleusia and Gwilym, who were scanning the mess area, looking for a place to sit. There was hardly any free space near a fire and most of the mercenaries were already seated in tightknit groups clearly used to, and comfortable with, their own company, free from outsiders.

'You sit with those blasted dwarfs if you want,' Eleusia was saying as Torben joined the conversation. 'But I, for one, would rather enjoy my gruel in peace rather than have to endure their brutish games after what we've just been through.'

'Well, I wouldn't be surprised if you wanted to sit in the dark and eat alone … at least then I'd get some peace,' Gwilym said.

'What about there?' Torben asked before the argument became more heated. He motioned with his bread to the other side, where Antauros was sitting alone in front of a fire. He was clearly the topic of conversation for those seated around the nearest campfires, because they constantly cast looks in his direction and leaned close to speak confidentially.

'With *him*?' Gwilym was shocked and his voice betrayed a hint of fear. 'You're mad, Torben. Just because you haven't seen the brute that he really is, doesn't mean that you should think of him as being a harmless cow!'

'Shut up,' Torben snapped. 'You should know better than to listen to idle gossip!' He pushed past the dwarf and made his way across the mess, towards Antauros. The other mercenaries appeared astonished as Torben marched past and took a seat next to the minotaur.

Antauros himself looked taken aback and then nodded a greeting, and continued to eat.

'That's it. He's finally lost it,' Gwilym said despairingly. 'I knew that this would happen; it's probably some brutal form of culture shock, you know. The poor lad's been plucked so sharply from his quaint, quiet environment that it's addled his brain. He hasn't had time to adjust. And now there he is, breaking bread with a veritable beast. What are we going to do El—hey, where are you going?'

Eleusia followed Torben's lead and headed towards the far campfire. 'At least it'll be quiet over there,' she said over her shoulder.

Gwilym stared at Eleusia as she took up a place with Torben and Antauros. He looked around, trying to find someone to express the madness of the situation to, but he was alone, stranded amid the islands of diners who took no notice of him.

'Oh, sod it,' he said to himself. 'Madness this is, complete idiocy. It'll get us all killed, I'm sure of it.'

He continued to grumble discontentedly as he made his way towards his companions and sat near Antauros. He tried not to take notice of the mercenaries' incredulous, dumbfounded stares as the three broke bread with the minotaur.

11

———————

Torben's heart pounded, blood thudding through his head as he shifted his weight from foot to foot. He lowered his shield slightly to get a clearer line of vision and then thrust the spear forward. A miss.

He wheeled right, shield up again to protect his head from his opponent's retaliatory blow. Sweat streamed down his forehead and stung as it seeped into his eyes, blurring his sight. He couldn't stop, couldn't afford to wipe his eyes and clear his vision. A second of lapsed concentration and he'd go down.

The light flashed off Torben's spear as it sliced through the air at his opponent, but the lunge was swatted away, the spear clattering to the ground when batted from his grasp.

Don't drop your guard, Torben thought as he drew his short-sword and prepared for the next attack. *Wait for it, wait for it.* He ducked, his opponent's weapon flying through the space where his head had been. *Now!* He charged forward and crashed into his opponent with his shield, sword at the ready to deal the final blow.

His opponent, however, did not give way and stood firm as mountain. For a second, they struggled, pushing against one another, trying to inch each other back. The muscles on Torben's shield arm bulged, veins and sinew pushing against his skin as he strained with all his might … but to no avail.

With a loud grunt, Antauros gave a mighty heave of his shield and sent Torben sprawling into the dust, the wind knocked from him. 'On your feet, boy,' Antauros thundered across the practice area, war-hammer held at the ready.

Trying to dodge out of the way, he scrambled to his feet, but Antauros had already predicted his next move and sent him rolling back into the dirt with another well-timed shield barge. He stood over Torben and laid a stout boots on Torben's chest, stopping him from rising. 'Dead, but that was much better.'

'I might as well be dead with the battering you've given me lately,' Torben said, staggering to his feet.

'It's good for you, as long as you remember what I tell you. Now, fetch your spear; you still need to work on those feints.'

Torben hobbled across the bare patch of earth they'd cleared to make a practice area. They were over two weeks into the journey from Karpella to the city of Ashmiltes, situated on the edge of the great Sonsuz Desert in the Sultanate of Fashaddon, the caravan's final destination. The caravan had set up camp for the night on the edge of a great forest, known as the Bar-Dendra, which sprawled before them as far as the eye could see. It would take the caravan at least nine days to snake its way along the road through the trees, and the merchants and mercenaries were lounging around, enjoying their last night in the open air.

Since leaving Karpella, Antauros had taken it upon himself to give Torben a grounding in military training, with Eleusia and Gwilym occasionally chipping in with their own pearls of wisdom, gained from decades of living a roguish life.

'Try not to spend so much time on the ground,' Gwilym chuckled, surveying the lesson over a large wineskin. 'You can't always play dead, you know.'

Torben threw a rude gesture in Gwilym's direction as he

picked up his spear and walked back towards Antauros, who'd set down his war-hammer and shield, and was standing with crossed arms looking his pupil up and down.

'Now, do the drill,' he ordered.

Puffing his cheeks and ignoring the aches that the relentless training had beaten into him over the nights, Torben began to bounce backwards and forwards, spear held out before him, its point dancing as he went through the training exercise.

Antauros walked slowly around, inspecting his technique from every angle, and commentating here and there. 'Keep the point up higher … make sure you keep your elbows in … you want to give your opponent only one obvious route of attack … and now parry! Riposte! Good, much better! Again, this time keep your feet properly square to your torso and lunge!'

As Torben launched into another sequence of movements, Eleusia emerged from a nearby tent and took a seat next to Gwilym to watch.

'How did your reconnaissance go?' Gwilym asked.

'I'm going in tonight,' Eleusia replied solemnly. 'The Superintendent's guards have been drinking ever since we stopped for the night. Once we start travelling through the forest, they'll be much more vigilant, so I reckon this is our best shot.'

'Aye, once we have a map to Gallenford, we can slip into the trees and lie low until the caravan has moved on. They'll never find us in the forest, if they even bother to look in the first place.'

'I doubt that. The Superintendent wouldn't risk halting the caravan in Bar-Dendra Forest for any longer than he has to. Too many places for watching eyes to peer from. The place is too arcane; you can practically smell the old magic in air.'

'I never had you down as the superstitious type, Eleusia. You know as well as most do that the last magic users are long gone, folks of stories and legends now.'

'Perhaps.' She stared intently into his eyes. 'But you know as well as I do that the things that the magic users made linger on. You carry one such item around in your pack.'

'It's nothing but a trick purse, barely any magic in it at all. Had it been of any significance, then the maker would have cast an enchantment on it that actually turned things into gold! Anyway,' Gwilym shrugged, changing the subject, 'I wish you'd let me come with you tonight. You should always have a partner on a job.'

'*You* may need a partner, but I don't. In any case, having you with me is too risky. With Antauros around all of the time, it would look suspicious if he noticed us both sneak off during the night. He's been watching us, you know. And he keeps asking Torben about the three of us, trying to catch him off guard.'

'The lad's been true to now. I don't think we should doubt him. His head has a damn sight more sense in it than I gave him credit for!'

'I know, but I want you to keep an eye on Antauros whilst I'm doing the job. Make sure he doesn't snoop around too much.'

'Don't fret,' Gwilym assured her. 'Torben and I will keep all four of our eyes on him, well provided he can keep his eyes open after the workout he's been getting.' Gwilym hopped to his feet and strode into the practice area. 'Here, Antauros. I'll give the boy a bout. I still owe him from when he beat me the last time.' Pulling off his shirt, Gwilym drew his seax and squared up to the sweaty, weary figure of Torben. He winked rakishly and began to circle. 'This'll be a fairer contest than the last time. I haven't had nearly as much wine this time.'

Eleusia watched the bout begin. Antauros looked on intently, issuing advice and instructions as Torben tried to best the dwarf. Since the altercation with Björn's men in the muster station, Antauros had barely parted company with the three of them. They patrolled together, ate and camped together. Eleusia was glad to have the minotaur in their company. Despite his bravado,

Gwilym was a spy and not a proper warrior, and Torben had yet to be tested in a true fight.

Björn's men were still tracking them. Eleusia had left the caravan's camp every night to scout their surroundings and every night she'd come upon their trail, and had gone right up to their camp on one occasion to assess their numbers—at least twelve. If they were caught away from the caravan, Eleusia wouldn't be able to fend them off by herself whilst looking out for the other two. They needed a proper fighter to help them and Antauros was the perfect candidate.

Only once had Eleusia broached the subject of letting Antauros in on the scheme with Gwilym, and it had been soundly rejected. Despite the help and companionship the minotaur provided, Gwilym didn't trust him and saw him as a threat.

There was a triumphant shout as Torben swept Gwilym off his feet with a well-timed swing of the spear, and the sound brought Eleusia back from her brooding. The sun had almost disappeared below the horizon, and it would be time for her to strike out soon. Pulling the hood over her head, she disappeared into to the city of tents to take up her station and wait for the right moment to make her move.

From out of the corner of his eye, Gwilym saw the folds of Eleusia's cloak vanish into the evening gloom as he was helped back to his feet by Torben.

'Perhaps you should have had more wine; it may have helped your performance.' Torben's face was warmed by a broad, victorious grin.

'Don't get complacent. It could have easily gone the other way,' Antauros chided.

'I don't know about that,' Gwilym said. 'He got me well and good tonight. Looks like I might have to have a few lessons with you, Antauros. The boy's getting too good for me!' He slapped Torben playfully on the back as he sat down by their campfire.

Torben and Antauros joined him and the three began to dig

into the rations the minotaur distributed from his large pack: salted meat and barrack's biscuit. The meat was tough and sinewy, and the barrack's biscuits hard as rocks, but Torben was so hungry he didn't care. Gratefully, he wolfed down the meal as fast as his teeth would allow. He'd noticed Eleusia wasn't with them, but he could guess where she was. Not only had she been checking on their hunters, but she'd relentlessly watched movement patterns and routines of the Superintendent and his guards as they performed their nightly duties.

Torben wasn't the only one that had noticed her absence. 'I see that Eleusia isn't joining us again,' Antauros said.

'Went to stretch her legs' Gwilym explained, not looking up from his meal. 'She wants to enjoy open spaces and fresh air before we enter the forest.'

'Strange, I wouldn't have said that she was someone who'd have been averse to travelling in woodland.'

Neither Gwilym nor Torben responded. Gwilym shrugged expansively, as if to indicate that he understood as much as Antauros about Eleusia's absence. Torben was too tired to offer an excuse; it was taking all of his energy to eat.

Antauros didn't push, but it was clear that he hadn't bought Gwilym's answer.

The sun was almost completely set and the only light that illuminated them was that of the campfire flickering before them. They could hear sounds of talking and some revellers enjoying their last night under the open sky.

Gwilym propped himself up against the wheel of a nearby wagon, holding the half-full wineskin as he sat in silence, staring at the glittering stars above. Nearby, Antauros began his daily routine of checks on his gear, running his wide hands up and down his shield to check for weaknesses, cleaning and oiling his war-hammer, and honing the points of his javelins. Torben didn't have the energy to do much other than pull a blanket from his pack and lie next to the fire.

The stars shone brightly and, staring up, Torben meditatively picked out constellations from the blackness. His father had often taken him into nearby fields to watch stars, pointing out the shapes they made, and telling him all about what they meant.

The history of our people is written up there in the sky. The Gods put all of our legends up there so that we cannot forget them. They can also tell us about the future, the past and the changing of the seasons. Torben could hear his father's gentle voice as clearly as if the man were sitting alongside him.

Directly above was the sickle; it sparkled dimly in the night sky. When it shone brightest, that was the best time to harvest. And there, next to it, hung the Warrior, who was said to always be striving to keep evil at bay from the world. When his stars shone most intensely, none needed be afraid, but one had to always be ready for when his stars waned as evil would be gain a foothold. Far to the east, the Wyrm coiled menacingly, its head poised to strike the Warrior as it searched for the best moment to overwhelm him.

Torben didn't really hold much stock in the tales and guidance that his father had pointed out in the sky, but now that he was so far away from home, thinking about the tales gave him comfort. After his parents had died, he'd spent night after night staring at the sky, trying to see a sign suspended in the heavens … but he'd yet to find one. Thinking of his parents, he absently fingered his silver arm-ring; it was as close a physical connection with them that he could get, and he took comfort in tracing its ever-familiar patterns.

From his spot against the wagon, Gwilym began to sing softly. It was a ballad about rolling fields and peaceful meadows, and the way that he sang it, the ease with which the words rolled off his tongue, made it feel as if the song was about his homeland.

The notes washed over Torben as his eyes began to shut, the stars growing dimmer and dimmer as sleep washed over him.

Like Torben, the eyes of the guard watching the entrance to

the Superintendent's tent were beginning to grow heavy, his head nodding further towards his chest as he leaned heavily on his spear for support. He had drawn the short straw of the last-night watch before entering Bar-Dendra Forest, but that hadn't stopped him having a few drinks with his compatriots before being called to duty—a few too many drinks.

His sight, already clouded by alcohol, went black as his eyes fully closed.

For a moment, everything was sweet sleep … until something jerked him back into bleary-eyed consciousness. The flap of the tent next to him fluttered quietly in the breeze, but there was nothing and no one nearby. After a moment of peering drunkenly from side to side, he propped himself up with the spear and settled back into shirking his duty.

On the other side of the tent flap, Eleusia crouched and held her breath as she watched the silhouette of the guard outside straighten and then relax again. Satisfied that he was going nowhere, she stalked silently into the tent.

Eleusia knew exactly where she needed to go. Since her first reconnoitre of the tent outside the walls of Karpella, she'd systematically watched the Superintendent's servants erect and disassemble the tent every morning and night. If asked, she could list exactly what pieces of furniture were in the tent and where they were placed.

She didn't need light to find her way. Making her quiet and swift way to the back, Eleusia approached a large writing desk, holding her breath again as she crept passed the slumbering figure of the Superintendent who lay on a travelling cot nearby. Drawing a lock pick from the folds of her cloak, she inserted it into the desk lock and, slowly but surely, began to manipulate the mechanism. Behind her, the Superintendent's heavy breathing sounded comfortingly regular and peaceful. When a loud snore erupted, Eleusia deftly made a final adjustment and the lock clicked open.

Inside the desk were rolled-up maps, every one kept within

its own leather tube to protect it from the elements. She felt the ends of each, running her fingers over the embossed numbers on the exterior of the cases. As her fingers traced the number VII, she slowly withdrew the tube from the desk, her other hand guiding the tubes above into new resting places.

She hovered, waiting for another snore from the Superintendent and, as soon as it sounded, the desk was shut with a soft click and she was by the tent flap again. Checking the coast was clear, she slipped out and disappeared into the wagons opposite.

It didn't take long for Eleusia to make her way back to the camp base. As she emerged from the wagons, she could see Torben sleeping in front of the fire, the massive bulk of Antauros lying across from him and facing away to warm his back near the flames.

'Success?' Gwilym asked quietly as he looked at Eleusia from his position by the wagon wheel.

'I thought you were asleep,' she whispered.

'Just keeping up appearances for the General over there. Did you get it?'

'Yes.' She pulled back the cloak to reveal the leather map case.

'And you're sure this is the right map?'

'Absol …' Eleusia stopped abruptly as Antauros snorted loudly and rolled over in his sleep. Her eyes scanned the minotaur for signs of consciousness and found none. Still, she crouched in silence for a full moment before continuing. 'Absolutely, I'm sure this is the map of the northern part of Bar-Dendra Forest, as Gallenford lies on the border to the east of here. This will do us.'

'I'd still like to check it first. I don't want to get away only to realise that we stole a useless piece of paper.'

'Fine, but not here.' Eleusia glanced at Antauros. 'We're too exposed here. Anyone could be watching.'

'Agreed. Let's find somewhere a bit more secluded.'

'What about Torben? Shouldn't we go over the plan with him again?'

'No, leave him to sleep,' Gwilym answered. 'That brute is pushing him too hard; he's barely got enough energy to manage the escape tomorrow, let alone go wandering about at night. He knows what the plan is. The boy's not stupid.'

Nodding, Eleusia followed him as they slipped amongst the wagons to verify the map.

Early the next morning, Antauros roused the three of them to take their guard duty shift. Despite her lack of sleep, Eleusia didn't complain as the four of them trudged around the perimeter, watching as the camp came to life and make itself ready for the day of travel. Merchants and mercenaries alike dragged their feet as they surveyed the menacing wall of trees before them. The draft animals were also forced into reluctant movement, nostrils flaring nervously as they lumbered along the road towards the tree line. As the caravan began to slowly roll along, Antauros led Torben, Gwilym and Eleusia to their allotted place at the front of the column.

Entering the forest, Torben tried to recall the tales his mother had told him about the place they were travelling through. There were many legends that surrounded the Bar-Dendra Forest, too many to count. Some thought that deep within the trees, in places where no creature had stepped for thousands of years, were primordial pools from which all life in the world had crawled, eons ago. Others thought that the forest was the source of the old magic of legends and that, one day, magic would once again flow unchecked from the centre of the forest, to be manipulated for both good and ill.

Bar-Dendra's reputation as a place of magic also meant that people spoke of the many beasts said to dwell within the trees. Since joining the caravan, Torben had overheard many tales of creatures setting out from the forest to wreak havoc upon nearby towns and villages. One mercenary swore on his life that the skull of one such beast hung on a castle wall in Karpella, a memento of a famous hunt that was still sung about by tavern bards.

The trees, Torben noticed, weren't too dissimilar from those that bordered Bywater, and the darkness of the forest filled him with the same sense of dread ... and of being watched. The other mercenaries marching on the caravan's edge must have shared Torben's feelings for they walked more carefully along the road, peering intently into the gloom of the forest, hands anxiously gripping weapons and shields.

It was approaching midday, or so Torben guessed, when Gwilym tugged at his sleeve and pointed down the road. Drifting slowly above the trees were thick tendrils of dust thrown up from the road just over the horizon.

'Strange,' Torben murmured. 'Surely there can't be enough wind to blow up the dust like that along the road? The trees are too close.'

'Aye, it's not the wind,' Gwilym responded. 'Like as not, it's horses hooves. There are mounted men coming this way and fast.'

He and Torben were not the only ones who'd noticed the dust swirling towards them. Antauros already had his war-hammer and shield at the ready, whilst Eleusia was fitting a bolt into her crossbow. All around, the mercenaries were moving up the column and forming a ragged line in front of the caravan, which had ground to a halt. The Superintendent himself appeared, mounted on an expensive bay stallion to suss out what might impede the progress of his charge.

As the dense dust cloud drew closer and closer the figures of horses and riders became visible as they pounded along the road. Surprisingly, the riders were bedecked in heavy armour, or so Torben guessed by the myriad reflections of light that bounced of the leaders. Above them, attached to lances, waved brightly coloured pennants.

The mercenaries around them shifted uneasily as the riders approached. It was unusual to see a column of knights such as this at the best of times, but to see them in the middle of the Bar-Dendra Forest was most unusual.

'Ghosts,' one mercenary near Torben muttered. 'They're the ghosts of the Fey Folk come to kill those who trespass in their territory.'

As whispers began to ripple around the caravan, a loud and shrill horn sounded, and the riders cantered to a halt on the road, a final flurry of dust drifting up into sky. Three knights spurred their horses onwards and covered the last stretch to within earshot of the caravan's vanguard.

To Torben, they looked like figures straight out of a legend. They were covered from head to toe in shimmering scale-mail that flowed with the movement of their horses. Heads were concealed by thick helmets topped with elaborate plumes, and shields were emblazoned with the sigil of a rearing white horse with a golden mane and tail on a crimson backdrop. The knights that rode on the outside of the trio carried long heavy lances, pennants fluttering above them, whilst the knight riding in the centre rode casually with his hands resting on the pommel of his saddle, clearly in command.

As they reigned in the horses, the middle rider removed his helmet, revealing a shock of fiery red hair and he smirked at the rag-tag group of mercenaries on the ground. Removing one of his gauntlets, he ran a hand through his hair, smoothing it from his forehead as his eyes set on the mounted figure of the Superintendent, doing his best to try and look intimidating.

'Look what we have here,' the knight sneered. 'I would have expected one of the esteemed Guild Houses to trust its goods and sundries with more than a band of vagabonds and thieves.'

'Might I enquire as to your business?' The Superintendent's

high voice quivered with nervousness. 'We have many miles to travel and can't afford to be delayed for long.'

'Look at some of these fellows,' the knight continued, addressing his companions and ignoring the Superintendent. 'Half of them look like they're about to keel over from exhaustion and the other half look like they're about to desert!'

'I'd do well to remind you,' the Superintendent tried to raise his voice above the knight's, 'that it's not wise for anyone to disrupt the business of Guild House Fisel, or hinder the progress of its goods on their way.'

'Well, well, well.' A smirk returned as he gazed back at the Superintendent. 'I wouldn't have expected this soft bureaucrat to pull out the threats so quickly. Then, I suppose, we shouldn't expect too much small-talk from a Guild House lackey. If you want to get down to business, fine!'

The knight clicked his tongue disapprovingly and drew a small scroll from a saddlebag and began to unroll it. A few mercenaries were already beginning to melt further back down the caravan, as if they could sense that something wasn't right. The Superintendent pulled nervously at his collar as he watched the knight deliberately unroll the scroll, sweat beading the large bald patch on his head.

'I am here to inform you, that by order of Her Majesty Queen Alliona IV, you are trespassing whilst bearing arms in the Kingdom of Sharisar.' The knight stared keenly. 'Either you agree to pay tribute to the Queen, lay down your arms and be escorted to the nearest stronghold so your goods can be impounded, or you reject the offer and suffer the consequences of your actions.'

There was stunned silence as what he said sunk in. The Superintendent sat on his horse, staring blankly back at the deputation, his mouth opening and shutting as he processed the information.

'Well, what is your answer?'

'But ... b-but ... you have no authority here. S-sovereignty over Bar-Dendra is claimed by the Kingdom of Dazscor and Aramore, and we … we are many, many miles away from Sharisar's border,' the Superintendent stammered. 'In any case, Guild House Fisel has held a trade agreement with the Kingdom of Sharisar for the last two hundred and fifty years. Under the terms of our agreement … we … we are entitled to move freely through the kingdom, as armed as the Guild House feels is necessary to protect its assets.'

'So you reject the terms of the ultimatum?'

'Well, no … yes … errm.'

'If that is the case then, our discussion is sadly at an end,' the knight stated flatly.

Before the Superintendent could say a word, the knight turned his horse around and rode back to his men, his guard following. All eyes in the caravan instinctively turned to the Superintendent, who was muttering confusedly to himself and not making eye contact.

As the three knights returned to their fellows, the sound of the horn echoed through the forest again and slowly drifted into the trees. The mercenaries drew closer together, arrows knocked to bowstrings and spears levelled, all eyes fixed on the column of knights that had formed into a solid block of horse and metal before them.

The horn sounded again and this time its call was answered by a distinct howl that broke out from the trees on both sides of the road. *Lupines.* Before any of them could react, screams and shouts came from the rear of the caravan, accompanied by snarling and barking.

'They're attacking the rear of the column,' the Superintendent squealed. 'Quickly, pull back and protect the merchants!'

The mercenaries peeled from the ragged shield wall they had formed and sprinted down the caravan; not many wanted to stay with their backs to the Lupines behind them. Before any of them managed to get very far, however, the horn blasted again and the knights charged.

Torben stared at the horsemen bearing down on the caravan. The front rank of knights had lowered their lances, the wicked points barely visible in the blur of movement and the dust that the horses were flinging into the air again.

'Get back!' Antauros yelled.

'What? Shouldn't we stand and fight?' Torben was mesmerised.

'Don't argue with him,' Gwilym shouted, pulling him down the caravan. 'For once, I'm inclined to agree with him; we can't stand against that!'

Few mercenaries stayed to receive the charge. Most had decided to try their luck against the Lupines that were swarming over the wagons and carts to the rear, killing the merchants and animals alike. Those that did stand their ground were swept away by the tide of metal that hit them. The knights instinctively peeled to the left and right of the carts as they met the caravan, swords and lances cutting down those mercenaries that crossed their path.

Gwilym didn't drag Torben far down the column, but darted behind the sturdiest looking wagon he could find to take shelter from the charge, Antauros following behind. Eleusia fired her crossbow at the knights before leaping behind the wagon with the others. For a moment, the four of them crouched, seeing nothing and listening to pounding hooves growing closer and closer.

Then the knights stormed past. From their hiding place, Torben watched as one of the mercenaries was ridden down, the knight's lance passing straight through him as the man rode by. A shower of blood and splinters spattered the four of them as the knight's lance shattered on impact and the mercenary's limp body was ground into the dust by horses.

'Easy, wait for it.' Antauros spoke soothingly, watching knights thunder past. 'Now … *run!*'

As the last of the knights galloped past, they burst from their hiding place and raced towards the tree line. In the confined space, it was hard for the knights to do anything but continue to charge down the full length of the caravan but, by now, the Lupines had pushed their way up, and more of them emerged from the trees to mop up the remnants of Guild House Fisel's trading caravan.

Ducking, Eleusia slashed her sword across the torso of a Lupine that confronted them as they left the hiding place, an axe raised to strike. Torben jabbed his spear at another that ran towards them and the beast recoiled as the point bit deep into his shoulder. Before the Lupine could react and retaliate, he jabbed again, ripping through the fur and flesh of the Lupine's stomach; he tumbled, convulsing, to the ground.

Now that they were in the open, they could view the entire length of the caravan; the scene was one of absolute chaos. Bodies were everywhere, mostly mercenaries and some finely garbed merchants, but here and there lay a Lupine with blood-matted fur.

'Make for the trees,' Gwilym yelled. As he sprinted across the road, he turned to check that the others were following, his sling whirring round his head, ready to strike. There was a shrill shrieking sound as the sling bullet whipped past Torben's head. It struck the Lupine's face that was stalking him, sending the creature smashing to the ground.

The forest was no more peaceful than the caravan. Battle sounds reverberated all around as the four plunged into the undergrowth and pushed their way to what they hoped was an escape route.

Almost immediately, they came across the bodies of several mercenaries, mangled nearly beyond recognition. There was also a large feral-looking Lupine crouched over a body. He snarled upon hearing them approach, jaws dripping with blood from where he'd been feeding.

The Lupine rose to face them, but Antauros moved quickly, his massive bulk deftly avoiding a wild sword blow aimed at him. There was another snarl, followed by a whimper as

Antauros' war-hammer found its mark. 'Come on, we need to keep moving!'

Eleusia chivvied the group from the rear, keeping a watchful eye behind them lest any Lupines were lured from the richer caravan pickings to search for stragglers. The others didn't need much encouragement, but sprinted through the trees, the sounds of dying souls echoing in their ears as they ran from the caravan.

12

Night was very slow to arrive that day and they were exhausted by the time it was too dark to press on without light. Eleusia had pushed them hard to escape the Lupines and, after the last few hours of wearily running, they'd not heard or seen anything that indicated they'd been followed.

When they finally stopped to rest, they'd made their way halfway up a large, tree-covered ridge that lay several miles from the road and the remains of the caravan. They sought shelter in a small cave that lay a short distance from the top of a hill and offered a good view across the landscape of Bar-Dendra Forest, now bathed in silvery moonlight. The only other light was the faint glow thrown out by the burning wagons that lay hidden on the road, visible as a dark line cutting through the trees.

For a while, the four sat in silence, catching their breath and eating whatever food they were able to find in their packs.

'Well, what now?' Gwilym asked, sighing softly. 'Do you reckon we should press on, or are we safe enough here for the moment?'

'I wouldn't like to tarry here too long,' Eleusia replied. 'We're still within a few miles of the caravan, which is far too close for my liking. We're well within the range of a Lupine war band, and it's never wise to take chances, especially where Lupines are concerned. I suggest we rest here for a little longer and then push on for a few more hours. I want us to get across this ridge before daybreak.'

'What then?' Torben asked tiredly. 'Where are we headed, other than deeper into the forest?'

'That's a good question and I'm sure Gwilym and Eleusia would be happy to shed some light on that matter.'

The features of Antauros' face were obscured by the night, but his huge frame was clearly visible. Soft moonlight reflected off his long polished horns.

'I'm not sure I know what you mean.' Gwilym's voice was soft and level.

'That's strange, because you seemed to know exactly where you wanted to go when Eleusia brought you that map from the Superintendent's tent.'

'Easy now, Antauros. You don't want to get involved in anything that doesn't concern you.'

'I think it rather does concern me now, considering that I'm stuck in the middle of nowhere with three co-conspirators. I don't fancy blundering around this dark forest with a pack of hungry Lupines hunting me on my own, but I'd also rather have those I've thrown in my lot with lay the cards on the table … *now*.'

'What's got you thinking like that, eh?' Forced jocularity was evident in Torben's voice. 'You must have misheard something or, like as not, you've been paying too close an ear to caravan gossip.'

'The boy's right. There's no point in us discussing pointless rumours; we haven't got time for that.' Gwilym's tone grew dangerous.

'If what I've heard and seen is pointless rumour,' Antauros said contemptuously, 'then how do you explain the fact that last night Eleusia returned to our camp with a map tube, and this morning I overheard the Superintendent berating one of his servants for losing the map of northern Bar-Dendra?'

'It's not what you think,' Gwilym growled.

'Really? Then how would you explain it?'

'I wouldn't care to have to explain our private business to the likes of you, brute!'

'That's a nice way to talk to the fellow that's saved your skin —how many times is it now? Two, three? And yet, I still barely know you. Gods know how you managed to survive for so long. A child would have more fight than you.'

'We would have been fine without you,' Gwilym snapped. 'In any case, why should I thank *you*—someone who's not only a murderer, but also a filthy eavesdropper!'

'Rich coming from a thief or, worse, someone who's too cowardly to do his own thieving and sends someone else to do it.'

'Look, Antauros, you can walk away from this now, forget everything you think you heard or saw, and we can go our separate ways with no hard feelings. Or you can continue to stick your snout into something that doesn't concern you, which will *not* end well.'

'Are you threatening me, dwarf?' Antauros hissed. 'I don't take kindly to being threatened. I'd have thought that you, of all people, would be careful to mind your manners around me, considering the reputation you've created for me.'

There was silence except for the grinding of Gwilym's teeth as he seethed with rage. Instinctively, four hands started to drift towards weapons in the dark.

'Gwilym, remember what I suggested to you the other day?' Eleusia's voice was calm and soothing in the tense air.

'What? No, I don't remember, and I hardly think this is the time to bring up past idle chitchat.'

'About how Antauros could be useful to us—'

'No! That's out of the question. You can't possibly think that's a good idea … and I thought I made it clear the last time that you brought this up, that it was a stupid idea. He can't be trusted!'

'You're not exactly portraying yourself as trustworthy at the moment either, dwarf,' Antauros rumbled.

'Think about it,' Eleusia said casually. 'Antauros was right when he said that we're stuck out here in the middle of nowhere … so no one's going to wander happily into the trees by themselves to be hunted by the Lupines. The only way this is going to end is if he kills us, or we kill him, and knowing his reputation, I wouldn't value our chances. Unless, that is, we invite him into the scheme—'

'Scheme, what scheme?' Antauros asked quickly.

'Eleusia, that isn't your decision to make,' Gwilym growled.

'You know what Gwilym? You're right. The three of us should vote on it.'

'Vote? Are you mad? We haven't got time to vote on anything. I never thought I'd here you spouting such rubbish at a time like this,' Gwilym muttered.

'And the last time I checked, you weren't the majority stakeholder in the Scheme,' Eleusia said softly.

'What? The whole bloody scheme was my idea!'

'Yes, but we all agreed that we'd share the profits equally; therefore you, Torben and I are equal partners and therefore, we should vote on it.' A triumphant smile spread across Eleusia's face, not that the others could see it in the dark.

'Bugger,' Gwilym spat.

'Can't really argue with that now, can you, dwarf?' Antauros chuckled.

'No, I guess I can't,' Gwilym replied dully. 'But the whole idea of a vote is pointless. Torben will obviously vote with me, so your plan won't work.'

'Whoa now. Hold on,' Torben said. 'What makes you think that I'll vote the same way as you?'

'Boy, after all we've been through, you'd vote *against* me?'

'If I thought it was the right decision, yes I would,' he replied defiantly.

'In that case, each of you should speak your peace,' Antauros said. 'We can't tarry here forever.'

'You know how I feel. He can't be trusted, no matter what he's done for us,' Gwilym said shortly. 'I've heard too many tales about what he's done to want to pal up with him, and have him profit from our scheme—*my* scheme. He's a coldhearted killer at the best of times and a downright bloodthirsty psychopath at the worst. That's the sort of reputation that can't be made up for you; sadly, it has to be earned. I'm against this stupidity!'

'I hardly see why,' Eleusia retorted. 'Clearly, Antauros has the potential and willingness to be a great asset to us. I vote we allow him into the scheme.'

'That's one for and one against,' Antauros declared. 'What about you, Torben?'

Deep in thought, he stood in silence, stroking his cheeks and the ragged beard that had taken hold there. 'Personally, I have no qualms about you, Antauros. You've taught me a great deal since we met you, and helped us out a good many times. You could have easily left us to be captured by Björn's men back at the muster station, but instead you helped. I vote that he joins the scheme.'

'Well,' Gwilym exhaled noisily. 'I can't deny that I'm disappointed, Torben, but if that's what the two of you want, I'll accept it. But it'll be on your head if he betrays us … and don't come crying to me when the bloodlust takes him, because I'll be well out of the way.'

'I assure you that no such thing will happen. Give me a chance to prove those rumours you've heard about me are unfounded, and put them to bed.' There was a certain smugness in Antauros' voice.

'Put them in their grave more like,' Gwilym muttered, throwing a dirty look at his colleagues in the darkness. 'And just because they've accepted you as part of the scheme doesn't mean that I have. I'm only going along with this because it seems like the most likely way of getting my gold … for now.'

'Gold?' Antauros almost whispered the word. 'So, what's this ever-so-secret scheme that you're plotting, eh?'

Before Eleusia could say anything, a high-pitched howl sounded from the forest near the ridge. A flock of birds burst from nearby trees, spooked by the horrible piercing noise.

'We can explain on the move,' Eleusia said hurriedly. 'They may have picked up our trail.'

They sprang to their feet and quickly picked their way through the undergrowth, making for the top of the ridge.

By the time morning had forced its way through the darkness, the group had reached the top of the ridge and followed its length for several hours. Every now and again, they could spy the vast expanse of Bar-Dendra, spread around them as far as the eye could see.

Eleusia had insisted on silence at first and had regularly stopped to listen intently for signs they were being followed, but they saw neither hide nor hair of a Lupine since leaving the cave. They had, however, heard battle sounds at the base of the ridge. Clearly, the Lupines had managed to track down another group of caravan guards who, like them, had managed to escape into the woods. The victorious baying of the Lupines made it clear which side had won, and the sound of revelry in their bloodlust sent shivers running along their spines.

Since then, the forest had been deathly quiet and, slowly but surely, their pace slackened as the threat of imminent attack diminished. Eventually, Torben began a whispered conversation with Antauros as he filled him in on scheme details, with Gwilym curtly correcting or adding details that Torben missed.

Stepping onto a large flat rock jutting from the edge of the ridge, they stopped to survey the landscape before them. From their vantage point, they could see the northeastern edge of the forest before the horizon.

'That's where we need to go.' Gwilym pointed, shielding his eyes from the bright sun and squinting into the distance. 'Gallenford lies on the northern edge of the forest.'

'That's all very well,' said Antauros, 'but how are we going to find our way? It's far too easy to lose our way in the trees.'

'Well, hopefully this will help us after all of the trouble that we went through to get it.' Eleusia reached into her pack and drew out the leather map case. Prying off the lid, she withdrew the parchment and unrolled it on the stone outcrop.

Torben peered at the yellowing document covered in thin spidery lines of black ink, most of which made no sense. Large parts of the map within the border of Bar-Dendra Forest were blank, but the area where the others focused their attention, was well relatively sketched out.

It was the first time that he'd ever seen a map; there'd been no need of them in Burndale. No one had ever ranged far enough to go beyond common knowledge regarding the roads and paths surrounding Bywater.

Gwilym's podgy finger blotted some map features. 'Here's Gallenford, about half a mile within the borders of Bar-Dendra.'

'Not a particularly safe place to settle a community,' Antauros commented.

'No, it wasn't,' Gwilym agreed. 'It was raided by Lupines nigh on a month.'

'Not a soul was left alive,' Eleusia added soberly. 'I passed through shortly after Gwilym, when I was on his trail. I barely made it out when the Lupines attacked. Their misfortune does mean that it will be easy for us to make our way about the town, provided that all of the raiders have moved on.'

'Where are we on this piece of paper?' Torben asked.

'Here.' Eleusia placed a dexterous finger on the map. 'This is the ridge and we should be roughly here, on the northern side.

There's no road access from the forest, so we'll have to make sure that we keep a steady course to the northeast.'

The map rolled up on its own as Eleusia let go of one end. She slotted it back into the tube and peered at the sky to get their bearings from the sun's position. With a murmur, she strode down the side of the ridge.

'Does that woman ever stop and rest?' Antauros grumbled, hefting his shield onto his back.

'Not from what I've seen,' Gwilym replied wryly. 'You should have thought about this before you demanded to join us.'

It was hard work getting down the side of the ridge. The ground around the trees was stony and shifted easily under their weight, causing them to cling to the vegetation around them as they descended. By the time they reached the bottom, they were out of breath and grateful to be on level ground again.

'Do you think anyone else from the caravan managed to escape?' Torben broke the silence as they walked.

'I doubt it,' Antauros answered. 'The horsemen and the Lupines between them will have made sure that there were no survivors.'

'We were lucky that there was another group of survivors so close to us last night,' Eleusia said. 'Otherwise, the Lupines may have continued to track us.'

'I'm sure I recognised the sigil that the knights wore,' Gwilym said quietly. 'I've seen the odd folk in Karpella bearing that sign: a white horse with golden mane and tail on crimson.'

'It's the sigil of the Kingdom of Sharisar,' Antauros explained. 'The knight who led them claimed to act in the name of their queen, and I have no reason to doubt that. There have been a lot of rumours drifting around that the peace between Aramore and Sharisar has been recently strained.'

'Well, clearly, that relationship is now a bit more than strained,' said Gwilym dryly.

'I've heard that Queen Alliona wasn't happy with their share of the victory spoils from when they fought with Aramore against Rahhail,' Antauros stated. 'Part of the bargain was that they'd agreed extended trading rights on Dazscor and Aramore's maritime passages through the Drexi Sea, amongst other things ... something Sharisar was in no way happy about.'

'Aramore has always been wary of conceding anything that might threaten their dominance of the Drexi Sea, hardly surprising that they didn't give Sharisar everything that they wanted,' Eleusia added. 'What's more, it's concerning that Sharisar has been able to move so quickly through Dazscor and Aramore territory, that they can claim to hold the Uplands of Ara and the Bar-Dendra without anyone in Karpella being aware.'

'Perhaps the more worrying part of this isn't that they've disagreed over spoils, or that Sharisar have gained so much ground so quickly, but the fact that at least one Lupine tribe is fighting for Queen Alliona now. War and strife between the kingdoms is a fairly regular occurrence, but peace between one kingdom and Lupines is unheard of!' Antauros snorted with disgust.

'Why would they willingly work with such barbarous creatures?' Torben asked with a frown.

'You can't deny that they're good fighters,' Gwilym said. 'Savage they may be, but they're ruthlessly effective at what they do.'

'Like as not, Sharisar is using the Lupines to cover their incursions into the territory of Aramore.' Antauros tugged his long mane-like beard thoughtfully. 'The increase in Lupine raids of late implies that Sharisar plans to take out any outlying settlements that could give them away ... if they intend to push for Karpella to the north, they'll want as many diversions as the Lupines can give them.'

'Is that why those knights were on the forest road?' Torben asked.

'Most probably. Raiding trading caravans in territory that's supposed to be right in the middle of the Kingdom of Dazscor and Aramore, and therefore relatively safe, is a good way to stir up discontent amongst the Guild Houses,' Antauros explained. 'No doubt Guild House representatives in Karpella will soon enough be banging on castle gates, demanding an audience with Emperor Hastel. The Guild Houses have been instrumental in turning populations against their rulers before, perhaps Queen Alliona thinks the same can happen in Karpella.'

Most of the political talk was lost on Torben but, despite this, he listened intently to the talk of the kingdoms, drinking in the information. The people of Bywater had been little concerned with the machinations of the kingdoms, and many of them would have struggled to tell you which kingdom Bywater and Burndale was actually claimed by, even if any of them had bothered to contest a claim on the area.

The conversation around him abruptly stopped as the party stepped from the cover of the trees into a large clearing choked with a thick mass of briars and brambles. In the centre of the clearing was a large stone tower, very much like the one he and Gwilym had climbed in Burndale. This tower, however, had clearly been through tough times. A huge chunk had been torn from the stonework, causing the viewing platform at the top to collapse, as if an explosion from within had nearly torn the tower apart. Littered amongst the foliage in the clearing were huge pieces of masonry, some which had been thrown right to the tree line.

Antauros whistled in surprise as they approached the ruin. 'What the hell happened here?'

'Who knows,' Eleusia answered quietly, 'but whatever it was, it was a long time ago.' She pointed to the interior of the tower, thick with ivy. Most of the masonry scattered across the open space were almost completely covered by vegetation.

In the shadow of the tower, Torben picked up the ragged remains of a book almost completely decomposed. Carefully peeling apart the remaining pages, he tried to decipher information that might reveal what the tower used to be, but he could only make out the occasional word. Dropping it, he made his way to Antauros, who was peering through the doorway, viewing the interior. There wasn't much to see. The door, almost completely rotted through, was propped upright by a wall of rubble that blocked the entrance to the inside of the tower.

'Ah-h.' Gwilym clapped his hands in delight as he peered over the map that he'd unrolled on a heap of rubble. 'This tower is marked on the map, and just beyond it is a stream that should lead us straight to Gallenford if we follow it.'

'Strange that this tower should be marked on the map,' Eleusia said, moving to stand behind Gwilym and look at the scroll. 'There can't be anything else around here for miles, and there's no road leading to it.'

'Perhaps it used to be visible from the town, before it collapsed that is,' Torben added.

'Maybe, but this tower is old … much older than the town I would guess,' Eleusia said. 'It still surprises me that anyone knew it was here.'

Using his fingers as callipers, Gwilym tried to estimate the distance, his tongue poking out of the side of his mouth as he did so. 'If we find the stream, then I reckon we'll be overlooking the town by nightfall.'

It didn't take them long to find the stream—or rather a stream bed. The channel was bone dry, but still clear enough that they could follow it through the forest, and as the bottom of the channel was clear of vegetation, they were able to walk down the middle, which allowed their pace to pick up considerably.

The channel followed the downward slope of the land as it fell away from the ridge behind them, and the land around them began to level when dusk drew in quickly around them. The forest ended abruptly as they drew closer to Gallenford and, from the tree line, they could make out the charred remains of the palisade wall that surrounded the town.

'We'll rest up here tonight,' Gwilym said. 'Just inside the cover of the trees. There's no point in searching for Meckel's hoard now; we'll see bugger all in this poor light. In any case, who knows what mischief the Lupines got up to inside the palisade. I want to know exactly where I'll be putting my feet.'

'Do you reckon they're still in there?' Torben's voice sounded nervous.

'No,' Eleusia replied. 'If there were still Lupines in the town, we'd be able to tell. They're not the most subtle of creatures when they're not hunting, and they rarely stay in one place for more than a few days, preferring to stay on the move.'

'What I'm worried about, Torben, is that they've been at work laying traps inside the town ... especially if they've laid out anything along the main thoroughfares,' Gwilym stated. 'I only know how to get around via the main roads in Gallenford, and Meckel's directions go by landmarks in plain sight. If the Lupines have booby-trapped the roads, then it'll make our life a lot harder.'

'What's the point in them doing that though? Surely they won't be back any time soon?' Torben asked anxiously.

'You'd be surprised.' Antauros' voice rumbled from the shadows above Torben's head. 'It's not unheard of for Lupines to send scouting parties back to check settlements they've raided haven't been resettled. Sometimes they set traps purely for sport, to see whether they can capture any stragglers they missed who've return to their homes. But, often, they'll use larger settlements like this one as a cache for their loot, and protect it with all manner of vicious set-ups.'

Retreating a little into the forest, the four hunkered down for the night in a small clearing. In the dim light, they weren't able to make out many details of the surroundings, but it seemed as good a place as any to rest.

There was much rustling as they tried to find comfortable places to rest. Every time Torben thought that he'd found a good position to sleep in, he'd become painfully aware of a twig or thorn pushing its way through his clothing and making sleep impossible. Gwilym was clearly having a similar problem.

'Argh,' he huffed. 'I might as well be trying to sleep on a bed of nails. Damn this blasted darkness!'

'Not as comfortable as your last stay in Gallenford I imagine?' Torben asked with a wry smile.

'When did you say that you passed through last?' Antauros asked as he peered through the gloom towards Gwilym's fidgeting figure.

'It must have been over a month, maybe a month and half ago by now.' He grunted as he pulled prickly vegetation from his backside. 'Why don't you ask Eleusia? The huntress probably has more idea of my movements than I do.'

'It seems strange that you didn't claim the Keystone last time you were here. It would have been damn sight easier—unless there's something that you're not telling us about this place?'

'You're right. I *could* have taken the Keystone when I was last here.' Gwilym's voice held a spiky edge. 'But I knew that I was being tracked … as I rightly suspected, by Eleusia, on Björn's orders. I thought it wise not to leave a trail going straight to the Keystone's hiding spot until I was sure that there'd be no unfriendly eyes in the vicinity. And I didn't want to be caught with the thing in my possession; otherwise, like as not, I'd be dead and Björn an infinitely large amount of gold richer.'

'But surely if you were trying to pick up Meckel's trail from the hoard, the faster you examined it the easier it would have been to find him?' Torben sounded confused.

'Quite right,' Eleusia chimed in. 'If we're supposed to pick up Meckel's trail from the heart of Gallenford after a tribe of Lupines have cavorted through it, then we might as well give up now. The task would be practically impossible.'

'Don't worry yourselves with these details,' Gwilym assured them. 'I know Meckel better than any creature alive, and I'm telling you that he hasn't been back. I asked after him in a few well-placed locations in the town and no one had seen hide nor hair of him, not even his own kin. If he's been through his hoard, I'll eat my seax!'

'Be careful what you wish for, dwarf,' Antauros growled. 'I'm liking this whole business less and less by the minute.'

'Believe me, the hoard will be untouched when we find it. Meckel would have known that I'd be hot on his heels and, as far as he knows, I could have had all of Björn's resources at my back to track him down with. Meckel was never one to get cornered somewhere and have to fight. He always picks his ground very carefully. He'll almost certainly be lying low somewhere, and the fact that the Lupines have torn Gallenford to shreds will, like as not, have kept him away for even longer than he intended.'

'Even so, you'll have a lot to answer for if this turns into a wild goose chase.' Antauros still sounded unconvinced.

'Gods, relax, won't you? Can't a dwarf get a bit of trust from his companions? Now, if you lot don't give over with the inquisition, then none of us will get any sleep.'

There was little conversation after that. They didn't dare light a fire, and as clouds rolled in, covering the moon and its feeble rays of light, there was little left to do but sleep. That said, they were all glad of the chance to rest.

13

The next morning, Gwilym woke them as dawn was creeping through the trees of Bar-Dendra. Silently, they gathered their things, ate a measly breakfast of barrack's biscuits, and made their way back towards the edge of the forest.

A thick mist had settled in the clearing between the tree line and Gallenford, rendering the distant buildings and palisade to little more than dark smudges on the horizon. There was no sign of life between them and the town, but each of them scanned the landscape for anything suspicious, any sign of movement.

Gwilym cleared his throat and took a step ahead. 'Here's the plan; we need to get to the town square and, from there, make our way to a tanner's yard at the back of a public house called the … errm … errm.' He ran a hand from his temple to the end of his short ponytail, racking his brain for the finer details of the directions Meckel had confided in him.

'Well, this bodes favourably,' Antauros muttered, watching Gwilym's thoughtful expression. 'Our guide can't even remember the directions.'

'It's in here somewhere.' Gwilym tapped his forehead. 'I'll know the place when I see it. I've visited the place many times when I've passed through Gallenford.'

'But you've been in so many taverns in your time, that they blur into one?' Torben asked with a grin.

'Something like that, I guess. In any case, the name's of no consequence as long as I can get us to the right area.'

'The right area?" Antauros asked with a snort. 'If the town is like any other in this area, there could be any number of taverns and public houses on the street. We're pushing our luck entering a town sacked by Lupines so soon after they passed through. We shouldn't push our luck even further by spending the whole day scouring every abandoned drinking hole in this forsaken place!'

'I agree, but it's hard to get the facts straight in my head when you're wittering on!'

'The Hammer & Tongs,' Eleusia said.

'What? How on earth do you know that?' Gwilym exclaimed.

'The Hammer & Tongs is the public house that you stayed in when you passed through last,' Eleusia replied with a smirk. 'When I was on your trail, I tracked you to that place, and the barman confirmed that a dwarf of your description had stayed there two nights gone.'

'How can you be sure the man meant Gwilym?' Torben asked.

'Let's just say that he gave a very colourful description of our friend here.'

'As entertaining as I'm sure his illustration was,' Gwilym cut in, 'we should keep ourselves focused. Once we get inside the palisade, we need to have our wits about us. The Lupines may have moved on, but who knows what may have moved *in*. If we're lucky, there'll only be a few stray dogs wandering around.'

'And if we're not?' Torben queried.

'Then we'd better watch each others' backs.' Antauros hefted the shield onto his arm, readying to move out.

The clearing remained silent as the party jogged lightly through the long grass that had grown up amongst the forgotten fields and paddocks of Gallenford. The dense mist pressed claustrophobically, even in the open spaces they hastened across.

As the dark shapes of the town became more defined the closer they came to the palisade wall, Torben grew increasingly aware of the eerie silence that was broken only by the sound of their movements. He had to remind himself that they were approaching what had been a settlement, but the lack of noise and the oppressive mist made him think he was approaching something more akin to a graveyard than a place where people had once worked, traded, lived. The feeling was emphasised when a huddled silhouette appeared from the mist before them, lying chillingly still.

The grass had grown so tall, it almost completely obscured the figure of the girl lying curled up on her side. The dark blue dress she wore was stained dark at the neckline, where her brown hair concealed the fatal wound. A cloud of flies buzzed into the air, sensing the party's presence as they passed; with them came the horrific stench of decay rolling from the girl's body. Torben gagged, turning his head and covering his mouth and nose with the sleeve of his coat to protect himself from the smell and sight. The others kept on walking, resolutely not looking at the crumpled body as they made their way towards the palisade. Staggering, Torben couldn't help but look back at the corpse disappearing into the mist. His gaze was met by milky eyes and death's lifeless stare. Shaking his head to dispel the image of the girl, he broke into a shambling run to catch up with Antauros and Gwilym, who were surveying the town through a hole punched in the palisade.

'You don't look well, lad,' Gwilym muttered darkly.

'Aye, well I wasn't expecting to see … you know.'

'Get used to it.' Antauros put one of his massive hands on Torben's shoulders. 'Sadly, I imagine that we'll see a lot of that within these walls.'

There was soft whistling from the other side of the palisade and Gwilym took a step forward, beckoning Torben and Antauros to follow. 'That's the signal!'

Stepping over charred timbers from the palisade, Torben

found himself standing in a narrow street lined with brick houses, whose roofs had collapsed and showed telltale signs of fire damage.

Eleusia stood a few steps away, her loaded crossbow in the crook of her arm. 'So far, so good,' she whispered. 'The main road is this way.'

They moved swiftly and silently along the palisade, avoiding the houses on the other side of the street and keeping watchful eyes on the darkened windows and doors they passed. The street was littered with broken furniture and all manner of household items thrown from within as Lupines searched for spoils. Here and there, sprawled amongst the buildings, were the bodies of Gallenford's inhabitants.

Before them appeared the towers and walkway of the town gate—or what was left of it. The large wooden gate doors swayed back and forth in the breeze, the crossbar that had once secured them hanging limply, shattered and splintered. Immediately around the gatehouse lay a large number of bodies, most wearing the crude, hardened leather armour of Gallenford's Town Watch. The occasional Lupine body dotted the dead. Most of the watchmen had fallen protecting the gate, but the ragged line of corpses that lay along the road indicated they'd not held out long before their bravery had broken.

Skirting around the side of the massacre, Eleusia led them onto the main street and they made their way slowly along the thoroughfare. Every now and again, she'd stop and examine the ground, watching and listening for signs of movement, or any signs that the way forward was a trap.

Despite the fact that they appeared to be the only living entities in the settlement, Torben couldn't help but feel as if he were being watched. Occasionally, he swore that he could see a figure from the corner of his eye following them or looking down from one of the many windows that lined the street. Every time he'd turn to spot the figure, however, all he'd see was

Antauros bringing up the rear. Still, the feeling made him decidedly uncomfortable.

Torben clearly wasn't the only one to think this. Eleusia kept stopping the group so that she could scan surroundings, clearly looking for a sign of their imaginary footpad, but no one, or nothing, made itself known.

Must be my mind playing tricks on me, Torben thought as they stood for a moment in the shadow of a large shop. Eleusia peered into the gloom of the interior. She shook her head; like Torben, she tried to convince herself that her imagination was getting the better of her. 'I'm sure I saw something move in there,' she muttered.

'Come on, don't get jumpy on us.' Gwilym's jaunty whisper seemed obtrusively loud in the quiet street.

She turned and glowered before leading them further into Gallenford.

Thankfully, the road ahead was clear and they made good time through the town. Soon the road opened up into the main square. The space was dominated by a small grove of pine trees surrounding a stone altar covered in a swirling pattern of runes. The square was also full of bodies. Small bands of city watch lay where they'd been cut down trying to keep the Lupines out of the square. The majority of the corpses, however, were of women and children. The Lupines had spared no one.

The air in the square was choked with the heavy, sickly-sweet smell of rotting flesh. Torben paled and Antauros bowed his head, his expression and tone sad. 'This is where they made their last stand.'

'Aye, well there's not much that we can do for them now,' Gwilym said, scanning the streets on the other side of the square, seeking the one they needed to take. 'We need Blacksmith's Lane and from what I can remember, it's on the other side of the grove. Let's get moving. Hanging around here is giving me the creeps. Eleusia?'

She was staring intently down the road from where they'd

come, her eyes flitting from door to door. She had instinctively raised her crossbow to her shoulder, the fingers of her right hand hovering over the trigger.

"I said, let's go!"

'Did you see it?' she asked in a hushed tone.

'What? See what?' He sounded impatient.

'There was a figure behind us. I only saw it for a split second and then it was gone. I'm sure of it.'

'Bloody hell, Eleusia. There's no one there … and if there is, we shouldn't stick around here, waiting for them to jump us. We need to keep moving. The sooner we get what we came for, the sooner we can leave this place.' With that, Gwilym started to pick his way through the mass of bodies, holding a hand over his face to keep the cloying smell of decay from his nose.

'I don't like this,' she said with a frown. 'We're being watched, I know it.'

'What do you think is following us?' Antauros crouched down and spoke softly in Eleusia's ear.

'I don't know,' she replied, 'but whatever it is, it's very good at keeping hidden. Too good. It's as if every time I think I've spotted it, the air swallows—him, her, or whatever—up.'

Eleusia, Antauros and Torben slowly made their way across the square after Gwilym. The dwarf was waiting for them in the shadow of the pine trees. As they joined him, he pointed across the square to a street marked by a large wooden anvil swinging from a house.

'That's the street we want,' he affirmed. 'Now, if I remember correctly, the tavern shouldn't be too far down the street, so keep your eyes peeled.'

As they turned to cut through the grove, Torben instinctively turned when he felt an unwelcome gaze behind him. He spun, shield up to cover his body and spear in the guard position, ready to receive an attack. There no one creeping up on them, but from the other side of the square he swore that he could see a figure, hooded and cloaked, standing in the middle of the street.

He and the figure opposite him stood transfixed, staring at each other. He couldn't make out details other than the voluminous cloak encasing the body. He opened his mouth to shout for the others, but before he could do so, the air around the figure rippled and they were gone. Torben blinked, rubbed his eyes with a sleeve, and looked back where the figure had been, but there was nothing there, save the bodies of the dead that hadn't moved from their resting places.

He shuffled back a few steps and bolted into the grove after the others, looking to return to the protection of the group.

The grove was lined with neatly shaped flagstones that covered the ground around the altar. They'd once have been pure white marble, but now they were stained by the blood of several people who'd either died trying to protect the sacred area or had sought refuge against the tide of death flowing through the town. A figure sprawled near the altar must have been a priestess of sorts. The woman was wearing long white robes embroidered with flowing patterns created in silver thread.

Torben had seen similar robes that the Bywater priest had worn on particular feast days—not that he'd attended the ceremonies at the Gods' Grove particularly often. The last time he'd stepped foot in the Gods' Grove, north of the village, had been for his father's funeral. His mother had been burned, with little ceremony, on Amos' farm. The old priest had made it clear that he'd not bless the passing of the 'witch' that had brought plague to the village in the Grove, lest her body pollute the sacred space and anger the Gods even more.

Gathering on the other side of the grove, the group darted into the shadow of the building that lay at the beginning of Blacksmith's Lane. Like all the other streets they'd passed through, Blacksmith's Lane was eerily quiet, occupied only by the bodies of the dead. At the end of the street, the palisade wall was visible in the distance, the white tips of sharpened wooden spikes standing out against the horizon.

It didn't take them long to spot the sign of the Hammer & Tongs public house swinging from chains outside a large house; it looked as if it had mostly escaped the blaze the Lupines had set in the town. As they drew closer, Eleusia broke into a jog and positioned herself on the far side of the closed door, crossbow held at the ready, lest anything be lurking inside. Antauros hefted his shield and stood directly in front of the door, covering Eleusia's body with the shield's immense bulk. He signalled to Torben, who carefully levered the half-open door with the butt of the spear.

They held their breaths as the door creaked open, and then visibly tensed when the door swung completely open. It took them a few seconds to adjust their eyes to the gloomy interior, but all they could see within were dusty tables and a long bar stretching into the gloom.

Gwilym entered slowly, seax drawn, and sniffed. 'It may look shabbier than I remember, but at least there's no smell of decay. This way.'

Antauros ducked under the building lintel after Gwilym and the room grew visibly darker as his huge frame blocked the light from the doorway. Stepping towards the door, Torben saw a flicker of movement high in his field of vision. His head snapped around, his gaze fixing on a first-floor window in the house opposite, but all he could see was the fluttering of tattered curtains. He turned back to the door and saw Eleusia staring at the same spot, her crossbow lined up with the window.

'Something doesn't feel right about this place,' Torben said uneasily as he stepped through the doorway.

'You're right,' Eleusia said, following. 'For starters, there's hardly a gust of wind about today.' As she entered, she swung the door shut after them and dropped the crossbar into place. 'Better safe than sorry,' she said to Torben, still standing in the taproom. 'I want to know that our backsides are safe.'

'Aye, sounds good to me. The others have gone out this way.' He pointed to an open door at the end of the taproom. Beyond it lay a small dishevelled kitchen, and past that was a long thin kitchen garden that snaked towards a large stone wall. There were no houses backing onto the Hammer & Tongs and as Torben entered the garden, he realised why.

The whole garden reeked of stale urine, which wafted over the wall from the tanner's yard. His eyes watered from the intrusive stench as he made his way to the bottom of the garden, where Antauros was giving Gwilym a leg up over the wall.

'Not long now, you'll be glad to hear,' Gwilym grinned as he poked his head over the wall to check if the coast was clear.

'Good, 'cause this place reeks,' Torben grumbled.

'Why would anyone pick a place like this to hoard valuables?' Antauros grunted beneath the strain of Gwilym's weight.

'The stench keeps people away.' Eleusia spoke through a large sprig of lavender she'd liberated from the garden and was holding to her nose to mask the smell.

'Well, Meckel was a bit of a smelly bugger himself,' Gwilym said wryly. 'He probably didn't notice it.'

Satisfied that the coast was clear, he dropped over the wall and disappeared out of sight. Antauros cupped his hands so that he could boost Torben over and virtually catapulted the young man over the obstacle. Torben had to windmill his arms to regain his balance when he landed on the other side, and narrowly avoided falling into a stinking tanning pit.

Eleusia dropped down nimbly beside him and then Antauros heaved himself over the wall and made the ground shudder when he landed.

The tanner's yard was pockmarked with several large pits, most still full of urine, with the rawhides of various animals still soaking in the noxious mixture. Dotted in between the vats were small brick sheds, and it was towards one of these that they could see Gwilym striding.

The three picked up their pace to catch up with him and, when they finally drew level, he was squatting near the base of the shed and tapping the lower bricks with the pommel of his seax. As he tapped, he began to shuffle along the base of the wall, muttering to himself.

'What's he doing?' Torben whispered, not wanting to break his concentration.

'Checking for cavities in the foundations,' Eleusia answered. 'If Meckel hid his hoard in the fabric of the building, then Gwilym will find it soon enough.'

He made his way along their side of the building and turned the corner, tapping the brickwork constantly. The others followed, wary of the fact that the sound of their footsteps might interfere with Gwilym's detective work.

As he disappeared around the side of the building, he stopped dead in his tracks, then suddenly sprinted out of sight. A moment later, came a strangled cry.

'Gwilym? Gwilym?' Torben called out anxiously and, not hearing a response, ran after the dwarf, all caution forgotten. Turning the corner, he saw Gwilym crouching, head bowed, over a body lying spread-eagled on the ground.

As Torben closed the distance between them, he could see the corpse was that of a dwarf, much slimmer than Gwilym and with a shock of bright red hair. Meckel.

A crash of footsteps sounded behind as Eleusia and Antauros rounded the corner of the storehouse. They'd clearly been expecting trouble; Antauros' shield was up and Eleusia had her crossbow raised to her shoulder. They relaxed when they saw Torben standing a respectful distance from the nearby mourning figure.

'He's dead then,' Antauros said softly, slinging his shield back over his shoulder and sliding his war-hammer into its belt loop.

'Looks like he had the same idea as us.' Eleusia pointed to the side of the building. The brickwork next to Meckel's body had been hastily prized from its place, revealing a small space in the building's foundations, which had clearly been the hiding place of his hoard.

The hoard, however, was strewn about the corpse. All manner of silver and bronze coins peeked up from the tanning yard dirt and, here and there, were large lumps of unrecognisable metal that had begun to weather and dull under the open sky.

Approaching Gwilym, Torben placed a hand on his shoulder. 'I'm sorry. It must be hard seeing him like this, given the two of you were partners for so long.'

'Aye, it is,' he said quietly. 'We got into all sorts of scrapes together ... so many times when one of us nearly bought it. It's surreal now, looking at him and knowing that his luck ran out, that one day mine might run out, too. The bugger must have tried to rescue his stash before the Lupines overran the town.'

'He needn't have worried that much.' Antauros's booming voice shattered the solemn atmosphere. 'They wouldn't have bothered rooting for a hole like us. And they certainly wouldn't bother scrabbling around on their hands and knees for the sake of a few pieces of silver.'

'Yes, but there shouldn't just be a few pieces of silver here.' Eleusia scanned the ground, moving methodically along the side of the building and looking for anything out of the ordinary.

'Come on, Gwilym,' Torben said, pulling the dwarf off the ground and back to his feet. 'There's nothing you can do for him now, and we need to move quickly. I don't like it here; we're too exposed.'

'Well said,' Eleusia said briskly. Drawing her knife, she bent over the body of Meckel, rolled him onto his back and made delicate incisions along the lining of his clothes and pockets.

Torben felt Gwilym tense as she went to work, but he moved no further when Torben squeezed his shoulder in warning. 'Come on, let's look over here,' he said, steering the dwarf to scattered coins and trinkets a few feet away.

They searched every inch of ground around the building, silence broken only by the occasional clink of a coin as it was thrown to one side or the soft tearing of Meckel's clothes as Eleusia continued checking every fold of fabric for hidden items. Torben forced himself to inspect the coins strewn at the edge of one of the tanning pits that lay against the building, but to no avail. He coughed and spat as he walked back to Gwilym and Antauros, now gathered around Meckel's body, watching Eleusia finish.

She sheathed the knife as she cast aside the mutilated remains of one of Meckel's shoes and let out a groan of frustration. 'He had a lot of coin hidden on him,' she said. 'Nearly twenty gold pieces and Gods know how much silver. He probably wouldn't have been able to run away if he'd had the chance.' She gestured the sizeable pile of coins next to the corpse she'd collected. 'No sign of anything else. I gather you've had no joy, either?'

Antauros snorted. 'Nothing but worn coins and slag metal.'

'There was nothing over there, either,' Torben said, leaning heavily on his spear.

'It must be *somewhere*.' Suddenly, Gwilym jumped towards the wall and ran his hands along the inside of the hiding place, desperation coming over him.

'Face it, Gwilym, we need to think of what to do next. Perhaps he had another hiding spot that you don't know about?' Eleusia picked over the pile of coins next to the body, and winced when she bit into one of the large gold coins.

'If that's the case, then it could be anywhere,' Torben said in exasperation. 'If there's another spot, it might not even be in Gallenford!'

'No, it's here. I know that the Keystone is *here*.' Gwilym had moved towards the tanning pit, scanning the ground they'd already searched, inspecting every coin and object he found with fierce intensity.

'How do you know it's here?' Antauros called after Gwilym.

'We can't just go on your gut instinct anymore. Eleusia's right; we need to regroup and think over our options.'

'This isn't just a gut instinct,' Gwilym snapped, turning to regard them. 'I know it's here because Meckel told me that it was, and clearly he's in no fit state to take it anywhere else now, is he?"

'What did you say?'

Slowly, Eleusia rose to her feet and stepped towards Gwilym, who continued to stare, horrified by what he'd just said.

'How could he have told you it was here? You said the last time that you'd seen him was when he stole the blasted Keystone in the first place.'

'Ah, yes well, what I meant was, erm-mm.' Gwilym paused and shook his head. 'Oh, bugger it! I guess it doesn't matter now, does it?'

'*What* doesn't matter?' Antauros growled.

'Meckel and I came up with the idea of the scheme together.' Avoiding eye contact, Gwilym spoke to the wall. 'We were tired of being pushed around by Björn ... reckoned that the only way that we'd be released from service was in a coffin. Like you said Eleusia, Björn had become too unpredictable; we couldn't go around looking over our shoulders the whole time, waiting for when he'd snap and lay us low ... for whatever stupid reason popped into his head.

'When Björn sent Meckel and me to find the Keystone, I was glad of going off on a wild goose chase. It meant we'd be out of harm's way for a good long while, even if it felt like a waste of time to me. Anyway, when we reached Makesh and saw the Keystone for the first time, Meckel and I both knew this was the chance we'd been waiting for. Had it been up to me, I'd have made the deal with the priest and slipped away with the Keystone on our way back to Karpella. Annoyingly, Meckel just snapped and attacked them, and what was I to do but help a comrade in arms?

'After the priest and his men were dead, we came up with the plan. Meckel would hide the Keystone here and I'd head back to Björn tell him that Meckel had lost it and done a runner. We hoped that Björn would buy the tale and send me to track down Meckel but, sadly, that wasn't the case.

'I'd arranged to meet Meckel in the woods outside of Bywater. He'd passed through your neck of the woods before, Torben, with a trading caravan, and knew that no one would look for us there. When he didn't show up, I guessed he'd been detained, or that I'd got the location of the meeting wrong, which is why I came into the village and bumped into you. Hell, I was half hoping that I'd really screwed up and that Meckel would be waiting at the top of the valley where that godforsaken tower was, which was partly why I suggested we go that way. When you told us about what had happened here, Eleusia, I guessed that the worst had probably befallen him.' He glanced over. 'I guessed right. He must have come to rescue the Keystone in case the Lupines discovered it, but he wasn't fast enough'

'So you've been lying to us all this time? Did you not think that it would have been useful if we'd known all of this to begin with?' Eleusia asked angrily.

'I didn't know whether I could trust you, especially given the fact that you brought me back to Björn in the first place … and once we got underway, I didn't know how many unwelcome ears might have been listening.'

'And you expect us to trust you after this?' Antauros took a long stride towards Gwilym, throwing the dwarf into his shadow.

'I hardly think the details matter now, do they? The situation is still the same. We have no Keystone and if Meckel had been alive, he'd have been a damn sight more useful than you!' Gwilym's eyes narrowed as he stared at Antauros.

'Ha. If you ask me, we're better off only having the one thieving dwarf in our company.'

'Watch your tongue! I would have given my life for him … and he gave his trying to keep our plan alive.'

'Thieves and cutthroats will always stick together.' Antauros met Gwilym's gaze and stared coldly back.

'Aye you're right, we do.' Gwilym's voice was full of venom. 'We steal and kill to survive, but only because those we kill would do the same to us given half the chance. Unlike you, we don't kill for sport!'

'What?' Antauros took another stride towards Gwilym and loomed over him.

'You heard me! I'd kill someone who stood between me and what I wanted, or someone who tried to kill me as long as they could defend themselves, but some of us draw the line at killing bairns and old folk who couldn't lift a sword if their life depended on it.'

'You should mind what you're saying before you sling accusations around.'

'And why's that, Antauros? Everyone knows what you did in that village in the name of duty. What did the poor villagers do to be slaughtered? Did one of them speak the truth to you as well? Though I guess some of them would have been too young to say anything to you.'

'Shut it!'

'Why? I thought we were being honest with each other? I've shown you how much of a filthy crook I am, so I only think it's right that we all know how much of a coldhearted murdering bastard you are!'

What next unfolded happened so quickly that Torben's head reeled. One minute Gwilym was squaring up to Antauros and the next the minotaur had picked him up by the throat and pinned him against the storehouse wall. 'You know *nothing* of what happened,' Antauros roared.

Eleusia and Torben sprang forwards, trying to separate Antauros and Gwilym and stop the situation from spiralling out of control.

'Let go of him,' Eleusia yelled, trying to drag one of his burly arms from Gwilym's neck.

The dwarf was looking decidedly red in the face and he lashed at Antauros, trying to kick him in the chest, even though he was suspended several feet above the ground.

'Give over, Antauros, ple-ease,' Torben grunted, trying to wrestle Gwilym from his grip.

'Get off me, all of you! He's tried my patience long enough,' Antauros snapped.

Some sense must have returned Antauros for he suddenly dropped Gwilym and shrugged off Torben and Eleusia, still hanging onto his arms in the vain attempt to restrain him. The sudden movement tipped Torben off balance and he staggered back, tripping over his own feet and falling next to the edge of a tanning pit.

He lay dazed for a few seconds, his head and shoulders hanging precipitously over the trough of fetid liquid. The fumes from the pit choked him, creeping into his mouth and nose.

Scrambling over the edge, he knelt on all fours and retched, trying to be free of the stench. He couldn't make out any words behind him, but did hear Gwilym's voice rise with indignity as he continued to argue with Antauros, and Eleusia's voice attempting to calm them both down.

As his head cleared, he noticed something glinting at the bottom of the dark tanning pit—a flash of silver.

14

Eleusia stood between Antauros and Gwilym, a hand on each, trying to stop them from scuffling. In reality, she knew she could do little to stop Antauros from laying hands on Gwilym again if he wanted. Both she and Torben had been shrugged off the minotaur as easily as if he'd brushed away two flies. Torben was still on the ground a few feet away. Out of the corner of her eye, she could see him slowly rise onto both hands and knees, and then pause. He must have knocked his head on the ground, she thought.

Gwilym was still struggling to get at Antauros, who was content to stand, arms crossed over his massive torso, and hurl insults at the furious dwarf straining to get around Eleusia and throw punches.

'Gwilym, calm down,' she exclaimed. 'It's no use. You can't beat him, you've tried that. Why not use words instead of fists? You're much better at that.'

'I could and would beat him in a fair fight, if he could deign to bring himself up to that level,' Gwilym snorted and gritted his teeth.

'Ha! Like you've ever been in a fair fight. I thought you just lurked in shadows and waited for someone else to do your job for you?' Antauros retorted.

'Why you lug-headed brute!' Gwilym managed to worm his way round Eleusia, slipping out of her grip and lunging towards Antauros, fists raised and ready to strike. His attack was thwarted, however, as she spun and grabbed the dwarf around the middle to hold him in place.

Antauros chuckled as he watched Gwilym, his angry face purple and his green eyes filled with hate.

'Torben, I could really do with a hand here!' Eleusia glanced in his direction to see whether he'd risen to his feet, but the young man was leaning over a tanning pit, his gaze fixed on the filthy liquid. A second later, he plunged his hand into the stinking pit.

'What the hell are you doing? Torben, get your hand out of that!'

Gwilym and Antauros turned to see what Torben was doing, forgetting their quarrel. They all watched in disgust as Torben withdrew his hand and studied whatever it was that he had rescued from the depths.

'I think that knock you gave him addled his brains,' Eleusia said to Antauros.

'Sometimes I forget my own strength,' the minotaur said grimly, studying Torben with a worried expression.

Gwilym took a step towards Torben, his head cocked, trying to see what he was holding. Sensing the dwarf, he looked up and held out his hand. 'I think I've found something.'

At first, it looked like Torben was holding another lump of scrap metal, but as he held up the object in the light and opened his hand, Gwilym could see what it was: *the Keystone*.

It was large, round and flat, almost as big as Torben's hand, and it was covered in a network of intricate runes and symbols that ebbed and flowed across the dull silver. Swirling across the Keystone's edge was the figure of a serpent devouring its own tail. The object appeared to emanate power, and Gwilym could saw the same fascination in Torben's eyes that he had seen in Meckel's when the priest had first revealed the Keystone to them.

'Gods alive,' Gwilym gasped. He took it from Torben's outstretched hand and turned the object over and over, watching runes ripple across the surface, the serpent around the edge writhing and snarling in the light. 'Meckel, you little bugger,' Gwilym said in a hushed tone. 'He must have thrown it into the tanning pit to save it from the Lupines; even they'd have enough brains to know that this thing is worth its weight in gold.'

'What do the runes say?' Antauros stood behind Gwilym, Eleusia at his side, the gleaming silver disc reflected in the black of his eyes.

'There's no language that I know of,' Eleusia stated. 'Perhaps it's the incantation that we have to use to get into the vault?'

'No. The priest said that all we had to do was place the Keystone on the plinth in the entrance chamber to the vault, and it would open,' Gwilym explained. 'I wouldn't worry about what the runes say; it's probably just archaic gibberish.'

'For once, I'm inclined to agree with you,' Antauros said. 'I heard that old sorcerers were obsessed with making their incantations and spells as visually complex as possible to dazzle the uninitiated.'

Torben had now climbed to his feet and was wiping the last of the stinking liquid off his hand. The Keystone did not look any worse for wear given it had spent weeks steeped in the stagnant water and malodorous urine of the tanning pit. The fine hairs on his neck prickled as he felt that horribly familiar sensation that he was being watched. Gazing away from the Keystone, he scanned the area. 'We should leave,' he said casually. 'We can't afford to stand here all day and gawp.'

'Why? What is it? What do you see?' Eleusia's head snapped up, a shadow of worry crossing her face.

'Rain, coming in from the south.'

Antauros looked at the sky and pointed to a bank of threatening clouds swiftly making their way towards them, the sound of rain drifting on the wind.

'Good spot. Let's get back inside the tavern. I don't fancy getting soaked to the skin,' Gwilym said.

Eleusia exchanged a wary glance with Torben. Unlike Antauros, she knew what Torben had meant.

Wrapping the Keystone in cloth produced from his pocket, Gwilym led the group towards the back wall of the Hammer & Tongs garden. He clapped Torben on the back as they walked. 'Well done, lad; you may have saved us all.'

In the few minutes it took them to walk across the tanner's yard, the rain began to hammer down, the rhythmic drumming of the teeming wetness on the ground and surrounding rooftops filling the air.

By the time they'd clambered over the garden wall and caught the shelter of the Hammer & Tongs, they were wringing wet. Outside, the percussive clap of thunder echoed around the ruined buildings of Gallenford.

'This doesn't look like it's going to clear anytime soon,' Torben said, peering out the kitchen door.

'Night is fast approaching as well,' Antauros added. 'There's little point trying to leave now. We'd only get colder and wetter than we already are, and we wouldn't get far with the amount of daylight left.'

'The upstairs rooms looked good enough from out in the yard,' Eleusia said. 'They'd be as good a place as any to barricade ourselves in for the night.'

'Sounds like a good enough plan to me, and it seems such a shame to cut our sightseeing trip short now that we've got what we came for,' Gwilym said with a wry smile.

'Fine. Gwilym, Antauros, you wait here and keep watch in the garden whilst Torben and I check upstairs … wouldn't want to stumble into any nasty surprises now, would we?'

Eleusia led Torben cautiously back through the tavern

taproom, pausing to triple-check that the barricade on the front door and windows still held firm. Satisfied that no one, nothing, had tried to force entry and follow them to the tanner's yard, she crept up the stairs to the second level. Torben followed close behind, his spear ready.

Up there, they found a large room with a single open door leading off it. The room was dusty, cold, and full of tables and chairs, much like the taproom downstairs. Eleusia navigated her way between tables, approaching the half-open door at the back with her crossbow raised. With a jerk of her head, she indicated to Torben where she wanted him to stand and, once he was in position on the other side of the door, she slowly pushed it open with her foot.

The room beyond was some kind of storeroom; most of it was taken up by rows of shelving and a large stack of barrels against the far wall. As the two of them stepped in, they could hear Gwilym's voice drift up from the kitchen below, punctuated occasionally by Antauros' bass rumble.

Now that he was fully in the room, Torben could see a single bed and a small table nestled amongst the shelves, near a fireplace. There was only one window and it was shuttered closed.

'Well this seems like a good place to spend the night,' Eleusia said, relaxing and letting her crossbow rest in the crook of her arm.

'Aye, it's positively cosy,' Torben said. 'And it looks as if we won't struggle to find something to eat in here.'

The shelves supported various jars and small barrels of vegetables and preserves, and had clearly served as the larder for the tavern's kitchen, as well as staff quarters.

'I'll go and fetch the other two. Why don't you get a fire going? The shutter looks good enough to stop any light from leaking and giving us away, so we might as well get dry and have a warm meal.'

Torben leant his arms against the wall and, fishing around his pack for a tinderbox, knelt by the hearth and began to build a fire from a large pile of neatly chopped logs and kindling stacked to one side. Below, he could hear Eleusia holding a muffled conversation with Gwilym and Antauros, and then the scraping of furniture being moved. *Must be securing the kitchen door, better safe than sorry.*

When the others entered the room, Torben's face was illuminated by the growing glow of the fire. He'd hung his overcoat over one of the nearby shelves, and his boots were already drying in front of the hearth.

'Looks like someone has made themselves comfortable,' Antauros said as he stooped into the room and dropped his pack next to Torben's by the fire.

'Well, you know, no point in wasting heat.' Torben pushed the sodden mop of curls from his eyes and grinned at Antauros, who was steadying himself against the wall as he pulled off his massive boots and dropped them with a heavy clunk onto the hearth.

'Give us a hand with this, Eleusia,' Gwilym wheezed as he lifted a heavy box to brace against the door. 'It looks like these two intend to be no more help whatsoever.'

'I think we deserve some rest now that we're at the end of this wild goose chase,' Antauros said, plucking an apple from one of the shelves and tossing it to Torben.

'We've still got a long way to go yet.' Eleusia stepped into the glow of the firelight, her face flushed from the effort of bracing the door, and took a seat on the bed, which sagged visibly. She stretched out her hands to the fire and gazed into the flames. 'We need to work out what to do next—how we get back to Karpella, how we break into the castle. We also need to work out how to find the treasure vault … and then there's the matter of the treasure. There are so many things that could go wrong and that's before we've even made it back to the city. Between the

Lupines and those troops from Sharisar, I'd be surprised if every inch of the countryside isn't being watched.'

'It's not all that much doom and gloom,' Torben said. 'I value my chances out there with you three more than if I were travelling with an entire army! And back in Karpella, we've got the base at Ivy House to work from, and hopefully the Madame managed to gather some intelligence and built some connections for us in our absence.'

'True enough, but there's a lot still in our way. It takes years to build the kind of connections we'll need to slip into the castle … and we need to *survive* long enough to get back to Ivy House. Who knows what plans have been set against us in our absence?' Eleusia continued to stare gloomily into the fire.

'I take it that Björn was not overly happy with your escape from the city?' Antauros asked.

'Not exactly, no.'

'Enough of this pessimism! I say we relax a little and enjoy our success. I'll warrant that it's a long and uncertain road that we're trekking, but now that we have the Keystone, we're a damn sight further along than we once were!' Gwilym stepped into the middle of the room and unwrapped the Keystone from the concealing fabric, and held it out to the others.

In the warm orange glow of the fire, the runes drifted lazily across the polished surface, as if relaxing in the warmth emanating from the flames.

'Just think. This bizarre chunk of metal is what will make the four of us richer than our wildest dreams. We'll be the envy of all but Sarper himself! And, if nothing else, I found something that will help take the edge off a little.' Tucking the Keystone and its wrapping into a pocket, Gwilym ducked behind a shelf and rolled out a large barrel. 'I did think to myself that there was a distinct lack of beer in this tavern, but it would seem that this is one barrel that the Lupines didn't get their hands on. Now, who'd like a drink?'

'Now, that's a good idea,' Antauros said, helping Gwilym heave the barrel onto a chair.

The four bustled around the cramped room, searching shelves for anything they could put to use. Soon, Torben was slicing vegetables into a large pot. Eleusia wrestled with the lid of a barrel of salted beef before allowing Antauros to smash the lid with his war-hammer.

There was a triumphant shout from the other end of the room as Gwilym knocked a dusty tap into the barrel of beer and filled large wooden tankards to the brim.

For what felt like the first time in years, Torben began to feel safe and even happy. The effect from the ale began drifting through his body, spreading warmth from his toes to his fingertips. By the time he dipped a chunk of bread into the steaming broth from the pot, his head was filled with the golden, warming glow of the good life. 'So,' he said, a slight slur creeping into his voice. 'What will you all do with your share of the treasure?'

'That's easy.' Gwilym set his bowl down in front of the fire and leaned towards them. 'I'd buy myself a ship and hire enough good men to crew her and sail away.'

'So you'd become a pirate?' Torben smiled to himself.

'No, I'd just roam the seas, probably carry out odd jobs, shipping and the like, I guess. I've never been the kind of fellow that can stay in one place. Wanderlust will never leave me, I reckon. Being able to set off on the open sea and wake up somewhere completely different every morning would be heaven!'

'I'm not sure I can imagine anything more disheartening,' Antauros said. 'I want to put down roots somewhere, buy land, start a family again. If I could, I'd lay down my arms right now and never take up the mercenary life for the rest of my allotted years.'

'Why don't you then?' Gwilym asked over the rim of his tankard. 'I'm sure most of the civilised world would breathe a sigh of relief when they found out that you'd laid down your war-hammer and taken up the plough.'

'Perhaps, but there are too many other people who think they have a score to settle with me,' Antauros replied. 'I can only set my weary bones down somewhere and call it home if I can afford to go somewhere isolated, with enough capital to invest in my safety and prosperity. There's not much chance of that happening on a mercenary's wage, especially when it isn't paid half the time.'

'What about you, Torben?' Gwilym turned his gaze to the young man, who sat close to the fire, his back against the bed. Eleusia was already curled up on the yellowing mattress, her chest rising up and down in time with slumber-heavy breaths.

'Huh, what is it?' Torben regarded Gwilym with half-closed, bleary eyes. He'd clearly been sleeping, like Eleusia.

'What would you do with your share?' Gwilym asked again.

'Oh, I don't know,' Torben murmured, his head nodding onto his chest.

'Looks like you won't be getting much more out of him,' Antauros chuckled.

'Aye well, he's had a hard time of things, the lad has; like as not, this is the safest he's felt for a long time.'

'He told me about what happened to his village. It was good of you to help him escape. I'm sure many people in your position would have bolted and left him there to die rather than risk helping another.'

'Maybe so, maybe so.'

Gwilym and Antauros sat in silence for a while, with only the sound of Torben and Eleusia's breathing and the crackling fire intruding on the quiet. Every now and again, one of them would take a long draft from their tankard.

'Now that we have the Keystone and we actually have a shot at pulling this off,' Gwilym said quietly, 'I was thinking that perhaps I owe you an apology for certain words and some actions that passed between us.'

'Like *all* our interactions, you mean?'

'Aye well, neither of us have had a particularly kind word to say about each other, have we?'

'I suppose not.'

'In my defence,' Gwilym said with a wry smile, 'until very recently, I was convinced that you would slaughter the three of us without a second thought. Though I'm glad to say that, so far, I've seen little of what people speak about in the stories told about you.'

'Well, well,' Antauros smiled broadly. 'I never thought that I'd hear you, of all people, say something like that. You must be getting soft!'

Indignant, Gwilym opened his mouth to reply to the jest, but before he could say anything, Antauros held out an arm towards the dwarf. 'Truce?'

'Truce.'

The minotaur and dwarf grasped forearms—Antauros' hand practically enveloping Gwilym's whole arm—and held each other's grip. As they slipped back into their seats, Gwilym reached over his shoulder and refilled his tankard from the barrel and then took Antauros' from the floor and topped it up, too.

'So, how many of the stories are true?'

'Well, I was where people said I was. Estair, the village was called. But I wasn't there in the name of duty.' Antauros took a long swig from his tankard and paused. He was staring deep into the fire; Gwilym could see the flames dance in his deep black eyes. 'Estair used to be my home. I led a prosperous life there on my few acres with my wife and daughter. I'd never once raised my fists in anger against any creature, and I thought that it would stay that way for the rest of my life.

'When the war between Aramore and Rahhail broke out, the village thought it was of little concern. Estair lay far to the south of Rahhail's border with Aramore, and we'd heard that most of the fighting was taking place in the north. Well, one day a small column of troops arrived at the village, not an uncommon occurrence. A large portion of Rahhail's army had already passed through on their way to reinforce the forces in the north. This time, however, the troops stayed. News had reached them, they said, of a spy tracked to our village, who was passing information to the Aramorians, helping them react to Rahhail's troop movements.

'At first, their captain contented himself with searching the village, politely and with little fuss; we were all cooperating. We just wanted them to up and leave as soon as they were satisfied. The longer that they searched without turning up anything, the angrier their captain became.

'His troops started arresting villagers at random and would question them for hours on end. They took me in one night and kept me for three days with their incessant questioning and accusations—how can we take your word for granted, how do we know you're not lying to us?

'Just after they let me go, things became violent. The people they'd been detaining appeared mutilated, half-dead in the streets. Our neighbour had his hands broken, several of his fingers cut off. He had been a carpenter, and a skilled one at that, but the Merchant Prince of Rahhail was overly suspicious and pushed his troops to keep beating us, torturing us.

'Several nights later the captain received orders from the Merchant Prince himself. Our little village had caused too much trouble, taken too many resources away from the war. If there was still a spy amongst us, then they certainly wouldn't leave alive, no one would.

'I tried to save my wife, my daughter. Told them to escape through the back of house whilst I held off the troops in our yard. Somehow, a fire was started, either a candle knocked over in the confusion or fire spilled out of the grate ... or maybe one of the soldiers started the blaze. I don't know. All I know is that they made me watch the house burn with my family still inside. Laughed at me and told me that if I'd only given up the spy, this non-existent phantom that they had imagined, then my family wouldn't be trapped inside that house … the other villagers would still be alive.

'I don't really remember what happened next. All I can recall clearly is seeing a veil of red pass over my eyes and the faces of the soldiers I killed that night. When morning broke, I was the only creature left alive in Estair, so I ran.

'Whenever I came across a group of Rahhail's soldiers, I threw myself at them, hoping that one of them would kill me and reunite me with those I'd lost. As it happened, I managed to make it all the way to the border and joined a group of mercenaries in the employ of the Kingdom of Dazscor and Aramore, people I thought had been my enemies.

'Rahhail's spy masters and spin-pedlars made out that what happened at Estair had been my doing—that I had slaughtered the villagers whilst their troops had valiantly tried to defend innocent lives. I wasted so much breath trying to convince people otherwise, I gave up. As long as I knew the truth, that could keep me going, so I thought.'

When Antauros finished speaking, Gwilym saw the glimmer of tears in his eyes, reflected by the firelight. Without saying another word, the minotaur stood and lay on the floor, drawing a blanket over himself and turning his back to the room.

Alone by the fire, Gwilym's eyes began to droop as he pondered what Antauros had said. Outside, the rain drummed against the shutters, but the warmth of the fire slowly but surely lulled him to sleep.

———

When Torben woke, the fire was burning low in the grate and casting the dimmest of light into the room, barely brightening the dark shadows enveloping the room. He had no idea what time it was, though he reckoned that it was still be night.

A thick silence filled the room, and no sound or light drifted through the cracks in the shuttered window. He rolled his neck, trying to ease the stiffness in his joints. He'd fallen asleep leaning against the hard bedframe and small aches had developed in most of his joints. He sat up and stretched, moving as quietly as he could for fear of waking the others. His back cracked in several places as he extended his spine, the noises as loud as thunderclaps. Settling back against the bed, he tried to find a comfortable position to fall asleep in.

Behind him, Torben could hear Eleusia's soft restful breathing; from the other side of the room, Antauros' heavy rumbling breaths sounded like waves lapping the shore. Since he'd fallen asleep, the room had become chilly, even with the heat of their bodies in such a confined space. Clearly, Antauros and Gwilym had forgotten to put more wood on the fire before they'd fallen asleep.

Leaning over quietly, Torben placed a few logs and kindling onto the embers, and prodded the fire back into life. As the flames grew in strength, he leant back again and closed his eyes, turning his head towards the fire, and enjoying the warmth on his face. It would probably be a good long while before he felt this cosy again.

One of the branches popped in the grate, causing Torben's eyes to open instinctively. The fresh wood smoke made his eyes water and, as he passed a hand across his eyes, he thought he saw something move. He wiped at the moisture in his eyes and scanned the other side of the room, the crackles and pops from the freshly stoked fire covering his movements. All he could see was the sleeping form of Gwilym, his head resting against his chest, rising and falling in time with his breathing.

Torben started to let his eyes close again when he saw movement again, this time more clearly. A figure stood stock still next to Gwilym, drifting in and out of focus in the flickering firelight. A large puff of smoke swirled from the fire and drifted over the figure, defining it for a second before whatever trick was concealing it seemed to pull the shadows back around it.

In that split second, Torben had clearly seen a face, a distinctly wolf-like face with bright orange eyes—staring directly at him. He half-climbed to his feet, reaching for the hilt of his nearby sword. He drew in a quick breath to shout, scream, *anything* to wake the others, but before he could, the creature's arm appeared out of thin air, pointing straight at him.

'Ashak,' the face hissed.

The breath that Torben had drawn to speak sailed from his lips and he began to breathe normally, quietly. He tried to move, but his arms and legs were fixed in position, one hand clenching the end of the bed, the fingers of the other hand brushing the sword hilt. In the back of his mind he heard the creature's word reverberate, felt it twist around his limbs, holding him in place and locking his tongue in position.

The creature moved slowly towards Torben. The shadowy shroud concealing it began to slip away, the spell broken as the creature's attention fixed on Torben, securing him.

He saw that the creature was distinctly different to a Lupine, but the similarity was still plain to see. The face had a canine-like snout, but the top of its head was crowned with two large ears that twitched and rotated of their own accord as the creature moved, scanning the room for alarming noises. The creature stood much shorter in stature than a Lupine, and would have been little taller in height than Gwilym; its fur was deep orange in hue, like its eyes. The large black cloak it wore rippled around it as it advanced on Torben, revealing a stained, threadbare blue robe beneath, several sizes too large.

'What have we got here then, my dear? Someone bent on causing trouble, it would seem. Someone who won't let me complete my work without interruption.' The creature crooned softly to itself, the voice sounding breathy and hoarse, like that of an extremely old man or woman. As it approached and inspected Torben up and down, the end of its snout brushed his face.

'I recognise your scent, you and that girl, too watchful, too alert. Stopped me from creeping close you did … from taking what is mine when you first discovered it. It can't be far away though; I can smell its aura filling this room … smell it on your hands. Where is it?' Long sinewy hands patted Torben's torso, reaching inside his pockets and feeling the seams of his clothes.

Torben still couldn't move, but his leg muscles were burning with pain from being contorted into one position for so long.

'Where is it?' the creature growled. 'Hidden it well, you have? Too well. Everything in this place reeks of it! Too many places to search, too little time.' The creature ran a hand through the fur on its head, eyes shut, clearly deep in thought.

Now that the creature was so close to him, he could distinctly view white and grey patches and streaks in its fur, and deep wrinkles around its eyes and mouth. As its focus shifted from Torben, he felt the effects of the spell losing its grip. He concentrated every atom of his brain on moving his hand, fighting the restraining force. Out of the corner of his eye, he saw his index finger twitch, felt it brush against the leather of his sword grip, but the creature also felt it.

Its eyes snapped open and once more fixed on Torben's face. Once again, he felt the invisible bonds tighten around him, and the word that the creature had spoken earlier began to grow louder and louder inside his head. '*Ashak, ashak, ashak.*'

'Yes,' the creature said, 'that is the answer. I don't need to find it myself; you and your friends can give it to me.'

Reaching into the folds of the baggy robe beneath its cloak, the creature drew out a battered quill and a small knife. Deftly, it cut a small incision on the back of its gnarled hand with the knife and squeezed the cut. A small pool of blood oozed from the wound. Taking the quill, the creature gathered a large globule with the nib and whispered to itself. The blood dangling perilously from the quill glowed golden, softly at first, but blazing with intensity with every passing second.

The creature leaned towards Torben and bent over his right

arm, which was still frozen and grasping the edge of the bed. Still murmuring the incantation, it used the quill to jab his flesh.

Torben could feel an intense burning sensation as the nib dug into his arm. From the corner of his eye, he saw the creature writing one long word in a language and script he didn't recognize; the golden light suspended in its blood disappeared into his arm. The burning sensation spread throughout his body as the spell coursed through his bloodstream. He thought his heart was would stop as his chest erupted in pain when the burning streamed through his torso and up to his head. He wanted to scream but, unable to move or speak, he had no way to voice his agony. His eyes blurred, his vision clouded with a golden haze; the spell had reached his head.

Just when Torben thought he'd go mad with pain, a flash of blinding golden light obscured his vision. The other spell that had been holding him in place was broken, and he thudded to the ground.

Eleusia's eyes snapped open. She had a vague recollection of being woken by an intense flash of light, a loud thud, and a heart-wrenching scream. She bolted upright, her dagger ready in her hand as she realised that she'd not been dreaming.

Torben was writhing around on the floor next to the bed, gasping in agony, his right arm covered in blood. She leapt from the bed, dragging bedclothes with her and began to stifle the bleeding.

There was the sound of frantic scrabbling from the other side of the room as Antauros struggled to his feet, rubbing sleep from his eyes with the back of a hand.

'Don't move, filth!' Gwilym held his seax at the throat of what appeared to be an incredibly old Lupine and one of his meaty hands was pinning the creature to the floor. Despite his warning, the creature didn't look as if it had any intentions of running away. A slight smirk pulled at its muzzle, revealing long yellowed fangs.

'What have you done to him?' Gwilym snarled. 'Tell me quickly and you may just stop me from slitting your throat.'

'I wouldn't do that if I were you,' the creature sniggered. 'He'll be safe as long as you don't do anything too rash … he's barely hurt at all.'

'Barely hurt? It looks like you nearly took his arm off,' Antauros rumbled. 'Kill her, Gwilym, before she tries to finish Torben off!'

'What do you know of such things, bull beast? The boy is fine for the moment—'

'What is she talking about?' Antauros took a step closer, his war-hammer clenched tight, ready to strike.

'How's he getting on?' Gwilym asked, not taking his eyes off the creature.

'He's … he's fine. He's not bleeding, I mean … but look.' Eleusia sat against the bed with an expression of deep surprise. She was clutching some bedclothes in her hand, stained deep red with blood.

Torben had calmed down significantly and had managed to raise himself into a sitting position. He was holding his arm stiffly from his body, the shock of what had happened clearly written on his face. His forearm was covered in gold letters that pulsed with dim light, penned in a flowing curling hand.

'Witchcraft,' Antauros exclaimed, stepping back.

'What spell have you put on him? Tell me!' Gwilym smacked the seax pommel into the creatures face, but she didn't flinch, just kept staring into Gwilym's eyes, the smirk spreading into a grin.

On the other side of the room, Torben yelped with pain when his head jerked to the side, as if by the force of Gwilym's blow.

'You're taking a dangerous path to discover the truth,' the creature grinned. 'As I said, he's fine for now, though he won't thank you for striking me. You should think very carefully before you do anything stupid.'

'You've bound yourself to him.' Eleusia was back at Torben's side, dabbing a cut that had appeared on Torben's cheek and was rapidly beginning to swell.

'Clever girl,' the creature whispered. 'Had you and the rest of the naive imbeciles walking this earth not turned your backs on the old ways, you'd not have needed such a brutal test to know what I'd done. My name was once revered and feared across the world, and none would have dared put a blade to the throat of Hrex!' The creature's gaze turned from Eleusia to Gwilym, the orange of its eyes burning like hot coals.

'Why have you done this?' Antauros demanded.

'Call it an insurance policy, bull beast; any hurt you try to inflict on me will be passed straight to him. Unless I sever the bond, there is *no* way you can free him—that is, unless you're prepared to kill him.'

'Why do this to him?' Gwilym asked, sheathing the seax slowly.

'Because,' Hrex replied quietly. 'You have an item in your possession of great value that I need.'

'The Keystone?' Eleusia blurted.

'Yes, girl. I'd meant to take it while you slept ... thought you were so safe you all did ... but perhaps you're sneakier than I anticipated. Once the boy spotted me though, I thought of a better idea. I don't necessarily need the Keystone in my possession; I just need it to go to the right place. What better couriers, thought I, than a group of hardened mercenaries. I'm glad I spared him. The boy is proving to be quite the useful bargaining chip.'

'What makes you think we'll help you?' Antauros snorted.

'If you don't, the boy dies.' Hrex lifted one of her crooked fingers to her cheek and dug into the flesh with a wickedly pointed claw.

Torben hissed in pain and recoiled, trying to twist away. A deep red line appeared on his cheek as Hrex slowly drew the claw through her fur, blood seeping as it scaled down Torben's face.

'Stop it! Please,' Eleusia cried.

Hrex removed the finger and cocked her head to survey the foursome.

'What do you want us to do?' Gwilym asked grimly.

'I want you to help me get to the vault beneath Karpella Castle.'

15

It didn't take long for the group to prepare to leave. They readied themselves in silence, Eleusia helping a still dazed Torben gather his things into his pack. All of them had one eye on Hrex at all times.

The witch sat next to the fire, eating the remains of the previous evening's meal straight from the pot; she was plainly unconcerned by the others. As Hrex leaned back against the fireplace and began to pick her teeth, Torben could feel a slight unpleasant, prickling sensation creeping up his back, as if he were sitting uncomfortably close to the fire. She was in control of the situation, and they knew it.

As they unbarred the door, light flooded in from the un-shuttered windows of the tavern beyond. There was no sign of how Hrex had gained entry into the room or even the building. The main door to the tavern was firmly wedged shut, as Eleusia had left it.

The street outside was still and quiet as if it, too, were apprehensive of what the new day would bring. The rain that had fallen the night before had settled in potholes and wagon tracks that pitted the road, and many of the houses that had lost roofs looked as if the rain was bringing them close to collapse.

Eleusia exited the tavern cautiously as ever, scanning buildings for signs of untoward movement. Hrex, however, strode purposefully into the middle of the street.

'No need to be so careful, the sun will drive away the worst of the creatures that come here in the night to feast on the dead. Besides, I was the only one following you when you entered this place, and you don't need to worry too much about me ambushing you now, do you?' Hrex surveyed them with a wicked grin and then strolled up the road, back the way the party had come the day before.

Eleusia, Gwilym, Antauros and Torben walked together closely, a good few steps behind. Torben felt the eyes of his three colleagues flicking between himself and Hrex, checking that he was alright.

Torben caught a glance of the letters Hrex had carved into his arm, shining through his coat sleeve. He pulled it down, gripping the edge with his hand, trying to obscure the marks she had left on him.

'Don't worry Torben, we'll get her for this … *somehow*, we will.' Antauros' voice was full of barely concealed rage as he trudged behind Torben, staring over his head at the figure in front.

The witch looked frailer now that they were in the starkly revealing light of morning. The shadows that had billowed around her in the tavern had provided bulk to the much slighter figure. As she moved, it was easy to tell that within her slender frame was an intense, otherworldly strength.

'Dammed Lupine scum,' Gwilym spat. 'Antauros is right, Torben, and when we work out how to pay her back for all this, I'll enjoy every minute of it.'

'Easy,' Eleusia muttered. 'She's got keen hearing, so don't go saying anything too provocative; remember, it won't be you that she makes suffer for harsh words.'

In front of them, Hrex's ears revolved and twitched. Clearly, she was listening for signs of danger on the road ahead and from surrounding houses, but every now and again one of her ears would twist in their direction, listening to their scraps of conversation.

'At this point in time, I don't see what we can do,' Torben spoke despondently. 'Seeing what she was capable of, what she could do just by whispering words under her breath, it beggars belief. How could we fight or hope to gain revenge against something so powerful?'

'There's always a way, lad,' Gwilym affirmed. 'I may not be the wisest of dwarves, but I know for a fact that no matter how big someone is, there's *always* a way to make them fall!'

'Not that we've seen you put that into practice yet.' Antauros chuckled involuntarily at his own joke, but his laughter was stifled as Gwilym aimed an elbow at his groin, forcing him to jump back to avoid connection.

'Oh, give over you two,' Eleusia sighed. 'I thought we'd moved past all this and that the two of you had kissed and made up?'

'I wouldn't go so far as to say that. No one can help but rise to such a flagrant insult,' Gwilym huffed.

'Eleusia, you're right,' Antauros said. 'Now is not the time to be making jokes, Gwilym. My apologies. I wasn't thinking straight.'

Gwilym turned his head and nodded curtly to Antauros, a grudging acceptance of the apology.

Torben had been oblivious to the exchange; he'd been lost in thought, racking his brains for anything that he'd read or heard about regarding the power that Hrex had been able to wield so easily. There'd been little mention of magic back in Bywater. Whenever the subject had cropped up in conversation, usually on dark winter nights in a corner of the Rusty Sickle, it had been spoken about in fearful whispers. As far as Torben could remember, however, no one had had a decent idea of what magic actually was, or what it was truly capable of. The village folk had spoken as if the fear of magic had been ingrained in them through years of terrifying mutterings … and sent shivers down their spines long after the origin of the fear had been forgotten.

Often, his mother had spun fantastic tales about witches and sorcerers, but he could barely remember the stories she'd told him. The magicians had always seemed wise and kindly, advising rulers on how best to govern their kingdoms and protect villages from evil beasts. Fairytales, stories, myths.

It had only been since his forced exile from Burndale that Torben had actually seen evidence for the existence of magic firsthand, and that had been Gwilym's trick purse, not exactly the stuff of nightmares. Gwilym himself had said there existed a few rare items imbued with magical power in the world, but had only mentioned wielders of magic in his tale of Sarper IV, and then had only told of one.

'How does she do it, do you reckon?'

The others stopped their quiet conversation and turned to Torben, who obviously hadn't realised that he had been speaking out loud.

'What?'

'How do you think she can do, you know, magic?' Torben asked, blushing. 'I was under the impression that there were no magic users left, so she must have learnt it from someone.'

'You do have a point,' Eleusia answered. 'As far as I can remember, there were once many magic users in the world; at one time, every large town could boast of having an arcane wielder of some sort living among them, and they were held in great esteem. My mother told me that kings and queens used to attract large numbers of trained magicians, witches, warlocks and others to their courts. It was a show of wealth and power, I guess, to be able to support so many interesting individuals, and they were certainly not without their uses.

'Indeed, they'd often give their magical entourages free rein to take anyone or anything that showed an aptitude for magic, and bring them back to the court for training. King Hastel still employs a Court Mage, though I'm sure they're only a shadow of what such a person used to be. Not to mention that there are still whole libraries of books inside the castle dedicated to such matters, though they're mostly forgotten now … their meaning and whatever obscure language they were written in lost. I doubt that anyone would be able to learn such skills on their own, from scratch, now.'

'What about *her* then?' Antauros' voice was barely a whisper. 'Unless she's hundreds of years old, then she'd appear to be the exception that proves the rule. Either that, or there are more magic users hiding out there than we'd like to think.'

'But why would they go into hiding?' Torben asked, bemused. 'Surely there must have been a reason why a whole community of people, stretching beyond the boundaries of any kingdom, would suddenly just disappear?'

'Disappeared, or destroyed?'

The four jumped as they realised Hrex had stopped walking and had turned to them in the middle of the road. Gwilym and Eleusia physically leapt back and nearly collided with her, leaving Torben and Hrex facing each other.

'You know little of what happened, boy. Few people remember the events surrounding the so-called "loss of magic" with any clarity and those that do, are wise enough to keep their mouths shut. All any of you need to know is that the faithful amongst us were spared from purification, and that our Master's memory and teaching is kept alive in the fortunate few of us, his servants, still alive to roam the earth and haven't been turned into purveyors of parlour tricks. We've all been searching for a way to access the legacy that he left us and, thanks to you, I am closer than any other to attaining this. Now, I suggest that you all stop your idle prattling lest you, boy, are acquiring a taste for personal suffering.'

Turning sharply, Hrex set off again through the streets of Gallenford, the others following, their tongues—if not their minds—quietened by the witch's speech.

When they reached the central square, the familiar stench of the town's deceased inhabitants slowly crept into their nostrils again. As they passed through the centre of the square, there were obvious signs that the corpses littering the flagstones had been tampered with. Many were more dismembered than they'd previously been and, here and there around the square, trails of dried blood told of where a body had been dragged into the protective shadows of one of the buildings.

As they passed one such trail, Eleusia stopped and knelt beside it, and then followed it to the edge of the square where it had entered a building through a sizeable hole. She peered inside and jogged back to the others.

'What is it?' Gwilym asked anxiously.

'A family of troglodytes, I reckon. They must have come in from the forest to scavenge food and supplies. There are no more than five: two adults and three children, judging by the debris in that house. Having said that, if a family is happy to come so boldly into Gallenford not long after it's been sacked, then I'd guess that their mob must be nearby, probably lodging in the other buildings roundabouts.'

Torben shrugged off the shield from his back and slid his arms through the straps, as if he was expecting an army to suddenly descend on them.

'Don't bother,' Gwilym said. 'Troglodytes won't come out in the daytime; they mostly live underground or in caves. The sunlight burns them something horrible. And, if nothing else, they're mostly harmless … scavengers and hoarders as opposed to hunters. I've only heard of a handful of folks being killed by troglodytes purely for food; their mobs are too small to risk open war with the kingdoms through doing too much hunting of the King's subjects. Having said that, I doubt any troglodyte could pass up a feast such as this. Must have been what drew them to the surface from whatever hovel they were squatting in. Poor buggers. It's no way for anyone to enter their eternal rest.'

Reluctantly, Torben slung his shield back over his shoulder, though he remained on guard and gripped his spear tightly in both hands as they walked. The others seemed sure that hungry troglodytes weren't a threat, but he'd been steadily learning *not* to take anything for granted.

The five of them moved quickly through the streets of Gallenford, their progress greatly accelerated by the fact that Hrex wasn't concerned with keeping their whereabouts hidden, and it didn't take them long to traverse the streets between the central square and the town's main gate.

Crossing beneath the battered wooden archway of the gatehouse, Gwilym stopped in his tracks, putting his arm out to keep Torben, Eleusia and Antauros from walking any further, and fixed his beady eyes on Hrex. 'Before we go any further, we need to talk about what's going on here.'

'What are you doing?' Eleusia hissed.

'Don't worry, it's nothing to be concerned about. We just need some answers is all.'

'You'd better not go and say anything too stupid, and please try not to provoke her!'

'Aye, I'm with you on that one,' Torben muttered.

'Oh shush you two. Trust me, I've got this covered.'

Slowly, Hrex turned to face them. Her orange eyes were reduced to narrow slits and her ears continued to twitch, seeking any sound or whisper that might be coming from their direction.

'Well dwarf, what is it? Speak quickly; my patience is far from boundless.'

'Ah, well, you see,' Gwilym started, then froze. Something about her piercing stare was deeply unsettling, sapping his confidence and robbing him of his usual eloquence.

'What is it?' Hrex's voice was full of malice.

'I … I only wanted to ask, wh-what we're doing. That's to say, what is the plan? To get back to Karpella? It would seem best to have some sort of plan, a … a strategy, so that our journey is as, err, efficient as possible. Don't you think?'

There was a moment of intense silence as Hrex eyed them intently, her suspicious gaze flitting from Gwilym, now practically quaking, to Antauros, then Eleusia and lastly Torben, checking for signs of suspect movement. Finally, she relaxed and a sly smile spread across her muzzle. 'Have no fear, dwarf. No one will stop us along the road, of that I can assure you. Just follow me and you'll be perfectly safe—that is, as long as you don't badger me with pointless questions. Now come. There isn't time for anymore time-wasting!'

She turned and walked purposefully down the road out of Gallenford. As she turned her back, Gwilym visibly shivered and passed an unsteady hand over his eyes and face.

'Are you alright?' Antauros leaned down to inspect the dwarf, who had stopped shaking, though his breathing still sounded short and sharp.

'Yes, I'll be alright, I think. Whatever she was doing to me, it's stopped. Gods, I've never felt fear like that before, and all because of a decrepit old crone. I'd be laughed out of every tavern in the land if word of that got about.'

'Better get moving then, before she shows off anymore of her tricks,' Torben said, gently encouraging Gwilym forward with a hand on the dwarf's back.

'This seems like a bad idea,' Eleusia murmured darkly. 'How can she be so carefree about taking the roads? I would think twice about taking the main road through Bar-Dendra, even in peaceful times. Given what happened back at the caravan, I think it's safe to say that we don't have the luxury of peace anyway. Like as not, Sharisar's cavalry will still be patrolling the road if Queen Alliona hasn't already committed more troops to her burgeoning war.'

'True, but I think whatever throws itself at her on the road wouldn't do much to harm her, even a company of well-trained, well-equipped horseman,' Antauros said.

'It's not her I'm worried about,' Eleusia stated. 'I wouldn't be surprised if she's hoping we'll all be killed; then she can search us at her leisure and take the Keystone.'

'Well, we'll just have to pray that we get lucky then, won't we?' Gwilym growled.

The road from Gallenford curled round the forest edge for several miles before plunging into the tree line proper, as if the people who'd built the road had needed to psych themselves up before intruding upon the borders of the forest.

By the end of that day, they'd made good progress though, given the situation, it was hard for Torben, Gwilym, Eleusia and Antauros to feel particularly elated by this.

When she finally called a halt, Hrex led them off the road, into the forest, the only sign that she wasn't being too reckless about their safety. Whilst on the road, the four of them had agreed that one of them should be on watch at all times during the night—to observe Hrex as much as watch for attackers.

Torben took the first watch, but he managed to get little rest after he was relieved by Antauros. His forearm still ached with a gentle burning sensation, just strong enough to keep him from falling into a fitful sleep. During the brief periods when he did manage to sleep, he was troubled by strange dreams and the ghostly echo of Hrex's words when she'd enchanted him.

With sunrise, they took to the road again and soon connected with a larger road, the main artery through Bar-Dendra, which they had been travelling along only a few nights previously. The trampled earth of the road was pitted and scarred by the vast numbers of heavily armed men, horses and wagons that had travelled it. At first sight, Eleusia had knelt and inspected the tracks, but even Torben could tell that this wasn't the passage of a trading caravan or a raiding party but of an army, marching north to Karpella.

After a few hours of walking, they reached the spot where the caravan of Guild House Fisel had been ambushed. The looted wagons had been tipped and rolled, and many of them were lying broken and upended in the dense undergrowth. What had remained of Fisel's guards had been unceremoniously thrown off the road, left for the forest and its creatures to slowly reclaim.

Once they'd passed through the battleground, the rest of the day passed in grim silence with only the occasional sound of an animal or bird breaking the monotonous drone of their footsteps. The road was well maintained, despite its isolation from the main hubs of civilisation in the Kingdom of Dazscor and Aramore. They were able to make quick time as their speed wasn't dictated by the lumbering pace of heavy wagons.

By the time that they stopped for the evening, they were near the edge of the forest; as darkness approached, they could see the dim orange glow of hundreds of campfires smudging the horizon, a worrying sign of how close they were to the Sharisian army.

'They'll be moving slowly, deliberately slowly,' Antauros said as he stared at the glow from their makeshift camp. 'They'll have scouts riding on all sides, a screen of skirmishers behind; they'll subdue any threat as quickly as possible, without committing the main body of their army. Nothing will be able to come within several miles of them on open ground without being spotted. This is no hit-and-run raiding trip, but an open declaration of war. They'll eliminate anyone that doesn't get well out of their way, lest spies are able to record their movements and count their numbers. We'll be sitting ducks once we leave this forest.'

'As much as I hate being stuck amongst these trees, you're right, Antauros,' Gwilym said, his gaze on the fire, attempting to coax life into it. 'With that army between us and Karpella, we haven't got much chance of moving anywhere quickly. Even if we were able to edge past them, we'd be at risk of being cut down as spies of the Aramorians. Like you said, better to guess that someone is snooping for the other side, rather than risk letting agents freely gather information in your country.'

'Fear not, young ones; there is no need for any of you to die yet.'

The proximity of the hostile army and the lack of direct interaction had tricked them into forgetting that Hrex was travelling with them. She'd not spoken since they had left Gallenford, except to herself in a hoarse whisper; the sound of her voice made them recoil, afraid of what she might say or do.

'I've made arrangements for us to regain access to the city, regardless of the games silly little kings and queens are playing with each other,' Hrex continued flatly. 'Just follow me and all will be fine.' She grinned evilly before disappearing into the undergrowth.

'I'd like to know what she's doing out there,' Gwilym said, staring at the place where she'd disappeared.

'Are you sure about that?' Eleusia asked dully. 'As long as she leaves us alone, I'd rather be oblivious to whatever mischief she's creating. I'd be more interested in knowing what arrangements she's made. If we're not careful, then Karpella will be under siege by the time we get there.'

'Surely there must be other ways of getting in though?' Torben asked.

'Well yes, of course there are, but most of those ways in are either known about by the City Guard, in which case they'll be very well protected, or they're extremely difficult to get to, especially when you're looking over your shoulder, expecting to see enemy soldiers.'

As the sun rose the next morning, the sounds of thousands of soldiers from the distant army camp could be heard readying themselves for the day's march. The noise and growing strength of daylight dragged Torben from a restless slumber. He rubbed sleep from his eyes as he sat up and tried to remember what it felt like to be human.

Hrex had returned from her nightly wanderings and was squatting near the remains of the small fire, trying to bring it back into life, clearly unconcerned as to whether it would give them away to watchful eyes.

Gwilym and Antauros talked quietly to one another, casting evil glances at Hrex, who seemed oblivious to the dreadful fate they were doubtless wishing upon her.

Seeing that Torben was awake, Antauros threw him some bread and water. 'Here, not exactly a delicious breakfast, but we haven't got much else.'

'Thanks,' Torben said with a grateful smile.

'Gods, but I wish we'd packed more of that salt beef.' Antauros sighed loudly. 'I'm sick of this diet of stale bread and bugger all else. No one says anything, you know, about the dire quality of the food when you sign up to be a mercenary. All they tell you is how heroic it is, how many stories you'll be able tell around tavern fires, the thrill of battle. Nothing about how the piss-poor diet will make you wish you'd never been born and that you'll break your teeth on terrible hard bread.'

'Where's Eleusia gone?'

'Scouting,' Gwilym answered. 'Assessing what our chances are of crossing the plain without being spotted. My money's still on that being slim to impossible, but I don't think we have any choice other than to give it crack now, do we?'

Gwilym had clearly aimed this last remark at Hrex, but the witch continued to stare into the steadily growing flames, apparently lost in thought. She was muttering inaudibly, her lips moving ever so slightly. Occasionally, the fire swelled up, as if in response to what she was saying; streaks of unnatural colour— purples, blues and greens—occasionally flashed amongst the flames.

It didn't take long for Eleusia to return, her face furrowed in thought as she descended into the clearing from the road.

'What's the situation?' Gwilym asked, springing to his feet.

'Bleak at best, but if we're going to make a dash for it, we should do so now. I reckon that the Sharisians will be ahead of us enough so that we won't be immediately spotted by their patrols, but not so far away that we can't slip past them during the night. If I remember rightly, small woods are about fifteen miles to the north. If we can reach there, then we'll have somewhere to hide until it's dark enough for us to sneak past the scouts—'

'No, girl, we shan't be doing that,' Hrex interrupted, looking at them for the first time. The fire spluttered and then went out, thin tendrils of smoke whirling around her head and partially obscuring her face. 'There is a village eight days walk to the northwest of here; that's where we shall go.'

'But that'll take us well out of our way,' Eleusia said. 'If we do anything but follow the tracks of the army, then we'll never make it back to Karpella before they lock down the defences and stop letting people in.'

'Don't worry girl. I told you, I've made arrangements.'

'What *arrangements*? Unless you're not planning to get into the city at all, then those *arrangements* are useless unless we overtake those troops … and we can't do that if we go strolling off into the countryside!' Eleusia's face flushed an angry red colour.

Hrex stood slowly and took a few steps towards Eleusia, who just managed to hold her ground as the witch approached. 'Tell me, did I ask for your opinion on my orders?'

'No, but you might as well use the expertise of those around you, even if you are holding them hostage!'

'Expertise, ha! The body of your expertise is smothered by the huge mass of your ignorance.'

'I beg to differ—'

'Silence!' Hrex screeched the word, the piercing sound sending a flock of birds flying in panic from a nearby tree. In her fury, her eyes glared wildly and she drew a wickedly pointed dagger from the sleeve of her robe. 'You seem to have forgotten that your opinions mean nothing now; they are worthless to me and I do *not* want to hear them being volunteered again. Perhaps you need reminding of the consequences for not doing what I say?'

Before any of them could move or speak, she slashed the side of her face with the dagger. Eleusia was spotted with flecks of blood as a wound appeared on Torben's face. He grunted in pain, but gritted his teeth, not wanting to show weakness.

'Next time you dare to cross me, girl, it'll be his throat! Get moving all of you. We leave *now*!' Hrex strode past them onto the road, not waiting for them to collect their things.

Torben swore as she left, checking his cheek to see how badly he was bleeding.

'I'm so sorry. I didn't mean for her to hurt you,' Eleusia said, dashing over to him.

'It's fine, just a scratch. I'll be alright.'

'We need to go—you heard what she said,' Antauros growled, staring angrily up the road where Hrex was waiting.

'I'll be fine, honest,' Torben said, taking the bandage Eleusia was using to dab his check and pressing it to his face. 'Don't worry about me; I'll enjoy it all the more when we work out how to get ourselves out of this fix.'

16
_____

The rain drummed the thatched roofs of a small cluster of houses that made up Findale. The dirt road that ran through the heart of the village had come alive with little streams of water that flowed down wagon ruts and disappeared into hedgerows that shielded Findale from the outside world. Little else could be heard over the rain.

House doors were barred shut and shutters had been fastened over all windows. The village seemed deserted but, here and there, small slivers of light could be seen shining through cracks in a shutter or illuminating frayed areas of thatch on roofs.

The villagers of Findale had not just barred themselves against the weather; all around, crops had been trampled, roads and tracks scarred by a myriad of hoof prints from a large body of cavalry that had swept through the countryside earlier that day. With no way to defend themselves, the villagers had retreated into their houses, praying at kitchen altars for the troops to pass by and leave them unharmed.

For the most part, the Sharisian cavalry had ignored the folk of Findale. They were just farmers, too young or old to be of threat. In any case, if Queen Alliona was to rule the Kingdom of

Dazscor and Aramore she needed stability, a large part of which relied on a cowed but very much alive peasant population.

The majority of able-bodied men and women had fled before the Sharisians arrived, fearful that they'd be killed as suspected spies or militia. Like as not, they'd gone into hiding in the fens that lay a couple of miles to the northwest, a place where cavalry wouldn't follow. They'd be back soon enough, and the Sharisians knew this; it would be far less trouble if they came back to find their villages and livelihoods mostly intact. Peasants who emerged cold and wet from their hiding places to find their homes still standing were much less likely to listen to a handful of renegades that would be rallying them against the invading force.

Having said that, the bald patch of dirt that marked the village centre was now home to a crude wooden scaffold. Swaying ever so slightly in the breeze were four bodies suspended by their necks. Three bodies were male—two humans and a dwarf caught by the Sharisian cavalry when they attempted to reach the safety of the fens. They'd not offered any physical resistance to the Sharisian soldiers, but a hard day of riding in the rain with little diversion had meant the troops wanted to blow off steam. Littered around the scaffold were empty wineskins and shattered mugs; the Sharisians had watched and jeered as their captives danced their last.

The fourth body was that of a woman, her hair streaming in front of her face in the wind, covering the grisly visage of death. She was the only one of the four who'd resisted, striking a soldier who had beaten her father into submission ... and for that act of selfless courage, she had died.

The village hadn't had time to mourn their loss yet. When the men and women returned from hiding, the scaffold would be torn down and used as a funeral pyre for the dead but, until then, all they dared do was remain in the houses and pray for the souls of the departed, lest the Sharisians returned to find their handiwork undone.

Late that night, a small group of people appeared on the road into Findale, not that any of the villagers saw them approach, nor heard them pass the houses over the din of the rain. Hrex had led the group for seven nights and eight days over the plains of Dazscor once they had left Bar-Dendra, unconcerned by the threat of marauding cavalry or the army they patrolled around.

With every passing mile, she seemed to grow bolder, stood taller, and her strides longer and longer. Behind her, the figures of Eleusia, Antauros, Gwilym and Torben looked tired and very wary of their surroundings. The past few days had been long and weary, the nights sleepless and nerve-wracking. The slightest noise had woken them, and often they stayed awake for long stretches, staring into the gloomy blackness, expecting to see a horseman charge forth at any moment.

Hrex, too, had appeared to be sleeping very little from what they could tell. Since they'd starting travelling, she hadn't spent the night with them, something that they were all grateful for. At first, Gwilym had proposed that they give her the slip, but it had become clear that she was never too far away. Occasionally, they'd heard her voice echoing through the night, speaking in the unknown language that she'd used to curse Torben. When she had re-joined them, her arrival had always been sudden and unannounced. She appeared very keen to keep her movements as unpredictable as possible, which added to their sense of unease. Even Eleusia, with her excellent well-practised tracking skills, found that the elderly witch eluded her. She told them that the few nights she'd attempted to trail Hrex, she'd simply melted into the darkness of the night without a trace.

As the group continued to make their way through the houses, Hrex stopped in front of the gibbet, surveying the grim display with a smile.

'We're not stopping here are we?' Gwilym's voice echoed around the dwellings, sounding far too loud, even over the rain.

'This is the meeting place, whether you like it or not.' Hrex didn't turn to address Gwilym, but instead walked up to the legs dangling above on the scaffolding. She reached out and caressed one of the pale feet, her eyes closed and her snout twitching as if she were trying to pick up a particular scent.

'That lot are giving me the creeps,' Torben muttered, his eyes darting nervously between the corpses and Hrex.

'Looks like a patrol passed through here not too long ago,' Antauros rumbled. 'I'd suspect that they were the horsemen that passed us in the morning. I knew they were up to mischief.'

'What are the odds they'd come back this way?' Eleusia asked, bending to inspect the debris the troopers had left behind.

'Slim, I would think. If the Sharisian army is still holding the course that you saw them taking at dawn, then I'd guess that they're at least ten miles away from us now. It would be a bold cavalry troop that would range so far from the safety of their army this deep into hostile territory. Anyway, I doubt there are many cavalrymen stupid enough to be riding out in this.'

'No, it would seem that only we and our four sorrowful companions here are stupid enough to be out in this weather.' Gwilym flashed a grim smile at Antauros.

'I'm not sure sorrowful is the way I'd describe them … ghastly more like, poor buggers.' Torben was still staring concernedly at the bodies, his back pressed to the wooden wall of a house, trying to get under the relative shelter of the overhanging thatch.

'You shouldn't fear death, boy' Hrex said absentmindedly as she inspected each of the bodies above. 'There's little point fearing what is inevitable, lest you spend your whole life looking over your shoulder. Often from death comes the greatest source of life.' Circling back round the gallows, she stopped before one of the men. His long brown hair and beard was saturated with rainwater, giving him the impression of a man who'd drowned rather than been hanged. 'This one is strong,' she whispered. 'I can feel the fire of his spirit still fresh inside him, vigorous but weak-willed.'

'What is she talking about?' Eleusia retreated from Hrex and moved towards the house where Torben was sheltering. Antauros and Gwilym also began to move back, hands straying towards weapons as the four instinctively bunched together.

Standing below the man's body, Hrex drew her quill from the folds of her robes and chanted quietly, swaying from side to side. The quill began to glow with a dull red light and the rain that fell on and around her began to hiss and steam, repelled by the magic being summoned by the witch. The light emanating from the quill grew brighter and brighter, until it was almost too intense to regard; it threw an eerie crimson glow over the whole space and the buildings round about.

Slowly, Hrex moved the tip of the quill towards the man's foot, as if she were afraid that moving too suddenly would shatter her concentration and break the spell. There was a horrid sizzling sound as the quill tip contacted the man's foot, and Hrex repeatedly drew a single intricate symbol on the grey flesh. The red light that had gathered itself in the quill's feather leeched into the body, twisting from the symbol up the man's leg and disappearing beneath his clothing. The corpse's muscles flexed and tightened as the light travelled from his legs to his arms, and finally to his head, forcing his mouth and eyes open; the man's head tilted back in what looked like a silent scream.

As the last of the red light entered the body, Hrex drew her dagger and, still chanting, leapt impossibly high into the air for such a small, frail creature, and severed the rope that suspended the man from the gallows. The body hit the ground with a heavy thud, its legs crumpling beneath; it stayed propped up, its head slumped on its chest with arms limp in grim mockery of sitting. Landing gracefully beside it, Hrex restored the quill and dagger inside her robes and cocked her head expectantly at the corpse, waiting.

The last of the red light had faded from the surface of the man's skin and all that could be seen of the magic inside the corpse was the symbol carved into its foot, burning with a deep rosy glow. Slowly the corpse raised its head, the broken vertebrae in its neck thumping into place, and looked at Hrex with eyes that were empty black pools.

'Rise thrall, I have a job for you.'

With the scraping and crunching of joints, the corpse rose unsteadily to its feet and continued to stare at Hrex, its mistress, awaiting instructions.

'There is a group of the living coming to this village. Find them and bring them to me as quickly as you can. Do you understand?'

The thrall clumsily nodded its head before turning on its heel and breaking into a clumsy run, disappearing into the shadow of one of the houses.

'Like I said, from death comes the greatest source of life. Pick the right host and you have a strong, relentless, obedient slave who will do anything without question … much more appealing than fickle living servants.' Hrex regarded Torben, Eleusia, Gwilym and Antauros who were huddled together, their backs to the house. Antauros and Torben had their shields up and Eleusia had her crossbow trained at the other corpses on the scaffold.

It didn't take long for the thrall to return, shambling into view of the uneasy party. The thrall looked considerably more ragged than when it had left, its clothes tattered and ragged, and its arms and legs covered with small cuts from blundering through obstacles in its path. There were also several arrows with black fletching sticking from its chest and one from its throat, not that this seemed to be a cause for concern.

Stopping in front of Hrex, the thrall raised an arm and pointed into the gloom from which could be heard the movements of an armed group making their way hurriedly towards them. Torben could feel Eleusia and Gwilym grow increasingly tenser as figures ran into view. Gwilym swore as an incredibly tall muscular figure strode into the space with a bald, stocky looking dwarf beside him.

'It's Björn,' Gwilym spat.

'Traitor!' Björn's hand whipped to his side, easily drawing his sword from his belt.

The small village square rang with the rasp of weapons being drawn as Björn's cronies readied themselves for a fight. Gord, grinned oafishly in anticipation as he shrugged his huge bearded axe from his shoulder and spun it casually in his hands, sending raindrops flying from the blade.

'I should have guessed that you'd have been involved in this damned escapade,' Björn snarled. 'Though I'm disappointed that the witch didn't come back with your head, instead of having you skulking in tow, like some whipped mongrel!'

'It's always a pleasure to see you too, Björn, though I must admit that the manner of our meetings continues to go downhill every time we run into one another.'

The air next to Torben began to whir as Gwilym swung his sling, preparing to fire if things turned nasty.

'What is the meaning of this, Hrex?' Björn turned his attention to the witch, who was watching the proceedings with passive interest.

Slowly, she locked eyes with him and he instinctively flinched as her gaze bore through him. 'I felt that they would be of more use to me alive. A great many challenges will face us in gaining access to the vault and their skills will come in useful, not to mention the fact that they still possess the Keystone.'

'What?' Even in the dim light of the village square, Björn's face had clearly turned crimson with rage. He spluttered, trying to keep himself from shouting in anger and drew a deep breath. He clicked his fingers and gestured the companions in the shadows. Silently, his men moved slowly towards them. 'When you came to me all those years ago and asked me to be your partner in finding this godforsaken lump of rock, you didn't just promise me the lion's share of the spoils—you said that with your ability to wield old-world magic at will, nothing would be able to stand in our way. Yet you were unable to steal the most pivotal object we need from a band of useless, washed-up failures? Kill them, and finish what this damned creature couldn't!'

Björn's men surged forwards, the ground shaking as Gord lumbered forward, bringing up the rear, his single eye flashing malevolently. Before he could take more than a few steps forward, however, Hrex shouted a barely intelligible word at the top of her voice, her arm moving quickly through the air, quill in hand. She drew a delicate symbol in fire, which hung suspended in the air for a moment and then shot forward towards Björn's men.

The symbol cut through the centre of the advancing thugs, a tail of fire dragging along the ground and casting up a wall of flames, cutting off Gord, Björn, and most of his men from their target.

'Keep going, kill them! Kill them,' Björn screamed at his men on the other side of the flames, shielding his eyes from the light that was blinding compared to the darkness of the square seconds ago.

Gord and his men staggered back from the flames, several of them scorched and desperately slapping out the tongues of fire that had managed take hold of their clothes. On the other side of the flames, the three fastest men looked back nervously. They could hear their master yelling at them to carry out his orders. For a split second, doubt crossed their faces; they were outnumbered and they knew the reputation that Eleusia and Gwilym had within the circle of Björn's employees. They didn't much fancy taking on the minotaur, either. Even the young man, the least threatening, had steely determination in his eyes; he was ready to kill.

Björn's voice rose again from behind the flames, prompting them to continue. One fell to the ground, his forehead caved in by a slingshot bullet, another had a crossbow bolt in his chest. The third man cursed, sheathed his sword, and placed his hands on his head. He didn't want to die that night.

'What the bloody hell are you playing at?' Hrex shuffled

slowly and purposefully towards Björn, moving her arms as if pushing back a curtain when she reached the wall of flames, which parted and then sealed up behind her. She stood defiantly, her back to the flames as Björn squared up to her, his knuckles white as he gripped the hilt of his sword, trying to contain his rage.

'I told you, dwarf; they are of more use to me *alive*.'

'And I don't bloody care. I want my revenge and if you insist upon standing in my way, then you'll very quickly learn what happens to business partners that disappoint me.'

Hrex threw back her head and laughed, the harsh sound echoing around the square. The laughter sent shivers down the spines of Torben and his friends; they knew the perils of confronting her.

'And what exactly makes you think that we're partners, Björn Ivanson? What makes you think that we're equals in any way, shape, or form? In the glory days of the Kingdom of Dazscor, I'd not have deigned to let a worm such as you scrape the dirt off my shoes, so be under no illusions that our business dealings are between people of parity in *any* way.

'I hired your services because I need your skills, just as I need theirs, but only to make my life easier. I could have done all of this by myself, but I couldn't risk putting myself at such risk for the sake of my Master. When I have what I want, I need to be able to vanish so that our plans can be put into preparation, not be hunted by half the kingdoms of this world!'

'If that is so, then why do you *still* not have the Keystone? Think of those bastards as being useful if you will, but that's no reason to leave such a valuable object in their hands.'

'Fool, you know nothing of the world that doesn't fall under the end of your over-inflated nose! If you were more educated in these matters, then you'd be able to tell, like I can, that I cannot simply take the Keystone from them. They've concealed it with magic.

'It's not a spell I recognize, so who knows what the

consequences might be of killing them without first securing the object? The Keystone may be teleported to a safe space; it might even be destroyed if you try to take it by force. Not that I'd expect a simple thug like you to understand.'

'Well, I guess that's the problem with trusting the apprentice; you say you know everything when in fact you know *nothing*! How do we even know you're right, eh? Why don't I just try my luck? It seems that you have more to lose than I do.'

'Don't try me, Björn. If you still doubt my powers, then you're a much bigger idiot than I gave you credit for. Beware, Björn, lest the next time you push me into demonstrating my abilities, *you're* the one that gets caught in the fireplace.'

The shuffling footsteps of the thrall were heard coming closer as it waded through roaring flames. Emerging from the maelstrom, it stood next to Hrex, a lifeless grin spread across its face. The trip through the fire had burned off its hair and beard; its skin was red and blistered, and the arrows sticking out of its body were reduced to blackened shafts.

It took a shuffling step towards Björn, stretching a hand towards him. The dwarf took a step back, but the creature kept staggering forward. Gord, sensing the danger, tried to intervene, swinging his massive axe at the corpse, severing one of the arms and sending it thudding to the ground—but then it continued to come, demonstrating not a twitch of pain, not a break in its awkward steps.

Björn tripped as he retreated and fell to the ground, vainly trying to bat away the remaining hand with his sword, to no avail. Gord stood dumbstruck, his thick skull struggling to work out what he could do next. The rest of Björn's crew edged back involuntarily, too scared to intervene.

'Enough!'

The thrall twisted its head unnaturally to look at his mistress, the fingers on its remaining hand inches from Björn's throat.

'I think he's learnt his lesson. You've served me well, but I will have no use for you in the city.'

Hrex clapped her hands and the thrall collapsed, the magic that drove it leaving the body with a hideous screech as its tortured soul escaped and vanished into the night.

Björn hurriedly kicked the corpse away and scrambled to his feet, desperately trying to reassert his usual aura of confidence and menace. 'Don't you ever try that again, witch,' he spluttered.

'I won't if you remember your place.' She turned towards the wall of fire, snapping her fingers to dismiss the flames. They sank into the damp ground with a hiss, throwing up a cloud of steam. 'Come, we're leaving.' She gestured to Torben, Antauros, Eleusia and Gwilym, who moved slowly towards her, putting as much distance between Björn and his men as they could.

'Gord, lead them to the tunnel.' Björn's grip tightened on his sword hilt as he strode across the scorched ground to where his one man still stood between the bodies of his former friends.

Gord gingerly glanced back as he led the way out of the village and into the woods. The man's screams ended only when the last of Björn's men had left the village.

The air was heavy with tension as they stumbled through the dark towards Björn's entrance to Karpella, at least Torben assumed that was where they headed. Now that they'd left the dim light of the village square, they were being led by Gord in near pitch blackness.

Björn's men had arranged themselves into a long line that snaked through the trees and scrub, each holding onto the belt of the person in front so that they'd not become lost. The rain still trickled through foliage and the ground was slick with mud. Several times, Torben lost his footing, his legs sliding from under him as the treacherous ground disappeared under his feet. Thankfully, Antauros' sturdy frame helped Torben steady himself every time, the minotaur barely reacting when Torben's weight hung from his belt as the man desperately kicked the ground, trying to get back on his feet.

As they crept closer to Karpella, the sounds of the city and the siege camp drifted towards them through the inky darkness.

Pinpricks of light appeared through the trees and, occasionally, the line slithered to a halt when Gord stopped in his tracks, checking that the coast was clear.

They stopped more often the closer they came to the siege camp. Patrols of armoured men and riders regularly clattered past, sounding as if they were right next to them in the dark. One patrol came perilously close, the soldiers barely twenty feet away from Gord at the head of the column. As they approached, they crouched down and buried themselves as deeply as possible in the thick undergrowth. For the first time in what seemed like an age, Torben could see light illuminating their surroundings, emanating from the torches that the patrol carried with them which cast a flickering light all about them.

Once Gord was satisfied that the way was clear, they crept forward once more. Not long after getting on their way, Torben no longer felt clammy slippery mud beneath his feet but stone. A shaft of light appeared before them, revealing the ruins of a small house, roof open to the sky; set in the floor was a trap door, spilling out warm light.

The passageway beneath the ruin was oppressively warm. Torches set into wall brackets all along its length were throwing out heat and smoke that hung thickly in the narrow tunnel. They didn't stop as they reached the tunnel floor, but continued to snake into and through the tunnel.

The journey through the passageway seemed as long, if not longer, than the trek through the dark woods. Nothing broke the monotony of the smooth walls, streaked with moss and algae, except for a torch bracket every few feet. By the time it sloped upwards, Torben felt he was close to going insane; passing through a thick iron-bound door into the basement room beyond was like pushing his head above water and taking a breath of air just before drowning.

It took a few minutes for them to file into the room, though most of Björn's men passed straight through and down another passage, out of sight. When Björn himself emerged from the darkness, only Gord was left of his men, and he stood scowling at Hrex, his thumb absentmindedly stroking the blade of his axe.

'What now, then? I suppose you've already mapped this out in your own head, haven't you, witch?'

'Watch your tongue, Björn, lest it condemn you by accident.'

His eyes narrowed with hate, but the threat made him instinctively take a few steps away from her.

'You have proven yourself to be quite the incompetent fool tonight,' Hrex continued dully. 'Consider this a termination of our deal; I won't be needing any further assistance from you from now on.'

'What? You can't go back on our deal—we swore an oath!'

'Ha, who cares about oaths? They have no real power, and now that you've seen real power in the flesh, I'd have thought it would have made you more respectful. If you're lucky, I'll still deliver some payment to you once we've accessed the vault, but your disobedience tonight is making me rethink even that.'

For a second, it looked as if Björn would attack her; the muscles of his arms were tense and his hand had strayed to his sword. His arm relaxed, but his face was still flushed with anger and a vein pulsed on his forehead. 'I won't forget this, witch, and you'll rue the day that you dared to insult me.' With that, he whipped around and followed his men down the other passageway.

Gord crouched to duck under the low ceiling.

'You know where to find me when you fancy a fair fight over this,' he called over his shoulder.

Hrex ignored the threat, but turned to face the companions behind her, fixing her eyes on Eleusia. 'Girl, you have a safe house in the city we can go to?'

'Yes, though I can't say how welcome you'll be there.'

'That doesn't concern me; lead me to it. We need to pull together the final strands of this business, because soon we will strike.'

17

Belts were beginning to tighten in Karpella. It had been nearly two weeks since the Sharisian army had laid siege to the city and, since then, their bands of swift-footed horsemen had formed an impenetrable barrier to the outside world. The few groups of desperate citizens who'd tried to flee were charged down, well within sight of the walls, and put to work digging the trenches and embankments of the siege works. The bodies of messengers, sent in a desperate plea for aid from the rest of the kingdom, rotted before walls, corpses still hanging from the scaffolds they'd been hung on, a stark warning of what would happen to those that resisted.

For guards posted on the walls, and the few brave city folk who ventured to take a look, each day was an agonising wait ... watching siege lines snake slowly closer, and catapults and siege towers being constructed in the distance. Everyone in Karpella knew what they were waiting for, but no one dared mention it. Down in the city, from Medallion Square all the way to the Karpella Castle, people spoke in hushed whispers about when they thought the assault would begin.

Walking through the streets, Torben could clearly see fear lurking in faces that walked past and nervousness in the eyes of the City Guard, who regarded everyone as if they were a potential spy, saboteur, or rioter. He'd been watching from his position on the street corner for days, observing a small postern on the east side of the castle.

At first, the castle had been buzzing with activity, extra patrols stomping along the parapet, double postings of guards at each watch point, and every guard with an arrow on their bowstring, their swords permanently drawn. Lethargy, however, had started to sink into the garrison; the extra vigilance and workload was making them visibly weary, and the guards before the postern leaned against walls, trying and often failing to stay awake.

Out of the corner of his eye, Torben caught the tiniest glint of sun in his eye and, looking up, he saw Eleusia lying on her stomach on the roof of a nearby building. In her hand was a small mirror with which she expertly manipulated the light to shine in short bursts on Torben's face. She gestured towards the ground and then wriggled her way out of sight.

Drawing his leather overcoat tightly around himself, he stepped into the flow of people on the street and began weaving a path through the crowd, back towards Ivy House. As he turned a corner, he was joined by Eleusia, who appeared from a nearby alley, and fell into step beside him.

'Same as yesterday?'

'Same as yesterday, though I counted nearly twice as many who'd dosed off on shift today. I thought at one point the Duty Sergeant would throw one of the sleepers into the river.' Eleusia smiled as she spoke, replaying the memory.

'Ah, so that's what all the commotion was about earlier? You're lucky being up on that roof. You get to see much more interesting stuff than I do. All I get to look at is the rank fellow who's always on gate-duty, picking his nose. You'd think he was looking for gold up there, the amount of time he spends rooting around.'

'Sometimes it's the simple pleasures in life that bring the

greatest joy. In any case, depending how things go, he might not have much nose-picking time left.'

'You think the assault will start soon then?' Torben flashed a worried look at Eleusia, who was scanning the guard patrols they passed.

'It won't be much longer. Sharisar is a kingdom of nomads, and the few people I've met from there have become restless after spending a week in the same place, especially when they're just sitting on their arses. My guess would be that they only need maybe one or two more days of preparation. Then, they can bring their catapults in range and hammer the walls to hell. We've just got to pray that they don't make significant headway during the night; otherwise, things will be a lot more difficult come tomorrow.'

Ahead, the large double doors of Ivy House had come into view and there was already a steady flow of people entering the courtyard beyond. Passing over the threshold, the pair could see a mass of people lounging around the space and in the tavern rooms beyond. Sweet-scented smoke drifted up from the braziers in the courtyard and mingled with the food and cooking smells wafting from bowls and platters of food carried to and from tables. The ladies of Ivy House were also weaving between tables, engaging patrons in conversation and trying to drum up business.

Several ladies smiled and greeted Torben and Eleusia as they walked past, causing him to grow distinctly red in the face when he awkwardly mumbled in response. Eleusia rolled her eyes in exasperation when a well-timed wink from one of the ladies sent Torben into a small coughing fit.

'Pull yourself together. I'd have thought you'd be used to staying here by now.'

'Yes, well … you know.' His sputtered words were lost as they stepped into the main building and the noise level spiked as a myriad of conversations echoed around the taproom.

The clientele of Ivy House had certainly not been made more

frugal by the siege of the city. Each table was practically groaning under the weight of platters and bottles. Many of the patrons looked as if they could afford the extravagancies on offer without a second thought. The room was a blur with brightly coloured silk, satin, and velvet clothes that were all the fashion amongst the nobles and affluent merchants of Karpella. Here and there, burnished plate armour of Imperial Guardsmen flashed in the candlelight.

Beyond the taproom, the House kitchen was a hive of industriousness as cooks and hands rushed about their business. The head chef, a slight dwarf with a clean-shaven face and neatly plaited hair, stood on a stool in the middle of the room, barking orders and directing his troops. He bellowed in frustration as a kitchen hand tripped, sending a tray of neatly arranged salad leaves cascading over the floor. As he closed the door to the Silent Room behind him, Torben could hear the chef's remonstrations becoming bluer and bluer, the unfortunate kitchen hand cowering under the tirade of curses.

There was a morose air in the Silence Room, which made Torben's heart sink. Antauros and Gwilym were there, having a hushed conversation over papers on the table. Alone in the corner of the room, Hrex sat cross-legged on a chair in a trancelike state. Her eyes were wide open, but had rolled back into her head so that they appeared white voids, and her muzzle twitched animatedly, as if she were holding a silent conversation with an unknown entity. Seeing her again, Torben felt the echoing, garbled whispering creeping into his consciousness again.

Since being cursed by Hrex, his mind had been clouded by her whispering voice swirling around his head. Mostly, the whispers were incoherent words muttered in languages he couldn't understand; occasionally, recognisable phrases would swim through his head, fragments of conversations he'd never had and he tried his utmost to ignore them. During the day, he was able to blot out the whispers, more or less, and focus on the task at hand, even one as dull as watching castle guards. However, when the night began to creep in or whenever Hrex was close, the noise in his head grew louder, sometimes to such volume he could barely concentrate. It was worst at night when he tried to sleep ... when the whispers converged into a single word bellowing through his skull. Ashak.

Antauros straightened as Torben and Eleusia entered the room. 'All clear?'

'Yep,' Eleusia replied. 'Even if they change their guard patrols tomorrow, we shouldn't have too much of a problem getting inside. Moral is so low there, I'd be surprised if they don't all run away as soon as the Sharisians attack. Did you get the stuff?'

'Oh aye ... pilfered the last uniform and armour from the barracks this morning ... and Antauros has just finished making the manacles.' Gwilym pointed to the corner of the room where a pile of Imperial Guard uniforms and armour was neatly stacked, enormous minotaur-sized manacles next to them.

'How long has she been out?' Torben was still staring at Hrex, subconsciously trying to match the movements of her jaws to the whispering in his head, but made little headway understanding the mutterings.

'Don't know. Ever since the two of us got back,' Antauros said, studiously keeping himself from looking directly at Hrex. 'I hate it when she does that, gives me the creeps. Who knows what she's doing, who she's talking to, what she's plotting and scheming.'

Gwilym lowered himself from his chair and spat viciously into the brazier in the corner of the room. Whether it was the conversation about her or the loud sizzle of spittle hitting charcoals, Hrex blinked several times and then surveyed the room, her amber pupils visible again. 'You've finalised all the arrangements?'

There was a moment of silence as Torben, Eleusia and Antauros glanced at one another, each holding out that the other would speak first. Eventually, Antauros took a deep breath, fixed his eyes on Hrex, and spoke through gritted teeth. 'Yes, everything has been arranged. Torben and Eleusia have just returned from the castle and we don't need to make final adjustments to the plan. We have all the disguises that we need, so unless there's anything else, I think the four of us would appreciate resting up before the morrow.'

'That is acceptable; you may go.' Hrex took a deep breath and closed her eyes, resuming her previous position. Slowly, her eyes crept upward, revealing white voids once again.

Antauros jerked his head in the direction of the door, his horns narrowly missing the candelabra suspended from the ceiling, and moved to leave the Silent Room. Hrex didn't move as the door snapped shut behind them, and Torben lengthened his strides in the narrow corridor to get away from the room as quickly as possible. He could hear the whispering picking up pace, almost chasing him, like a wave of madness spilling from the room and threatening to overwhelm him.

'You all right, Torben?'

He only just managed to stop from walking right into Antauros, who'd stopped at the second door and turned to survey the group. 'What? Sorry ... yes, I'm fine. I'll be fine.'

'You're a terrible liar,' Gwilym said. 'Only have to look at you to know you're not all right.'

'Thanks for the supportive words,' Torben bristled. In truth, he knew exactly what Gwilym was referring to. He could still feel his hands shaking in his pockets, and he was intensely aware of sweat beading in his hairline. Every now and again, when the whispers drifting around his head would swell in volume, a nexus of barely visible runes pulsed from the wound Hrex had left in his arm and shimmy across his body.

'Come on, let's not linger here. We need food and rest. It's a big day tomorrow and I for one want to be in as good a form as possible.' Eleusia took Torben's arm and half guided, half frogmarched him through the door and into the kitchen.

The four made their way back through the kitchen and took the back stairs to the servants' living quarters. Madame Fleurese had been putting them up in a large but cluttered storeroom, where enough floor space had been cleared to allow them to lay their bedrolls.

A large tray of food had been left on a large upturned washbasin that served as a table. They ate mostly in silence, the combined apprehensiveness of what the morning had in store and the ever-present shadow of Hrex stifling conversation. The night drew in quickly and, before long, they were sitting in nearly total darkness. Torben felt exhausted and rather than try to prolong awkward, stilted exchanges about the next day, he lay on his bedroll, as if going to sleep.

The others took their cue and kept mostly quiet. Eleusia got up from her space on the floor and disappeared back down to the kitchens with the empty tray, her soft footsteps quickly receding. Gwilym lit a small candle and went over the sketch plans of the castle one more time, carefully studying each parchment diagram, trying to visualise every corner and corridor. Antauros checked and re-checked his gear, making sure everything was in its place before lying down with his back to the room. Soon, his snoring rumbled through the floorboards.

Torben didn't really sleep; he was concentrating so hard on suppressing Hrex's muttering in his head that it was impossible for him to let his brain relax. Every time his exhaustion felt as if it would finally pull him into unconsciousness, Hrex's voice crescendoed in his head, jolting him back into wakefulness. He lay on his bedroll for what seemed an eternity and long after Gwilym and Eleusia had retired and joined Antauros in sleep, Torben conceded defeat and sat up.

As silently as possible, he left the room and climbed the backstairs until he reached a small door at the top of Ivy House. The door was stiff, but with a firm shove swung open with a groan of the hinges. Before Torben was a small balcony, nestled amongst the pitched roofs of the building, and giving a vast view of Karpella. To the east, he saw the looming castle, beams of moonlight reflecting off its polished stone walls and casting pools of pale light on the buildings nestled at its base. To the south, was the orange glow of fires in the siege camp. Firelight flickered and swelled, sometimes disappearing from sight all together behind the curtain wall, at other times looking as if the defences would be engulfed in flame. The solitary torches of the guards on the curtain wall and castle parapets looked distressingly feeble in comparison.

Hearing footsteps coming up the stairs, Torben pressed himself against the roof tiles, trying to sink into the shadows. A few seconds later, the silhouette of a woman stepped onto the balcony, her frame picked out by the moonlight.

'I know you're there, Torben.' Madame Fleurese's voice held that instantly recognisable sing-song tone, even when speaking quietly. She didn't turn to look as he moved sulkily from the shadows and drew level with her, leaning his arms on the balcony's bannister.

'How did you know I was there?'

'You've been coming up here every night ever since you came back from Gallenford. Very little happens in my establishment that I don't know about. In any case, I always come up here when I have something on my mind, too.' She placed both hands on the bannister and took a deep breath, staring across the city. Her blonde hair seemed more like silver in the moonlight, and made her pale skin appear almost luminescent. 'There was a time when I would come up here every night to try and forget the worries that were keeping me up at night … to lose myself in the bigger picture. Looking down from here, you can trick yourself into thinking that life's problems are often so very small, meaningless when compared to size of the city, the world. Why worry about something trivial when the world itself is shifting seasons and turning day to night without a second thought … when life and death can appear without a moment's notice?'

'Does it work?'

Madame Fleurese gave Torben a wry smile. 'Only sometimes —if you're just trying to make yourself look beyond the more mundane things in life. But it's much harder to suppress that feeling of worry when it concerns someone you love. I don't think you can truly stop worrying then, even when there isn't anything you should be worrying about.' She eyed him closely. 'Eleusia told me what happened in Gallenford, what that witch did to you. If it was up to me, she'd never have darkened my doorstep.'

'If it was up to me, I'd do more than throw her out,' Torben growled.

'People sensitive to magic and arcane forces often wonder why the rest of the world treats them with such mistrust—but when you have the power to wield something that can be so hurtful, so destructive, that can change peoples' lives in so many horrible ways in the blink of an eye—it's no wonder they rarely find a friendly face amongst us more mundane folk.' She sighed softly. 'It's hard seeing you suffer and it's hard seeing those around you trying everything in their power to help you, but to no avail.'

'Help me? If they've been trying to help me, I've seen neither hide nor hair of it. We've all been too busy, and rightly so. I'd much rather they concentrated on preparing for tomorrow. I wouldn't want anything to go wrong or be missed because of me.'

'You never wondered why the room you're sleeping in smells of sage, then?'

'What?'

'Gwilym has been burning sage in the brazier of your room every day since you arrived back. Gordon the cook told him his grandmother burnt it to ward off evil. Every night, Eleusia has been sneaking into the City Infirmary and scouring records and archives for hours, trying to find references on how to remove a curse or hex. Antauros has been trying to track down other magic-sensitive people in the city to get their help. He spent more money than I care to mention the other day for a vial of potion that vanished from his pocket by the time he arrived back here. Not stolen: *vanished*.'

'Why didn't they tell me this? I would have helped them or gone out myself if I'd had any idea of where to start looking!'

'They don't know how the link Hrex has set up between you works. All we know is that you can hear her voice in your head. That voice might be repeating thoughts she's having, conversations she's having, memories she has. It might work both ways; she could be using the link not only as a way to keep herself safe from harm by threatening your life, but also to spy on those she's forced to work with her.'

'Then why are you telling me this? Aren't you putting them in danger by telling me? What if she *is* listening?'

'Then let her do her worst!' Madame Fleurese's eyes flashed angrily and the knuckles of her hands were even whiter as she gripped the banister tighter, as if it was Hrex's throat.

Torben took a step back, not expecting such a harsh venom to seep into the cheery, bubbly voice he knew.

Taking a deep breath, she composed herself and winced slightly as she removed neatly manicured nails from the damaged bannister. 'You're all too important to her plan. Any one of you could be hiding the Keystone, and all of you have skills that are very useful for her in gaining access to the castle and the vault. If she's going to hurt anyone, it would be me and only me, and I'd be damned if I didn't try and find a way to do the same to her first.'

The two of them stood in silence for a few moments, punctuated only by the few sounds drifting from the streets below. Torben returned to leaning over the bannister, and watched a drunk make his awkward, stumbling way home. He lurched from one side of the street to another, muttering threats to the walls as he bounced off them, as if expecting them to make way for him. He painstakingly continued on his way, seemingly confident in his ability to get home, whatever the odds.

'Why did Eleusia tell you about all of this?'

'Because I asked her. I could see the same worry in her eyes that I've had ever since I took her in over fifteen years ago. I found her sheltering in the doorway, a little girl of four or five. She wouldn't tell me who her parents where at first, but eventually she opened up enough for me to connect some of the dots. Her father was an elf from the Republic of Castar, whilst her mother was a human from the Sultanate of Fashaddon, though I'm still none the wiser about what happened to them and why Eleusia ended up on our doorstep. I suspect that she couldn't being herself to tell me, couldn't bear to put herself through that pain again but, regardless, we gave her sanctuary, food and a bed.

'She's been with us ever since. First, she was washing pots in the kitchens, then she was waiting tables. Before long, she was beating patrons at cards, honestly and dishonestly, but whenever they suspected foul play, the extra cards always ended up in their own sleeves. Even if they had caught her in the act, Gods she could fight like the wild animal she was … made everyone who came in here think twice before having a go at her, or anyone else for that matter, which was no bad thing.

'We used to have a more rough-and-tumble crowd come in then and they all liked her, taught her all manner of things, knife work, sparring, shooting. They saw in her one of their own, a child of the streets, kept alive by their own sheer force of will to survive. That's certainly what Björn saw in her.

'It didn't take him long to ask me if he could take her under his wing, give her a chance to make something of herself and make a fair bit of money along the way. As I said to him, the choice wasn't mine to make, and I wasn't surprised when Eleusia went to work for him, but she never forgot us and, if nothing else, I'm glad that all this nonsense has brought her home for longer than she normally stops now.' She drew a deep breath. 'Now though, she has her own people to worry about, just remember that, Torben.'

With that, Madame Fleurese put a hand gently on his shoulder and then left the balcony, pulling the door shut behind and leaving him alone at the breaking of the dawn.

18

A vortex of words and whispers swirled around Torben's head and blazed with the same golden fire he'd seen surging up his arm. The rasping tones of Hrex's voice was everywhere, wrapping itself around every part of his being.

Piercing the noise was a dull regular thud that scattered the flames, sending the words spiralling out of control before they slowly drew themselves back together. A volley of panicked shouts and cries accompanied each thud as it rocked his battered subconscious. Far away, in the distance, beyond the cacophony, he thought he could hear a different voice calling his name.

'Ashak.'

'Torben.'

'Ashak.'

In the haunting dream, a shadow descended over him, growing larger and larger, snuffing the light of the golden flames and stifling Hrex's horrible voice. He looked up, tried to sprint as the shadow bore down on him faster than he could run, threatening to crush him.

'Torben!'

He jolted awake and flinched instinctively, trying to save

himself from the crushing force of whatever was about to land on him. He cried out in desperation. 'No!'

'It's alright; it's only me. You were having a bad dream.'

Opening his eyes, he saw Eleusia peering at him, concern visibly painted on her face. 'Oh, right. Sorry, you must have taken me by surprise.' Sitting up, he realised he was still on the balcony of Ivy House, where he'd finally fallen asleep.

His forehead and hair were dripping with sweat, and he hastily wiped both with the sleeve of his jacket. It was still early. The pink and purple lights of dawn were just peeking over the walls of Karpella, but it was enough to dispel the oppressive rasp of Hrex's voice in his head. However, he could still hear shouts and screams drifting from the street below. The noise was swelled as a loud thud and crack split the air, sending reverberations through the building itself. 'What the hell was that?'

'The Sharisians have started their bombardment of the city. They finished bringing up their catapults late last night. Are you alright?'

Torben cleared his throat and tried to inject a note of confidence into his voice, but it cracked slightly, betraying him. "No worse than normal, I guess."

Eleusia's brows furrowed, but her face relaxed as she extended a hand to help him to his feet. 'Come on, it's time to go.'

The Silent Room was busy as they entered. The table was covered with Antauros' neatly organised equipment. He tightened the strapping around the handle of his war-hammer and the newly honed points of his javelins gleamed wickedly in the firelight. Gwilym, on the other hand, was hopping frustratedly around the room, struggling to fasten one of the buckles on a greave. The rest of his Imperial Guard uniform and armour lay in a disorganised pile on the floor. 'Best get a move on, you two. These things are an absolute bugger to get into! I don't see the point in all this clobber anyway; it's far too heavy and makes you into an immobile target!'

'Stop complaining, Gwilym, you have to look the part.' Eleusia moved to her own pile and dressed far more elegantly.

From behind the table, Antauros smirked at Gwilym's grumbling figure. He wore his own chainmail as easily as a linen shirt. 'You'll be glad of that armour when someone's trying to plant a halberd in your chest.'

'Unlike you, I don't often get myself into those situations.'

'Stab first and ask questions later, more like.'

'Perhaps more focus is called for … from *all* of you!'

The conversation had roused Hrex, who sat cross-legged on the same chair she'd occupied the day before. She glowered and they averted their gaze, and continued preparing in silence— silence heavy with anger and resentment.

The downstairs rooms of Ivy House were quiet and still as the party made their way from the Silent Room to the front courtyard. Here and there, the occasional patron from the night before, too inebriated to make his way home, slumbered fitfully in partially hidden corners.

In the courtyard, they stopped and Antauros grudgingly passed his shield, war-hammer and javelins to Torben and Eleusia, and turned to face a grinning Gwilym.

'Guess I can't put this off much longer,' he grimaced.

'If it's any comfort, Antauros, I can assure you that I won't enjoy this a single bit.'

Antauros grumbled as he knelt down low enough for Gwilym to place the large, specially made manacles over his wrists and secure them shut. He took a hold of the long chain and led the minotaur towards the gate, pulling and rocking the chain as if trying to coax a dog to follow him on a leash. 'Come on boy, time for a walk!'

'Shut it, dwarf!'

'I hope the shackles aren't too tight. Wouldn't want them to chafe now, would we?'

'Shut it!'

Eleusia sighed and caught Torben's eye as the odd couple weaved their way through tables. The chain Gwilym was leading Antauros by scraped wooden tabletops and threatened to knock over the remaining detritus that had yet to be cleared up.

Hrex began to follow, muttering to herself as she walked, her hands drawing strange symbols in the air faintly picked out via strands of blue flame. As the symbols multiplied in the air, they stuck to Hrex's body and clothes, making her form shimmer and fade until all that could be seen was an occasional ripple of air as she moved through the courtyard.

'Great,' Torben muttered, 'now we don't even know where she is, or what she's doing.'

Eleusia nodded grimly in agreement as she hefted the straps of Antauros' shield over her shoulder. Torben followed her lead, picking up the rest of Antauros' things. He nearly tipped over as he picked up the war-hammer and, with the extra weight of the weapon, felt his belt slipping down his body, threatening to drop his trousers. There was a soft squeaking noise from the Ivy House gate as Gwilym swung it open and the foursome were in the street, Hrex presumably close behind, hidden in her web of sorcery.

As they made their way through the streets of Karpella, Torben and Eleusia flanked Antauros to give the impression that he'd been arrested by the Imperial Guards. The guard uniform and armour Torben was wearing felt tight and hot, the chainmail coat rubbing his neck uncomfortably; after a few minutes, it felt as if it were rubbing away skin.

Even at this early hour of the day, plenty of people were out and about; however, rather than the hustle and bustle of people going about the business of a working day, they moved through the streets looking decidedly panicky. The commencement of the bombardment had brought home the reality of the situation, with residents trying to secure their homes and businesses as best they could, and many streaming towards the castle in hopes of shelter.

The party made slow progress, pushing their way through the crowds that thronged the streets; a normally twenty-minute walk took over an hour. Torben, Eleusia and Gwilym were constantly harangued by passersby as they inched through, people berating them for not being up on the ramparts defending the city, appealing to them to take them to shelter; one appeal came from a lavishly dressed merchant, offering them several thousand gold pieces to smuggle him and his family out of the city.

When they finally reached the foot of Karpella Castle, a huge crowd had flocked to the banks of the channel that separated the castle and its island from the rest of the city. The main gate was shut, with the drawbridge raised against the tide of refugees. Torben drew a sigh of relief as they inched close enough to see that the postern was still open, surrounded by a large cordon of Imperial Guard keeping crowds back from the drawbridge via a close formation of guardsmen sporting tower shields. As they approached, a cry rang from behind the wall of shields: 'Patrol returning, make way!'

Two guardsmen pulled their shields to one side, and those around levelled spears to keep back the crowd, which surged towards a gap in the formation to follow the party through the barricade. As they squeezed through the gap, Torben heard panicked shouts and screams of those at the front when people behind pushed them into the shield wall. As the two guardsmen forced their way back into position, and the others raised their spears, several of sharp points were stained with fresh blood.

Inside the defensive crescent, a young worried-looking officer stood on a barrel, surveying the increasingly angry crowd. He jumped down as Gwilym tugged Antauros before him and waved his hand limply towards his temple in recognition of the dwarf's flourishing salute.

'Prisoner for incarceration, is it?'

'Yes sir. Caught him trying to stir up trouble in Thirsty Bear on Weaver Street,' Gwilym responded.

'Gods, he's a big fellow! I'm glad he's not egging on the crowd to mischief. They're already getting hot under the collar and I'm not sure how much longer we can hold them back. We've still got five patrols in the city and once we're forced into shutting this gate, there's no way to get them back.'

'Yes sir, bad situation through and through, sir.'

The officer continued to mutter worriedly as he pulled out a battered notebook and a stub of pencil tucked into his belt, and scribbled down a short message.

'Here's your warrant to admit the prisoner into cells. Report to Captain Sudthorpe at the main gate for redeployment once you've delivered him.'

'Thank you sir, good luck!'

Gwilym yanked on the chain to get Antauros moving and they proceeded over the narrow drawbridge of the postern, leaving the officer to mount his barrel again and nervously watch the crowd.

The air cooled quickly as they entered the arched corridor that lead from the postern into the castle proper. Gwilym and Eleusia took torches from a box beside a large brazier and ignited them, lighting the way down a corridor that was almost pitch-black. They walked in silence for some time as Gwilym led them through a maze of corridors before they finally arrived at a large junction.

'That's your exit,' he said, pointing at stairs that ascended into darkness.'

'Good luck, all of you.' Eleusia handed Antauros' immense shield to Gwilym, who could barely hold it. 'All being well, it won't take me long to get into position. Just remember, kill as much time as you can before the alarm is raised. Once the garrison is distracted, you should be able to make your way to the Great Hall with ease.'

'Look after yourself, and don't get caught!' Torben blushed in the darkness as the words blurted from his mouth.

Eleusia looked at him with a sly smile. 'Don't worry, I know how to handle myself. See you on the other side'. With that, she bounded up the stairs and disappeared from sight.

Torben stood looking into the gloomy void she'd ascended before being jolted back to reality by an elbow to the leg from Gwilym.

'Come on, lad. This is not the time for you to go all mushy on us. Let's keep moving.' He led the way down another corridor, away from the stairs.

Torben reluctantly followed Gwilym and Antauros and, as the light from his torch illuminated the passageway stonework, he saw a distinctive rippling of air: the invisible form of Hrex was following his friends. Deep in his mind, he swore he heard Hrex laughing at him.

The four of them moved through corridor after corridor, worming their way up from the bowels of the castle. They passed innumerable rooms and antechambers that made up the underground complex, but didn't see another soul. It was only after they'd climbed a spiral staircase, barely wide or tall enough to accommodate Antauros' bulk, that Torben heard voices echoing through the halls around them.

Above the much more utilitarian basement levels, the castle's corridors where more elaborate. Grey-white marble covered the floors, with pink marble columns continuing down the much wider thoroughfares. As they emerged from the staircase, a group of fraught bureaucrats in flowing black robes scuttled past, their ink-stained hands clutching rolls of parchment and quills. Several of them yelped in surprise and sprinted down the corridor as Antauros' bulk emerged from the inconspicuous staircase. The cries of fear and shock from the rapidly retreating bureaucrats drew the attention of a small squad of Imperial Guard standing watch over a doorway further down. After a few seconds of staring confusedly at the strange party that had appeared before them, they advanced on Torben, Gwilym and Antauros, hands resting on sword hilts.

'You there! Why is this prisoner above ground?'

'We've, err … we've got orders to bring this beast up to the City Marshall's chambers for questioning.' An air of self-assuredness developed in Gwilym's voice as he grew more confident in the lie that he'd plucked out of thin air. He cleared his throat and puffed out his chest as he continued to spin the yarn. 'We apprehended this piece of scum trying to insight rioting in a crowd at the Dancing Bear on Weaver Street. With all of the commotion going on with the siege and all, we were ordered to bring him straight to the Marshall so he could ascertain whether this is part of a Sharisian plot to undermine the city's morale, and cause rebellion against the crown.'

'Who gave you your orders?'

'Officer on duty at the postern gate.'

'Who was that?'

'I … I don't know, but I have the order dispatch here.' Gwilym placed a fumbling hand in a pouch hanging off his belt and produced the crumpled piece of paper the officer had given him. The leader of the group guards, who had three gold roses embroidered on the sleeve of his uniform, took the paper and studied it carefully.

'This is just a warrant for incarceration in the cells. There isn't anything written here authorising you to transport the prisoner to the Marshall's chambers.'

'There isn't?' Gwilym took a few steps forward, feigning interest in the paper, but the guardsman took a step back and his sword scraped through the scabbard as he half-drew it, sensing something was amiss.

'Those orders were given verbally.'

Seeing that Gwilym was beginning to flounder, Torben stepped forward, looking the lead guardsman straight in the eyes and standing to attention. 'We're new recruits, sir, and we didn't take proper care to insist that the officer wrote down all their orders. It's pretty chaotic out there, sir, with the crowds trying to gain access to the castle. I believe the officer was preoccupied with locating the whereabouts of his last patrols; that's why he omitted to write down all his orders.'

'Is that so, eh?' The guardsman looked hard at Torben for several long seconds.

Torben, guessing that the three roses indicated the guardsman was a sergeant of sorts, adjusted his gaze so that he was staring above the man's head, and tried to do his best impression of a soldier standing to attention on parade.

'New recruits? Makes sense, I thought you both looked a bit too green. Take the prisoner to the cells and the officer in charge will send a runner to the Marshall's chambers to see if he's free to question the prisoner, but take him down through the passages. We have enough to deal with without idiots like you, who haven't got a clue what you're doing, wandering through the corridors.' With that, the Sergeant thrust the piece of paper into Gwilym's hand and walked back towards his station, the other guardsmen following.

Just as the guards returned to their posts, one of them turned around and walked back towards Gwilym, hand once more on his sword hilt. 'Where did you say you arrested the prisoner?'

'The Dancing Bear on Weaver Street.'

'The Dancing Bear isn't on Weaver Street; that's the Thirsty Bear. The Dancing Bear is down past the Spice Market and isn't on any of our patrol routes. That's City Guard jurisdiction.'

The other guards, who'd been listening, all turned to face the party. Torben heard Gwilym curse under his breath and he could see the dwarf moving his hand slowly behind his back to the hilt of the seax.

The tension was shattered as bells echoed all around the palace—so loudly that Torben nearly dropped his spear and shield in shock to cover his ears. The guardsmen looked worriedly to their sergeant, who pushed his sword back into its scabbard and jogged down the corridor, away from the party.

'Fire bells. Get to the emergency stations,' he bellowed over the peal of the bells. 'You lot, get that prisoner down to the cells sharpish and report for fire duty. Now!'

The other guardsmen sprinted after the sergeant, leaving Gwilym, Antauros and Torben alone.

'Well, that could have gone better,' Antauros' deep voice rumbled around the corridor.

'Don't you start! You're supposed to be a prisoner still, remember? So save your judgement of the situation for later. What matters is that Eleusia caused her diversion in time, so let's get moving before it's too late.'

With the alarm bells ringing out around them, the group made their way through the castle's ground floor. Unlike in the subterranean levels, activity could be heard all around—the clatter and shouts of guard patrols pounding through corridors, servants dodging between rooms with hurriedly packed belongings, and elaborately dressed courtiers softly discussing how they could best survive the siege.

Because of Antauros' bulk and intimidating presence, Gwilym was able to lead the group relatively quickly through the marbled corridors and halls. Thankfully, the other groups of Imperial Guards that ran past were too preoccupied with getting to the emergency stations to question Gwilym and Torben about Antauros, and why they were above ground.

As they progressed, Torben could almost hear Gwilym counting turnoffs and corridors they passed over the din of the fire bells and commotion. Eventually, Gwilym brought them to a halt in front of an inconspicuous wooden door and, after quickly looking up and down the corridor, he lifted the heavy latch and disappeared inside, Antauros and Torben following quickly behind.

The door led through into a large antechamber filled with piled chairs and tables, along with feasting paraphernalia, large brass candelabras, tablecloths and boxes of candles. By the time that Torben had shut the door quietly behind, Gwilym was already peering through a door on the other side of the room. There was a dull thud as Antauros released himself from the manacles and placed them carefully on a nearby table. He nodded with thanks as Torben handed him his equipment, and stealthily navigated his way through the maze of straps and buckles.

'Right, the coast is clear. Let's go!'

Opening the door just enough to allow them through, Gwilym slipped through and was gone. Torben could see the air in the doorway shimmer as Hrex likewise passed through … and, then, he himself was in the massive room.

The Great Hall of Karpella Castle was an immense structure of architecture. The room was a giant open space with an arched roof supported by pink marble columns lining the walls, creating a covered walkway around the hall perimeter. In the shadows of the rafters, the ceiling was painted a deep blue colour, with bright white stars in the pattern of the constellations. The ceiling was so high above them that Torben stopped dead in his tracks and marvelled at the structure he was standing in. He'd never thought such a building would have been possible, let alone that he'd one day be standing in it.

Amongst the columns, intricate mosaics had been set into the walls, each depicting an event in the history of the Kingdom of Dazscor & Aramore. Torben felt the stern gaze of the kings and queens of old glowering at him from all four walls, as if judging him for his trespass.

Torben's eyes were drawn to a mosaic at the end of the hall set into the wall behind a large ornately carved and highly polished wooden feasting table; it was of a queen with arms outstretched in welcome. Her features had been picked out through the intricate placement of gems and precious stones— her eyes were two bright, clear sapphires that flashed in the light and seemed to follow Torben around the room. The figure was only slightly larger in stature than Torben, but her feet were set several feet off the ground so that the mosaic could be seen above an elaborate chair behind the feasting table: the Imperial Throne.

Antauros and Gwilym were behind the table, weapons drawn, scanning the length of the hall in case someone should enter. As he moved towards them, Torben's view of the mosaic queen was partially obstructed by Hrex, who materialised before the artwork. She reached out and placed a hand on it, and looked into the face of the queen smiling benignly above.

'I have waited years to be back here again.' As she whispered to herself, Torben could have sworn he saw a tear trickling slowly from Hrex's eye, down the ginger facial fur.

Ever so gently, almost reverently, she pressed a deep red ruby set in the centre of the queen's belt. As Torben, Gwilym and Antauros looked on, the ruby disappeared into the wall and was followed by a harsh grinding sound when the wall opened like a set of double doors, splitting the mosaic queen in two. Beyond, a dank and dusty corridor plunged below the ground.

Hrex turned to face Torben, a smile spreading across her muzzle. 'This is the way we must go. Don't be afraid, boy. You've nearly finished your time of servitude.'

19

As soon as all four of them had stepped into the tunnel, the mosaic door closed behind, causing the light that filtered in from the Great Hall to rapidly diminish. Desperately, Torben looked around to see if there was a torch or candle he could grab —anything to light the way through the pitch darkness.

As the doors shut, the last ray of light bounced off one of the queen's sapphire eyes, casting her final judgement upon the party before they were enveloped by blackness.

Torben felt as if he were utterly alone. He knew, however, that Antauros was right in front of him. If he stilled his increasingly panicked breathing, he would have been able to hear the minotaur's breathing, his lungs working like blacksmith's bellows. Instead, his ears filled with the thud-thud-thud of his own desperate heartbeat. This, he thought, was what death must feel like ... or what it would feel like to simply cease to exist.

His panic was broken as the corridor filled with pale blue light. A swirling nexus of runes had formed in Hrex's hand and, as she continued to chant, joined the sphere until it rose slowly from her palm and floated above her head.

Wordlessly, she walked down the well-worn stone steps and

Torben, Gwilym and Antauros followed, keeping as close as they dared to the light for fear of being left alone in the dark.

The staircase plummeted for what felt like miles. As soon as they'd lost the daylight, Torben's concept of time had completely vanished and the descent might have lasted minutes, days, or years. There was no way he'd have been able to say for sure. The constant rhythm of his footsteps down the stairs lulled him into a trance-like state, which he was jolted from when they stepped onto the level floor of a large underground chamber.

Before them was a huge barrel-vaulted chamber—the treasure vault of Sarper IV. There was a large marble alter in the centre of the vast room's and immediately beyond that was a low, greenish-white marble wall with thick gold railings rising from it at short intervals and reaching to the ceiling. In the middle of this barrier, directly behind the alter, was a set of ornately wrought golden gates that appeared firmly closed.

Hrex's light wasn't the only thing illuminating the space; a wall of swirling greenish-blue light was seen surrounding the railings and gate, obscuring the view beyond and bathing the antechamber in an alien glow—it was an odd quality that illuminated the antechamber, but also blurred and obscured things, rather like a desert mirage.

It took Torben quite a while to notice cracks that ran down the walls, a caved-in passage that branched into the depths below the city, and a huge chunk of masonry that had fallen from the vaulted ceiling near the entrance to the stairwell. He recoiled instinctively from the fallen masonry when the light shifted and revealed a partly mummified, skeletal arm protruding from beneath it.

'Don't be alarmed,' Hrex chuckled to herself, 'that's only the old Lord Chamberlain. He's far past doing you harm now, of his own accord anyway.' Still sniggering, she approached the altar and turned to face the three of them. 'Now is the time for you to give me what I want. Give me the Keystone so I can open the vault and, once I've claimed my prize, you can take whatever you want, and your friend here will be released from his bondage to me.'

As if to hammer home the point, Hrex drew her knife from the sleeve of her robe and caressed her cheek with it, in turn gouging a thin red line across Torben's face.

Torben and Antauros' gaze drifted to Gwilym, who stood defiantly in front of the altar, glowering at Hrex from under his severe brow-line. For a moment, the look in Gwilym's eyes made Torben think that the dwarf was going to try his luck and attack the witch, but then his face softened and he took off his pack.

'I want it to go down on record that this is the first time I've been backed into a corner like this.' He rooted around in his pack and pulled out the brown leather trick purse he had shown Torben the first time they'd met. This time, however, the purse looked distinctly misshapen and the seams between each leather strip bulged, almost to breaking point. As he loosened the string at the purse's neck, Gwilym teased a large cloth-covered object from inside.

When the Keystone was extricated, all those in the room were suddenly keenly aware of its presence and felt its power creep into their consciousness. Gwilym removed the cloth wrapping to reveal the Keystone' silver surface. Bathed in the weird green-blue light of the chamber, the runes on the surface glowed a brilliant fiery blue colour, and the serpent on the edge began to thrash around as it devoured itself.

Slowly, he approached the altar and placed the Keystone on the stone work. As soon as the silver surface of the Keystone contacted the marble, the runes peeled off and swirled in the air around the Keystone whilst the object itself visibly vibrated, letting off a low hum.

As the Keystone became more animated, the grin on Hrex's face widened, revealing yellowed, pointed teeth. 'Thank you dwarf. For once, you've done something vaguely helpful. I'm impressed that you had the necessary resources to shield the stone's aura from me. It's surprising the things that vagabonds like yourself manage to acquire nowadays. Now, all I need is for you to stand back and keep out of my way.'

From behind the altar, her right hand lashed forth and gold strands of light erupted from her hand, speeding across the room towards Gwilym, the light stretching like a net to ensnare the dwarf.

'*Ashak Mabourta*!' Hrex spat the incantation, her smile replaced by a snarl.

Gwilym tried to jump out of the light's path, but it shifted course as if tracking his movements, and enveloped him with radiant threads. As soon as the strands touched him, he was frozen in place, in mid dive to one side; his body crashed to the stone floor. His body was immobile, but his eyes could be seen moving wildly from side to side, seeking a way out.

A roar of anger echoed around the chamber as Antauros charged the altar and Hrex, but the witch calmly turned her gaze on the minotaur and spoke the words of the incantation again. Again, the golden threads of light shot from her hand, and hit Antauros square in the chest. The momentum of his charge carried him forward several more steps before freezing him in position, like Gwilym. There was a clatter as the javelin he'd started to throw fell from his grasp and skidded several metres across the floor.

'That was lucky.' Hrex smirked and turned her gaze towards Torben, standing transfixed by what had happened. She approached him, the light from the Keystone's runes illuminating the top of her head with an eerie halo. 'It would seem that in the heat of the moment, your friend forgot what would have happened if he'd tried to kill me.' She picked up the javelin, which was almost as tall as she, and pricked her finger on its point.

Torben flinched and felt a bead of blood forming at the tip of his left index finger. 'Why don't you just take what you want and leave us be? We gave you the Keystone … we fulfilled our part of the bargain. Now take what you want and we can go our separate ways.'

'How bold of you to assume that I have *everything* that I want. That's the problem with you laypeople who have no comprehension of the arcane. You don't know the price needed to break such a powerful enchantment as was placed on this vault.

'Did your dwarf friend addle your brains so much that you were convinced all you had to do was waltz down here and use the Keystone, as if you were unlocking a trinket chest? I suspect he knew as little as you.

'Good King Sarper was a very exacting task-master and he demanded only the best and the finest things in life, and the most stringent and effective ways of protecting those things. Such high demands naturally come with a cost.' Hrex continued to walk slowly towards Torben, who backed away, his eyes darting from side to side, looking for something, *anything*, that might help him.

'When my Master and I were tasked with safeguarding the King's treasure, we knew that we had to do whatever we could to keep it safe, and that meant calling upon powers few in this mortal realm have ever dealt with ... powers that would destroy those who weren't prepared to look upon them ... powers that wouldn't be satisfied with the return of a mere lump of metal. They require a greater form of payment.'

Torben's retreat ceased as he backed into the large chunk of masonry. His head snapped back to see what the obstacle was, and Hrex ceased her moment to strike.

'Ashak!'

The familiar cold sensation descended upon Torben and his limbs locked into place; he was rooted to the spot. Out of the corner of his eye, he saw her produce the battered quill from her robes, and she began to sketch runes in the air, which formed themselves into a long golden thread.

As she finished the spell, the thread wrapped itself around

Torben, plucking his petrified body with ease from the ground and carrying him to the altar.

Hrex walked behind Torben's hovering body, directing the course of the thread with the end of her quill. As Torben was pulled over the centre of the altar, she flicked up the end of the quill and the free end of the golden thread leapt high into the air and sank into the ceiling stonework, suspending him a couple of feet over the marble.

From this vantage point, Torben spotted a round indentation in the centre of the altar, an exact match of the Keystone that was still humming and glowing to one side. From the side, he saw Hrex ascending a small set of steps built into the back of the altar, bringing her almost to Torben's level.

'As I said before, I didn't need the Keystone to be in my possession, I just needed it to be here ... along with someone who can pay the price of opening the vault for me.' As she spoke, she brought the quill towards Torben's face and then jammed the point into the flesh of his shoulder.

The stinging pain as the quill stabbed him was overshadowed by a huge sense of relief as he felt Hrex dispelling the bonding curse she'd placed on him. The golden runes that had flowed over and sunk into his skin when she'd initially cursed him, were drawn out and sucked into the quill, which continued to glow with the same golden light.

Hrex's voice, which had been present in his head since that fateful night in Gallenford, grew dimmer and dimmer, until all that he could hear was her muttering in the real world. When the last of the golden runes were removed from his body, she yanked the quill from his shoulder and wiped the blood from the nib on her sleeve. 'I'm sure it feels good for your mind and body to be free for your final moments.'

Before Torben could speak, her knife came hammering up, and pieced his belly, passing through the guardsman's uniform and chainmail coat as if it were made of silk. The relief of freedom was crushed by intense pain as black blood flowed freely from the wound, into the indentation of the altar. He screamed inwardly with pain but, unable to move or speak, outwardly his face remained fixed with the same expression.

Picking up the Keystone, Hrex chanted, moving her hands over the silver object and then through the node of runes floating above it. Torben had no idea what she was saying; his brain was too shocked by the pain coursing through his abdomen to process anything.

Carefully, almost reverently, Hrex placed the Keystone in the altar indentation, Torben's blood welling onto the white marble and staining the silver as the Keystone locked into place. She raised her arms high above her head and finished the final words of the chant, her voice affected by the magic flowing around her.

At first, nothing happened. Then slowly, ever so slowly, the green-blue force-field wrapped around the railings and gate that led to the vault proper, drew towards the altar. It oozed across the floor and clawed its way up the side of the marble altar, and was sucked into the silver body of the Keystone.

As more of the force-field was absorbed, the louder the humming became and the stronger the vibrations it emitted. The vibrations swiftly strengthened and the chamber began to shake as if experiencing an earthquake. Dust and small pieces of stone fell from the ceiling, and Hrex had to grip the altar with both hands to steady herself.

As the last of the force-field was absorbed, there was an explosion of blue light and an immense sound like a thunderclap ripping through the chamber. Huge cracks appeared in the antechamber ceiling and rippled through the stairwell, surging towards the castle and city above.

The blast dispelled the magic that Hrex had cast, causing Torben to fall from his place in midair as the golden thread dissolved. As he crashed onto the altar, his body was freed from the spell, but contorted as he was beset by pain. His screams of agony were joined by Antauros' war cry, and a surprised shout from Gwilym as their voices were released and able to sound again.

It took Antauros a couple of seconds to collect himself as the net of golden energy dropped from his body, and he thundered to the altar, drawing bandages and dressings hurriedly from his bag. With incredible delicacy, he tended Torben, assessing the situation and applying pressure to the wound.

Gwilym stumbled up behind and craned his neck to see the surface of the altar. 'How is he? Is it bad?'

Antauros didn't answer at first, his mind too absorbed in saving their friend. 'She lifted the hex from him. Follow her, find her, and make her suffer for what she has done!'

Gwilym didn't need to be told twice and he jumped from the foot of the altar and hurried towards the gate to the vault.

The golden gate was ajar and beyond it stretched an immense space lit by torches and braziers that flickered in stilted, stuttering way, as if they'd been frozen in time and were only now coming to terms with being active again. As the light they emitted strengthened, it was reflected by a huge quantity of gold, silver, and gems that littered the floor and lay in great piles.

Gwilym stopped dead in his tracks, transfixed by the treasure hoard. It was larger than his wildest imagination had conceived, so much grander and far more beautiful. He knelt and let some of the fat gold pieces fall through his fingers, the mounted knights emblazoned on their surfaces dancing and prancing in the flickering light.

He was brought back to earth by a strangled cry of pain from the antechamber. *Keep it together, Gwilym. Focus on the task at hand! We'll all gain satisfaction from hunting that furry hag down.* He rose carefully, into a crouch, and stalked into the vault. In the distance, he heard the chink and spill of coins and gems as Hrex made her way hurriedly deeper into the hoard.

Picking up his pace, Gwilym moved through the heaps of treasure. There were bodies, he noticed—armoured men and women that looked as if they had just laid down and gone to sleep, even though they'd been lying amongst the treasure for over 170 years.

Rounding a large stack of overflowing chests, Gwilym caught sight of Hrex. She was bent over the body of a man dressed in long flowing robes, lying flat on the ground. In the dim light Gwilym thought he could spy pointed ears peeking from the man's dishevelled blonde hair: an elf.

Hrex was cooing softly as she lifted the elf's head with one hand and held a small unstoppered bottle beneath the figure's nose with the other. The elf coughed, spluttered, and came to.

As Gwilym inched closer, he could hear the elf's clear, cold voice. 'Hrex, what happened? Did the spell hold?'

'Yes, Master. There's no need to worry, but we must hurry and get you to a place of safety so you can recover.'

'What of my research and equipment? We *must* move them before they're destroyed in the siege.'

'Fear not, Master, I've moved them and made all necessary preparations for you to continue your work in safety. But we must move now. Much has changed whilst you've been slumbering here. Dazscor isn't how you remember it.' Hrex helped him to his feet and supported him with an arm around his waist as he swayed unsteadily, clearly unused to being vertical again. Clumsily, she produced the quill once more and sketched a large, complex symbol in the air.

Realising that his chance was swiftly disappearing, Gwilym threw caution to the winds and sprinted across the vault towards her. His feet slipped on the treasure as he surged forward, sending coins and gems flying in his wake, which clattered to earth behind. He drew his seax as he closed in, but the witch only smirked as she completed her spell; the two figures vanished into thin air.

Gwilym crashed to the ground as his wild thrust at Hrex met no resistance, and he cursed foully as he collapsed onto a bed of coins. As he rose slowly, tears of frustration and anguish formed in his eyes, and he became aware of the intense silence that surrounded him.

Torben wasn't yelling out anymore.

The dwarf spun to make his way back to his friends, but was stopped dead in his tracks by the wicked end of a sabre pointed at his throat. The wielder, a regal and stern-looking young woman with thick cascading auburn curls, looked as if she meant business.

Gwilym could see and hear more figures approaching, dressed in the same armour as the young woman. They hefted shields, spears, and swords as they rallied around their princess, casting the dwarf into shadow.

'You trample on the legacy of my father and my people. Give me one good reason why I shouldn't take your head, thief!'

Dear Reader,

We hope you enjoyed reading *Legacy*. Please take a moment to leave a review, even if it's a short one. Your opinion is important to us.

Discover more books by C.J. Pyrah at

https://www.nextchapter.pub/authors/cj-pyrah

Want to know when one of our books is free or discounted? Join the newsletter at

http://eepurl.com/bqqB3H

Best regards,

C.J. Pyrah and the Next Chapter Team

AUTHOR BIOGRAPHY

Born and brought up in the Newcastle Upon Tyne in the northeast of England, C.J. Pyrah has since moved south to Oxford, where he studied Classical Archaeology and Ancient History. Since graduating, he has spent most of his spare waking moments writing and tinkering with the minutia of the many fantasy worlds that he has created.

You might also like:

A Chronicle of Chaos by D.M. Cain

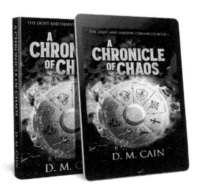

To read the first chapter for free go to:
https://www.nextchapter.pub/books/chronicle-of-chaos-dark-fantasy

Legacy
ISBN: 978-4-86747-739-7

Published by
Next Chapter
1-60-20 Minami-Otsuka
170-0005 Toshima-Ku, Tokyo
+818035793528

24th May 2021

Lightning Source UK Ltd.
Milton Keynes UK
UKHW012059030621
384904UK00001B/174